HELL DIVERS XI
RENEGADES

BOOKS BY *NEW YORK TIMES* BESTSELLING AUTHOR

NICHOLAS SANSBURY SMITH

HELL DIVERS XI
RENEGADES

NICHOLAS SANSBURY SMITH

BLACK
STONE
PUBLISHING

Printed in the United States of America
Originally published in hardcover by Blackstone Publishing in 2023

ISBN 979-8-212-38666-1
Fiction / Science Fiction / Apocalyptic & Post-Apocalyptic

Version 1

Blackstone Publishing
31 Mistletoe Rd.
Ashland, OR 97520

www.BlackstonePublishing.com

This one's for Ace, our red-nose pit bull that left us last November. My wife rescued Acey-boy from a fighting ring in Joplin, Missouri, fifteen years ago and gave him the best life. Ace was the sweetest, strongest, and most gentle soul—a truly special dog that enriched the life of everyone that knew him.

"Battle not with monsters, lest ye become a monster, and if you gaze into the abyss, the abyss gazes also into you."

—Friedrich Nietzsche

RECAP SINCE
HELL DIVERS X: FALLOUT

The fight for the Vanguard Islands is over, and once again King Xavier has managed to pull off a victory. But things are different this time. After a brutal year of battle after battle, he has decided to pass the torch of leadership to a younger man—Hell Diver Kade Long. Hanging up his crown, X departs the islands in the *Sea Wolf* with Magnolia to search for Michael Everhart and his family, who narrowly escaped captivity under the silver-tongued, stonehearted Charmer on the airship *Vanguard*. X believes they are headed to Rio de Janeiro.

On the airship, plans have changed. Michael and his family, along with Steve, Victor, and the AI Timothy Pepper, are no longer heading to Rio but across the Atlantic to Victor's home—a place called the Canary Islands. If they make it through the storms, they hope to find a bunker filled with vital resources.

At the Vanguard Islands, Kade Long is sworn in as king before all the dead from the battle against his own people are buried. Some rebels still remain at large—supporters of Charmer, who hangs in a cage, awaiting his fate. Kade treads carefully, trying to bring peace while knowing that a war with the Forerunner and the Knights of the Coral Castle could be on the horizon. General Forge, the newly promoted Commander Slayer, Lieutenant Wynn, and Gran Jefe prepare the defenses, looking west for any sign of an attack.

In *Hell Divers XI: Renegades*, life for the survivors hangs by the most tenuous of threads. But these heroes aren't done fighting yet.

PROLOGUE
TEN YEARS AGO . . .

Strong winds blasted the ten prisoners with stinging grit as they trekked across the wastes. Kade Long tried to wipe his goggles on his scarf but just smeared ash over the lenses. He tried again, finally clearing them enough to see the massive rock looming in the distance.

Kilimanjaro, they had called it in the Old World. The last time he saw the distant foothills, he had imagined himself escaping with the other survivors from his crashed airship, *Victory*. He had pictured himself as a free man, helping Tia escape and trying to find a place where they might survive.

"Move or die."

The synthetic, robotic voice reminded Kade that he would never be free, and neither would Tia. The failed attack on the machines had caused more deaths of his people. For some reason, the machines had spared him and Carl "Charmer" Lex despite their involvement in carrying out the assault. Captain Rolo, who had ordered the attack, was also spared.

It seemed the machines either didn't know who was behind it, or didn't care. Or perhaps they simply weren't threatened and decided to keep the rest of the prisoners alive.

Still, Kade wasn't sure what happened to Charmer after their visit to the infirmary. All he remembered was that Charmer had a patch over one eye. He assumed that the machines had taken one of his eyes to punish him for the attack. Since then, Kade hadn't seen or heard anything about him.

Nothing really made sense, though it did seem that the machines had kept them alive for a reason. Kade was just lucky to be alive. *Lucky, or cursed?* he wondered.

This was his first trip outside the camp after the attack.

They trekked with two DEF-Nine units behind them. They were the typical models, with orange visors built into their human-oid skulls. These units had some miles on them, as evidenced by the dents and dings in their armor. Draped over their chest rigs were the cracked bones of animals and humans, some looking more recently alive than others.

Kade remembered hearing a rumor that they did this for intim-idation—something programmed into their CPUs from centuries ago. He didn't understand why they would need that now.

Everyone was terrified of them—everyone except for Kade.

He looked back at the defector wearing the horns of some ancient animal that had once roamed the plains bordering the mountain. Some kind of antelope—he wasn't sure—but the rib cage attached to the front of the machine was undeniably human.

Maybe his own bones would be hanging on one of these war droids soon.

Maybe the machines didn't need him. Maybe they were lead-ing him somewhere to gun him and the others down and leave their flesh for the mutant creatures that roamed these plains.

Kade wouldn't run if that happened. Nor would he fight. He had long accepted that he would die here, one way or another.

Fighting was futile, but a part of him had yet to fully cave to the machines. There were still people he could help survive, even if they might never escape. People like Tia, other kids too. The promise he had made to her father, Raph, on a dive years ago kept him accountable. An image of the Māori Hell Diver's final moments surfaced in Kade's mind as he trudged forward. The image of his friend being hacked apart by the mutant feral humans was seared in his mind along with too many other horrible images that he could never purge.

More of them surfaced in his tormented head: Johnny popping like a bug in the air when they arrived at this blasted mountain. Kade finding his family's charred remains. And the attack that resulted in Joey's being erased much as Johnny had been.

"Where do you think they're taking us?" asked the man trudging alongside Kade.

It took him a second to place the voice as Captain Rolo's. It sounded far too timid, too fearful, to belong to the proud, strong captain of the *Victory*.

Kade ignored the question and kept walking, partly because he had no idea where they were going. He didn't remember ever taking this route away from the camp on other errands for the machines, but this was mostly the same group he usually went with.

Donovan, Beau, and Woody were all here. They had become a tight-knit group from working and living together. All three men had done their best to keep Kade alive and his spirits up. Woody was a jokester. Beau was a quiet man, father to a nine- and a seven-year-old boy that he loved more than anything. Donovan was an angry, aggressive man. He had whispered of trying to attack the machines again, but Kade had talked him down.

Beau and Woody were also against it, Beau trying his best to preserve the lives of his sons, who were being held in the same building as Tia.

"This is definitely a new route," Woody said. "Anyone see a dunny?"

"You take more shits than a squirrel," Beau said.

"It's the bloody soup they feed us, mate. Comes out unchanged from when it went in."

"Don't talk about food. I can't stand it anymore," Donovan said. He cursed the machines under his breath.

For the next two hours, the group of men plodded through the whipping wind, which seemed to be growing worse. Rain sheeted down on the hills in the distance. It would be on them soon.

"Hell, do y'all see that?" Beau asked.

Kade turned to the sprawling dunes west of them, where two modest-size twisters had formed. The vortices snaked and danced across the dry dirt, churning up more grit.

"Keep moving," said the soulless voice of a defector.

Another salvo of wind-driven grit slammed into the group. Kade lowered his head and braced against the onslaught. A few minutes later, the rain hit them all with cold, hard drops.

If not for Woody and Beau, water would now be leaking into the suit Kade wore. They had patched up his black suit when he was sleeping. Back when he dived, his gear could be the difference between life and death. That was before he lost his family.

The twin tornadoes roared closer, and again the line halted—this time, because Woody had slipped and fallen to the ground. A machine raised its laser rifle.

Kade hurried over with Donovan and helped Woody up.

"Don't shoot!" Beau said.

"Move or die," the machine said.

The group pushed on, winding down through a valley as the twisters finally spun back up into the clouds. For another hour, they trekked through the harsh terrain, moving into another area unfamiliar to Kade. He ended up on point, following the lead robot to the base of the mountain, where giant boulders blocked their advance.

Kade plotted a slope curving up and around the rocks. He started that way, moving between wind-polished boulders whose slick surfaces made travel all the more treacherous.

He tried to navigate a safe way up. For him, the hostile conditions weren't anything new. He had dived into frozen cities blanketed in snow, and red zones that were not just radioactive but also still burning. Places with coal deposits deep underground that would burn for centuries and never go out.

Despite his efforts to lead the group safely to its destination, he heard grunts and cries as prisoners behind him slipped and fell. He kept focused on the climb, becoming much like his machine captors.

At the command of a robotic voice, they halted. Glancing up, Kade saw they were under a vertical wall of rock. It protected them from the wind but did little to keep them dry. They huddled together for warmth.

Kade turned to look over the valley below. He could see much of their route, but not the prison camp. It was well on the other side of the mountain now.

One of the machines reached over its back and took off a cylindrical plastic pack. It placed the pack on the rocky ground, then stepped back after the lid clicked open. Inside was a large metal bottle.

"Drink," the machine commanded.

The crowd of prisoners surged toward it, with Rolo in the front of the line. He didn't seem to want to be the first to sample whatever was inside, though.

Donovan twisted off the lid and brought it up to his lips.

"What is it?" Rolo asked.

"Soup," Donovan said.

Rolo reached out. "Give it to me."

Woody stayed next to Kade while the prisoners fought over the bottle.

"More soup—what a surprise," Woody whispered. "I'm already gonna have the runs."

"Best clench up, then," Beau said.

Months ago, Kade might have laughed—he might still if he weren't so focused on something up the mountainside. He wiped the rain from his goggles for a better view. Just under the cloud cover, something protruded from the side of the mountain.

From here, it looked almost like a wing.

"Kade, you want some?" Beau asked.

"Nah."

"Come on, you need it," Woody said. He took a drink and handed it back.

Kade ignored it, still staring up as the clouds parted to expose the rocks hundreds of feet above them. Through the rain on his goggles, he could make out debris from an airship.

The burned remains had been there a decade, perhaps longer. They were within view only a few moments before the clouds shifted again, obscuring the wreckage.

"Hey, there's none left," someone in the back of the line said.

"Return the bottle to the pack and keep moving," said one of the defectors.

The group set off again. Kade hung back a little, letting Donovan take point behind the machine guiding them up the curving path, into the clouds.

As they got higher, the path narrowed to about five feet wide.

"Careful," Kade called back. "Hug the wall. Keep away from the edge."

His warnings were passed back but did little good. Beau lost his footing and fell to the ground.

"Gotcha," Woody said. With Kade's help, he pulled Beau up to his feet.

"No stopping," said the defector ahead of Donovan.

"Put your hand on the man ahead of you, and your other on the wall to guide you," Donovan said.

The group approached the cloud cover, all of them slowing in anticipation. Kade put a hand on Woody's shoulder, and Beau put a hand on Kade's. They trekked slowly, a human chain, melting into the clouds.

"Careful," Donovan called back.

The line slowed.

Rolo moved past Beau and grabbed Kade's shoulder.

"Take care, Commander Long," Rolo said.

"I got you . . ." Kade almost called him *sir*, but something stopped him. Watching Rolo devolve into a coward was really starting to infuriate Kade.

Pushing his feelings aside to lead Rolo, he hung on to Woody, whom he could hardly even see two feet ahead of him.

At a turtle's pace, the group advanced.

"Doing good," Kade said. "Everyone, keep moving. We do this together."

This was why he stayed alive, he thought to himself: to keep others safe.

Still, he wondered if there was a point.

What good was a life of nothing but scratching by?

What was this instinct to survive that kept people fighting through the harshest of situations? Something ingrained in all DNA to claw, scratch, and gnaw for survival.

Maybe it was also the hope that somehow they might once again be free.

A gust of wind snapped him from his philosophical musings.

A scream rang out, and Rolo pulled on Kade's back. Kade let

go of Woody and turned as the cry faded into the abyss. A distant smack marked the impact of a body against the rocks.

For a moment, no one moved.

"Who was it?" Kade asked.

He couldn't see past Rolo but feared for Beau.

"Beau, you back there?" Kade asked.

"Yes," came the reply.

"Move or die," the machines at both ends of the line said in unison.

The group pushed on. It was death by laser rifle, or take your chances on the path.

"Careful, Kade," Rolo said. "Please be careful."

Kade guided the captain higher into the clouds, tensing as another gust of wind slammed them.

Cries rang out, but the line held and no one went over the edge.

The march continued higher. It seemed that with every step, the wind picked up as Kade felt his way along, taking short, deliberate steps.

Terrified of upsetting the defectors, the prisoners were obliged to stop a third and fourth time to hunker down against the howling wind. When they started off again, Kade ran into the back of Woody, who had stopped abruptly.

"Sorry, mate," Kade replied. Stepping around his friend, he looked into a wide tunnel chiseled out of the bedrock. Glowing orange eyes pierced the darkness as the lead machine waited for the prisoners to gather. They all moved into the lip of a man-made—or, rather, machine-made—tunnel.

Train tracks stretched into the darkness.

The defector waited for its confederate to enter behind the humans.

"Forward," said the lead machine.

Lights in its metal shoulders clicked on. The visor also glowed brightly, illuminating the tunnel ahead.

Kade started after the defector, eager to see where the tunnel led.

"What is this place?" Beau asked.

"Shut up," Rolo said.

"Oh, now you want us to be quiet?" Woody said over his shoulder. "News alert, you ain't captain up here, mate. You're just one of us peasants."

"Quiet, all of you!" Kade hissed.

The machine inserted its finger into the center lock. Kade heard a click, then the clank of something bigger, and then a long, low whine as the massive round door cranked open.

Whatever it opened to, Kade couldn't see until the defector unit strode inside with its glowing orange visor.

"Move or die," the machine said.

Kade walked after it into a cavernous room. He flipped his goggles up and brought down his scarf to take a breath of stale air.

The machine kept moving, glowing like a beacon in the center of a chamber so vast that Kade still couldn't see across it. He glanced up. Couldn't see the ceiling either.

The tracks extended across the floor, making him think this was just one part of a facility built inside the mountain. The prisoners started across the chamber.

After a few minutes, Kade noticed something along the tracks ahead—clumps that brightened in the light emitted by the defector in front.

As he got closer, Kade recognized bags. Suitcases. Crates. Hundreds of them, heaped into mounds. Some were tattered from age and use, covered in cobwebs. The edge of the orange light illuminated the dusty windows and interior seats of a decrepit train that must have sat empty for decades.

The defector opened the first car and waved everyone in with its rifle barrel. As the prisoners piled inside, Kade noticed an imprint in the dust where someone had sat recently.

The door closed, and the train powered on. A dashboard in front of the seats flashed to life with gauges that looked even more old fashioned than what Kade had seen on the airship.

A strip of lights in the overhead clicked on, capturing the frightened faces of the passengers around Kade. Even Donovan looked spooked.

The train started down the tracks, quickly picking up speed. Its headlights speared outward, capturing an open blast door ahead. The train went through, whining louder as it picked up speed.

The defectors stood statue still, watching everyone. Most passengers kept their heads down, eyes on the floor. Kade glanced to the windows and the windshield, hoping for a view of their destination.

One of the machines raised its rifle just as the train began to slow. The ancient brakes screeched, and beams from the train shot out over another vast chamber. What Kade saw took his breath.

"Bloody hell!" Woody said.

As the train came to a stop, the passengers all rose to their feet and looked out over a vast city built inside a mountain.

"Out," said a defector.

The machine left through the car's open door and waited as the prisoners shuffled out onto a raised concrete platform overlooking the underground metropolis below. Kade walked over to the rail and took in the remarkable sight. Buildings six stories tall rose toward a rocky ceiling that sparkled with some sort of recessed lights that looked like stars.

Kade counted four of the larger structures and a dozen two-story buildings, plus a massive water cistern and what looked like a medical facility.

What he didn't see was movement. No one walked in the streets, but something was down there. Debris, perhaps. It was hard to tell in the dim light from the "stars" in the ceiling.

Questions rose in Kade's mind. Why was this place empty and not being used to house the prisoners living in squalor back at the camp?

And where were all the people who came here with the bags?

Anxious for answers, he followed the lead defector to an elevator off the platform. It was an industrial car, made for carrying lots of people, equipment, or both. The prisoners filed inside and rode it down to the bottom. Doors opened to a view of abandoned streets.

Clearly, they had not always been this empty.

Kade realized what he thought was debris when looking down from above was actually bodies. They lay on the road and the sidewalks outside the buildings. Most were just skeletons with tattered clothes, but here and there some of the remains had been disturbed.

Kade saw a corpse missing its entire rib cage.

The defector wearing one strode out of the car. "Move or die," it said.

Slowly, the herd of prisoners exited from the car, with Kade at the front. Beau suddenly held back, shaking.

"No, I can't be here," he said. "I have to get back to my boys. They need their father."

Kade grabbed him as he turned. "If you don't come with us, your boys won't *have* a father," he said.

"They'll be okay," Woody insisted.

Donovan put a hand on Beau, urging him to keep following the machines.

"You'll see them again," Kade said soothingly. It was his turn to try to help Beau. "Tia is with them; she'll watch over them. They know to stick together."

"Yeah," Donovan said. "Kade's right. You gotta stay alive right now, is all."

"Come on," Woody said.

They started down the center of the road, through the scene of death. Many of the skulls Kade passed bore wounds from laser bolts. He thought about what must've occurred here, and the scene played out in his mind as his boots crunched on empty shell casings.

This place had been built by humans before the war and was probably occupied by military officers and staff when the machines rose up around the world. The defectors had then found this place, infiltrated it, and used their laser weapons to slaughter everyone inside armed with obsolete guns. They later decided to use the mountain as a lure for more humans.

Using bait to bring us here, instead of hunting us down, he thought. *Ingenious and evil.*

Kade looked down to see footprints in the dust. There were two other tracks too, left by the mechanical feet of defectors.

Someone had been here recently.

He looked to a sign mounted on a pole at the first corner ahead. It showed a few bullet holes, no evidence of rust. Kade read down the list.

Ration Center
Hospital
Barracks
Apartments
Command Center
Maintenance Wing 1
Maintenance Wing 2

The first building they came to was the ration center. Most of the windows were shot out. Kade could see bare shelves inside and an empty counter with a white flip sign displaying the numerals 52.

Kade figured it was the number of the last person who had come for their rations.

The lead defector rounded the corner and continued to the hospital next, following the tracks of the recent visitor.

A crater obliterated the road where an explosion had blown open the front of the building. Limbless remains lay outside.

Not slowing, the machine strode past what must be the barracks. The second story had collapsed, flattening much of the first, and pieces of rubble had slid over much of the road.

The defector took a path through the debris toward three apartment buildings—four stories, all intact.

"Crikey," Beau said. "They're gonna keep us here, aren't they?"

There were courtyards outside, with withered trees and what were once garden beds and playgrounds. He could imagine the laughter of kids playing on the slide and swings.

The group pushed on, passing the water tanks, the sewage treatment center, the two maintenance buildings, and a tower with satellite dishes.

Railroad tracks led up to the open front doors.

"Stop," said the defector.

The group complied, huddling again, some shivering from fear.

"We are bringing this facility online," said the robotic voice. "Due to your skills, you have been picked to operate it."

"No, no, no," Beau said.

Kade and Woody turned to console their friend. They couldn't let him crack, not after making it this far.

"You all have specific trades that will be utilized," said the machine.

"Why not operate it yourselves?" Beau said through clenched teeth. "Why do they need us?"

Kade had wondered the same thing, but the answer seemed to be labor.

"Follow," said the defector.

The group moved into the command center. Its heavy doors were scarred by laser bolts. Inside, shell casings littered the floor. The humans had fought back.

The train tracks continued through the doors.

The defector marched them down the hallway, past open office doors. Kade saw a family picture on a wall—a husband and wife surrounded by their four kids.

Memories of his own family made his chest tighten.

"Here," said a defector.

The machine opened a pair of heavy doors to a room with three rows of connected desks in a half-moon shape. The stations faced a large wall-mounted monitor and a dozen smaller ones.

The captives followed the defector to the front of the room. The monitors flicked on, showing maps of the world.

Asia. North and South America. Africa. Antarctica. Hawaii.

On each map were red skulls with dates ranging from the beginning of the war to just a month ago.

It didn't take long to figure out what they were.

They represented places where humans had been tracked down by the defector hunter-killer units and eliminated.

On the other side of the room, the second machine had flipped switches labeled WATER-TREATMENT CENTER and ELECTRI-CAL GRID. The SATELLITE switch was already flipped.

As more screens blinked on, a voice echoed through the facility.

Kade turned and looked up at a window overlooking the room

where it seemed to be coming from. The harder he strained to hear, the more it sounded familiar.

"If you're listening, we have food, water, and safety," the voice said. *"We are the hope you have been longing for, the star in the sky that will lead you to your salvation. To a new world and a life you have only dreamed of."*

The voice trailed off, and a slender person with a patch on one eye emerged from behind the glass above them.

"What the shit," Woody said. "Is that Carl?"

Rolo turned and looked. "It can't . . ."

Kade couldn't believe it. But this was indeed Carl.

He felt another jolt of anger—for once, not at the machines. It was obvious now why they had been spared after the attack. They all had skills the machines needed to keep this place running.

It seemed they had picked Carl for his ability to convince people to do things they shouldn't—for his charm.

He stepped up to the window, raised a hand, and waved with what looked like a crack of a smile on his face.

ONE

I should have beat the smile off that bastard's face until he had no face, thought Xavier Rodriguez.

The Hell Diver and former king of the Vanguard Islands stood behind the wheel of the *Sea Wolf*, thinking about Charmer. The cunning snake was hundreds of miles away, hanging in a cage at the capitol tower rig. X would have preferred to hand him over directly to the Octopus Lords, but Kade had insisted that not killing him could save lives.

X had agreed, knowing that Charmer would get his eventually. Maybe X would even be back to witness it—and with Michael too. That was the mission that mattered most to X: finding Michael, Layla, Bray, Victor, Steve, and the airship.

He had lost Michael once before, and he wasn't going to do it again.

Gripping the wheel, X guided the catamaran over heavy chop. The hull rocked from side to side. They had been on the open water for over two days straight and were nearing the isle of Grenada. Miles snored peacefully on the floor beneath the dash. Magnolia was also resting, but X could find no peace wherever he tried to take his mind.

He'd had plenty of time to think on whether he was doing the right thing since he left the Vanguard Islands. Their home was in the hands of Commander Kade Long, who would soon be crowned king if he wasn't already. With General Forge's help, they would protect their home from any foreign threat, including this mysterious Forerunner and his knights.

According to the info Kade had given X, the knights' odds of even reaching the islands weren't good. And if they did arrive, General Forge would be able to repel them.

Still, X's leaving the islands was a decision that some might criticize. Some might see it as weakness. But X believed in his heart that he was doing the best thing for the islands. He had done everything in his power, first to lead his people to a new home, and then to protect that home by expanding and by securing a new food source.

And he had failed at the latter.

Panama had turned out to be a disaster. They lost hundreds of warriors setting up Outpost Gateway. Then they lost the outpost and, with it, Rodger.

On the Sunshine Coast of Australia, the Vanguard military had suffered more losses, some due to the terrain and its mutant denizens, but most due to Captain Rolo. The destruction of the supercarrier *Immortal* and the two hundred souls aboard was a blow that shattered not only the military but also the survivors' confidence in X. Gran Jefe and a squad of other Cazadores had put X to the test, nearly getting him killed by a gigantic water bug on the assault ship *Frog* during their return trip home.

X had survived and had taken the islands back from Rolo and Charmer, but he had decided that his reign was at its end. The islands needed new leadership that everyone could trust. Kade and Forge were the two best people for their roles.

In his heart, X felt he owed this not only to the people back home but also to Michael. He had abandoned the young man and his family twice: on his quest to form an outpost in Panama, and again on his journey to search for the Coral Castle, leaving Michael to fend for himself against Charmer and his henchmen.

But it was the orders to hide the food that had given the plotters their opening to turn public opinion against Michael. If it weren't for Layla and Victor, her husband would be dead and Bray would be without a father. X owed it to them to bring them back into the sunshine.

Hearing a grunt from outside the cabin, X looked back at the weather deck. Jo-Jo, the three-hundred-pound monkey, was down there slamming something against the slippery deck. Here in the sunless wastes, she was only an indistinct shadow, just as she had been aboard the *Frog* when she ghosted down the super-structure of the ship and flung Charmer to the deck, effectively ending his tyrannical rule.

X almost laughed when he saw that her prey was a fish.

Jo-Jo smacked the scaly body against the deck again until it quit wriggling. Then she raised the carcass and took a bite out of the belly. The monkey didn't seem to mind being on a boat in sloppy seas, but X was already getting tired of it. And they were still a long way from Rio de Janeiro.

X checked their route on the digital dashboard. According to the map, it would be another seven to ten days before they got there, depending on the wind. Right now they were using only the sails and moving at just over twelve knots.

So far, the trip had been smooth, with only one major storm, which had knocked their radio booster loose. He had yet to fix it, but he would as soon as Magnolia felt good enough to take the helm.

She had spent much of the trip belowdecks, mourning Rodger and recuperating from her injuries. X didn't bother her except to make sure she was eating and drinking. She needed nourishment and hydration to recover fully from the radiation poisoning she had suffered back on the Sunshine Coast.

X checked the gauges. To conserve battery and fuel, the hybrid engines were both offline. From what he could tell, everything was tip-top thanks to the Cazador engineers who had serviced the ship just before departure.

He took a seat on the cracked leather captain's seat and stared at the radio, desperately wishing he could use it to contact the Vanguard Islands for an update.

Soon, he thought.

X reached down to Miles to stroke his coat. The dog looked up groggily, then pushed himself up, trembling slightly. He was getting older and having a harder time getting around. He was also sleeping a lot more.

It hurt to think about losing him, but X was preparing for that every day.

"Go back to sleep, bud," he said. "I'm going to catch some shut-eye too."

X scanned the sky for storm clouds, then the surface for any kind of threat. Aside from sporadic flashes of lightning, the dark sky was mostly clear.

Satisfied, he adjusted his body in the comfortable chair and closed his eyes.

It wasn't long before he drifted off. Memories of the past haunted X. Diving through electrical storms. Battles against eyeless Sirens and deformed beasts that defied nature. They weren't all nightmares, though.

He remembered the sunshine of the Vanguard Islands. His head filled with images of farmers sowing and tending crops, sky people and Cazadores bartering goods at the trading post.

A new dream came. Miles was walking across a frozen tundra with X, both of them dressed in thick gray hazard suits and fighting a brutal wind. Snowflakes peppered their visors as X scanned the terrain.

At first, he thought this was Hades. But there were no partially buried buildings of Old World Chicago sticking out of the snow. No high-rises lying in pieces like broken toys.

The sun broke through the gray mass of clouds to spread over a sprawling icy landscape of rolling dunes that looked like frozen waves. This wasn't a dream but a vision of a place X had never seen.

He kept walking with Miles, crossing into a valley carved by a glacier. They trekked through the center, but X stopped when he felt resistance. He realized then that he was pulling a sled of supplies, which was caught.

The dream flashed ahead. They were out of the valley now, standing in front of a mountain chain. An enormous satellite dish looked up from the jagged peaks. No, not one but three dishes.

The weather-modification units. General Forge had shown him blueprints of them what felt like ages ago now.

He staggered against the screaming wind, closing his eyes.

When they opened again, he was back in the cabin of the *Sea Wolf.* He groaned as he awoke, wondering whether this was dream or premonition. He used to have the same type of dream about the Vanguard Islands before he ever knew of their existence.

Rain tapped at the window, and X got up to see storm clouds on the horizon. The wind wasn't from any dream or vision. It was real, and it was knocking the catamaran around like a child's toy.

He went to the hatch over the stern weather deck and opened

it to a surprising sight. Magnolia had climbed the center mast and stood in the crow's nest, working on the radio dish booster.

"What are you doing?" he shouted.

"What it looks like!" she yelled down.

X watched her fiddling with the dish. He was glad to see her up and active, but she should have woken him.

"Be careful!" X yelled. "That wind is getting—"

The boat rocked hard, nearly sending X over the gunwale. He held on and looked up to Magnolia. She was holding steady.

"I'm almost done," she called down.

X stayed where he was, just in case she needed his help. He finally relaxed when she got halfway down the rungs on the mast. Jo-Jo met her at the bottom, now holding a new half-eaten fish. The animal knuckle-walked after Magnolia to the ladder leading to the second deck cabin, where X now stood.

"Stay put," he said to Jo-Jo.

The animal went down in a squat, watching as Magnolia climbed up to the cabin.

X shut the door, sealing out the rain and wind. "How you feeling?" he asked.

She shrugged. "How about you?"

"Fine until I saw that storm."

Lightning speared the horizon.

"Looks like a big bugger," he said. "Static might cut us off, so good thing you got the dish up and—"

"Not sure if I got it running," Magnolia said. "Go check." She took the wheel while he took a seat in front of the dashboard. He tuned to the encrypted channel.

"Vanguard Command, this is Ki— This is Xavier Rodriguez and the *Sea Wolf*," he said. "Does anyone copy?"

Static filled the cabin, drowned out at the end by a thunder-clap. Miles groaned and put his head down.

"I feel the same way, boy," Magnolia said.

X raised the transmitter again.

"Vanguard Command, this is X and the *Sea Wolf*. Does anyone copy?"

He looked to Magnolia.

"Want me to go fiddle with it again?" she asked.

Just as X was about to answer, the radio crackled.

"Xavier," said a voice.

It was muddled, distant sounding, and he didn't recognize the voice.

"Copy, this is X," he replied. "Who is this?"

"Good to hear your voice, sir. This is General Forge. I thought you should know, Kade Long has been sworn in as king."

The radio crackled again, the channel going in and out.

"How is everything else back there?" X asked.

"Our defenses are in place," Forge said. "How is your journey?"

"It was going well until a few minutes ago. We're about to hit a big storm front."

There was a long pause.

"How are things there?" X asked.

"We're still tracking down the last of the holdouts, sir."

"Charmer still lives?"

"Yes, for now."

X snorted. He wasn't sure what King Kade was waiting for, but there had to be a reason for it. "Guide the cowboy," X said. "He will need you every step of the way."

"I will do my best, King Xavier. Be safe on your travels."

"We will. I'll be in touch soon." X put the transmitter back on the station as Magnolia glanced over.

"Should we make a run for Grenada, maybe wait it out?" she asked.

"No," X decided in the moment. "We've been through worse than this. We're gonna run right through it."

"You're sure?"

"We got the sails up," he said. "Full speed ahead."

X looked at the dark-blue clouds as lightning shot through them, illuminating them from within. The airship was out there somewhere, and on it, the only family X had left besides Mags and Miles.

"We're coming, Tin," X said. "We *will* find you."

Magnolia put a hand on X's forearm.

"I guess we're like them now, huh?" she asked.

"How so?"

"Renegades."

X grunted. "Your parents should have named you that, kid."

"*Kid?* And look who's talking! What about *you*?"

"Okay, both of us." He grinned. "Renegades for life."

*   *   *   *   *

Pockets of turbulence shook the airship.

The *Vanguard* was dead in the water—or, rather, air—210 miles north of the southern tip of Florida. Michael Everhart shook his head in frustration.

An ocean of storms flashed below them on the digital screens. He stood in front of them with his wife and their son, who was sleeping in a sling across her chest. The boy was getting big and would soon outgrow it. He was already starting to prefer walking around, exploring everything in sight, rather than riding around at his mother's whim.

Michael focused on the task at hand. They had to fix the ship, then find water. Then they had to cross the Atlantic to the Canary Islands and find a place to live.

A place to live… Michael recalled the dread he always felt as a kid, wondering if his family would ever be safe. After his father died and X took him in, he doubted it. Then X led them to the Metal Islands.

Michael tensed up thinking of X. For the past week he had tried not to think too much about him. But it was at times like this that memories of his best friend and mentor entered his thoughts.

He missed X terribly.

It was also times like this that the anger filled Michael. If not for Rolo and Charmer, X would still be alive.

Michael focused on the living. Not just his family but Steve and Victor as well. Victor was resting in sickbay, still recovering from wounds sustained during the escape from the Vanguard Islands nearly six days ago.

He had provided more information about the Canary Islands and the specific location of the place called Jameos del Agua. Michael pulled it up on the computer again to go over the blueprints that the archives had on the former Centro de Arte, Cultura y Turismo. If they could get there, he wanted to be ready.

A man named César Manrique had built the place. According to data, the volcanic tunnel and caverns had been home to a resort with an underground concert hall and salt lake. Victor had lived there with Ton and ten friends before eight of them fled on a ship to America. The other four stayed behind, which meant they could still be there.

Michael looked up from the blueprints.

"Pepper, where's Steve?" he asked.

The ship's AI emerged, dressed as nattily as ever with a bow tie and impeccably trimmed beard.

"Steve's trying to bring the water-treatment plant back online," Timothy said. "He said he has everything under control, and I've checked in three times."

"Sounds like the Schwarzer," Michael said. "Tell him I'll come help soon."

"Yes, sir."

Michael thought about everything they needed to do before they could brave the storms. From Outpost Gateway, they had scavenged parts to repair the plant and patch up *Vanguard*'s exterior. But so far, they had worked only inside.

"Damn," Michael said.

"What?" Layla whispered.

"Someone has to go topside and repair the damaged panels, or we'll never make it to the Canary Islands."

"We're not going to make it there without water either," Layla said.

She was right. They had lost a fifth of their reserves when Charmer ordered his forces to fire on the ship during its escape from the Vanguard Islands. They had lost another 30 percent to storm damage after leaving Panama. Fire had broken out during the ascent to twenty-five thousand feet, requiring precious water reserves to douse it.

He looked to the dashboard. They had just under half their water. Even with the recycling system and only five passengers, the farm needed more in order to keep alive the crops that would feed them should they fail to find food in the Canary Islands.

Assuming they could even get there.

For the foreseeable future, this was their home, and that meant they had to find the most important resource.

"We'll figure everything out, Michael, don't worry," Layla said. "I'm going to put Bray down now. Back soon."

"If I'm not here, I'm in the archives."

"Okay."

She kissed Michael on the cheek, and he smiled at Bray.

"Love you, little guy," he whispered.

Layla left quietly, and Michael turned back to the monitors. He lost himself in thought again until a voice pulled him back.

"Chief," Steve said.

He stood at the top level of the bridge, gripping the rail. Grease streaked his forehead.

"Got the treatment center working, I think," he said.

"Already?" Michael replied.

"Yeah, wasn't too bad. Want to try it out?"

"Timothy, let's test it."

"Okay, sir, but it will take a few hours to run tests before bringing it fully online," replied the AI.

Steve dragged a rag across his face. "I'm ready to start fixing the exterior panels whenever," he said.

"You deserve a break," Michael said.

"I'd go for a shower and a nap." Steve smiled and stuffed the rag into his pocket.

The old engineer always did whatever needed doing, and had risked everything to get Michael back to his family. He had also taken the lead back at Outpost Panama, endangering his life to gather the parts to keep the airship in the sky.

"Thanks," Michael said. "I couldn't do this without you."

"You got it, Chief."

"Go take care of yourself. You deserve it."

They parted ways, and Michael went to the quarters that once served as a library. The metal door whisked open, revealing a dark space with desks and mounted monitors. The room had changed since Michael came here years ago with Layla seeking information about the surface. The bolted-down bookshelves and built-in carrels were gone, taken out long ago when Rodger Mintel and his crew retrofitted the *Hive* and transformed it into the faster, nimbler *Vanguard*.

The thought of Rodger, and everyone else who had perished

over the past month, threatened to distract Michael from why he was here.

You can't help the dead, he thought.

As it was, the living had problems enough and to spare. He must get his family to the Canary Islands. That meant finding clean water before setting off across three thousand miles of Atlantic Ocean.

"Timothy, please mark the location of all ITC facilities along the Eastern Seaboard of the United States," Michael said.

"Certainly, sir."

A digital screen with a forking crack that looked like lightning came online somehow. On either side of that inky purple crack were listed locations of ITC campuses on the coast of the old United States.

The massive facilities had once been the home of groundbreaking technologies, from robotic design, research, and production to chemical and biological weapons.

ITC was also the leader in artificial intelligence.

Underneath the labs and production lines were bunkers built to house survivors of the apocalypse, just in case geopolitical risks should boil over and war rage through the fragile civilization of the twenty-first century. Little did they know, it would be their own work that enabled the destruction of all they held dear.

Michael had always found that ironic, but it was no surprise really.

Fortunately, ITC had prepared for the end with plenty of food, water, and resources to keep large numbers alive through a nuclear, chemical, or biological holocaust.

But there was something they hadn't prepared for. Deep beneath the research labs and bunkers of stockpiled goods were *monsters.*

Michael scoured the archives for hours, taking notes on

the locations. This was his fourth time going over them. He had created a list based on a battery of criteria.

First: the type of radiation zone they were in, ranging green to red.

Second: whether they had been visited before by the *Hive* or any ship that had contacted the *Hive* over the years.

Third: the function of the facility, and what supplies might be there.

Michael remembered many of these places, like Hades in what was once Chicago, and the Hilltop Bastion in the dead city of Charleston, South Carolina. The bunker was where they had found Timothy during the disastrous reign of Captain Leon Jordan on the *Hive*. It was also where they had discovered a second airship, which they named *Deliverance*.

The Hilltop Bastion was a place he knew intimately, and it was likely still packed full of supplies.

He shuddered recalling their narrow escape into *Deliverance* after the bone beast crushed Commander Rick Weaver's skull like a melon.

That wasn't the only monster that prowled the dark corridors and cavernous storage spaces a hundred floors under the main facility.

He remembered discovering the first cryo-chamber, where hundreds of humans and various animal species had been frozen. Most of the glass pods were broken and empty. He'd thought it strange at the time that some seemed to have been broken from the inside. Now he knew exactly why.

The genetically modified humans were created in a lab to survive the radiation.

Inside their tubes, they had evolved into abominations of nature.

"Michael."

He turned from the computer screen to find Layla standing in the open hatch to the archives. She smiled and walked over.

"Hey," he said.

"Do you know what time it is? You could use some sleep."

Michael rubbed his eyes and looked at the screen. It was after midnight.

"Time got away from me. Sorry," he said.

"What are you looking at…" Her words trailed off when she saw the screen. "The Hilltop Bastion? You're not seriously thinking about going there for the supplies."

Michael shook his head. "I was considering it. Too risky."

"*Everywhere* is too risky."

"I've got it narrowed down to a few locations," he said. "Here, take a look."

She pulled up a rolling chair and looked at the notebook.

"Is that Captain Rolo's?" Timothy asked.

"What?" Michael looked over as the AI's hologram flickered to life.

"The captain kept a notebook while he served on this ship," Timothy said.

"I don't give one single shit about what that filth had to say," Layla said. "Never mention—"

"Wait," Michael interrupted.

Layla glared.

"I want to hear this," Michael said. "Where's this notebook?"

"Why do you care?" Layla asked.

"I want to see it."

They followed Timothy out of the archives and through the retrofitted ship, stopping outside a hatch in the officers' barracks. Though they had searched the ship for stowaways, they had not looked for anything else.

Inside, they found a perfectly made bunk with a single blue

pillow. A desk with a chair secured under it was the only furnishing besides a bookshelf. Michael scoured it for any kind of notebook but found only hardcover books.

"It's in the bottom drawer," Timothy said.

Layla went to the desk, bent down, and pulled out two note-books. Michael hovered behind her as she flipped through a collection of sketches. The first was an image of Mount Kiliman-jaro, just as Michael remembered it.

Next was a sketch of a defector unit with a glowing orange visor.

"Old bastard is something of an artist, huh?" Michael asked.

"Who cares?" Layla said. "Timothy, is there anything in these that might help us?"

"Yes. Try the red notebook," said the AI.

Layla opened the second notebook.

"He kept logs of places the airship *Victory* traveled before Tanzania," Timothy explained. "I wonder if any of these might be useful to us before we make the trip to the Canary Islands."

Michael leaned down as Layla flipped through the log. There were ITC facilities, but also spots Michael had never heard of before.

"This dive was to a museum," Layla said.

"What did Rolo write?" Michael asked.

"He writes, 'We lost Raphael on this dive, but Kade and Johnny returned with intel that led us to Mount Rushmore. That is where we learned about Mount Kilimanjaro and the so-called safe zone there.'"

Layla kept going, pausing at a section called *Resources.*

"He marked areas where they dived for power cells, ammu-nition—all sorts of supplies," Layla said. She came across a page labeled *Water.*

"Looks like they stopped in the Blue Ridge Mountains for water," she said.

"They landed there?"

"No, they hovered over Mount Mitchell and dropped a tube down for divers to fill up."

Layla showed Michael an image that Rolo had drawn of the airship hovering over a mountain range.

"They must have had a tube long enough to stretch down and a pump powerful enough to suck the weight of water up to the airship."

"Do we have anything like that?" Layla asked.

"We did, but I'm not sure we still have long enough hoses or a strong enough pump system."

"We do, actually," Timothy said. "And here's good news. I just got an alert the water-treatment plant is about to come back online."

"Excellent! Now all we need is some water to fill it back up."

They looked at the map of Mount Mitchell.

"The area's a green zone," Layla said.

"I have maps of the different waterfalls at Mount Mitchell, also the facilities that were there before the war," Timothy said.

"No radiation, no monsters," Michael said.

"Famous last words," Layla said.

"Either way, we still have to fix the ship before we can go anywhere."

"I'm ready," Steve said. He stood in the doorway, his face clean but eyes still heavy and tired. "I'll dive too if you teach me how."

Michael and Layla exchanged a glance.

"That's mighty brave of you—and, if I'm honest, maybe a little crazy," Layla said with a grin. "But one of us needs to go."

"We'll figure it out after we fix the ship," Steve said.

"Okay, let's get moving, then," Michael said. "We got a ship to fix and water to find."

TWO

After the sun went down, a fifty-foot yacht pulled out of the marina at the capitol tower. It took a southerly bearing toward the invisible wall separating the light from the dark. The average onlooker would have missed it as it carved through the dark water, but Kade Long knew exactly where to look, because he was the one who had ordered it deployed. He stood on a balcony with binoculars to his eyes.

Onboard the yacht, three Cazador scouts under top-secret orders were prepared to be away indefinitely. Their mission: reach the Panama Canal and watch for the Knights of the Coral Castle. Based on what Kade had seen when he was a prisoner there, he believed that if the Forerunner were to deploy his troops, they would come by sea, which meant coming through the canal. In the unlikely event that the knights did have another pilot and could repair one of the other helicopters, it would be dealt with the same way the first chopper was dealt with.

Kade surveyed the machine guns and cannons spread out across the rooftop where that helicopter had been shot down. Soon, he would visit the knight who survived the crash, Lieutenant

Lucky Gaz, to see if he could get him to talk. The more Kade could find out about the Forerunner's forces, the better he would be at protecting the Vanguard Islands.

He looked away from the arrayed weapons, back out to sea, where his eyes fell on the container ship *Osprey*. It was hard to miss with the deck lit up like an airstrip from fires burning in open metal barrels. In a few hours, Kade would be crowned king of the Vanguard Islands on that very deck.

He wasn't ready for this. He didn't even *want* to be king. If he had known that pulling the trigger and ending Captain Rolo's life was going to result in this, would he still have done it?

Kade wasn't thinking about the Cazador custom at the time. He hadn't realized that killing Rolo would make him a shoo-in for the next king. Of course, it got muddy, considering Rolo was made king when everyone *thought* X was dead. If X wanted to, he could have fought it, but he seemed happy to hand over the reins.

This is just temporary, Kade reassured himself. *You're just a steward of the crown—just caretaking it.*

He thought of words from his Hell Diver commander, Raphael, Tia's father.

Sometimes, the best person for the job is the guy that doesn't want that job.

Kade had learned something of his own over the years: experience was what made a man good at something. He had also learned that a man had to know when to accept his fate, or be ruined by it.

This was his job now, his *duty*.

The crescent moon peeked out of the storm clouds as Kade left the balcony with the two Cazador soldiers who had been awaiting him there.

All told, fifty-two people had died during the whirlwind civil war two days ago. Six were civilians caught in the cross fire, including three from oil rig 14. Tonight, they were scattering the ashes of one of them, a young man named Cooper, Beau's oldest teenage son.

Kade saw his old friend from the machine camp standing in the crowd with his other son, Roman, by his side. Woody was also there, doing his best to comfort Beau.

From what Kade understood, Cooper had been fishing by himself in a rowboat the night of the attack and was mistaken for an enemy. He had been shot more than ten times.

Kade stood with his guards as the funeral ended. Beau, holding a hat in his hand, walked past, hardly even looking up while Roman and Woody escorted him away.

"Beau," Kade said.

Woody gave a sad smile. "Ah, Kade," he said, "nice of you to come."

"Kade?" Beau said. He squinted, as if he were having a hard time seeing.

"I'm sorry about Cooper," Kade said.

"The Cazadores kill anything and everything," Roman said. "They murdered Cooper."

"No," Beau said. He put a hand on his son's shoulder and looked in his eyes. "Your brother is dead because of *our* people. Because of Charmer, Rolo, and Donovan. *They* betrayed our people."

"They didn't shoot him."

"What happened to Cooper is a tragedy, but your father is right: this would never have happened but for Charmer," Kade said. He thought of Donovan, his old friend and ally from the machine camp. It broke his heart that Donovan had sided with Charmer and even fought for him. He was still out there somewhere with the other plotters, hiding and perhaps even awaiting the chance to strike.

"So what are you going to do about Donovan and Charmer, then?" Roman asked.

Beau and Woody both looked at Kade. After all, he would be in charge soon. If he wanted, he could have Charmer skinned alive and burned to a crisp before being ripped into pieces and fed to the Octopus Lords.

But that would make Kade no better than his enemy. And right now he had another enemy to worry about: the Forerunner. He had to move cautiously, especially in finding the last of the holdouts who had allied with Charmer. Donovan and the others still posed a threat to the fragile peace in place. For that reason, Kade needed Charmer alive.

"They will all be held accountable," Kade said. "You have my word."

The clank of armor caught his attention. General Forge strode up with an entourage of two praetorian guards in heavy armor. From what Kade understood, these soldiers were trained specifically in hand-to-hand combat and to prevent assassinations. Forge definitely had enemies.

"Sir, they're almost ready for you on the *Osprey*," he said.

"I'll be ready in a minute," Kade said. He turned back to his friends and Roman. The younger man stared at Forge with anger in his eyes. *This is how the cycle of violence continues*, Kade reflected. As king, his two main jobs were to protect the Vanguard Islands from external enemies and to break that pernicious cycle of suspicion, blame, and bigotry.

He reached out to Beau. "I'm sorry, mate. I'm truly sorry."

Beau took his hand. Then Roman too.

"If there's anything we can do, we're here," Woody said.

"Yeah," Roman said.

Beau nodded. "Just say the word."

There was new strength in his voice. Losing his oldest son ·

had changed Beau in some of the same ways that losing his family had changed Kade—often the case with people robbed of their loved ones.

Kade took a second to look at his two old friends from the machine camp. Before the crash, Woody had worked as a pilot on the airship, and Beau in the water plant. Both of them had served as maintenance workers on the oil rig since their rescue. Neither had joined Charmer, but they had done little to stop him. It seemed that now they were ready to step up. He could use their support, and he could use some friends, especially with Magnolia and X out there in the wastes.

"You know what? Why don't you come to the ceremony?" Kade suggested. "If you feel up to it, of course."

Beau and Roman exchanged a glance.

"You're both welcome, and you too, Woody." Kade looked at Forge for confirmation.

"No problem," Forge said, "but we shouldn't keep everyone waiting."

"Come on," Kade said, waving his old friends toward the elevator car. Then he stopped short. Charmer was still in the hanging cage, and seeing him there would upset Beau and Roman even more. "General Forge, take Beau and Roman down the internal stairs," he said. "Woody, you come with me."

They parted ways, and Woody and Kade hurried to the cage. After securing the gate, Kade pushed the lever down, lowering the elevator toward the marina. Halfway down, dangling from a pole that jutted like a bowsprit over the waters below, was the cage holding Charmer. Both arms were still in casts.

The fallen tyrant glanced up at the car with a grin on his face—that same sly grin Kade remembered from that day inside Mount Kilimanjaro when he had discovered that Carl was the "voice" of the machines.

"So this is it?" Charmer said. "You're going to be the new king? All because you blew off Rolo's crazed wig?"

Woody looked to Kade, who had nothing to say to Carl right now. And that was the worst possible punishment for a master manipulator: to be ignored.

"Rolo deserved what he got," Charmer said. "I was planning to do the same thing to him. You and I are the same, Kade. We—"

"Oh, we're *nothing* alike," Kade said calmly, but unable to let that one slide. "Like Rolo, you killed innocent people for your own gain. And like Rolo, you will pay for your crimes."

"I've sacrificed *everything* for our people, Kade!"

"Spare us the sniveling, Carl," Woody said. "You've only ever been in it for yourself."

"What have *you* done, Woody?" Charmer yelled back. "Nothing, that's what! You sat on that rig and did nothing, just as you did nothing at the machine camp!"

"That changes now." Woody turned to Kade. "Whatever you need, mate, I'm at your disposal. I've got your back, no matter what."

The elevator clanked to a stop at the bottom, and Kade stepped out to join the soldiers waiting for him on the pier. Soon, Forge, Beau, and Roman emerged from a door onto the pier, where two more Cazador soldiers escorted them to a small boat that would ferry everyone to the *Osprey*.

"Defenses are almost finished," Forge said. "We have boats on the perimeter of our territory, watching. We also have redistributed our soldiers. If the knights come here, we will have plenty of time to react."

"And the final holdouts?" Kade asked.

"Still searching for them," Forge said, the frustration clear in his voice. "We have a full list now. Here."

The general handed Kade a piece of paper. Kade recognized

everyone on the list, though seeing Donovan's name still surprised him. He wondered what had gone wrong. Perhaps, it was when he had served on the jury for Michael Everhart's trial. A sham trial that Charmer had used to spread lies and frame the very hero who had rescued them all from the machine camp.

Kade hoped Donovan was still alive and not lying at the bottom of the ocean. Maybe it wasn't too late to bring him back to reality.

He handed the paper back to Forge.

"Any idea where they could be?" Kade asked.

"After searching all the rigs and every boat and ship, I believe they went into the storms," Forge said. "We have several boats unaccounted for, though they could have sunk in the fight."

Kade looked out over the dark water.

"Bastards!" Roman said. "I'll kill them myself."

"No," said Beau. "I won't lose you too, damn it. You will keep your head down and—"

"That's all we've done since we got here, Dad, and it didn't save Cooper! Maybe if we had tried to stop Charmer, Cooper would still be alive."

Beau turned to look out the windscreen at the *Osprey*, now only a hundred meters out.

"We'll find Donovan," Kade said. "Justice will prevail."

As the boat pulled up to the *Osprey*, a rope ladder dropped down to the soldiers. Kade followed them up to the deck. The fiery orange glow from the barrel fires reflected off the polished armor of a dozen Cazador warriors on the deck.

They were the best of the best, the elite Barracuda warriors.

Commander Slayer, a battered but resilient Sergeant Blackburn, and Sergeant Jorge "Gran Jefe" Mata. Facing them were militia soldiers pulled from the former *Hive*, *Victory*, and several other airships with survivors rescued from Mount Kilimanjaro.

Lieutenant Wynn was also here, commanding a unit of militia guards. Kade hardly knew him, but he knew that Wynn had been held captive by Charmer and the Wave Runners. X had trusted Wynn and the Barracudas—except for Gran Jefe, who Kade would deal with at some point.

Tiger was also here. Promoted to captain after the loss of Captain Two Skulls, he was now one of the highest-ranking sailors left in the navy, and also one of the youngest. That didn't bother Kade in the slightest. The kid was capable, and he had experience under his belt.

Corporal Valeria stood in the same group. A good decade older than Tiger, and also with plenty of fighting experience.

Kade walked down the center of the deck to the final group: the Hell Divers.

Sofia was here in a wheelchair. Tia stood beside her, along with twelve greenhorn Hell Divers who had been aboard the airship *Vanguard* when Rolo nuked the supercarrier *Immortal*.

None of them had known what happened, and all were sleeping in the launch bay when the missile fired. Only Eevi had tried to stop things on the bridge, and she later paid the ultimate price. Ensign Dmitri Vasilev and Lieutenant Olga Novak said their own lives had been threatened.

Knowing how unhinged Rolo had become, Kade was inclined to believe them, but this was partly because General Forge had personally interrogated them. Over the past two days, he had vetted fifty-five people to see who they could trust.

As Kade walked down the deck to Imulah and the scribes preparing to start the ceremony, his mind harkened back to everything that got him here.

It was hard to understand the cascade of events that had led them to this point. A lifetime, really, even though it seemed only months ago that Kade was taking diving orders from Captain Rolo.

The camp at Kilimanjaro, and then coming here, had changed all of them, but it had turned Rolo and his right-hand man into murderers.

"Kade Long," the scribe said. "Tonight, we gather for a tradition two and a half centuries old. Tonight, you will be crowned king of the Vanguard Islands. Are you ready to accept this great honor?"

"Yes," Kade said.

"Follow me."

Imulah walked across the deck of the ship. A second scribe held out a knife wrapped in a purple cloth. He unwrapped it, and Imulah took the knife.

"Hold up your hand," he said.

Kade did as instructed. He saw Woody, Beau, and Roman all watching. Having his old friends here was a great support, and he hoped now they would become a bigger part of his life.

Tia nodded at Kade when he looked at her. He winced slightly as Imulah ran the knife's edge across his palm.

"I present the blood of King Kade Long to the Octopus Lords," Imulah said. He took Kade's wrist and shook it. Droplets of blood flew off, falling into the ocean.

"With this blood sacrifice, you are swearing an oath that you will protect these islands and lead the people with honor," Imulah said. "Do you swear to this?"

"I swear to lead with honor and to protect these islands and every man, woman, and child who calls this place home," Kade said.

Imulah gripped his wrist harder, then let go. He turned to the soldiers.

"Hail King Kade!" Imulah proclaimed.

"Hail King Kade!" repeated the soldiers in unison.

Imulah gestured for Kade to follow him down the aisle framed by soldiers beating their chest armor in rhythm. The *clack, clack-clack* echoed across the deck.

Forge joined him and Imulah. "Do you know what that sound means?" the general asked.

Kade shook his head.

"It means they will fight and die for you."

"I will do my best to make sure they don't have to."

Forge snorted. "In this world, fighting is a way of life, but there are ways to minimize death. King Xavier tried to protect life by taking us to Panama, but it cost us greatly. You must find a way to keep us all alive without making us weak. There must be a balance."

The general stopped at the end of the file and motioned for two praetorian guards. They stepped out, thumping their spear shafts against the deck.

"Meet Dakota and Zuni," Forge said. "They will stay with you at all times. Dakota is one of the most skilled hand-to-hand fighters in our ranks, and Zuni is one of our best trackers. He was instrumental in killing a breeder in Panama. If someone wants to hurt you, Zuni will sense it, and Dakota will slit their throat before they get close."

Both soldiers tapped their chests in salute.

Kade nodded at them in acknowledgment. If he was being honest with himself, he was glad to have them watching his back.

They followed Kade and Forge across the deck, the thump of fists on armor reverberating around them. It continued even as they climbed down the rope ladder to the boat. The sound reminded Kade of the burden and the responsibility he had inherited by pulling the trigger and killing Rolo. It was time to fix what Rolo and Charmer had done. To make the islands a place of peace and equality. That meant keeping people fed and figuring out how this place worked. After all, they had made him king knowing that he had no experience.

As the boat thumped over the waves, Kade thought back

to the dread and depression at the machine camp. How he had wanted to die. Those days were behind him now that he had a greater purpose. His duty was to protect the people of the Vanguard Islands—not just from each other but also from exterior threats like the Knights of the Coral Castle. The defenses were in place, but there was something else Kade could do to prepare.

He lifted his wrist computer. Two days had passed since he crash-landed with Lucky and Bulldozer on the top of the Capitol Tower. Below that was another number: the number of days he estimated it would take the Forerunner to reach the islands in a fleet of ships, if that was his goal. By Kade's calculations, it would be a minimum of three weeks traveling at normal speeds.

Time was ticking away, and he had a lot more preparing to do.

"General Forge," Kade said.

"Sir."

"I want to see Lieutenant Gaz," Kade said. "It's time we got him to talk."

"Right away, King Kade."

THREE

The *Sea Wolf*'s spotlights guided it through heavy seas. The storm was getting worse, and they had already fought it for twelve hours straight.

X was exhausted, cold, and starting to worry. All he wanted to do was go belowdecks, crash in a bed, and sleep. Miles was down there now with Jo-Jo, probably green from the motion.

Though X was used to storms in the sky and on the sea, he didn't feel much better than his dog. The constant up and down was starting to give him a headache. It didn't help that his head had taken a beating just two weeks ago when a water bug the size of an oil drum almost crushed his skull.

Heading into the storm was a bad idea. X had abandoned it and was now making a run for Grenada, which meant turning around and *losing* time.

He didn't like it, but it was better than ending up at the bottom of the ocean, like Rolo.

He gripped the wheel of the catamaran with his hand while keeping his prosthetic arm hooked between the spokes for balance. The boat rose up and up before starting to slide down the other side of a mountainous wave.

Just after the bow hit the trough and water sprayed the glass, he saw a reflection in it. Magnolia, drenched from the rain, opened the hatch behind him and stepped into the cabin.

"Wanna trade off?" she asked.

She pulled her helmet off and shook her newly pink-highlighted hair.

"Are Miles and Jo-Jo okay?" X asked.

"Fine, but I feel like I'm gonna puke."

"Sorry, I'm doing my best," X said, running with the waves.

Magnolia braced herself as the boat tilted up, then slapped down.

"This slop is getting worse by the second," she said.

"I know. We got two options," X said. "Reef the sails and use the engines, or deploy the sea anchor to keep us oriented with the waves."

"How far to Grenada?"

"Thirty miles."

"Holy Siren shit," Magnolia said.

She was looking in the direction of the dashboard, but not *at* the dashboard. A brilliant fork of lightning turned the horizon to day for nearly two seconds. X expected maybe to see land, but he saw something else that took his brain a moment to confirm.

"Well, screw me sideways," X muttered.

To the east, a waterspout spun across the ocean. X had never seen one on water, but he had seen tornados on land. The enormous storms that had ravaged the planet for the past two and a half centuries produced all sorts of extreme events like this one.

And there wasn't just one.

"There are two… wait, three of those things," Magnolia said.

She stepped back from the window. "We got to get the hell out of here. We need to switch to the engines."

X grunted. He didn't want to furl the sails and use precious battery power, but the waves were simply too big. They needed speed to get around the waterspouts.

"Reef the sails, and I'll turn on the engines," X said. He had never done this before during a storm, but he had once while training with the boat back at the Vanguard Islands.

With a push of a button, he began retracting the sails of the center mast. But the other two masts were manually operated and would require Magnolia, who had the use of both hands, to do the work.

"Take a rope," he said. "Tie in and make sure it's secured—bowline *and* a barrel knot."

She nodded. Then she was gone.

X looked back at the ocean, where the spotlights blasted over the water. Farther out, maybe a half mile away, one of the waterspouts skittered like a top over the surface. He turned the wheel too late and a wave hit them broadside. It felt like dropping into a waterfall. He knew from experience that a single cubic foot of water weighed sixty-plus pounds. The *Sea Wolf* had just been hit by several tons.

"Mags," he said over channel. "Mags, do you copy?"

"I didn't break my neck… yet, if you're wondering," she said.

Cold spray blasted the cabin's windshield, sluicing down in rivulets as the boat climbed up the next wave.

When the water cleared, he saw Magnolia winching down the foresail. Despite her injuries and the sorrow of losing Rodger, Mags's movements were fast and agile as ever.

X focused on keeping them perpendicular to the waves and away from the waterspouts. Two of them had spun back up into the clouds, and the third was meandering away from them.

He tried to relax his breathing. He had known they would face plenty of challenges on this journey.

He lost sight of Magnolia as she moved to the stern of the boat for the mizzen sail. When he looked back up at the horizon, one of the waterspouts had changed course and was barreling right at them.

"Well, chop me into shark chum!" X said.

He turned the rudder a bit too hard and caught a wave on the port side.

X caught a glimpse of Magnolia sliding toward a railing covered in razor wire. She went down on her butt and used her boots to stop her against the hull. Pushing herself up, she stumbled back to the stern.

"I'm good!" she called over the radio.

"Copy," X said. "Hold on to something, and prepare to come about."

He checked the waterspout's progress. The spinning vortex had to be forty feet wide. X couldn't let it get close.

"Here we go," he said over the comm.

X spun the wheel, turning the boat again. The lights speared out into the darkness, where he searched for the dark bulk that signified land. But all he saw was another twister.

The dashboard flickered, the digital map suddenly going offline.

"That's just out-fucking-standing," X said, resisting the urge to smash the screen with his prosthetic arm. Without the navigation system, he was blind out here. For all he knew, they were going in circles.

Another wave slapped the boat, turning it to port. X turned them again to get some distance from the waterspout.

The vortex screamed closer, as if they were about to be sucked into the turbofans of an airship.

"X," Mags said over the comms. *"X, do you—"*

"I see it," he replied. "Hold on, going to turn us again!"

"Almost got the mizzen down."

X studied the waterspout. They had a minute, maybe less.

"Do it," he said. "Then get back up here."

"Copy."

X steered into the waves, trying to keep steady. He took his hand off the wheel just for a second to switch on the battery-powered motors. The boat began to pick up speed. He tacked away from the waterspout, but it seemed to have locked on to them like a shark to blood.

That was impossible, of course. Just bad luck, but it was coming at them nonetheless.

"Mags!" X shouted. "Mags!"

"Got it!"

He turned to see the final sail down.

"Now, get back up here!" X yelled.

He spun the wheel, and the catamaran turned away from the twister—right into the path of the second spout.

"Bucket of Siren shit," X growled. His heart dropped in his chest. "Hold on!"

He braced himself by hooking his arm in the wheel. The waterspout spun toward the boat, whipping up thousands of cubic feet of ocean in front of him. The raucous noise roared closer.

X removed his arm from the wheel and tried to turn out of the path. He thought he heard Magnolia scream something over the comm.

"I'm sorry," X said. He closed his eyes, unable to watch as the waterspout whipped in front of the bow. The boat rose out of the water.

Something slammed into the glass, cracking it and popping

NICHOLAS SANSBURY SMITH | 49

his eyes open. It took him a moment to realize that the crack was covered in blood.

"Mags!" he shouted.

X stared in horror at more cracks around the glass windshield, but then he saw something beyond, in the glow of the spotlights. Dozens of meaty, scaly creatures swirled around the boat as it rose into the air.

Fish, hundreds of them, one the size of a human!

The flight out of the water was over almost the moment it began. They slapped back down into the ocean with such force that it almost dislocated his shoulder.

He winced from the pain as the waterspout roared away.

For a moment, there was a sense of utter weightlessness, like during the first moment of a dive. It was quiet, almost still.

But then everything came crashing back over X. The wind slammed into the boat, rain pelted the windows, and lightning flashed across the relentless waves. In a sudden fright, he searched the stern weather deck for Magnolia.

This time, he didn't see her or the safety rope.

"Mags!" X shouted into the comms.

No answer.

"MAGS!" he yelled at the top of his lungs.

He left the wheel and lurch-walked to the hatch. Just as he turned to back down, a voice called out.

"Watch it!"

X got out of the way as Magnolia climbed up the ladder. He grabbed her by a shoulder pad and helped her into the enclosed cabin. Then he scrambled back to the wheel, grabbing it and correcting.

"Are you good?" he asked.

"I'm alive," she replied.

The boat rocked and shook in the howling storm. The

spotlights lanced through the darkness, hitting waves and climbing them ahead of the catamaran. The bow of the portside hull hit something that sent a vibration through the boat.

"What was that?" Magnolia asked.

X reached up to redirect one of the lights attached to the cabin. He angled it down on the deck of the bow, where he saw a dozen flopping fish, ranging in size from Miles to X.

But the source of the impact was much bigger. Draped in the barbed wire at the front of the bow was a mutant shark some ten feet long with two heads. Even more shocking, the damned thing was still alive.

The tail lashed the water as the creature tried to free itself, the razor wire ripping across its flesh. Blood sloshed out onto the deck.

"X," Magnolia said, "you seeing this?"

"Yeah, I see it," he replied.

He could see her reflection in the mirror, but she wasn't facing him.

"X," she said again.

The glass lit up with a yellow glow, and he finally responded.

"Oh, you gotta be fucking kidding me," he said when he saw the glowing monstrosity beneath the waves. A leviathan.

"Go, go!" Magnolia reached for the wheel.

X turned it but wasn't sure what good that would do. If it was going to eat them, there was no outrunning it in the dinky *Sea Wolf*. The boat was a fraction the size of the ships the leviathans back in Panama had taken down.

The shark on the deck flipped harder, as if it too sensed the danger. X glanced over his shoulder, his heart pounding. The monster seemed to light up the entire length of a wave as it swam toward the bait trapped on their deck.

The waterspouts had stirred up the fish, making the

disoriented and injured sea creatures easy prey for the hybrid whale–giant squid abomination.

"Take the wheel," X said.

"What?" Magnolia asked.

"Just do it!"

X grabbed his helmet and threw it on before bursting out of the hatch. He slid down the ladder to the weather deck and plucked a spear out of a rack.

A wall of water rose up as the beast broke through the surface, exposing the deformed whalelike face. Squid arms whipped out of the water, each over forty feet long and rimmed with barbs. Many of those barbs had already found prey—sharks and large fish hung from the sharp hooks.

X slung the spear over his back and grabbed a rope tied to the deck. He tied it around his waist, then used it to walk across the bow while the boat bobbed in the heavy chop. By the time he got there, the deck was covered in blood, but the two-headed shark was still alive. One of the mouths snapped at him.

Letting go of the rope with his good hand, X unslung his spear. One quick stab took out the near head, but the other still had bite.

A high-frequency whistle pierced the storm, rising over the clap of thunder and howl of the wind. X glanced over his shoulder to see the monster surging right toward them. He had seconds to get this beast overboard.

In several swift strokes with the spear blade, X cut through the razor wire trapping the shark. Finally it flopped free, snapping rows of jagged teeth at his boot. He jumped back, then thrust the blade into the belly of the beast.

He set the shaft of the spear on his prosthetic arm and tried to lever the shark. The weight coupled with the thrashing made it impossible. Instead, he heaved it toward the side of the deck, just as the boat rode up another wave.

X lost his grip on the spear shaft. He fell backward, sliding with the shark toward the port gunwale. The animal flipped on its back, right into another section of razor wire. Still sliding, X was heading right for the snapping mouth.

"*X!*" Magnolia shouted over the comms.

The boat lifted up again just as his boots were about to go into the open maw of the shark. It was the rope that saved him, catching and jerking him back. He slid across the bloody deck.

The whistling leviathan was drawing closer, its orange glow brightening as it swam toward their boat. Limbs shot out of the water, flailing back and forth.

"*X, it's almost on us!*" Magnolia shouted. "*Hold on!*"

She turned the boat sharply. X slid down the foredeck, back toward the shark. It was still struggling but had slowed down.

With the leviathan bearing down on them, this was his last chance. Holding on to the bow rail, X worked his way over to the dying shark.

He grasped the spear shaft and pulled it free. Blood welled up from the spear hole in its belly. The boat started up another wave, and X pulled the multitool from his duty belt and snipped through the razor wire, freeing the creature. As the catamaran crested a wave, he thrust the spear into the back of the shark.

Levering the spear against the gunwale, he heaved the beast into the water. Then, as he scrambled back across the slick weather deck, a wave of water hit him from behind, knocking him facedown.

He turned to his back, sitting up and staring at the bulbous eyes of the leviathan as its head loomed over the boat. An arm rose out of the water with the shark, the spear still stuck in its back.

The massive jaw opened. A low groan came from the gullet,

shifting into a melancholy call loud enough it hurt his ears. Barking answered in the distance.

The cold eye stared at X, then flitted away, and the barnacle-covered head lowered into the water, the glow slowly fading away into the darkness. X collapsed on the deck.

"I'm getting too old for this shit," he muttered.

FOUR

"All hail King Kade!"

The voices echoed from the piers of the marina under the capitol tower. Kade arrived at midnight, still feeling strange with a crown on his head, not to mention two Cazador praetorian guards as shadows.

As their boat docked, an exuberant young voice greeted them all.

"Cowboy Kade!"

Alton ran up the dock, brown locks bobbing up and down.

"Hey, pal," Kade said. He searched for Katherine, who had taken Alton in at Layla's urging. From what Kade understood, Layla believed Katherine would be the best person to look after the boy.

"Alton!" Katherine called out.

She came running down the dock with her daughter, Phyl. They caught up with Alton just as Kade's feet hit the dock.

"You got to stop running away from us," Katherine said. She grabbed Alton and pulled him back as General Forge and the guards spread out to watch for potential hostiles that might want Kade dead.

As he scanned the faces on the dock, he saw Beau walking away, shoulders slumped, head down. Roman seemed to have lost his fighting spirit and now appeared solemn.

Kade called after an old friend and his son.

"I'm very sorry for your loss," he said. "If there's anything I can do…"

"Bring Donovan to justice and kill Charmer would be a good start," Roman said.

"Let's go," Beau said. He nodded at Kade, then left with Roman.

Woody lingered for a moment, looking up at the cage where Charmer dangled over the marina. "I'll do it if you want," he said. "It should be one of us. I'm sorry we didn't stop him when we had the chance."

Kade considered his friend as he stared up at the cage. Woody wasn't a killer. He was a jokester and a peaceful man.

"Killing a man takes a piece of you," Kade said.

"I can spare a piece for that bloody devil," Woody said. He looked back to Kade. "I'll see you tomorrow, King Kade."

Woody hurried after Beau and Roman, allowing space for Alton to move back up.

"So you are the king now?" Alton asked. "The cowboy king!"

Kade nodded.

"You don't seem too excited." This voice came from behind Kade. He turned to Tia, walking with the greenhorn Hell Divers.

"*King Kade*," she said, smirking. "This is wilder than a bone beast drunk on shine. I wish my dad were here to see it."

"So do I. I know he would be very proud of you," Kade said.

"For what?"

"You helped us get those seeds in Brisbane."

Tia shrugged.

"You did good. You survived!"

"I was scared, Kade."

"If you weren't, I'd be worried."

She smiled and flicked a dreadlock over her shoulder. It took him a moment to realize she was eyeing one of his praetorian guards.

"Thanks," she said. "I'll be better trained for the next dive."

"Next dive?"

She looked Kade in the eye and said, "I'm a Hell Diver."

An audible sigh came from Katherine—not surprising from one who had lost both her son and her husband to the skies.

"Yes, you are indeed," Kade said. "A Hell Diver without an airship."

"King X will find Michael and bring him home in the *Vanguard*." Tia said it so confidently, Kade was afraid to say anything in response—especially since he doubted that X would find Michael in Rio. It was possible, of course, but it was also possible that Michael had flown that ship to the other side of the world.

If Kade had a chance to be with his family again, it wouldn't matter where. In the sky for the rest of their lives, in a bunker—anywhere safe.

Either way, Kade wasn't counting on the airship's return anytime soon, and he was already starting to think about what to do if that was the case. Somehow, they needed to replace the *Vanguard*.

"I really miss Michael," Alton said. "I'm glad you're back, though, and now you're the king! Is there anything I can do to help you, Your Majesty?" He bowed and then grinned.

"Yeah, you can go get into bed, pal," Kade said.

"I'm not tired. I want to go fishing."

"That would be fun," Phyl said. "Mom, can we?"

"Maybe tomorrow," Katherine said.

The kids both protested, but Tia helped Katherine corral them.

"The king has important business," Tia said.

Alton threw up a salute. "See you later, Cowboy King."

Kade smiled, but his face hardened as he turned back to Forge. They had important business.

Dakota led the way with his shield, followed by Forge, then Kade, and Zuni on rear guard. They went up an interior stairwell to the hospital. Dr. Huff greeted them in the lobby, holding a clipboard.

"Can I help you?" he asked.

"We're here to talk to Gaz," Forge said.

"Gaz needs rest, General," said Dr. Huff.

"This won't take long," Kade said.

The doctor hesitated.

"*King* Kade said he needs to talk to the prisoner," Forge said.

Huff looked from the general back to Kade. "Follow me," he said.

He led them through the lobby, where a militia soldier with an assault rifle stood guard. Three more stood inside the hallway of individual rooms occupied by injured soldiers. There were five surviving Wave Runners from Jamal's forces, all of whom had declared their loyalty to the Vanguard Islands after learning of Captain Rolo's evil deed.

Huff stopped halfway down the corridor and motioned for a guard to unlock the door.

Kade turned to Forge.

"I'll talk to him alone first," he said. "Wait here."

The guard unlocked the door, but Huff blocked the way. "He suffered extreme damage to his spine in that crash. Try and go easy on him."

"The man is our enemy," Forge said.

"Which is exactly why we want to make sure he recovers, so you can get more out of him," the doc replied.

Kade was glad to hear that the doctor understood the importance of gathering intel.

"I won't hurt him, don't worry," Kade said.

Huff stepped aside, and Kade entered the room to find Lucky on his back, eyes closed.

"Gaz," Kade said. He flipped on the light and closed the door.

The knight blinked as Kade walked over and stood by his right side. Lucky squinted up at him but didn't seem to recognize him at first.

"It's me, Kade," he said.

"Hell Diver," Lucky mumbled. "How long have I been out?"

"Two days. How do you feel?" Kade looked Lucky up and down. He couldn't see beneath the blanket pulled up to his chest, but his square jaw was bruised and scraped.

"I still can't move my legs," Lucky said. He reached out and grabbed Kade by the arm.

"Take it easy," Kade said.

"What's wrong with my legs?" Lucky asked. "No one's telling me jack."

"You have a spinal injury, but we're providing the best medical care we have. Try to relax, Lucky."

The knight tightened his grip, then let go and stared up at the ceiling.

"What do you plan on doing with me?" he asked.

"We want to help you heal, but before that can happen, I need you to talk to me. To tell me what activating the Trident did."

"You know what it was for."

"Do I?"

"To locate this place."

"The Forerunner plans on coming here, then? Bringing more knights?"

"I'm a soldier. I follow orders, and those were the orders

I was given. What further orders might be given are unknown to me." He cracked a pained grin.

"What?" Kade asked. "Something funny?"

"If you consider where you stand now and where I'm lying, yes." Kade mused at the irony.

"You were my prisoner; now I'm yours," Lucky said. "The only thing that hasn't changed is, you're still taking care of me and making sure I don't cark it."

"You're a good man, and I told you my people would kill those responsible for what happened in Brisbane."

Lucky looked toward the closed door.

"So where is this king of yours, this Xavier?" he asked. "I'd like to meet him."

"He's gone," Kade said.

"What do you mean, 'gone'?"

"King Rolo was killed, and King Xavier decided to move on."

"He *retired*?"

"Not exactly."

"So who's king? Who's in charge of this barbaric place?"

Kade was unsure whether to tell Lucky the truth. He decided, for now, to keep his coronation a secret.

"Rest; you'll need it," Kade said.

"For what?"

"For your journey home. As soon as you're better, I'm going to give you a boat and turn you loose."

"You're just setting me *free*?"

"I told you my people aren't barbarians, and now I get the chance to prove it."

Kade patted Lucky on the shoulder.

"Rest up and heal, mate," he said. He went to the door and flicked off the lights.

"Wait, Kade…"

"Yes?"

"Nothing," Lucky said after a beat. "It's nothing."

Kade hesitated, wondering if he should push. He decided it was better to take small steps with the knight. Gain more of his trust.

"Get some sleep," Kade said. He shut the door and took in a deep breath. Then he went to General Forge and Dr. Huff.

"When will you know if he'll walk again?" Kade asked.

"Walk?" Huff said with a laugh. "That would be a miracle unless you can get me YS8, the ITC nanoparticle treatments we ran out of last year."

"That would help him walk again?"

Huff shrugged. "It would be the best chance to heal his spine."

"Then we better find some," Kade said. "Keep me updated on his condition."

Kade and Forge walked out of the medical bay to the balcony overlooking the marina. Dakota and Zuni remained inside, making sure no one approached.

"Did he talk?" Forge asked.

"He confirmed what we thought: activating the Trident sent a beacon to the Coral Castle," Kade said.

"So they know where we are."

Kade nodded. "Soon, we'll know where they are."

"What? How?"

"Find the drugs and get a boat ready to send Lucky home."

Forge stopped and stared at his king. "You're letting him *go*? Sir, with all due respect—"

"I'm sending him home with a tracker to locate the Coral Castle, General."

Forge squinted, then nodded with realization.

"What about Charmer?" he asked. "Do you have a plan for him yet?"

"Working on that."

NICHOLAS SANSBURY SMITH |

61

"And Gran Jefe?"

Kade's brow rose. "What about Gran Jefe?"

"I fear … rather, I know he can't be trusted."

"He killed Ada and lied about it, I know, but X saw fit to give him a second chance, like he gave Ada a second chance after she dropped the container of Cazadores in the ocean."

"I believed that was a mistake, and Xavier is not the king now, sir."

Kade scratched his jaw.

"On our way back to the islands, Gran Jefe and several soldiers loyal to him nearly killed Xavier," Forge said. "I advised the king to deal with Gran Jefe then, but he let him live because he felt we needed him and the other men to win the battle for the Vanguard Islands."

"It worked. Without Gran Jefe, we might well have lost to Jamal."

Forge nodded.

As Kade stood there, he realized more than ever that kings must often grapple with decisions that were not black and white but a vast palette of grays. There were friends to the crown, and enemies, and some in the middle. Gran Jefe stood firmly in that middle section.

Kade didn't trust the warrior either, but the real question was whether X had been right about his usefulness. Did they need him for future fights, or was Gran Jefe too much of a liability?

"Keep an eye on Jorge," Kade said. "I'll give you my decision soon."

*   *   *   *   *

"*¿Dónde está la medicina?*" Gran Jefe asked.

"I don' got, don' got!" Pepe shouted.

The gaunt, heavily tattooed man cowered, holding a bony hand up above his beady eyes. Gran Jefe reached down and plucked Pepe off the ground by the neck with one hand.

"Don't lie, *amigo,* or we no longer *amigos,*" Gran Jefe growled. "You tell me where to find the medicine, or I go from amigo to Cazador hunting monster."

"*No, no, por favor,*" Pepe pleaded, gasping and kicking the air.

"I don't believe you," Gran Jefe said.

He tightened his grip and lifted Pepe higher off the deck. Trying to ignore the whiff of leaky sewage pipe in the small but fancy quarters that Pepe called home. They were in the bowels of a Cazador rig where the poorest of the poor lived.

The casual observer wouldn't know by the leather couch, wooden table, and chest of drawers, which were all in good condition.

The trader had done well for himself at such a young age. What Pepe lacked in size and experience, he made up for in brains, buying and selling goods on the black market from Cazador raiders who didn't declare everything they brought back from the wastes.

Many warriors were guilty of it, including Gran Jefe. It was a perk that came with joining the military under el Pulpo. The tradition had carried on since the very beginning days of the Cazador army.

"Well?" Gran Jefe said. He made a fist of his free hand while giving Pepe a chance to consider his words.

"I have no medicine," he stammered.

Gran Jefe cocked his fist, ready to bash Pepe if he smelled a lie. From what he could tell, Pepe was telling the truth. Hurting him would be a waste of energy, and Gran Jefe was tired.

He let go, and Pepe sank to the floor, choking for air. Then he scrambled backward out of reach.

"*Gracias, gracias, Jorge,*" Pepe said.

Gran Jefe went out into the dimly lit corridor, where several heads popped out of doorways for a look. Seeing the hulking Cazador, they ducked back into their holes.

Door locks clicked as he lumbered by. Anger boiled up in him. Beating on the locals was a job for the militia or wannabe soldiers. It was not a job for a Barracuda.

But the orders had come through Commander Slayer, handed down from King Kade himself. They were looking for special medicine, and Gran Jefe had been sent out as the muscle to shake it out of crooks like Pepe.

It was a stupid, wasteful job when Gran Jefe should be out looking for the last holdouts loyal to Charmer. Forge had put together a group of hunters that didn't include Gran Jefe. No surprise there. The general clearly didn't trust him, even after he demonstrated his loyalty by killing his own cousin.

Gran Jefe respected the chain of command, but that didn't mean he was happy about it. He had made mistakes in the general's eyes. Killing the Hell Diver Ada. Forcing X into the chamber to fight the giant bug. Various other disrespectful things over the years.

But babysitting errands like this, after what he had done for the Vanguard Islands by killing his own blood?

Gran Jefe halted at a ladder down to the corridor where a few ne'er-do-wells lived. Some might have medicine stowed away or would know where to get it for the king.

He had served two kings in his life and wasn't sure what to think of this third one. He liked the sky cowboy well enough. But he wasn't sure if Kade liked him after everything that had happened. X had cut Gran Jefe a lot of slack. But Kade was not X. And Jorge was no errand boy. He had done his part. He needed to blow off some steam.

"No más," he said with a snort.

He turned abruptly and went in the opposite direction. What he needed right now was a stiff drink. Followed by a stiffer one. Happily, he wasn't far from the Pit.

Still wearing his armor, he walked across the bridge connecting the two main Cazador rigs. He took a hatch and went down a few floors to a ladder. Even at this late hour, a small group of teenagers loitered outside, hoping somehow to gain entry or at least cadge a drink from those who came and went.

Music and shouting echoed out of the multilevel bar.

A guard named Alfredo stood in front of the black hatch. The sixty-year-old naval veteran's crossed arms bulged with heavily tattooed biceps. Gran Jefe tramped forward, drawing the attention of two kids.

"Out of the way," he growled.

Their eyes widened and they stepped aside.

"Jefe," one of them said.

Alfredo gave a stern, respectful nod and opened the hatch, letting out rowdy voices and the thump of amplified bass. Torches guided him down a stairwell into the cylindrical pit that was once used to store excavating equipment. The cavernous space had been retrofitted into what the Cazadores referred to as "the Pit."

The place served many functions. Some came to converse on the many balconies wrapped around the silo-shaped structure. Others came to drink at the bars, some to dance, and a few to venture into one of the pleasure corridors in the darkness below, where almost any desire was catered to.

Gran Jefe didn't frequent the Pit as much as he once had, but tonight it beckoned him like a lighthouse in the wastes.

He stepped over to the railing and looked down five stories to the bottom. Half-naked, sweaty men and women clung to one another, drinking away their inhibitions.

Sky people knew not to come here. This was for Cazadores only.

Martino was one of them, sitting with his current entourage of whores in a booth at the very bottom level. He plucked berries from a silver goblet and crushed them in his mouth.

"*Hijoeputa*," Gran Jefe whispered.

He made his way down to the bottom floor and sat at his usual spot at a bar counter made from the mandible bone of a blue whale. This was just one of many bars at the bottom of the Pit. All of them surrounded a central dance floor that generally saw more fighting than dancing.

It wasn't crowded, but the night was young. The moon still hung low in the sky. Gran Jefe sat down by himself.

The bartender passed him tequila in a clouded glass. It was some of the best, Gran Jefe knew, because he had been on the raid in Tabasco, Mexico, where his squad liberated ten barrels of the delicious liquid from a bombed distributorship. He had been drinking it for free ever since.

After swirling the liquid, Gran Jefe lifted the glass just as a memory from the battle on the docks surfaced. In his mind's eye, he could see Jamal holding Magnolia with a knife to her throat, ready to cut off her head and toss it to the Octopus Lords.

In his younger years, Gran Jefe had respected his cousin, even looked up to him in some ways. Jamal was fearless, but he had made a vital error teaming with Charmer. An unforgivable error, which resulted in his demise.

Gran Jefe slugged down the liquor and pounded the glass down on the counter as the liquid ran down his throat. Warmth ignited inside his chest still covered in bandages from the battle. One of the arrow wounds burned like a jellyfish sting. The tequila numbed the physical pain, but not the other.

Images of battle filled his mind: the wars for the islands; fights in the wastes; battles with monsters, machines, men.

The images were etched in his mind as vividly as the tattoos on his flesh. In many ways, they were more painful than the physical wounds.

He finished off the next glass and tapped it again.

"*Otra, por favor*," he grumbled.

The bartender held up the bottle of tequila, but Gran Jefe waved it off.

"Shine," he said.

The homemade stuff the sky people brought here was far more potent. And *potent* was what Gran Jefe wanted.

The bartender poured a mug. Gran Jefe had just brought it to his lips when he heard a moan of pleasure. He turned to see two women kissing in a shadowy horseshoe-shaped booth. Martino watched from the next booth, still popping fruit into his maw.

One of the women looked at Gran Jefe and winked. He was used to the attention. Any Barracuda who came down here had his pick. There were plenty to choose from. So many had become widows over the past two years.

They should have known better than to look at him. He had long since given up on having a family. That life was not for him. And he knew he would be a lousy father.

Gran Jefe took a long slug of the shine as a memory from his own childhood surfaced. His father wasn't a bad man, but neither was he a good man. He had spent most of his time on the open seas as a raider. His wife died in childbirth with Gran Jefe's brother, who also perished in the traumatic birth.

Two years after that, his father had gone out on a raid and never returned.

Gran Jefe took another swig of shine, then a third. On the fourth, he was feeling nothing but bliss. He eyed the corridors to the pleasure dens. In one of them, he could see more shadowy figures grinding against one another.

He watched, tempted to go in but finally deciding, not tonight. Lowering his head, he tried to chase away the memories that the alcohol had yet to erase.

At some point, a finger tapped him on the back.

"*Vete a la mierda*," he said.

He looked up to see a woman reflected in the mirror. He smirked. Maybe he would be visiting the pleasure dens after all.

He turned and saw a woman with a pale complexion and bright-blue eyes. Judging by her glare, she wasn't here to seduce him.

"*¿Qué?*" he asked.

"You're a disgrace for what you did to Jamal."

"Ah," Gran Jefe said, grinning wider. "So you're one of his whores."

She bared her teeth like a wild animal. That told him she was more than a whore. This *puta* had been special to his deceased cousin. Jamal sure liked the English-speaking sky women.

"You betray your own blood," she said.

"Careful," Gran Jefe said.

She spat in his face.

"Or not," he growled.

Lifting a hand to wipe it away, he watched as she raised her own hand to hit him. On a normal night, Gran Jefe would easily have caught it before she connected, but the liquor hadn't just numbed his senses; it had affected his motor skills. He didn't bother trying to defend himself. The hand connected with a loud slap to the side of his face.

He laughed, which only made her angrier.

She slapped him again, then raked at him with her nails. A scratch across his cheek finally got him to respond. He pushed her away a bit too hard, and she fell backward, crashing into a booth and falling to the floor.

For a moment, she crouched like a cat, baring her teeth again, ready to pounce. But she must have thought otherwise, because she got up, stumbled, and left.

"Go back to your hole," Gran Jefe said in Spanish.

Turning back to his shine, he felt eyes on him from men across the bar, including Martino.

"You want some too?" he asked in Spanish.

All the eyes flitted away, even Martino's.

Gran Jefe sat back down and had another swig of shine. Closing his eyes, he had just started to relax when he felt a hand on his back again.

"Back for more?" Gran Jefe asked in Spanish.

He opened his eyes to see the bartender step back. And in the dirty mirror, Gran Jefe noticed a fully armored Cazador soldier standing behind him. He had been too drunk to hear the man approach.

Gran Jefe stood and faced Commander Slayer. The Barracuda leader put a hand on the hilt of his sword.

"King Kade wants to see you," he said.

"*Un momento*, or..." Gran Jefe blinked, trying to squeeze his double vision into a single field. "You mean now, I think."

Slayer nodded.

Gran Jefe tossed back the rest of his drink, not bothering to ask Slayer for more info. If the commander knew, he wouldn't say. Either this was about Ada—which meant his neck—or the new king had a neck to break and needed Gran Jefe for the job.

FIVE

"Airship at twenty-five thousand feet," Timothy Pepper announced over the comm channel.

"Copy that, moving into position," Michael Everhart replied.

Michael climbed one armed up a ladder behind Steve, heading to the top of the airship. They both wore backpacks containing their equipment and a roll of sheet metal.

"I hate to sound like a coward, but what do you think our odds are of getting fried up here?" Steve called down.

"Oh, it's a possibility, but most lightning strikes occur between five thousand and fifteen thousand feet," Michael replied.

"Not a bad way to go, I guess, but we got no choice."

He was right about that. The ship had taken major damage to the exterior panels as they departed from Outpost Gateway, this on top of the damage they had taken during their escape from the Vanguard Islands just a week earlier.

It was just a matter of time before the storms did them in, which was the reason Michael and Steve were headed to the roof. It was either put the airship down to make repairs, or do them in the air. And without a security team to protect the ship, the first option was just too risky. The second was risky too, but it was the only way.

They couldn't travel another mile without repairing the damaged rooftop panels. Timothy had found a weak area in the storms that would give them a shot at making the repair in midflight.

While climbing the rusted old ladder, Michael reflected on how lucky he was even to have made it this far. He had been granted a second chance thanks to the brave actions of Layla, Steve, Victor, and Pedro. If not for them, Michael would be dead just like X and everyone else they knew: Magnolia, Rodger, Les, Arlo… The list kept growing.

They were beyond lucky to have escaped. Michael also knew he was lucky to have Steve up here. His can-do expertise was key to keeping the ship in the air, especially after Michael lost his prosthetic arm. He shook his head in amazement that the old warhorse was still in the air.

"Ready?" Steve called down. He had reached the top of the shaft and was reaching for the hatch.

"Ready," Michael replied.

Steve popped the hatch open and climbed out into the darkness. Then he bent down and helped Michael up. As soon as he emerged, a gust of wind slammed into both of them, nearly knocking Michael back into the shaft.

Steve kept a grip and pulled him forward.

"Whoa, steady, Chief," he said.

Michael took a moment to catch his breath as he looked out over the horizon. Bulging dark clouds flashed from sporadic bursts of lightning. Just one of those strikes in the damaged hull section would take down their entire ship.

They moved cautiously out onto the spine of the airship. The beetle-shaped vessel hovered in relatively calm skies, surrounded by violent storm clouds.

Michael unslung the coil of braided nylon rope from over his shoulder while Steve opened his pack. Inside was a tube of adhesive and a gun to apply it. In a better situation, they would weld the metal sheet to the side of the ship, but there was no way to do this in the air. For now, the adhesive was all they could manage.

By the time Steve had the adhesive tubes and gun unpacked, Michael had the rope shaken out, and carabiners ready to anchor it to the rings on the roof.

"Here, take the end," Michael said.

Steve took the rope, fed it through the belay loop on his duty belt, and tied himself in with a figure-eight knot. Then Michael played out fifteen feet of rope and tied himself in with a butterfly knot. Now they were anchored to the roof, with Steve at the end of the rope and Michael a dozen feet above him. Once they were secured, they moved out into the gusts.

"We're topside," Michael reported over the comms. "Heading toward the first damaged panel."

Michael thought he heard Bray saying "daddy" in the background. He had recently graduated from "da-da."

Lightning flashed across the horizon, gilding the scalloped edges of the storm. The two men pushed against the gusts to the port side of the long airship. As he moved, Michael couldn't help thinking of the people who had built it over two and a half centuries ago.

Those men and women would have had no idea that the ship would be a lifeboat to house some of the only survivors of World War III. Or that it would become a bastion for generations of their descendants.

After a minute battling their way across the airship's aluminum spine, Michael and Steve reached the point on the curving roof directly over the damaged panel. Static charge caused the hair on the back of Michael's neck to stand up. He turned to look behind them at the sprawling storm that seemed to be closing in from all sides.

"There's the panel," Steve said, pointing.

The damaged ten-by-four-foot shield section had broken loose and was completely gone, exposing the wire mesh and other secondary layers of protection like the wire-bundle shields. Seeing the ship's open wound reminded Michael just how remarkable it was that they could still be in the air.

"Couldn't have been in an easy place, could it?" Steve said with a laugh. "Guess I'm up for a little adventure today."

"Ha, *adventure*—I guess you could call it that," Michael said with a snort.

Steve bent down to take out the roll of sheet metal. Getting it down to the damaged section and securing it was going to be a son of a bitch.

"How do you want to do this?" Michael asked.

"Very carefully and together is how," Steve replied.

A savage blast of wind slammed into them, knocking Michael back a step. He muttered a curse and hunkered into the wind.

"Timothy, I need you to keep us as steady as possible," Michael said into the comms.

"Copy, sir," replied the AI.

Suspended on the rope, one above the other, as Michael played out the slack, they backed their way down the sloped hull to the damaged section. When they got there, Steve went directly below it and pulled out the metal sheet from his pack. Hanging from the ropes, he managed to flatten the bottom end over the opening.

Michael planted his boot on the top end of the sheet metal.

"Good, hold her steady," Steve called up. Using one hand to hold the bottom of the sheet down, he squeezed a bead of adhesive around the edges with the glue gun.

Thunder shook the hull. Michael tried to focus on the mission, but that was hard knowing that every second could be his last.

"Come on," he whispered.

He watched as Steve worked his way around the sheet metal with the adhesive, bonding it to the panel. The wind howled, drowning out a transmission over the comms. It came again a moment later.

"What's your status?" Layla asked.

"About halfway there," Michael replied.

Wind pummeled them as Steve stowed the adhesive gun in his pack. When the gust abated, he climbed up to start on the top half of the panel.

Thunder cracked like a gunshot at close range. Michael flinched but kept his boots firmly planted on the top of the sheet and kept his light on the area Steve was working on. The electrical storm seemed to be intensifying.

With the bottom and sides secured, Steve quickly made his way to the top. He had almost finished securing the piece when an errant gust hit them hard, lashing Steve to the side.

"Hold on!" Michael shouted.

The wind pushed the two dangling men sideways, away from the panel. Then suddenly, the line jerked downward. Michael felt his guts drop and realized that one of the anchor rings had failed. If the second one failed, they would free-fall the three miles to Earth.

Another blast of wind hit them, swinging them left, then back toward the metal patch. They swung like a pendulum, back and forth, flailing for something to grab on to.

Each time they swung, the rope connecting them creaked and strained. It couldn't take this punishment much longer. Michael tried to keep calm as they finally stopped swinging.

"You okay?" he called down. He carefully shined his helmet

light down on Steve, a dozen feet beneath him. He hung there, looking up, knowing better than to move in this moment.

Michael gently rotated his body back around, facing the hull.

"We have to climb back up, slowly," he said.

"No," Steve said.

Michael looked down. The bladesmith had to know what was happening. Their combined weight on that rope, in this wind, was too much. It had already broken one of the two anchors, leaving them hanging from a steel ring not much bigger than a wedding band.

"It's not going to hold us!" Steve yelled.

Reaching down, he pulled a knife from a sheath on his belt.

"What are you *doing*!" Michael yelled back.

Steve brought the knife to the rope. "It's been an honor working with you, Chief. One of the greatest in my life."

"Don't do it!" Michael shouted.

Steve brought the blade to the rope above his body.

"Stop!" Michael shouted. "We can make it!"

Steve held his gaze for a long moment.

"Save your family," he said. "I believe in you."

The knife edge touched the weighted rope, which parted like a filament of gristle. And where Steve had been just a moment ago, there was only the wind.

"NO!" Michael screamed.

Steve didn't scream. He simply vanished into the abyss.

Michael hung there for several moments, hot tears blowing in the wind. The comms flared with frantic messages, but he ignored them, still staring into the black.

"Steve," he murmured. "Steve, I'm so sorry."

"Tin, what's happening up there?" Layla said over the comm.

Her repeated calls finally snapped him from the shock. Steve had died so they might live. He gave them another chance, and Michael wouldn't waste it.

"Tin, do you copy? Please, please respond."

"I'm okay . . ." he said.

He fitted his mini ascenders onto the rope, a couple of feet apart, clipped a sling to the lower ascender, and stepped into the sling, weighting it. Then he pushed the upper ascender about three feet up the rope and pulled himself up.

A gust of wind caught him, twisting him violently from side to side. He closed his eyes and held still. When it passed, he slid the lower ascender upward and repeated the process. About thirty slide-and-pulls later, he was back topside. Looking down at the battered airship, he wasn't sure how he was going to keep it in the air without Steve, but he couldn't give up. He had to finish the work.

* * * * *

The *Sea Wolf* tacked away from the storm's center, toward Grenada. There was no telling how far they were from the island, with their digital map still offline from storm interference. The only way Magnolia knew they were heading in the right direction was by watching the dashboard-mounted compass.

There was also no way to tell how long the storm would last. It battered the catamaran with a vengeance, but somehow, the plucky little vessel held together.

She couldn't say how, exactly. The waterspouts had nearly done them in, and the leviathan could have swallowed them as easily as a whale swallowing krill. It had moved on, diving back into the mysterious depths.

Hours after the attack, she still had a vise grip on the wheel. X had brought Miles and Jo-Jo into the cabin, where he could keep an eye on them. Neither animal was injured, but the monkey didn't like being stuck inside the small space. Miles didn't seem to mind. He was camped out under the attached table where X was going over maps.

"Relax, Jo-Jo, damn!" X kept saying.

The monkey grunted at him and then pawed at the hatch to get out. Miles looked up and whined.

"Jo-Jo, sit down," X commanded.

"Yeah, that's going to help," Magnolia said. "She doesn't know the words."

X stood up and nearly fell as the boat yawed from a wave hitting at an oblique angle. He patted his thigh the way he did to call Miles over. Jo-Jo didn't seem to understand, or completely ignored him. She hammered on the hatch again with her fist.

"That is pretty annoying," Magnolia said.

"Jo-Jo, sit your furry ass down!" X yelled.

The animal finally looked away from the hatch and knuckle-walked over to the table. She grunted into his face.

"That smelled like some rank fish, wow," X said.

Magnolia couldn't help but chuckle.

The boat bobbed and pitched over the relentless waves. They were using both engines to leave these turbulent seas.

When the catamaran leveled off in a fleeting moment of steadiness, she took one hand off the wheel and shook it out. Her fingers tingled from the continuous gripping.

"What are the batteries at?" X asked.

Magnolia checked the gauges.

"Ninety-five percent on meter one, ninety-two on meter two."

"Shit, that's a lot of juice for a few hours."

"Want to switch back to the sails?"

"No, just get us to Grenada."

Jo-Jo went to the corner and slumped against the hull, letting out a heavy sigh. She lowered her head in apparent despair. Maybe she was thinking of her dear departed Ada.

Magnolia felt bad for the animal and began to think of her own losses as she piloted the boat. Her mind drifted back to Rodger, unable to steer away from the painful memory of finding his remains.

It was her fault that he was ever at Outpost Gateway. Her fault that he decided to take the position and not stay back at the islands, or perhaps go to Brisbane. Her selfishness had gotten him killed.

She had also failed Arlo in Brisbane. Maybe if she had kept eyes on their surroundings, she would have seen the bats before they got him. Same thing on the docks at the capitol tower, where Jamal had sneaked up on her and Edgar. Edgar didn't even stand a chance.

The memories flashed in her mind, each one adding to her anxiety. Only the flicker of the digital map kept her from slipping into the dark abyss that accompanied those painful images.

She glanced down and watched the map solidify.

"Check it out. We're only three miles away from Grenada," she reported.

"Hell yeah, finally some good news." X moved in for a look. "Should we thank the Octopus Lords?"

"I'd *kiss* one of those gross things if it meant we get to rest."

"Yeah, well, before we can rest, we've got to find a safe place to dock." X took his hand away. "Want me to take over yet?"

Jo-Jo grunted and went back to pounding on the hatch.

"No, just do something about Jo-Jo."

"Okay, I'm gonna let her out now since we're almost there."

He opened the hatch, and Jo-Jo hopped down to the stern weather deck.

Magnolia held the wheel steady as they rode up another wave and came crashing back down. When they popped back up, Magnolia steered them right into the next wave. It was constant work and required an endless store of focused attention. Having the monkey out of the cabin helped her concentrate on the task at hand, but it also forced her mind back to the painful memories of people she had lost over the years.

"You okay?" X asked.

She didn't even realize he was standing beside her again.

"Yeah," Magnolia lied.

"You ever going to talk to me about shit, or you just going to keep holding everything in?"

"I'll talk to you when you talk to me."

"About?"

"Maybe why we're on the open sea heading back to Rio."

"Uh, because we're looking for Michael."

"Exactly. Because you feel responsible for what happened to him."

X sighed. "Okay, I understand where you're going with this, but what happened to Rodger was not your fault, Mags."

"And what happened to Michael wasn't yours. At least he may still be alive."

X got up and walked over to the wheel.

"I sure hope he is, but you and I both know the airship might not have made it to Rio," X said. He studied the dark ocean waves through water-streaked windows. "If it went down, I'll never forgive myself."

"Just like I will never forgive myself."

X put a hand on her shoulder. "You're gonna have to, or you'll never be happy again."

"I'll be happy when we get there," Magnolia said. She pointed just as two almost simultaneous lightning bolts lit up the shore.

Miles got up and walked over, growling under his breath.

"Nothing to fear, boy, we're almost out of this squall," X said.

The dog barked, and Jo-Jo answered with a howl.

X went over to the hatch and looked through the porthole.

"What is it?" Magnolia asked. "Something wrong with Jo-Jo?"

"Nah, she's just eating a fish," X said. He returned to the wheel. "Let's just find a place to dock. Those two are as tired as we are."

X went to pet Miles, but the dog growled again at something off the starboard beam.

"It's okay, pal," X began to say. "We're almost—"

Jo-Jo howled again. This was not her casual frustrated tone. This was a howl of fear. Magnolia felt a stab of fear herself when the sea off the starboard bow took on a yellow glow.

"The leviathan's back!" she shouted.

The immense barnacled back surfaced, pushing up a wave. It was maybe a thousand feet away but closing fast.

"Can we make it to land?" X asked.

"I . . . I don't know," Magnolia said. She reached for the throttle, and X gave her the nod. It was their only shot. She pushed it down, and the boat surged toward the dark landmass.

X went back to the hatch and opened it.

"Jo-Jo, get up here!" he yelled.

Magnolia kept working the waves—trickier now with the boat's increased speed.

"I have to get her," X said.

"X!" Magnolia shouted.

It was already too late. He shut the hatch and climbed the ladder down to the weather deck.

Magnolia turned to the starboard viewports to watch for the leviathan, but the beast had sounded. She searched for the telltale glow before the storm forced her gaze back to the steady onslaught of waves.

The land was so close, she could see a rocky beach. Waves slapped against it, rising up toward a tree line. If she could get to the break, they could ride the surf in to shore.

Another howl came from the afterdeck. The yellow glow of the leviathan reflected in the window.

Magnolia turned in horror to see that the creature was trailing them. She pushed the throttle down all the way, the engines purring. From her vantage, she couldn't see X or Jo-Jo, but she couldn't abandon her post at the helm.

"X," she said over the comms. "X, what are you doing?"

A muffled reply crackled over the radio. Miles barked, standing at the back hatch and pawing to get out.

Magnolia took a calming breath. The catamaran rode up another wave, raced down the other side, and went up again. Grenada was a dark mass dead ahead. She could see the tops of the trees.

They were so close!

She sneaked a glance over her shoulder to see long, barbed arms snaking out of the water. Miles barked viciously.

"X, get back inside!" she shouted.

A figure moved out on the foredeck. It was Jo-Jo, and X was right behind her with a rope in hand. He was waving at the beast and screaming.

The yellow glow suddenly lit up the water all around the *Sea Wolf*. The gigantic body was swimming directly under the catamaran.

It breached the surface in front of them. The limbs whipped through the air, one of them finding Jo-Jo's leg and lifting her up. X fell to his back and scrambled away from another barbed arm as it felt about on the deck.

"Get out of there!" Magnolia shouted.

She tried to turn the boat, but they were aground on top of the monster. Letting go of the wheel, she reached for her blaster. The weapon wasn't there.

Cursing, she looked for something to use as a weapon, when a wave dashed against the cockpit. The catamaran rose up, and

Miles slid across the cockpit deck and slammed into the control panel. He got right back up and placed his paws on the dash, trying to get a view outside before falling back down.

The bright glow of the beast suddenly faded. Magnolia lunged for the wheel. Three of the arms were still whipping about above the surface, and to her horror, she saw X enwrapped in one. He was stabbing the meaty arm with his knife, over and over.

"Bastard's . . . got me!" X grunted over the comm channel. "Mags!"

The arm swung past the windshield with X still wrapped in a thick coil. The limb bent him, his body arching backward.

A yelp of pain cut across the open channel.

"Watch . . . out . . . for Miles!" X yelled.

He hit the water, and static sizzled on the line. A column of water splashed up where the limb had taken X under.

"X!" Magnolia screamed in horror as the glow in the water dimmed. She turned the boat, trying to gauge where the beast would resurface. Miles jumped back up, trying to see outside the viewports.

"X," she said. "X, do you copy?"

Her eyes remained locked on the surface as the last of the glow faded to black.

"X," she whispered.

Waves beat at the hull, making the boat bobble and shimmy. Just standing was nearly impossible.

She watched the surface, searching for her best friend, her mentor, and the father she never knew.

And this time, she knew, the Hell Diver legend and former king—the Immortal—was finally gone. And same with Jo-Jo. There was no escaping the leviathan. If X and the monkey weren't ground into chum by the teeth, the digestive acids would kill them almost as quickly.

Miles realized something was terribly wrong. He whined and nudged up against Magnolia, but she couldn't reach down to calm him. In this moment of devastation, she couldn't do *anything*. All she could do was think of X and Jo-Jo dying a slow, torturous death inside the monster's belly. Horrible as it was to think of, she hoped they were both already dead.

SIX

Footsteps and voices shook Kade out of a fitful sleep. He reached to the nightstand and drew from its holster the Monster Hunter, an ancient revolver he had found in a museum.

At the sound of a fist hitting his door, he thumbed the hammer back.

"Who's there?"

"General Forge," said a gruff voice.

"Hold on."

Kade swung his legs over the bed. Outside his open window, the moon was still high in the night sky. He had fallen asleep in his uniform after returning from the ceremony.

He buckled the gun holster around his waist, then opened the door. General Forge stood there, flanked by Zuni and Dakota.

"We found them, sir," Forge said. "The final holdouts, including Donovan."

"Where?" Kade asked.

"Holed up in a fishing trawler ten miles out into the storms. How do you want me to handle them?"

Kade went to his hanging armor.

"Sir, we can handle this," said Forge. "It's too dangerous for you to come."

"Would you have said that to King Xavier?"

"Yes, and he would not have listened."

"I appreciate your honesty, General, but these traitors are people I know. I should deal with them."

"I would argue that is why you should not come, sir. Some of these men, like Donovan, you consider friends, yes?"

"Yes," Kade said.

"If you insist on coming, you must not let any personal bias affect your decisions. We may need to deal with these traitors forcefully."

"Maybe, maybe not."

Forge raised a brow but said nothing.

"I'll share my plan at the marina," Kade said.

The general hurried out while Kade dressed. This wasn't his first time second-guessing what X would have done, or wondering whether Forge would have treated X the same. All the more reason he must make his own way, just as Imulah had recommended after the coronation ceremony.

He donned his Hell Diver armor and grabbed his submachine gun and sword. Zuni and Dakota escorted him down to the marina in silence.

Under a silver moon, they joined Forge and the other fighters on the dock. Lieutenant Wynn came with six militia soldiers. Commander Slayer had ten Cazadores, including Corporal Valeria and Sergeant Blackburn, who still walked with a slight limp.

Gran Jefe was present, as requested, but reeking of booze.

"*Su Majestad*," he slurred.

"Are you drunk?" Kade asked.

"I found him in the Pit," said Slayer. "He drank enough tequila to pickle a dolphin."

"Dolphin no handle tequila," Gran Jefe said with a laugh. His grin vanished and he pounded his chest.

"I fight," he said proudly. "*No más* running errands."

"Errands?" Kade asked.

"I find no medicine for you, *lo siento*, Cowboy."

"That's King Kade," Forge growled.

Gran Jefe turned and saluted as the general strode over.

"My apologies," Gran Jefe said. "I mean no disrespect."

Kade looked the hulking Cazador up and down, gauging his level of intoxication. It was surely a risk bringing him in this condition.

Also a risk not *bringing him,* Kade thought. He motioned for Forge and Slayer to follow him to the edge of the dock.

"Can he fight?" Kade asked.

"I've seen him fight in worse shape," Slayer said.

"Worse shape?" Kade didn't see how the man could *stand* if he were any drunker.

"One time, he took some irradiated mushrooms before a battle. He was high and sick as hell."

"Ha ha!" Gran Jefe said.

"He can't be trusted even when he's sober," Forge said.

Kade considered all Gran Jefe's actions: killing Ada, testing the king, killing his own criminal cousin, saving Magnolia.

Could he be trusted? Time would tell. But first, a test.

"He comes," Kade said.

"All due respect, sir, but—" said Forge before Gran Jefe cut him off.

"No, I can fight!" Gran Jefe sulked backward after receiving a one-eyed death glare from Forge. The eye flitted back to Kade.

"We will lose men if we attack—even if Gran Jefe was one hundred percent," Forge said. "It can't be avoided unless we simply sink the boat."

"I don't plan on attacking," Kade said. "I plan on them surrendering."

"How?" Forge asked.

Kade looked up at the cage where Charmer was imprisoned.

"Bring the scoundrel," he said. "I kept him alive for this very reason."

Forge glanced up at the hanging cage, then ordered Slayer to get him down.

Farther down the pier, Lieutenant Wynn had soldiers carrying automatic weapons and crossbows onto two assault boats and four Jet Skis.

"I want Gran Jefe with us, just in case I can't find a way to negotiate peace," Kade said.

Forge hesitated a beat before waving Gran Jefe over.

"Don't do anything stupid," Kade said.

"*No estúpido*, sir," Gran Jefe said, and fell in line.

Soon, Slayer had Charmer in leg shackles, shuffling across the piers.

"You going to kill me now?" Charmer asked.

"I suppose that's up to you," Kade replied. "Load him up."

They shoved Charmer into a boat. Kade got in the same one. Props hit the water, and both assault boats pushed away. Seconds later, Jet Skis roared ahead, leading the way.

Kade looked up at the capitol tower. Scars from the battle remained—a reminder of the terror Charmer and Rolo had caused. It was time to cut out the rest of the cancer and look to the future.

The boats raced away under a bright moon for half an hour, then plunged into the darkness beyond the border. Rain lanced down as the soldiers prepared for battle.

"You're just going to toss me into the sea?" Charmer asked.

"That would be too easy," Kade said.

Charmer scowled and glanced over his shoulder before clamming up. Finally, the guy knew when to keep his garbage hole shut.

Or perhaps it was the sight of Gran Jefe at the starboard rail with his double-bitted axe. He seemed steady enough to Kade.

"We're closing in," Commander Slayer reported. "Everyone, get ready."

"Hold your fire unless I give the order!" Kade shouted.

"No one fires a bullet or launches a spear until the king says!" Forge yelled.

The general put his helmet on, its red plume whipping in the wind. The soldiers in both boats made their final preparations. Spears were honed, rifles loaded, armor tightened.

In the sporadic lightning, a dark shape coalesced into a fishing trawler. The scouts who had located it were not in view, but they radioed Kade they were standing by for orders.

Forge gave a hand signal, and four Jet Skis fanned out. The lead rider fired a parachute flare. Its red glow captured the full length of the trawler. On the deck, five men stood with rifles aimed at the boats.

The assault boats and the Jet Skis began to move around the trawler.

"You're surrounded!" Kade said. "Lay down your weapons!"

The guns on the trawler didn't move.

"Get me closer," Kade said.

"Sir," Forge said, "any closer and we'll be in firing range."

"I kill all those *hijoeputas*," Gran Jefe said, shaking his axe. "Gut 'em all!"

"You will stand down until I tell you," Kade said.

"Stand... down?"

"It means you listen to me," Kade said. Perhaps he should have left the big drunken lunk back on the pier to sober up.

"Talking *es para cobardes*," Gran Jefe said. "For cowards."

"Watch your tongue," Forge said.

"If you can work things out another way, fighting is for fools." Kade looked back and motioned to Slayer.

The lieutenant grabbed Charmer and hauled him to his feet. Holding him up like a shield, he made his way to the front of the assault craft. Kade kept right behind them as the boat purred closer to the trawler.

Flashlight beams hit the rust-stained hull. Several of Charmer's followers held up their hands in the bright glow.

"Put down your weapons and surrender!" Kade repeated. "If you swear allegiance to the Vanguard flag, you will be spared."

"You're not the rightful king!" one of the men shouted back. "You murdered King Rolo!"

"Rolo betrayed us all! I killed him because he murdered hundreds of Cazadores and tried to murder the Hell Divers and King Xavier."

"That's a lie, Kade!"

The voice belonged to Donovan.

Kade saw his old friend step up to the railing of the trawler. Zuni and Dakota crowded around Kade with their shields to protect him from incoming fire.

"Donovan," Kade called out. "Listen to reason. You know me, and you know I would never hurt our people."

Donovan shook his head. "King Xavier led us on a path of destruction. Something had to be done! Charmer was trying to protect our new home."

"Think back to the machine camp," Kade said. "Rolo and Charmer were out for themselves then. Don't you remember the voice of the defectors?"

Donovan nodded. "That doesn't excuse what Michael Everhart did. I was there for his trial. He killed Oliver and his boy. I can't let that go. Charmer was right."

"Charmer fought for our people! You have fallen for lies!" someone else shouted from the fishing trawler.

More angry voices rang out.

Kade had anticipated this reaction from the holdouts, so he had brought the one man who could change their poisoned minds—the poisoner himself.

"Carl, you have ten seconds to tell the truth before I let Gran Jefe break the rest of your bones," Kade said.

"You stupid son of a bitch, Kade, you have no idea what you're doing," Charmer said.

Slayer smacked him in the ear. "Next time, I let Jorge bite it off."

Gran Jefe laughed.

"Tell them the truth, Carl," Kade said. "Save lives. Do something good in your life."

Charmer squirmed until Slayer grabbed him by one broken arm and twisted. He howled like a dying bone beast.

"Speak," Slayer said. He held Charmer by the cast, ready to give another twist.

"Part of what they say is true," Charmer coughed out.

"Louder. And what part?" Kade said.

"Rolo dropped a nuke on King Xavier and left the Hell Divers behind to die in Brisbane," Charmer said. "I, however, had nothing to do with it!"

Kade shook his head.

"Charmer knew all this and didn't tell you!" he yelled. "He tricked you into defending the islands under a lie, and *he* killed Oliver and Nez—hired Jamal, the Wave Runner you all fought alongside. Michael had nothing to do with those murders. Charmer framed him so he could remove him!"

Kade saw several of the men on the deck exchanging glances.

"Is that true, Carl?" Donovan asked.

"You'd best chose your words carefully," Kade said. "Isn't that what you told Michael to do?"

Charmer stared ahead.

"Tell the truth, and I'll grant you mercy," Kade said.

"You let them live, and they can still come back and kill you," Forge said. "I've seen it before. You cut off a hand, and they stab you with the other. You cut off both, and they kick you to death."

Kade had already decided. Some of these men were good people he had grown up with on the airship *Victory*. Charmer had deceived them. Kade would do what he could to help them.

"Mercy, or a painful death," Kade said. "Your choice, Carl."

Charmer drew in a breath and turned back to the trawler.

"Listen to me, and listen to me now!" He paused a moment, then shouted, "They're all liars. They came here to murder you! Kill them before they kill you!"

Gran Jefe yanked Charmer back from Slayer and launched his axe through the air at the holdouts before Kade could stop him. A second later, the first gunshot cracked. Kade wasn't sure who fired it, but it didn't matter.

"Fire!" Forge yelled. "Open fire!"

Zuni pulled Kade backward, and Dakota moved in front of them with a shield. He fell to the deck as shots zipped all around them. Muzzle flashes of return fire sparked from the trawler.

By the time Kade got up on one knee, he saw that Donovan was gone, along with most of his fellows. A few got off a shot or two, only to have their skulls burst in explosions of red mist.

"Hold fire!" Kade yelled. "HOLD FIRE!"

It took a few beats for the shooting to stop and the noise to fade away. Ears ringing, he looked over at General Forge, who held up a fist.

Kade tried to push past Zuni and Dakota, but they stuck close, shields up. He walked back to Charmer and brought a boot down hard on his chest. "You talking pile of Siren shit!"

Charmer grunted in pain.

"You killed them all!" Kade shouted.

"Wrong again, Cowboy King," Charmer managed to choke out. "*You* killed them."

Kade stared down, his heart pounding, realizing his mistake in trusting the snake. He wanted to stomp both broken arms into pulp.

"Medic!" someone yelled.

Looking toward the voice, Kade saw Valeria on the other assault craft, working to remove the armor from a downed Cazador. Anguished voices rang out. It wasn't just one injured soldier.

The Jet Skis zoomed past the assault boats to board the trawler. Kade's boat sped toward it, too. Slayer threw a rope ladder up over a rail and boarded. Zuni led the way, with Kade right behind him. He hopped over the rail to behold a sad sight. All but two of the original seven holdouts were dead.

Dakota and Zuni stuck to Kade as he approached Donovan. He writhed in pain, gripping the handle of the axe that Gran Jefe had hurled into his chest. They could do nothing to stanch the blood pouring from his body. Even if they could, the medics were busy with wounded Cazadores.

Kade thought back to the Coral Castle, when General Jack killed the injured knight rather than see him suffer.

"Kade," Donovan whispered.

Kade bent down next to him. "I'm sorry it came to this," he said.

"I was…" Donovan reached up with a bleeding, shaking hand. "I was wrong. You will…"

He broke into a coughing fit, blood bubbling from his mouth. He used his final breath to finish his statement. ". . . make a good king."

Blood spread away from his inert body, merging with other dark pools across the deck. Kade slowly got to his feet, looking out over the blown-open heads and bullet-riddled torsos before his eyes locked on Gran Jefe.

The big man strode over and plucked his axe from Donovan with a sucking sound.

"You gave second chance," Gran Jefe said. "He picked wrong."

Then he walked away.

Kade grabbed him by the arm. "I told you to stand down!"

Gran Jefe turned and yanked his arm free.

"If we hadn't fired, more of us would be hurt or dead," Forge said. "Charmer doomed your peace mission with his poison."

Chest heaving, Kade looked from Gran Jefe to the general.

"And now I must return to the islands to tell the wife and son of another warrior that he has passed to the underworld," Forge said.

His eye went to the boat where a Cazador lay on the deck with Valeria crouched over him. She had removed a plate of armor and held a sopping pad of gauze against a chest wound. It was obvious from the sheer volume of blood that the man would not make it home.

"Mario will leave behind a wife and two kids," Forge said. "He didn't have to die."

Kade clenched his jaw as dread replaced the adrenaline rushing through his blood. His first action as king had gotten people killed.

"I did what I thought would save lives, not take them," Kade said.

"Life cheap in wastes," Gran Jefe said. He wiped the blood off his axe. "King must be *muy duro*—strong, like blade—and never weak in face of *enemigos*."

*   *   *   *   *

A field of sunflowers the height of a man blew gently in the cool breeze. X stood on a hill overlooking a prodigiously fertile meadow that seemed to stretch across the horizon to a thicket of dense woodlands. Barking pulled him in the opposite direction. Miles came running up the hill, tail wagging, eyes as clear as the limpid brook tumbling through the woods behind them. A pair of birds chased each other through the canopy, climbing into a cloudless blue sky.

This was surely the most beautiful place he had ever seen.

Miles raced down the other side of the hill, toward the sunflowers. X felt a smile forming. He reached up, touched his face. He had no beard, no scars.

He glanced down to find his prosthetic arm gone, in its place his own arm of flesh and bone. He had no armor on. Instead, he was dressed in brown dungarees with a button-down white shirt.

This had to be a dream.

Or else he was dead.

Still, if he was dead, at least he didn't appear to be in hell. He would take this place over fire and brimstone in a heartbeat. He chased after his dog, who ran faster than X had seen him move in years. Like X, Miles seemed to be a younger version of himself.

The mutant husky bolted across the field of sunflowers, stopping here and there to sniff. He lifted his leg and watered one of the long sunflower stems before taking off again. X ran after him, clapping his hands.

Miles turned around, circling him just as he used to do. The dog jumped in the air, planting his paws playfully on X's chest and licking his face.

Then he was off again, bolting into a lush green meadow where he ran and ran. He went down in the lush grass, lolling with his tongue out. He kicked up in the air, grunting and pawing at the sky. X caught up with him and bent down to rub his soft, furry belly.

A quake shook the ground beneath them. Miles flipped from his back onto his feet, ears perked. Alert.

The tremor came and went, and Miles lazily wagged his tail again. Guard down, he jumped back up on X, licking him again. Then he took off running, glancing back as if urging X to follow.

They ran across the field, closing in on the woods.

"Miles, come here!" X yelled.

Some of the trees bore fruit. He ran over and snatched a ripe pear off a limb. He tossed it in the air, and Miles leaped up and caught it in his mouth. X picked another pear and took a juicy bite as he walked after Miles. Birds chirped from the canopy of healthy, normal-looking trees. A pair of squirrels raced up the trunk, chasing each other.

Rabbits nibbled the grass, eyeing X and then darting away from Miles. The dog chased one back into the meadows. The bunny finally escaped into a hole. Miles dug at the opening, pawing to get at it.

"Here, boy," X said, tossing the pear like a ball.

Miles hesitated, looked back to the hole, then bolted away for the pear.

The ground rumbled again. X turned toward the forest, where it seemed to be coming from. But now he heard something.

Faint voices, like whispers. None that he could make out.

He saw a tree towering above the others. The trunk was thick and covered in bulbous growths that were smoother than the surrounding bark.

Miles returned, growling in the direction of the tree.

The voices whispered back.

"Come," one said.

X started toward the forest, Miles trotting by his side. They neared the edge, where the tree's thick roots coiled and twisted along the surface like snakes.

Unlike on the other trees, no birds or squirrels frolicked on these limbs.

"Hello?" X called out.

He took a cautious step, noticing the strange growths on the bark. They looked almost like…

A pair of eyes in the center of one of the bulbous growths opened their lids and found X. He froze at the horrifying sight. This couldn't be real. The growths were indeed what he thought: human faces.

Faces of people he had known.

All across the wide trunk, eyelids opened on the trapped heads.

Katarina. Les. Ash. Weaver. Rhino. Arlo. Rodger…

"Help us," they whispered. "Set us free!"

The voices combined into a hissing chorus.

Miles whined and backed up toward X.

Seemingly out of nowhere, storm clouds rolled across the sky, dumping sheets of rain over the forest. Lightning flashed downward, striking a tree somewhere with a deafening crack. Thunder boomed like a shotgun.

Miles yelped, though not from the noise.

X whirled about to find his dog enwrapped by roots that had pulled him to the ground. He pawed and squirmed as X ran over to help.

"Miles!" he shouted.

Roots burst from the ground, one of them snagging X by the leg. He tried to kick it off, but a second root grabbed the other leg.

"Help usss," hissed the voices. "Ssset usss free!"

X reached out to Miles as the roots pulled him toward the tree of faces. Another snaking limb wrapped around X, dragging him down. He fought as hard as he could, but these roots and vines were more powerful than the muscular arms of a Siren.

"Miles!" he yelled again.

The dog snarled and bit, fighting to get free. The roots pulled them both closer to the trunk of the tree, its many faces peering over them.

Kicking and squirming, trying to break free, X noticed a shadow striding out of the forest. The man or woman held a sword in one hand, raising it up as they approached Miles.

"NO! STOP!" X screamed.

He watched in horror as the person brought the sword down. Miles hopped up, free, and ran over to X. Only then did X see the face of the man.

It was Michael. He bent over and hacked the roots off X, freeing him with three swift strokes, then reached down and helped X to his feet.

"Tin," X said. "Where are we? What is this place?"

"Find me," Michael said. "We still have work to do."

He walked back into the forest, which dimmed now under the growing shadow of a mountain. Snowcapped peaks rose up in a violent quake that shook the ground. Gusts of icy air swept out of the woods, howling over the hissing voices that pleaded to be set free.

The pastures froze all around X and Miles, the flower petals shriveling and stems turning to ice. In seconds, the world transformed from a green oasis, brimming with life, to frigid tundra.

Storm clouds swept over the snowy terrain. Above those humps of snow, X saw something else—something human made.

Airship-size dishes, attached to the tops of structures that looked like oil rigs, angled up at the clouds. But these weren't Cazador homes. These were ITC weather-modification units.

X had had this dream before.

He crouched down with Miles, shielding the dog from the gusting wind. It was as if they had been transported back to Hades.

"It's okay, boy," X said.

He closed his eyes, and when he opened them again, there was darkness behind his visor. This was no dream or vision.

Warning sensors beeped in his helmet. Water streaked down the cracked visor. His eyes flitted back and forth as he tried to make sense of his location on his HUD. He finally managed to focus on one of the alerts.

Toxins present.

He tried to move against squishy but firm constraints. He seemed to be on his side, with his prosthetic arm tucked under him. He used his real arm and hand to reach under him and activate the wrist computer on the prosthetic arm.

It took a few tries before he activated his helmet lights. The bright glow illuminated a pink surface with grooves and ...

Blood vessels?

Snaking blue veins protruded from the fleshy floor he was pinned against.

Fog blurred his mind as he tried to remember where the hell he was. Using his free hand, he tried to push against the floor, wall, or whatever this was ...

Vibrations rumbled all around him, followed by a distant groan that grew louder. The faint but intensifying noise of rushing water followed.

The constraints around him suddenly loosened, and he freed his trapped prosthesis. The overhead rose up, allowing him to get up on his knees, finding the blood vessels both above and below him. It was as if he was in a living tube of some sort.

The rushing noise grew louder. He managed to turn his helmet. The lights illuminated the fleshy tunnel. That groaning came again, but this time it transitioned to a roaring whistle like the high-frequency voice of some gigantic monster...

"Oh my God," X said, remembering those eyes.

Those bulging mutant eyes of the leviathan had looked at him right before the monster swallowed him whole.

He wasn't dead, but he may as well be.

You're really fucked now, old man.

SEVEN

"We're almost in position over Mount Mitchell," Timothy announced.

His hologram stood in the center of the airship's launch bay. Across the space, on a bench near the row of lockers, Layla stepped into her jumpsuit, heart pounding at what she was about to do.

The flight to the mountain Captain Rolo wrote about in his journal had been unremarkable, and for that Layla was glad. She wasn't sure how much more they could handle after the accident that killed Steve.

Michael had managed to fix the other damaged panels with her help, even though he had tried to insist on doing it himself. After they completed the work, he vanished into the lower decks, working on various projects during the two-day trip to Mount Mitchell.

It was his way of dealing with the grief, and Layla gave him that space.

He was also inside the launch bay, preparing the hundreds of feet of coiled hoses that would pump water to the ship from the mountain streams—assuming that the water was clean. With the airship's water-treatment center up and running, it didn't need to be perfect. But Layla knew from experience that most water from the surface was far too polluted even for their system to cleanse.

She would find out soon enough.

In a few minutes, she would dive to the surface.

While Michael got the hoses ready, she opened her locker to grab her boots. It was odd, standing here again. When she gave birth to Bray, she had sworn she would never dive again. Back then she had a choice. Now there wasn't one.

You're doing this for your family.

Layla sat on a bench and laced up her boots. Then she went to the armory. Her old chest armor rig was inside one of the cages, used last by one of the greenhorns.

She checked the other stuff, including the cracked wrist computer and rusted shin and thigh guards. It took a few minutes of searching—time she tried to spend not dwelling on the divers who had once donned this armor. People she had called friends.

Dents, shrapnel holes, and deep scratches—not just from the claws of beasts but also from machetes and spears—reminded her of those battles.

Layla hoped today she wouldn't have to worry about violence, but she was going prepared with her blaster, a pistol, and a laser rifle.

Finally, she located her armor in a nook. She unfolded it and put her head through. The rig still fit like a glove over her chest and stomach. Returning to the bench, she put on shin guards, elbow guards, and the plates that connected everything together.

When she was finished, she grabbed her helmet and went to her weapons.

"Ma-ma, Mommy, Mommy."

Layla turned to find Victor standing in the launch-bay

entrance with Bray. The boy ran inside, with Victor limping a little just behind him.

"Victor, you're supposed to be taking it easy," she chided.

"I am."

Bray reached out as he approached his mother. Then he stopped and put up his forefinger.

"Hi, honey." Layla met his fingertip with hers. He chuckled when their fingertips met. It was a game he enjoyed playing with everyone lately, and was what Michael referred to as their son's *handshake*.

Layla bent down and kissed him, her heart pounding with anxiety at the thought of not returning from the dive. She had reminded herself many times that it was in a green zone, but that didn't mean it was safe.

Hearing noises behind them, Layla checked to find Michael kicking one of the hoses in frustration.

"Another damned pinhole," he said. "I've got to patch that up before we can lower it, or we'll never get water to the ship."

"Shouldn't be too hard, right?" Layla asked.

"No, but I worry there are more I missed."

Michael walked over to Layla. He couldn't hide the worry in his eyes.

"Don't say it, Tin, please," she said. "I'm not as rusty as I look."

"I can't let you go alone."

Bray reached out to him, then pulled back, sensing his father's despair.

Michael sighed. "I'm sorry, I just… we can't survive without you."

"Look, I'll be fine," Layla said. "And Ti—sorry, Michael—you know your mind isn't in it right now." She left off the fact that he was missing his prosthetic arm, not that he needed reminding.

The worry transitioned to sadness on his face, and now Layla felt guilt. She didn't want him to feel *broken*.

"You don't always have to be the hero," Layla said.

"Ha! You're the hero. You risked your life to save me. I couldn't even save Steve."

"It wasn't your fault, Michael."

"No," Victor chimed in. "It was accident."

"I failed a good man, plain and simple," Michael said.

Bray babbled and then reached out with his finger, this time to Timothy. The AI met it with his own glowing fingertip. That made Bray smile. He pulled back, then reached out again.

Michael and Layla both smiled.

"I'll be fine," she said. She leaned in and kissed Michael. "Besides, we need someone up here who knows how to operate those hoses."

"Yeah, right."

"We're in position," Timothy announced.

Layla welcomed the distraction. She hated seeing her husband like this and wanted to help, but right now she had to focus on the dive. She squatted in front of Bray and kissed him on the head. "I love you. I'll be back soon."

Michael gave Layla a one-armed hug and kissed her on the lips.

"Watch your six," he said.

"Good luck," Victor said.

Layla put on her helmet. The heads-up display activated with a digital topo map of Mount Mitchell and the surrounding terrain.

"I've downloaded the maps from the archives to your HUD," Timothy said. "There are several different waterfalls in the area with suitably deep pools below them. I believe the most accessible is Crabtree Falls. There's also an observation post at the top of Mount Mitchell if you care to search it for supplies. Records show it once had a general store that might have some preserved items."

"One thing at a time, Pepper," Michael said.

"Indeed, sir."

As soon as Layla walked away, Bray began to sob.

"It's okay," Michael said. "Ma-ma won't be gone long."

Layla finished prepping her gear and walked to the launch-bay doors. Bray's wailing broke her heart, but she would be back with him soon enough.

She secured her helmet with a click and drew in a whiff of plastic. As she neared the yellow line on the deck, the comms flared.

"Testing, Raptor One," Timothy said.

"Copy, comms working," Layla replied.

She stepped on the painted line in front of the double doors. A bead of sweat rolled down her forehead. It had been a long time since she had actually dived into the wastes.

"Drop zone is confirmed clear of major storms," Timothy said. *"Green light to dive."*

A Klaxon blared, and the doors yawned open into darkness. Layla glanced over her shoulder at the exit doors, where she could see Michael holding Bray. Victor was next to them, also watching.

She raised a hand and then, with a deep breath, leaped into the black void.

Her training kicked in as she fell. For the first few moments, she felt the old sense of weightlessness. Then she hit a pocket of turbulence that rocked her out of position.

The view went topsy-turvy, and she caught a glimpse of the beetle-shaped airship above her. In a way, it was chilling to see the ship from this angle again. She had never thought she would be diving again to keep it in the sky. But as long as she was with her family, she would take it in stride.

Layla fought her way back into stable position: facedown, arms and legs bent at right angles. A puffy mattress of clouds stretched across the field of her night-vision optics. So far, electrical interference was minimal and everything was operating properly.

She checked her altitude at twenty-two thousand feet. Her falling speed was stable at 110 miles per hour. The HUD flickered for a second when lightning flashed across the shelf of clouds to the west.

Thunder clapped two heartbeats later, reverberating through her body. She bit down on her mouth guard and pulled her arms in to her sides, straightening into a nosedive. Within fifteen seconds of jumping, the old skills were back.

As she speared through the clouds, a message from Michael crackled over the channel.

"Layla, you okay?" he asked.

"Everything's good," she replied.

"You got this, Lay—" Electrical interference cut him off. The wind screaming past her drowned out the static crackle from the speakers in her helmet.

At fourteen thousand feet, she was streaking down at 180 miles an hour. The wind buffeted and tugged her body, but she kept arms tight to her sides and held steady.

Another jagged fork of lightning blasted across her flight path, and the thunderclap rattled her bones. The data on her HUD fizzled, then solidified.

Down to 10,400 feet. Out of nowhere, turbulence knocked her out of the nosedive and sent her cartwheeling like a rag doll in a hurricane.

A voice surged over the comms. She could hear Michael's voice but couldn't make out what he was saying. Chances were, he had seen her heart rate ramp up.

By the time she had pulled back into a nosedive, her heart was thumping loud in her ears.

"I'm okay, just some bad turbulence."

"You're almost to the surface," Michael said.

At five thousand feet, the clouds below her had all but vanished.

Seconds later, she saw the twin camel humps that had to be Mount Mitchell. Forests carpeted its slopes. Looking closer, even from three thousand feet up she could see that most of the trees were dead, their skeletal limbs upraised in a silent plea to the heavens.

But there was life down there too—here and there a canopy of thriving foliage offered some small respite to the barren terrain. Checking her HUD, she saw her altitude fast approaching two thousand feet.

Layla pulled the rip cord and stuffed it in her jumpsuit as the chute inflated, giving her the sensation of being yanked upward. She grabbed the toggles and checked the digital map on her HUD to locate the DZ.

Crabtree Falls was to the west. She steered her chute toward it. Passing over the forest, she turned off her night vision to have a look unaided. Sporadic flashes of lightning provided the necessary light to see Crabtree Falls, cascading into a pool that fed a rushing stream.

Gliding over a patch of bright-carmine foliage, she looked for an open spot to flare and land.

It was difficult to see through the dense vegetation around the snaking watercourse. Along its banks grew dense bushes and vine-laden trees. Beside the pool of the falls, the purple and red foliage opened up into a glade. The white noise of rushing water grew into a roar, and a moment later she sailed over a silvery cataract down a rock face some fifty feet high.

"Tin, you copy?" Layla asked over the channel.

"Copy, Raptor One."

"I'm almost to the DZ. Looks clear. I'll send a sitrep ASAP."

Bringing up her knees, she performed a two-stage flare and stepped out of the sky onto a floor of flat river pebbles. The chute and shrouds floated down behind her and rippled in the breeze. The faint cry of a bird carried on the wind.

As soon as she had freed herself from the parachute, she unslung her rifle and took cover behind a boulder on the stream bank. A quick life scan of the area revealed only birds and a few rodent-size animals.

Still, she stood quietly peering into the shadows with her night-vision goggles, looking for movement. She rotated her optics over the shoreline and found only a small bird. She zoomed in on brown feathers and a white chest. The creature didn't look the least bit scary or mutant in any way. It was similar to birds she had seen in picture books growing up.

Her pounding heart calmed, and she lowered the rifle barrel. Cautiously she turned and walked down to the stream.

Crouching, she pulled out the water-testing kit from her pack. She set it down, propped it open, and took out the test tube. Then she twisted off the cap and dunked it in the water. After filling it, she dripped the testing solution into the water, put the cap back on, and swirled it around inside.

She repeated the process with three more tubes. When they were all side by side in the testing kit, she walked away for a closer look at the area. Her boots crunched on dead branches that lay strewn across the rocks.

The birds abruptly ceased their chirping.

Layla brought up her rifle and surveyed the dead trees. In the forest, nothing stirred.

Returning to the testing kits, she crouched down to examine their findings. A smile crossed her face when she saw that the water levels were clean. It seemed almost too good to be true.

"Tin, I've got good news," she said into the comm link. "I think the water's good."

White noise surged over the channel.

"Michael, do you copy?"

She glanced up as lightning speared across the horizon. Her

joy faded at the sight of a dull, reddish fog drifting across the mountain. It was moving fast.

"Michael, do you read?"

A faint voice crackled. *"Layla, we have some sort of interference. I didn't get your last."*

"I know, but listen, the water test is good. You can lower the ship and the tubes."

Static crackled in her helmet. She heard what sounded like acknowledgment about the water, but she couldn't be sure.

"Michael?" she said in a louder voice. "Tin, do you copy?"

The reddish fog rolled over the hills east of her, toward the stream. Was *that* the reason for the interference?

Seeing the flash of electricity branch out across the fog bank, she realized that the fog was the source. The smokelike curtain swallowed up the forest at the bottom of the mountain and kept on rolling, right toward her location.

"Michael, do you copy?"

She stared at the sky in anticipation of a response, but there was nothing. The channel seemed to be completely offline—no static, no white noise. The birds had stopped chirping. The only thing she heard was the sounds of falling, rushing, trickling water.

A stillness fell over the woods. Layla raised her rifle as the creepy sensation of being watched hit her.

The wind picked up behind her, whispering through the branches of towering trees. She turned, only to hear a raucous, almost laughing sound coming from the woods.

Watching the dead trees, she moved her finger to the trigger.

The cackle echoed through the forest, making it difficult to pinpoint. She switched on her infrared optics and searched for heat signatures. Nothing moved across her field of vision, but she did notice something dangling from a lower branch of a pine tree with purple ferns growing on its bark. She approached with her rifle shouldered and stopped in front of the stand of towering trees. The skeletal limbs creaked in the wind. The object she had seen on one of the lower branches spun in the air.

Layla took a step into the forest, her boot sinking into soft moss and leaf litter.

Another step brought her within ten feet of the tree. Before her, a hoop hung from a rope on the branch. Feathers adorned the bottom of the hoop, and beaded wires formed a hexagonal pattern in the middle. She could tell that it hadn't been hanging here for long—certainly not years. Someone, or something, had put it here.

She took another step as a loud static crack over the headset made her jump.

"Layla, do you copy?" Michael asked.

"Yes, I copy," she said, panting.

"What's happening?"

"There's a weird red fog blanketing everything... and I found some sort of hanging ornament in a tree. I think it was put here recently. I heard a voice."

"A voice? Human?"

She spun in all directions with her rifle, searching for the beast that had made the hyena-like call.

"No, I don't know what it was," Layla replied.

"It's going to be okay. We're lowering the airship," Michael said. *"We'll get the water and get out of here. Just hold tight and watch your—"*

Another flash of electricity bloomed through the blood-tinted fog, cutting off the transmission. Layla stared for another moment and felt a twinge of fear. She had to get out of here. But that meant running into the forest—toward the source of the animal noises.

With maybe a minute left before the fog reached her, she

had to decide fast. She searched the stream for an escape route, and then she saw it—the waterfall.

"Michael, do you copy?" she asked.

Nothing.

She ran out of the woodland glen, to the pool below the falls. Loose rocks made moving difficult, and twice she almost fell. She glanced over her shoulder. The fog was almost to the stream. Sizzling bursts of electricity shot out from the edges of the moving curtain.

The hair on the back of her neck stood up as she reached the pool under the falls. As the water cascaded down the featured rock, Layla looked up to the slopes on either side of the falls. The sides were too steep for her to climb without a rope and protective gear. And even then she wouldn't have time.

She was trapped.

Heart pounding, she thought of another option. She could hit her booster, but if she couldn't reach Michael on the airship, she would just keep rising and rising into the sky.

Standing at the edge of the pool, she thought she saw something through the rushing water. There appeared to be a passage on the other side. A cave, maybe?

She took a step and again hesitated. To get there, she would have to cross through the pool. If the fog was carrying a powerful enough electrical charge, it would be the last step she ever took.

Maniacal cackling erupted in the distance. Layla scanned the blood fog, searching for some clue to whatever creature was making it. It seemed that the creature was inside the curtain now.

Just standing here, she was a target. She decided to take her chances in the water.

She removed her left glove and touched the surface with her finger. No electrical shock came. Holding her breath, she stepped into the shallow pool, half expecting a powerful jolt. Nothing happened. She waded out toward the bottom of the falls. The water came up to her waist. Another laughing cry erupted behind her, but this time she didn't turn to search for whatever monster had made the noise.

Layla pointed her gun toward the waterfall, took a breath, and walked into the cascading veil without looking back.

EIGHT

At three in the morning, the two assault boats were closing in on the capitol tower. The journey back had been mostly silent after the adrenaline settled, but Kade still felt his heart pounding.

Valeria had tried her best, but Mario was dead. She stood up on the blood-slick deck of the assault craft and shook her head. Kade heaved a silent sigh and turned to look at the fishing trawler behind them. Two Cazadores piloted the boat with its cargo of Charmer's seven dead henchmen. It could have been worse, but it could also have been a lot better.

Kade had taken time on the ride back to consider what he would do with Charmer and also with Gran Jefe. There was also the growing tension between Kade and General Forge to consider. Especially after losing Mario in what should never have escalated into a fight.

Charmer was to blame for that. Bringing him out here had made things worse.

Kade should bloody well have known better than to enlist Charmer to make things right. Keeping him alive had been strategic up to this point. Kade had followed the flawed logic that he could get Charmer to admit his crimes and persuade Donovan and the others to surrender without bloodshed.

He looked in the stern, where Charmer was curled up in a ball on the deck, looking defeated. But Kade wasn't deceived. The snake still had a bite.

Gran Jefe sat across from Charmer, snoring with his head slumped against his chest. He didn't seem at all fazed by the killing. Not a big surprise to Kade.

He was trained to spill blood, just like Kade's praetorian guards, Zuni and Dakota, whose faces Kade had yet to see behind their masked helmets.

"Prepare for docking!" someone shouted.

Kade got up and went to the bow as the assault craft approached the marina at the capitol tower. Torches burned on the piers, casting an orange glow over the faces of a waiting crowd.

"What the bloody hell are they doing out there?" Kade asked. "Clear those docks!"

General Forge radioed an order to the guards posted at the marina. They quickly herded the people away from the piers. Kade spotted Beau, Roman, Woody, Tia, and many other sky people among those watching.

They all wanted news.

Kade let out a sigh. He was exhausted, but he knew there would be no sleep for him this morning. He had much to do to repair things after the latest cycle of violence at the islands, and to prepare for the threat of the Forerunner's knights.

The boats pulled up alongside the pier, and Kade hopped out.

"Get them back," he commanded.

The people were being moved away, but some were still on the docks. Only three Cazador guards and two militia soldiers were around to help.

Shouting erupted from the gathered civilians. Something flew from the crowd and landed on the deck behind Kade. When he turned, he saw the putrid mango, and its target—Charmer, who was now standing up in the boat.

More objects flew across the docks. Rotting fruit, a fish head, a rock. Things were one knife or gunshot away from escalating into more bloodshed.

"Hang Charmer!" someone screamed.

"Yeah, by the 'nads! Cut him up into chum and feed him to the fish!"

The crowd was getting even more worked up. Mourning family members and enraged citizens who had heard the news broke free of the guards trying to hold them back. Zuni and Dakota raised their shields and stepped in front of Kade.

Everything seemed to shift into slow motion. Maybe the exhaustion from the past few weeks had finally caught up to Kade.

"Hold them!" Forge yelled.

The crowd surged down the pier, and a new voice carried over the others.

"Mario! No! *NO!*" A woman stood watching the body of her husband being lifted from the boat. Two young children clung to her sides as Valeria and another soldier carried their dead father away.

Kade held up his hand when two guards tried to get them to move. It was too late now, and he wasn't going to hold them back.

"Let me go, you bastards!" shouted Charmer, squirming in the grip of Slayer and Blackburn. "You won't get away with this, Kade!" he screamed. "You murdered them all in cold blood! Gunned Donovan and the others down like dogs!"

The onlookers grew quiet, even the sobs winding down.

"You're going to execute me too, like you did Rolo!" Charmer shouted. "I should have a trial, just like we did for Michael Everhart!

I did nothing wrong! Everything I did was to protect our people! To protect this PLACE!"

"Shut that poisonous yap of yours!" Slayer yelled. He smacked Charmer in the back of the head, but that only revved him up.

"Your new king is a murderer!" Charmer yelled to the crowd. "He did the same thing at the machine camp!"

Kade stepped away from Zuni and Dakota, drawing his cutlass from his sheath. Slayer and Blackburn held the prisoner still as Kade brought the sword up to his mouth. He grabbed Charmer by the jaw with one hand, forcing his lips open. He angled the blade up into the mouth that had spewed so much venom.

"No," Charmer squeaked. "No, no … *Stop!*"

"Hold him!" Kade shouted.

"See, he's a murderer!"

Slayer grabbed Charmer's broken left arm, eliciting a yelp. Kade put the tip of the cutlass into his mouth and turned it, chipping a tooth.

"King Kade!" a young voice cried.

Through his rage, Kade recognized the voice as Tia's. He pulled the blade back. She was standing in the crowd with Katherine, Phyl, and Alton. Beau was holding Roman back from Charmer.

"Slit his throat, King Kade!" Roman yelled. "Let him bleed out in front of all to see what we do to traitors!"

Woody stood at an angle, an arm slightly out, clearly trying to make sure Roman didn't break free from Beau and cause more chaos.

"I'm all for gutting this scum," Tia said. "But here? Like this?"

"Do it!" Alton yelled. "He's evil! He killed Oliver and Nez and tried to blame Chief Everhart!"

"Shut up, runt!" Charmer shouted.

Kade squeezed his mouth shut again and brought the blade up to his throat.

"He's crazy!" Charmer squeaked. "Someone help me!"

Kade looked back to Alton, who had a fist raised.

In a moment of clarity, Kade looked past his vengeful rage. This was not the example he wanted to set for the boy.

He faced Charmer again, still holding the blade to his throat.

"You say another word, and I swear on my family, I'll cut your tongue out and jam it down your gullet," Kade said. "Nod if you understand."

Charmer hesitated, then nodded.

"I'll give you your trial," Kade said. "But it won't be another kangaroo court like the one you trotted out for Michael. This trial will be conducted according to Cazador customs. A trial by combat."

Charmer's eye flitted down to his casts, as if to say, *How can I fight with two broken arms?*

"Use your bloody teeth and toes—no, wait, why don't you just *talk* your opponent to death?" Kade said. He backed away and pointed his sword at the capitol tower. "Put him in the brig."

"What? No, he needs to die!" Roman shouted. "You have to kill him!"

Beau pulled his son back with Woody's help as Slayer and Blackburn dragged Charmer away.

Exhaling, Kade sheathed his cutlass. Zuni and Dakota kept their shields up, facing the crowd and the upper balconies of the tower.

Kade gestured to Imulah, who had joined them on the docks.

"Call a council meeting," Kade said. "I'm going to go clean the blood off my armor and then explain to everyone how we're moving forward as *one* people."

He walked away from the assault boats and over to the now-silent crowd.

"Donovan is dead," Kade announced loudly. "Everyone who

supported Charmer is dead. I tried to stop it. I tried to give them a chance, but Charmer lied to them yet again, and there was a shootout…"

He shook his head.

"Please, go home to your families, mourn the dead, and get up ready to face a better future," he said.

No one said anything, and the crowd began to disperse.

Not everyone moved, though. Woody and Tia lingered. Roman had calmed down, and Beau gave Kade a subtle nod.

Seeing the gesture and knowing he had his friends here gave Kade a sense of support that he desperately needed. He walked over to them while the assault teams remained behind to unload the boats.

Dakota and Zuni walked with him, but Kade asked them to stand back. They obeyed but remained close.

"Donovan's gone?" Beau asked.

Kade nodded. "I tried, but—"

"He made his own choices," Woody said.

"We'll deal with Charmer too," Kade said. He faced Roman and Beau. "The bastard won't get away with what he's done, but I need him alive a bit longer."

"I trust you," Beau said.

Roman glanced up, then nodded.

"Okay," Kade said. "So you guys still want to help?"

"Do dolphins like to screw?" Woody asked.

Kade raised a brow.

"They do, is the point," Woody said. "I see 'em going at it a lot. Things really like to pork. Why, they'd fuck the crack of dawn if they could!"

"What a weird observation," Kade said.

"What Woody means to say is we ain't no bludgers and are ready to help," Beau said. "What ya got in mind?"

"Well, much as I like these two guys following me around, I'd appreciate having friends nearby," Kade said.

"Told ya, I'm happy to be court jester," Woody said.

"I think the king's looking for bodyguards more than laughs," Tia said.

"We'll watch your six," Beau said.

Roman didn't respond, which was fine by Kade.

"Does this mean I get to follow royalty around and dress like one of *them*?" Woody gestured to the praetorian guards.

"They look like they've killed a lot of people," Beau said.

"Dakota, Zuni, come here a minute, please," Kade said.

The guards clanked over, popping their helmet visors.

"Beau, Woody, and Tia, meet Dakota and Zuni," Kade said.

"We've met," Tia said, giving Zuni a sly grin.

He grinned back at her, then stiffened as Kade looked over.

You've met, huh? Kade knew what that meant, and as much as he wanted to keep Tia out of danger, who she saw was not his responsibility.

Apparently, it wouldn't matter anyway. Tia blushed for the first time that Kade had ever seen, just because Zuni winked at her. He was a good-looking young man with a bronze complexion and a mane of wild black hair tied back with a thong.

Dakota, on the other hand, was built on the Gran Jefe body plan, only a bit smaller. His beard was dyed orange, and he had a dark tattoo of a breeder on his neck.

The same beast from Panama that nearly killed Forge, Kade realized.

"Did you help bring down one of those breeders?" he asked.

Dakota nodded. "I throw spear tied with a grenade—blow up the *mierdita*'s belly. Big mess." He grinned.

"Holy shit," Tia breathed.

"And you're a tracker?" Kade asked Zuni.

"Yes, I learn as *muchacho*." He had decent English. "I come from Texas. Same bunker as the legendary General Rhino."

It occurred to Kade that Zuni had Native American blood in his line. He had read about the indigenous Zuni people of the North American Southwest when he was a kid, but had never met one.

"Beau and Woody are going to be spending a lot of time with us," Kade said. "I want you to help train them to fight."

"What about me?" Tia said. "I need something to do until we get an airship."

"I need your help with something else, and also making sure Alton stays out of trouble," Kade said.

"You got to be kidding me. Isn't that Katherine's job?"

"I just want a second pair of eyes on him, especially after that scam trial and—"

"Didn't I prove myself in Brisbane?"

"Yes, of course, but—"

"You're not my dad, Kade," she interrupted.

"Tia," Kade said loudly. "Walk with me."

The others moved on as Kade strode out. For a moment, he worried that Tia wouldn't follow. But she trotted after him.

She had learned a lot in Brisbane, and Kade was just happy she had made it out in one piece. He wanted to make sure she stayed that way.

When they were a few steps away, Kade turned to her.

"I have a plan to save this place, but I need your help, and most important, I need you to trust me."

"I'm not a babysitter, and I'm old enough to do what I want."

Kade gently put a hand on her wrist. "I know you're a young woman now. You can see who you want and do what you want. I just ask you to help me with Alton, and listen to what I say."

She met his gaze.

"Can you do that?" Kade asked.

She looked away. He didn't need to turn to know she had her eyes on Zuni.

"More people died tonight," Kade said. "This place is hanging on by a thread, and I need your help."

"I hear you," she said. "I'll do what you say, but when the time comes, I'm diving again."

✶   ✶   ✶   ✶   ✶

X woke to a whooshing sound. He lifted his head from where it had been slumped against his chest armor. The HUD display beeped with an array of warnings.

Suit integrity compromised.

Foreign toxins detected.

Battery level dropping.

X tried to remember what had happened, but his mind was groggy. He recalled a dream of green pastures, a forest, and . . . that tree. A tree of faces of people he couldn't save.

Another image entered his mind—not from a dream, but a vision of the weather-modification units.

X reached up and turned on his helmet lights. The beams hit a strange, ribbed pink roof. His situation came crashing back down on him.

He was *inside* the leviathan. Not the stomach, which was the reason he still existed. He was trapped in the throat, his prosthesis jammed into a groove.

That wasn't a dream or a vision after all. He remembered it swallowing him and Jo-Jo. A moment of dread passed over him as he realized that Jo-Jo was probably dead. The animal wouldn't have lasted long without a suit. Then again, she surely died when the thing ate them.

Dumb luck he didn't die then.

Or maybe Jo-Jo was the lucky one.

The whooshing noise that had woken him came again, louder this time. He angled his lights down the tunnel of flesh as a wave of yellowish water surged up the corridor, hitting him. The force tugged on him, but his prosthetic arm remained jammed inside the groove.

He grabbed it and tried to pry it free. Finally the hand popped out. Then he was moving with the current—not fast, but slowly rising.

Was this thing going to puke him out?

It beat the alternative—being dropped down into the stomach—but if he was puked out in the ocean, he would likely sink to the bottom and die from the water pressure. Unless, of course, he could get his armor off, but with no air supply he would drown.

He flailed for something to hold on to as he rose up the creature's throat, but found no purchase on the smooth, meaty walls. The warning box on his HUD flashed with a new message.

Danger. Danger. Danger!

"Uh, no shit!" X grunted.

He had just righted his body in the current when he saw the smoke rising off his armor. This liquid—it wasn't seawater.

X flailed to get himself out of the corrosive stomach acid. If it ate through his suit, he was dead.

His fingers slid over the floor, then ceiling, then walls until he tumbled head over feet again. The force of the acidic wave sent him surging up the widening tube. His lights speared into an opening.

What the glow revealed took his breath away.

He was blasted into the closed mouth of the monster. The jaw was filled with what looked like long strands of super-stiff fur.

His prosthesis caught between two of those strands. For

a moment, he just stared as his helmet lights revealed, at the bottom of the mouth, the biggest tongue he ever hoped to see. Seawater sloshed beneath him.

He realized he wasn't the only thing stuck in these long, stiff strands. The two-headed shark with X's spear still sticking out of it floated belly up a dozen feet away.

The warning block on his HUD flashed a new message.

Suit integrity compromised.

X kicked and squirmed, trying to get free of the bristly lattice-work in the creature's mouth. His boot slid against the carcass of a large fish below him.

He grabbed a piece of his strange prison, trying to free himself. The material felt like thin, hard, leafless branches or fronds. Grabbing a chunk, he pulled as hard as he could.

A tremor rumbled through the mouth in response.

X let go of the bristles. He couldn't let himself be swallowed again, but neither could he afford to get puked out and sink to the seafloor.

He blinked, trying to marshal his thoughts.

Think, X. Think!

His helmet light danced over the roof of the mouth, far above him, then across, where something was moving in the parallel rows of bristles. The beam shot away when the leviathan began to move. The water in the bottom of the mouth swirled, and the tongue rose up toward X.

Oh, no, no, no!

He hugged the bristle, hanging on for dear life now as the enormous tongue licked at him, trying to pluck him free. No matter how hard he tried, the thing was just too powerful. It yanked him free—all but his prosthetic arm.

Once again it was stuck.

Dangling by the metal arm, he looked down again at the

tongue. It batted him like a toddler tired of its toy, dislodging him and sending him flying into the opposite jaw. He slammed into the rows of coarse bristles, once again ensnared.

The tongue settled back down.

He waited a beat before moving. Then he played his light over the mouth. It was easily the size of the trading post on the *Hive*. His beam hit the esophagus that he had just been vomited up through.

Luckily, his suit had handled the stomach acid, but his air reserves wouldn't last forever.

He bent down to examine his boots and suit where they were exposed under the armor. Most of it was holding up, but a place on his right shin guard had burned through to his leg. The flesh was red and burned like hell. The compartment on his thigh armor that held patching supplies and a medical kit was out of reach.

He did a scan of the mouth again and noticed something he had missed earlier—fish caught in the bristles were being fed on by hordes of snakelike creatures.

A loud howl made X jump. He knew that animal cry. It seemed to be coming from the strands above him.

X recognized the black, furry body wedged between the rows of bristles. As he watched, Jo-Jo tugged at the slithering creature that had her ensnared. Ripping free, she dropped down to X, where she promptly stuffed the head of the snakelike thing into her mouth and started chewing contentedly.

The leviathan's tongue moved again, smacking her aside before X could react. It knocked him free too. The next thing he knew, he splashed down into the water below with Jo-Jo.

Again the tongue whipped at X. He rolled under it and lunged over to the speared shark, yanking the spear free just as the tongue swiped at him again.

He jumped back, then thrust the spear.

Jo-Jo howled, growing more agitated.

Water rushed in, slamming X and Jo-Jo backward and swirling them around.

X noticed a blue glow in the darkness outside the leviathan's half-open jaws. They weren't far from the surface. He flailed with the spear, trying to stop this merry-go-round ride from hell. The blade snapped off.

Everything went topsy-turvy as a force slammed X in the back. It seemed the monster was done messing with these annoying animals in its mouth and had decided to spit them out.

X went cartwheeling through the water, his helmet lights raking back and forth. He saw Jo-Jo spinning away too. After a few moments, X righted himself, but he was already sinking.

He let go of the spear shaft and pulled for the surface, his heart hammering at the sight of the baleful eyes staring down at him. The creature let out a long, low whistle.

The jaws parted slightly as if preparing to eat him again.

Turning, he kicked after Jo-Jo, who was already swimming in what looked like an underwater graveyard of vessels. Finally some good luck!

X didn't look over his shoulder as he swam after her, pulling as hard as he could toward the open stern of a ship.

A light broke through the darkness, but it wasn't coming from behind them. Or above. It was coming from *inside* the ship.

Jo-Jo kept kicking toward a large opening and vanished under a mangled bulkhead. X grabbed it and pulled himself up as the leviathan submerged back into the shadows of the bay.

The monstrous eyes watched him from a distance.

Another stroke of luck. He wasn't going to waste it.

Ducking down, he followed Jo-Jo up into the guts of this sunken vessel. She had stopped ahead, still kicking to keep from sinking. Bubbles rose from her nose. Her wide eyes centered on several glowing figures at the other end of this open deck. Five or six—X couldn't be sure, but he could be sure about those squid arms reaching outward in the water.

X stopped kicking and stared in horror. This wasn't good luck at all.

The leviathan had spat them out right in front of a sunken ship full of its hungry calves. And it seemed X and Jo-Jo were to be the next meal.

NINE

"Layla, do you copy?" Michael said into the comms.

Static crackled and hissed in his earpiece as he stood in the bridge of the airship, hovering five hundred feet over the stream that Layla had dived down to just three hours ago. A dense curtain of reddish fog had blanketed the area, and within it, lightning flashed sporadically.

"Pepper, run a life scan again," Michael said.

"Stand by," Timothy replied.

Michael and Victor were still awaiting an update from Layla. They could only hope that she had found shelter from the fog. But it wasn't just the lightning and the strange red mist that worried him. She had said something about repeatedly hearing a strange voice and finding an object that appeared to have been placed there by intelligent—possibly human—life.

"I'm picking up some very odd readings in this fog," Timothy said.

"Life-forms?" Michael asked.

"No, I'm not detecting anything *within* the fog. The odd readings have to do with the fog itself."

"How so?"

"Even dense fog cannot conduct an electrical charge, but this fog seems to be carrying a current. Although… well, that's odd."

"What?"

"Chief, the electrical charges seem to be originating consistently in certain areas of the fog, which means—"

"Something or someone is causing them?" Michael asked.

"Yes, I would agree, that is the most logical conclusion."

The thought sent a chill through Michael. What on earth could be causing an electrical charge in the fog? It seemed impossible. But then again, he had seen stranger things in his years of diving.

"The fog is *alive*?" Victor asked.

"I have to find her," Michael said. "Pepper, if Bray wakes up, let Victor know. And, Victor, please comfort him until we get back."

"But, sir, you can't go into that storm," Timothy said.

Victor turned to Michael, but he was already on his way up the stairs from the bridge. He couldn't wait another second. He had to find Layla and extract her—something he should already have done.

Michael rushed to the launch bay, already suited up to dive. It took some work to get his armor on—a much more difficult process with just one arm. He grabbed a pistol and a blaster from the weapons locker. They were the only things he could effectively fire with one hand.

"Maybe I go," Victor said. "You stay here with Bray. Just in case something bad happens."

Michael thought on it. He was worried and not thinking it through. If he should be killed and Layla died too, Bray would be an orphan. Victor could probably raise the boy, but…

"May I opine?" Timothy asked.

His hologram emerged between the two men.

"Victor, you're injured and in no shape to go down there,"

said the AI. He turned to Michael. "And, Chief Everhart, you must consider your son, and—"

"I *am* considering my son!" Michael snapped.

"I'm sorry, sir, but please let me finish. You must consider your son, and your wife," Timothy said. "Your wife has the survival skills to take care of herself. Your son does not. The chances of Bray surviving without at least one of you aren't very good. If he loses both of you, the chances dwindle considerably."

"Without water, *none* of us will survive," Michael said. "Except you."

"I understand, but may I make a suggestion?"

Michael bent down to grab a harness from a locker while looking up at the same time. "Yeah, what?"

"The drone I've seen you working on should be able to survive in that fog, even if it is hit with the electrical charges," Timothy said. "Perhaps sending it down there is a better option than you going personally to find Layla. It would also help us see what we're dealing with."

Michael gave an exasperated sigh. "I'm not finished with it. I'm not even sure we can get it to work."

"I ran some tests—I hope you don't mind. It's airworthy. Whether we can get a signal is another story, however. We'll find out soon."

"What do you mean, we'll find out soon?"

"Sir, I deployed the drone forty-nine minutes ago."

Michael stared in shock at the hologram. "Timothy, if we're going to survive, you can't be making rogue decisions."

"Sir, with all due respect, if we are going to survive, you will have to trust me. I ran some calculations and found a ninety-five percent likelihood that you would have given me instructions to deploy the drone if you knew it worked."

Michael started to respond, but Timothy cut him off.

"Sir, you lost Steve in an accident, Victor is injured, and you're missing an arm," the AI said in a serious, firm tone. "The crew's chances of survival are dwindling, and you will need my help to keep your family and Victor alive. Now . . . wait one moment."

"What is it?" Michael asked.

"I'm sorry. I was distracted by the first images from the drone."

"Bring them online in the training center."

"Yes, sir."

Michael and Victor rushed past the launch-bay lockers and into the room that once served as a briefing center for Hell Divers. The wall-mounted monitors remained. One of them came to life, and the hazy view from the drone appeared.

The first thing Michael saw was the stream meandering under the blanket of fog. The thick crimson haze drifted across the water, the shore, the surrounding woods.

"I located the water-testing kit," Timothy said.

The drone hovered over the case, which Layla had clearly abandoned.

"Follow her tracks," Michael said.

"Stand by."

The AI piloted the drone over footprints in the mud and rocks, to the edge of the woods. There they stopped, turned, and went back down to the shore.

"Looks like she went this way," Timothy said.

The drone stopped where the tracks ended, right at the edge of the water.

"She went in?" Victor asked.

"It seems that way," Timothy said.

The drone flew along the bank, stopping at the catchment pool under the waterfall.

"You think she went in there?" Victor asked.

"Yes," Michael said. "Because that is exactly what I would have done."

"Sir, I've located more footprints," Timothy said.

The drone footage zoomed in on tracks in the muddy embankment around the pool. As the image grew larger, it was clear these weren't from Layla's boots.

"Those don't match her prints," Timothy confirmed. "In fact…"

Michael swallowed. "Well? What made this one?" he asked.

Victor also looked to the AI for an answer.

The image zoomed in closer, and right away Michael could tell this wasn't made by a boot at all. It was much wider than a human shoe and ran in a continuous track.

"What walks on one foot?" Michael asked.

"The spacing is very odd," Timothy said. "I've run some comparisons in the database and haven't found a match."

"Maybe it's a really big snake." The thought sent a chill through his body.

The drone footage suddenly crackled, then went topsy-turvy. The water came closer and closer until the device splashed into the pool.

"What happened?" Victor asked.

Michael knew right away: the droid had taken a blast of electricity that knocked it offline. He hurried out of the room to the launch-bay doors.

"Victor, help me with this harness," he said. "I'm going down there."

Victor limped over and started rigging Michael up to a cable that would lower him down.

"Sir, that fog will electrocute you just as it did our drone," Timothy said.

"I'll take my chances," Michael said. "I'm going down there to find Layla before whatever made that track does."

Victor locked Michael in, then grabbed the helmet.

"Be careful, Chief," Victor said.

Michael nodded.

"Sir, if my theory is correct, then the danger in the fog is greatest near whatever is causing those electrical currents," Timothy said. "If you can avoid them, you will have the best odds of survival."

"Got it. Thanks, Pepper."

Victor lowered the helmet over Michael's head and secured it with a click. The launch-bay doors cracked open, letting in the flash of the distant lightning that captured the worried gaze on both Victor's and Timothy's faces.

"The tubes are ready to deploy," Michael said. "Get me as close to the waterfall as you can. Once I'm down, lower the tubes and start sucking up water. As soon as I find Layla, I want to get the hell away from this strange mountain."

*   *   *   *   *

Kade awaited Forge outside the council chamber's hall, where the statues of heroes loomed and portraits of former generals hung from the walls.

He had stopped in front of the statue of the late General Rhino. Kade had never met Rhino, but he had heard much about the man who served as X's top commander before Forge.

General Forge had combat and leadership experience under his belt. Everything he did was calculated. He had been loyal to X, but that relationship had taken time to work. Kade realized that the same would be true now.

Being a successful king meant finding a way to work with General Forge to keep everyone in the islands safe.

He heard footsteps behind him. Forge had arrived a few

minutes early for their meeting. Two Cazadores in red ceremonial armor flanked the general, who held his red-feathered helmet at his side. The two soldiers held spears and wore cutlasses, and each had a submachine gun slung over his shoulder plates.

"King Kade," Forge said with a salute. "You asked for me?"

"Yes, General, I'd like to talk to you in private."

Forge walked with Kade down the hall, past the statue of Les Mitchells. The famous airship captain and Hell Diver from the former *Hive* had willingly given his life to rescue Kade and his people—an act that earned him Kade's eternal gratitude.

Thank you for your sacrifice. I'll make sure Katherine and Phyl are safe.

Kade looked Forge in the eye.

"I was wrong last night," he said. "I tried to save lives, but in the end I put all our lives at risk, and Mario paid the price."

"You're a Hell Diver," Forge replied. "You were trained to save lives, not take them."

Before Kade could add another word, the general said, "Last night taught you how fast things go bad in war, and with the threat of the Knights of the Coral Castle on the horizon, you must trust me in defending what's left of our home."

Kade nodded. "I hope you can trust me too, as I have plans that I believe will improve our safety. That's why I'm sending Lucky home with a beacon."

Forge lifted his chin. "I'm afraid the recent deaths have only divided us further in the face of this new threat."

"Maybe, and that is why we must speak the truth about the knights."

"What?" Forge stepped closer. "You do that, and we'll have chaos on our hands."

"I believe the truth will actually bring us together."

Again Kade surveyed the statues and portraits in the hall.

HELL DIVERS XI: RENEGADES

132

He thought of history books he had read as a young man, where enemies came together to fight as friends.

"Sun Tzu," Kade said. "Do you know of his teachings?"

"Yes. One of them is 'The enemy of my enemy is my friend.'"

"Precisely. There is a new enemy who threatens us all. The Forerunner. I plan to announce it at the council meeting. And I will ask every Cazador, sky person, and refugee that we brought here to unite under one banner and fight them."

Forge looked uncertain. He moved even closer, until they were inches apart.

"There will be warriors who want your head," he said. "For leading an enemy to our home. In all our history, that has happened only once, and look how it turned out for el Pulpo."

"I'm willing to accept whatever my fate is, but I believe transparency will bring us together in the face of a common foe."

"You are my king. I will serve your wishes."

Kade reached out and shook hands with the general, but it seemed Forge still wasn't convinced. It would take more than words. He was a man of action, and actions were key to winning his respect.

They parted ways, Forge heading into the great hall to prepare for the council meeting.

Kade went back to his quarters to change into his Hell Diver armor. He combed his hair first, slicking it back. In the mirror, he looked exhausted, with dark circles under his eyes, and new lines on his forehead. Grays were starting to take over his beard. He decided to cut it off, then shave.

When he was finished, he looked back in the mirror at his haggard face and square jawline. There stood a lonely, sad man. Hardly a king.

He looked like a Hell Diver.

"You better be doing the right thing," he whispered.

Kade grabbed his cutlass and left his quarters. Zuni and Dakota escorted him back to the great hall outside the council chamber. They led the way to the double doors engraved with images of sea creatures, among them an octopus. Two Cazador guards in red plate armor with black capes stood outside with crossed spears. They drew them back, stamped the left boot, and opened the doors for Kade and his two guards.

Brilliant light spilled across the throne and the stone floor. Kade walked down the center aisle between the pews. Fifty people in the front rows all stood and bowed their heads as he approached the throne. They were Cazador scribes, soldiers, Hell Divers, and businesspeople like Martino. Pedro and his people were here, and Yejun too. All brought here as refugees.

There were also farmers, fishers, and technicians who kept the gears of the islands turning. Most of them didn't know much about Kade and might have seen him only in passing, or perhaps never before. He could see in their gazes that they were skeptical, and scared after the violence that had occurred yet again.

Imulah walked over to stand in front of the throne platform.

"Today, we welcome King Kade Long to the hall," he said. "Remarks from subjects will proceed after the king has spoken. All hail King Kade."

The words filled the chamber, becoming more real each time Kade heard them. He remained standing, but a glance from Imulah indicated that he was supposed to sit.

Kade didn't want to sit. People sat because they were weak or tired. He walked out to the end of the platform and put his hand on the hilt of his cutlass.

"For those of you who don't know me, I'm Kade Long from the people of the airship *Victory*," he said. "I served as a Hell Diver for most of my adult life. But more importantly, I am—rather, I was—father to three boys, and husband to the love of my life."

Kade tried hard not to choke up. This was the first time he could recall that he had spoken about his family publicly, and simply mentioning them brought back their faces, voices, laughter…

Imulah glanced back slightly at Kade—another cue, this time to continue.

"Over a year ago now, I was rescued from the machine camp at Kilimanjaro by Hell Divers—Chief Michael Everhart and Captain Les Mitchells, among others. When I was brought here, I knew I had to help protect this place, and when King Xavier asked me to dive again, I did."

Kade paced in front of the throne.

"What I'm about to tell you is a condensed story of what many of you have already heard about the former king in name only, Rolo. The former captain of the ship I dutifully served my entire life. This is also the story of his henchman, Charmer, who still refuses to accept responsibility for framing Chief Michael Everhart for murder. We have the evidence to prove it was not Michael but rather Jamal who killed Oliver and his son, Nez, under orders from Charmer. I've sentenced Charmer to trial by combat, to proceed as soon as possible."

Kade looked to Forge, who gave him the slightest nod to proceed to the next part of the truth.

"In Australia, I was captured by the Knights of the Coral Castle," Kade said.

Many in the audience exchanged glances at this news. Others whispered in hushed voices. He told about what had happened with the seeds from the ITC facility in Brisbane, and then the nuking of the supercarrier *Immortal*, and the Hell Divers being left behind to perish.

"I was trying to reach the king with the other divers when I was separated from them and captured by these knights," he said. "Men who have sworn allegiance to the Trident—they are the protectors of the Coral Castle. I was held captive and ordered to find King Xavier in a journey that led us back here. I believed we could work together, to find common ground and even start a trading network. When we arrived, the knight accompanying me was injured, and the pilot was killed, but not before they activated the Trident, which we believe to be a beacon—"

A voice cut him off. "So they know the location of the Vanguard Islands?" It was Martino.

"We aren't sure," Kade replied.

"The military is ready to meet any foe," Forge announced. "Fear not these knights."

Tia stood. "If I were these knights, I would be coming here for Rolo's head, and when they don't find him, I'm sure they will settle for yours, King Kade."

"We will have advance warning if they come," Kade replied without going into detail. "That was the first action, but there are two more I've put in place to prepare us for any attack. I've authorized weapons to be distributed to every able man and woman, and training to take place on each rig—"

"*¡No más guerra!* We don' survive more war! Not now. Weak!"

The booming voice that cut Kade off came from the last person he expected.

Gran Jefe, still dressed in his bulky Cazador armor, stepped forward.

"Cowboy King, we fight many years," he said. "We fight each other. Fight *las máquinas*. Fight Horn *y los piratas*. We low in warriors to fight *más enemigos* if they come here—enemy you invite."

"Careful with your words, Mata," Slayer said.

Gran Jefe glared at the commander of the Barracudas.

"I like cowboy king, but he made bad judgment leading knights to our home," Gran Jefe said. He pounded his chest. "If enemy come, we could lose many innocents. We could lose the *islands*!"

"What are you saying, Jorge?" Kade asked. "That you won't fight?"

He pounded his chest again with rage in his eyes. "No, I die for Metal—Vanguard—Islands. I give all my blood, but a big fight now will destroy us."

"These knights are weak in numbers," Kade said. "The one working aircraft they had was destroyed on the rooftop of this very rig, and their one pilot died."

Gran Jefe narrowed his eyes. "And if you *estás equivocado?* What if enemy stronger than you see?"

Kade caught Tia looking at him. He saw in her eyes a trust that not everyone shared. The faces around hers were full of concern, fear, and anger. And why wouldn't they be? They had all hoped the daylong civil war would be a fresh start, and now they were hearing about another threat.

Chatter broke out around the room as Kade hesitated.

"Silence!" cried a female voice.

Kade looked at the standing crowd, to the aisle where he could see Sofia moving her wheelchair out. She rolled up to the platform, stared at Kade, then turned her chair toward the audience.

"King Kade has risked his life for us since day one," she said. "I've dived with him on multiple missions, and I have watched him fight for what he believes is right. He is a good man, with a good heart."

She looked over her shoulder, meeting Kade's gaze.

"I believe in King Kade, and so did King Xavier," she said. "We must give him a chance and trust his plan."

"I agree," Pedro said. "We must come together, fight side by side."

"Yes," Slayer announced. "I stand with King Kade to fight these knights if they are fools enough to come."

"We're with you, King Kade!" Woody shouted.

One by one, more voices pledged their support. Gran Jefe snorted his disapproval.

Kade had a feeling that sooner or later, he must make a very hard decision about this renegade warrior.

TEN

Gran Jefe could tell by the look in the king's eye that he didn't trust him. He had seen that look before in the eyes of men who wanted to slip a blade between his ribs. Now it seemed one of Jamal's former whores wanted his head. Slayer and General Forge also seemed to have turned against him.

But it was the cowboy who had Jefe the most concerned. Not because he was an evil man, but precisely because he was the opposite—a man who believed in justice, laws, and, perhaps, eye-for-an-eye justice.

Gran Jefe walked across a platform at his home oil rig. The smells of body odor, raw sewage, and fish cooking in oil drifted across the deck. He had returned to his humble dwelling after the meeting to sleep, but on the way he decided to visit a woman who once would have cut the throat of any man who wanted to hurt Gran Jefe—a woman who had loved him deeply.

Now she was likely to cut his throat if he showed up. Years of a tumultuous relationship had pushed her away, into the arms of the man she married.

With targets on his back, Gran Jefe felt compelled to see her again. Even if it got him a palm across his face, or a knife in his dark heart. Better by her hand than by some Cazador soldier or a monster in the wastes.

Gran Jefe took a ladder down to the corridor where he owned an apartment. Two scantily clad women in their twenties were loitering in the hallway. Normally, they might raise a seductive brow to him, but both turned away when he approached.

It seemed not even the whores were interested in him after word spread about his slaying Jamal. The islands were a close-knit community, where rumors spread like burning arrows fired from rig to rig. It didn't matter that Jamal was in deep with the enemy. Taking the life of one's own blood kin was taboo.

He stopped at his door, unlocked it, and looked over his shoulder to make sure he wasn't being followed. Seeing no one, he stepped inside the single room that he called home. It wasn't much: a mattress, table and chair, and small kitchen space. In a curtained-off corner was a small bathroom with a shit can and a sink.

Most soldiers of his caliber could afford a multiroom dwelling, but he had frittered away his loot over the years—on booze, women, dice, and frivolous purchases he didn't even remember. He didn't have much left.

He went to the bathroom and pulled back the rug over the rotted wood floor. At first glance, a would-be thief would miss the trapdoor. Gran Jefe had spent a lot of time camouflaging it. Reaching into his vest, he pulled out a multitool and inserted it into a crack that was actually a key lock.

He gave it a twist and lifted a piece of the rotted wood floor away—along with the steel safe door that it was glued to. Inside the small vault were five fragmentation grenades, a gold necklace with a cross pendant, two bars of silver, a single diamond ear stud, and a leviathan of a diamond ring.

He pulled it out, marveling at the sight. It was just shy of three carats, according to the jeweler he had brought it to after finding it on a raid a decade ago. One of the biggest and most beautiful rings in the islands. El Pulpo had offered to buy it from Gran Jefe, and Gran Jefe was prepared to sell it. Then the sky people had arrived. Apparently, the king had wanted it for Sofia or perhaps one of his other wives.

Gran Jefe had once planned on giving it to his own flame, until he got annoyed one night after drinking and smacked her for lipping off to him. She could put up with the other women, the lies, and his absence when on raids, but not the hitting. He felt bad about it. She deserved better.

He slipped the ring into his pocket and closed the safe. Then he got up and left his quarters. The two women he had seen earlier were back in the hall again. They both glared at him.

"*¿Qué pasa?*" he asked.

No response.

After leaving his floor, he came out in the open space before the bridge connecting the two main Cazador rigs. He crossed it, nodding to a militia soldier who was coming the other way.

Gran Jefe took an exterior stairwell, where the wind whistled over his armor. The horizon swallowed the last of the orange fire in the west. Torches flared up across the rig.

He climbed up to the fourth level, a broad space where the tents and shacks of the less fortunate stood. Open latrines with buzzing bugs produced a lingering scent of feces and urine, and a low droning of flies.

The people here had gotten used to it over the years, and while Gran Jefe didn't mind it, he did hate seeing kids grow up in such grim circumstances and filth. People on this section of the rig got sick more than they did elsewhere, and medicine was even scarcer than fresh fruit.

Two old guys sat on plastic crates playing a game of dominoes.

He knew them by name. Both men were born right here and had lived on this single level their entire sixty-plus years. And here they would die.

Faded tattoos illustrated their sun-weathered flesh, portraying the only things they knew off the rig: fish and fishing trawlers. Now they were retired, their bony limbs too arthritic to haul in a catch or throw out a net.

Most of the people here were fishermen or maintenance workers. Those jobs kept the population fed and the rigs working, but pay was terrible unless you were one of the men and women who raided and scavenged in the wastes.

Men like Gran Jefe. The brave were rewarded with loot like the diamond ring in his breast pocket. But the brave also lived only half as long as these two old fishermen setting up their dominoes.

Gran Jefe made his way down an aisle of flimsy shacks made of rusted metal sheets and wood brought back from the mainland. Lines stretched between posts were hung with drying clothes.

Whimpering came from a tent on his left. He glimpsed a pale, skeletal woman in the arms of her adoring husband. He rocked her like a child, soothing her disease-wrecked body. Gran Jefe remembered seeing her years ago, when she had life in her. Based on her condition, he doubted he would ever see her again.

He kept going until he reached the communal open space, where benches and tables were set up around a huge black iron cauldron. Three people stood around it, stirring the stew and tending the fire. Across the way, he saw his destination: a hut with a metal roof.

Gran Jefe felt a lump in his throat—normally the result of fear when facing monsters in the wastes. But this fear stemmed from something else entirely: guilt.

Go, asshole.

He crossed the open space, past people waiting meekly with

their tins for their rations of soup. Some of them looked up as he crossed by, nodding in respect.

Approaching the shack, he cleared his throat. The tarp that served as a door drew back, and the most beautiful woman in the islands stepped out.

Jada Herrera, who once could have been Jada Mata.

She stood barely five feet tall, but what she lacked in stature she made up for with passion. Passion in how she spoke, in what she believed, and in who she loved.

"What do you want?" she snapped in Spanish.

She wore a yellow dress that did more to emphasize than to conceal her spectacular breasts. Her freckled face had tightened the same way when they first met. He had loved her at first sight. Loved her little hands that she would sometimes wave when she was upset. And he loved the warm beating heart in her chest that was kind and empathetic to all.

That heart had once pounded for him, but that ardor had long since cooled.

"Jorge," she growled.

"It's been a long time," Gran Jefe said in Spanish. Three years almost to the day, he realized. "I came to say . . . goodbye."

A small boy, maybe two years old, peeked out from behind her. She waved him back inside the little apartment.

The boy tried to look around her, but Jada moved to block the entrance.

"Everything okay?" said a voice behind him.

Gran Jefe didn't need to turn to know that it belonged to Jada's husband, Chano Herrera. He walked over and stood next to Jada.

"Jorge," Chano said.

Gran Jefe gave a half nod in acknowledgment, doing his best to suppress his anger that this man had married his one true love.

But deep down, he knew whose fault it was. Gran Jefe had done everything to push her away, including the unthinkable: hurting her physically. At least Chano treated her right.

He was thin and tall but had a handsome face and thick black hair. Like most of the men here, he was a fisherman, working long hours to provide for her and the son that Gran Jefe hadn't even known about.

Jada seemed to soften then, and her tense shoulders relaxed. She whispered something to Chano, who gave Gran Jefe a hard look before stepping away.

"I didn't know you had a son," Gran Jefe said to her in Spanish.

"I didn't want you to know," Jada replied, "but I guess you do now."

She had done a good job hiding it from him, because no one had told him.

Gran Jefe looked over his shoulder at Chano. The gaunt man stood across the communal space, one hand on the handle of a knife. That almost made Gran Jefe laugh.

"Why you looking at him?" Jada asked.

She stepped aside, giving Gran Jefe a view into the shack. Seeing the toddler with the ruffled brown hair, Gran Jefe looked him up and down, from his round, happy face to his husky little frame and fat little feet.

He looked nothing like Chano.

He looked like ...

The kid was a spitting image of Gran Jefe.

"Oh," he whispered.

"Yes," Jada replied. "I had Pablo when you were away on a raid."

"Pablo," Gran Jefe said.

The boy looked at him, then reached to Jada and said, "Mamá."

She scooped him up.

"I deserved to know I'm his father." There was quiet rage in his voice, and Jada stepped back, shielding Pablo from him. Right then Gran Jefe understood why she had kept this a secret. She was afraid of him, and afraid for her family.

Jada's eyes shot out toward Chano, who was standing closer to her now, hand still on his knife.

Gran Jefe considered asking him if he fancied wearing it in his ass, but suppressed that urge in front of the lad.

He still couldn't quite believe he had a son.

Slowly Gran Jefe counted silently to ten, then turned back to Jada and Pablo.

"I'm sorry," Gran Jefe said. He reached into his vest. Again she stepped back.

"It's okay, I'm not going to hurt you," he said. "I want you to have something."

He pulled out the ring and held it out. Jada eyed it, then scoffed.

"I don't want your charity," she said. "Your blood money."

"I know, but... I won't need it when I'm gone, and I'd rather it went to you and Pablo."

Her lip twisted to the side—a thing she did in moments of uncertainty. Then she did something else he recognized. Her nose wrinkled.

She was gonna blow.

"I said no, I don't want anything from you," she snapped. "We don't need it."

"What about Pablo? What about our..."

He couldn't finish his sentence. The boy stared at him with wide, scared eyes.

"I messed up," Gran Jefe said. "A lot, but I'm begging you, take this one thing from me."

Gran Jefe held the ring out to her, but she did not soften.

That wasn't unusual. When she made her mind up, she would not be moved.

"Fine. Have it your way, but Pablo deserves better than this slum," Gran Jefe said.

Oops, he thought.

"Pablo has love, and people who care about him. We don't need fancy things to be happy." She poked her finger at him as if pointing a dagger. "I was wrong even letting you see him."

"Jorge, I think you should leave," Chano said.

Gran Jefe felt pain worse than anything a blade could do to him. It was the pain of regret, of missing out on something that could have been special. He stared at his son, and the boy stared right back.

Tears welled around those innocent brown eyes, but the kid didn't let them fall.

"I'm sorry," Gran Jefe said. "For everything."

He started to walk away, focusing all his intent on not smacking Chano to the deck. When he was ten steps away, Jada called out for him to wait.

Gran Jefe halted and turned back to Jada and his son. Chano stood next to them now, an arm around each of them.

"Why did you come to say goodbye?" Jada called out.

Gran Jefe just shrugged. "Take care of them, Chano," he said. "I know you will."

Chano nodded. The tall, wiry man had a good heart, and that was worth more than any jewels. Someday he would be holding Jada in her final hours, or vice versa.

Gran Jefe had given up his chance of being that lucky by craving adventure, riches, and women.

With a sigh, he started the trek back through the squalor. The scents and sights reminded him why he had wanted to escape from this life. But even this life was better than the one he had now.

By the time he got to the railing on the open deck outside, he felt tears in his eyes. For the first time in as long as he could remember, they blurred his vision. He took in a deep breath of sea air and turned when he noticed someone in his peripheral vision. A man stood near a pillar, a cowl over his head. The bulge in the midsection of his cloak said he was armed.

Gran Jefe had been right about people coming to kill him. But this wasn't a small army of Cazador or militia soldiers sent by the king. This was a faceless assassin, perhaps paid off by the Cazadores to make it look like a drunken brawl.

He could go down fighting right here, but what if he lost? He didn't want Pablo to see his absent father dead on the deck of this rig.

Well, he wasn't dying tonight.

He felt the wind back in his sails, filling him with a ferocity he hadn't felt since he was a young man. He had a son!

He hurried over to an outside stairwell that wound up the decks to the rooftop. A glance below told him his shadow was also on the move and had slipped back into the building, trying to flank him.

Gran Jefe worked his way up the stairs to the top floor of the rig. There would be guards up there. He hoped they might deter this assassin until Gran Jefe could somehow figure a way to get an advantage.

Sure enough, when he got to the top of the rig, he saw a single militia guard. He carried a crossbow and had his back to Gran Jefe as he patrolled along the rows of crops. Behind the man, dozens of solar panels angled up at a dark sky.

Gran Jefe reached behind him and pulled out one of his battle hatchets. His other hand held a revolver. The guard had yet to see him, and Gran Jefe took off toward the solar panels for cover.

A big moon shone down on the plants growing around him.

He had always imagined dying in the wastes, his decomposing remains feeding the mutant weeds where his body fell. Certainly not here, at his home, and not to another Cazador—or even a sky person.

An arrow zipped through the air, shattering a solar panel. Pistol up, he turned to look for the shooter. Another arrow flew past his ear.

This bolt was fired by a militia guard. A second assassin, he realized.

Gran Jefe ducked behind the rows of solar panels, hatchet in hand. He froze when he saw the cloaked man from belowdecks, also armed with a crossbow, emerge at the end of the row.

Cocking his arm, timing it, Gran Jefe threw the hatchet. An arrow whizzed by his face. The axe blade just as narrowly missed the head of the militia crossbowman.

In a fit of rage, Gran Jefe charged as the man loaded another bolt.

"Halt or you get one in the back!" someone called out in Spanish from behind.

Gran Jefe saw the assassin in front of him abandon the crossbow and pull out a machete. In that moment, he considered his options and decided there were two: surrender and get his throat cut, or die fighting.

Enraged, he chose the latter. The man with the cutlass raised it in one hand and lowered his hood with the other. Moonlight fell on the scarred, one-eyed face of General Forge.

Gran Jefe slowed and stopped, chest heaving. "Ah," he said between breaths. "The king sent you to kill me."

"No," Forge replied.

Gran Jefe looked back to the guard behind him, who had lifted up his helmet. It was a Cazador soldier named Rero, who had recently been promoted to one of the general's top officers.

"Get on with it, then," Gran Jefe said.

Forge held out the blade. "That's up to you."

"How's that?"

"This place has changed, Jorge," Forge said. He spat in the dirt. "We are weak, as you said back at the council meeting. We need a Cazador back on the throne."

Gran Jefe narrowed his eyes at the general. Forge had supported King Xavier with unflagging loyalty, but it seemed he was no fan of the cowboy king.

"We must take back the islands, and with X gone, this is our chance," Forge said. "I need you to help me kill him."

"What about the knights? If we kill Kade, there could be chaos. We could be even weaker if the enemy—"

"We must kill Kade *because* of the knights. He opened the door to bringing them here, and I fear he doesn't have what it takes to defend us."

Gran Jefe stared, considering everything he had just heard. He wasn't sure killing Kade would make things better, but it would put the Cazadores back in charge.

"You want to keep your son safe?" Forge said.

"How do you know about my son?"

Forge snorted. "Because I still have an eye that can see. Help me kill Kade, and restore the crown to the Cazadores, where it belongs."

ELEVEN

"He can't be dead," Magnolia whispered as the *Sea Wolf* beat against the storm. After finally abandoning the area where the leviathan swallowed X and Jo-Jo, she steered for the southern shore of Grenada. The beast had gone under and never resurfaced. Neither had X or the monkey.

Tears streaming down her face, feeling numb, Magnolia kept her grip on the wheel. Miles whined by her side, looking up at her every few seconds with concern in his dimming blue eyes. There was nothing she could do for the pain they both were feeling.

The Immortal was dead. Inhaled by a sea monster. It seemed fitting almost, that it took something that big to finally bring him down.

Memories returned, of their dives, adventures, and battles over the years. Was it really all over?

She wasn't sure she could go on without X. Without Rodger. Edgar. Arlo. Katrina. Ada… All the other divers from the past.

"*GOD DAMN IT!*" she screamed at the top of her lungs.

She pounded the wheel with her hand, over and over. Miles backed away, barking first, then whining.

Magnolia felt so numb, she feared she might collapse. A wave of anger hit her with the force of a sea wave. The warmth of the anger was something she could feel.

Unable to stand it any longer, she let out another mournful wail that she didn't even recognize. Miles howled in response, lifting his head to the storms. Something about his plaintive tone brought her back to reality.

She bent down to him. "I'm sorry," she said. "Miles, I—"

Thunder drowned her out.

Looking out the viewports again, she saw the shore. Lightning flashes captured the mutant palms and mangroves along the water's edge. They had made it to Grenada.

She gripped the wheel and pushed toward the line of surf less than a half mile ahead. Beyond it, she could see structures rising over the jungle. Some had been taken over by the dense tropical vegetation. She could only imagine what kinds of monsters awaited them there. Sirens certainly, bone beasts, the breeders and their spawn, snakes that could swallow a man.

Maybe it would be better just to shoot Miles with her blaster and then turn it on herself. They were alone at sea, heading toward an island that was no doubt home to its own share of mutant beasts. Having lost the two most important and beloved men in her life, she wasn't sure she had it in her to face the monsters alone.

But she had to consider what the dead, as well as the living, would want her to do.

Magnolia recalled the last words X uttered to her before vanishing. *Watch out for Miles.*

So what if she felt like giving up? Big whoop, she couldn't. Giving up was weak. Giving up was a *betrayal* of those she loved.

She had her marching orders: to protect Miles. And to find Michael, Layla, and Bray and bring them back to the Vanguard Islands.

Rodger would have wanted her to live on. To experience life. To plant a garden and bask in the sunshine while the plants grew.

Tears rolled down Magnolia's face, and she wanted to scream again—scream and scream until she couldn't anymore. But beyond all the pain, she felt something stirring inside her, telling her to keep going. A tiny thread of willpower.

Giving up wasn't in her makeup. She wouldn't even know how.

The *Sea Wolf* rode the surf in toward the line of waving palm trees and the ancient structures beyond.

A fresh wave lifted the catamaran, and Magnolia let it take them in. The hulls slid up on the beach, pushing up a mound of sand before them. She hurried outside and ran the bow rope out, hitching it around a big mutant palm with clusters of purplish fruit.

Magnolia looked through the glass, searching for any creatures that might have emerged from the jungle to have a look at this odd new sight.

Seeing nothing unusual, she checked the gauges on the dashboard. The batteries had fallen to 70 and 75 percent. With the flip of a switch, she killed all power.

"Let's go, Miles," she said. "We'll wait out the storm below-decks."

She opened the hatch and started down the ladder. At the bottom, she lifted the dog gently down to the deck. Miles followed her into the lower level, where she shut the hatch, sealing out the wind and rain.

The dog wagged his tail, perhaps thinking X was down here.

Magnolia halted to look at the little galley table where she had shared so many meals with them both. Clothing, maps, and gear lay scattered across the wooden deck, jostled loose by the storm. Miles went to the blanket X had used, sniffed it, and whined softly. Magnolia nearly broke at the sight.

She sat and took off her helmet. A swatch of blue hair hung

down over eyes swollen from crying. She brushed it back and wiped away the new tears. Then she patted the seat beside her.

Miles jumped up and curled up on the blanket. She pulled it over his wet coat. For a few minutes, they just sat there in silence, listening to the howl of the storm.

Magnolia gave herself that time to get her head straight. Then she got up and went over to the closet that housed their weapons. She pulled out a laser rifle, a machine gun, and a crate of ammo with magazines, shotgun shells, and flares.

Next, she went to her bunk and pulled out the box beneath it to retrieve her curved blades. Fully armed now, she looked out the portholes at the beach. If something came down here to investigate, she would see it first.

She propped the rifles against the hull and took a seat beside Miles again. She leaned down to check the tear in her suit from falling into the razor wire in rough seas. With the power off to her main operating system, she had no idea how bad it was.

Bringing up her wrist computer, she checked the display: SUIT COMPROMISED.

But another thing caught her attention. A green dot beeped on the small digital map.

"It can't be," Magnolia whispered.

She stared at the impossible dot, wondering if her eyes were playing tricks on her. If it was real, it was about the most beautiful thing she had ever seen in her life. For this wasn't just a blinking dot. It was a beacon, and it meant that somehow, X was still alive.

She put her helmet back on and bumped the comm channel.

"X, do you copy?" she asked.

White noise answered.

She tried again, and again heard static.

Magnolia raised her wrist computer and tapped the screen for the exact location of the beacon. The blinking dot was faint, which meant it wasn't close. According to the digital map on her HUD, it was in the port of Grenada.

She wasted no time repairing the tear in her suit as Miles looked on.

After double-checking the repair job with a tap to her computer, she hopped to her feet and got the dog into his hazard suit. Then she started slinging the various weapons over her armor.

Miles trotted after her onto the weather deck, where Magnolia pulled out her binos and scanned the horizon to the northwest. She couldn't see the port from here, but it wasn't far. With the boat moored on the beach, she decided to go on foot with Miles.

"Let's do it, boy," she said.

Miles followed her to the gap in the razor wire where X had freed the two-headed shark. She jumped down and then turned to help Miles. The animal was old, but he moved with surprising speed, perhaps realizing that X was still out there.

She still couldn't believe it herself, and while she wasn't sure she could save him, it filled her with hope. Hope was good, but only in moderation. Too much, she had learned, was the way to heartbreak.

It wasn't long before she saw the bay. A half-dozen ships were still in the port, half-sunken or leaning on their sides. The bows of smaller craft jutted up from the water.

She checked X's beacon. It was getting closer—only about a thousand meters away now. She crossed a badly cracked asphalt road that had lost the fight to the weeds. Debris from destroyed industrial buildings had eroded into scree slopes that ran down almost to the beach. They would have to pass through that area, which looked like ideal cover for Sirens and other mutant beasts.

Miles paced while she confirmed that the beacon on her map was indeed in the port. But it wasn't near the shore. Which meant…

X was on a ship.

Magnolia lowered the wrist computer, trying to understand. Before she had a chance to make sense of it, she noticed a faint yellow-gold glow out in the water. The leviathan still had him, or it was at least close.

She started out a moment later, with Miles following. They moved past the collapsed warehouses and boats half-buried in the dirt. An impossibly big ship's screw. A foghorn.

Ten minutes of cautious movement got her through the port area to the beach. Magnolia stopped at the road that once curved along the shore, separating the port from the industrial area inland.

The bright glow from the leviathan lit up the deeper waters of the port, but strangely, she saw other lights as well. Holes in the hull of a wrecked ship glowed like internal lights. Were there more of the monsters?

Magnolia ventured out onto a pier with Miles for a better look. The glow seemed to be coming from several locations. Could it be…

She paused and tapped on her comms. "X, can you hear me?" she whispered.

A faint voice broke over the channel.

"Mags? Mags, is that you?"

"Yes, you bastard!" she hissed, trying to keep her voice low. "Me and Miles. We can see your location, but I don't understand. Are you…"

Static obliterated any words.

Miles moved up to her side, growling at the water.

"I'm with Jo-Jo, inside a ship," X grumbled. "But that thing is still out here, and it's got calves—and they're hungry. We're stranded here."

"I'll find a way to get to you," Magnolia said.

"No, stay put. Watch over Miles. I'm working on a plan to get us out of here."

*   *   *   *   *

Woody let out a low whistle. "That's a lot of bloody boom sticks."

The low morning sun's rays fell across the weapons arrayed on the deck of the *Osprey*, a container ship that had been home to Yejun's people.

"I get my pick?" Beau asked. He seemed to brighten at the prospect.

Kade was glad to see his friend coming out of the darkness after losing his son Cooper. But it was going to be a long road ahead. Kade knew all about it.

"We're with King Kade—of course we do," Woody said. "Right, Your Majesty?"

He raised a brow to Kade.

"Within reason," Kade said.

"You mean I can't have a flamethrower?" Woody asked. "I'm kidding. Those things look scary as hell. I'd probably roast everyone around me."

"Dakota, Zuni, you fellas got any suggestions?" Beau asked.

The two guards hung back while Kade examined the crates of weapons. Overnight, the militia had gathered up every weapon and bullet in the armories and brought them to the container ship where Yejun had lived for years in the wastes. Once Imulah's three scribes had finished inventorying those weapons, they would be distributed to every able-bodied Vanguard Islands adult.

"King Kade," Lieutenant Wynn said, saluting. He hurried over, clad in black riot armor, with a rifle slung over his back.

"Looks like things are going well," Kade said.

"Yes, from our initial count, we're going to have a weapon for every person who can wield one," Wynn said.

Kade took the opportunity to ask the lieutenant's thoughts. Judging from the anxiety in his features, he was worried about something.

"You don't approve of this?" he asked.

Wynn sighed. "This is a violent place, King Kade, as you know, but I'm less worried about people blasting one another than I am about you, sir."

"How do you mean?" Woody asked.

Wynn looked over his shoulder at Zuni and Dakota. The two soldiers were out of earshot, but Kade still moved away with Wynn.

"What is it?" he asked.

"I worry for you, King Kade. When X was king, he always had his fair share of enemies, but you may have him beat."

His eyes flitted away from Kade to Beau and Woody.

"Charmer and Rolo gave your people a bad reputation," Wynn said. "With X and Mags gone, I fear for all of you. We'll do our best to keep you safe, but keep your head on a swivel, as they used to say."

"I appreciate the honesty," Kade said.

"I'm sure General Forge would tell you the same thing."

"Lieutenant, we got the first boat approaching!" yelled a militia soldier.

"I'd better leave you to it," Kade said.

Wynn saluted and hurried off.

"Crikey," said Beau, "maybe you *should* take a flamethrower, considering that all the locals seem to hate us."

"I didn't come here to fuck spiders," Woody said, pulling from his waistband two pistols with extended magazines.

Beau had selected a scope-mounted assault rifle with an extended magazine. He held it up, studying the weapon of war.

"If I'd had this thing when Charmer was creating chaos, maybe my boy would still be alive."

"You can't think that way," Kade said.

"We should've helped, though," Woody said. "We should have done something."

"Yeah, well, I might not have dived again if it weren't for King X asking me," Kade said. "The past is the past; I'm just glad we're back together again."

"King Kade, I have the report you requested," Imulah said. He had approached quietly with his clipboard tucked under his arm.

"Go ahead," Kade said.

Imulah flipped to the second page and traced down it with his finger.

"There are nine hundred fifty-two sky people," he read. "There are two thousand three hundred four Cazadores, though the fighting population has dwindled. I'm still working on estimates, but over half those numbers are children and elderly."

"Of the fighting population, how many are male?" Kade asked.

"Four hundred, many of them fishermen who have never fired a gun."

Kade looked out over the motley flotilla of approaching boats, all transporting people coming for weapons. Even if he could give each of those people a gun, most of them had never fired one.

"Almost an entire generation of men has been wiped out," Imulah said.

"Many of them by our heroic Captain Rolo," Woody said. "And by *hero,* of course, I mean *cowardly shit stain.*"

Kade understood all too well why his people had a bad reputation, and he hated Rolo and Charmer all the more for it. Everyone had good reason not to trust his people. And he wasn't entirely sure that having a common enemy in the knights would be enough to keep them from fighting each other.

He saw the leader of the military, who had suffered perhaps the most. General Forge came across the deck with his guards.

"Have you found Gran Jefe?" Kade asked.

"Not yet. He's probably sobering up somewhere," said the general. "I do have an update on the scouts we deployed. The team's closing in on Panama. They plan to set up in a lighthouse we once used in Colón."

Kade recalled that lighthouse. He had been there with Lucky. The knight's father had died there, killed by Cazadores.

The cycle of violence seemed never ending.

"And the meds I requested?" Kade asked.

"Slayer located them, and the injured knight will be given the treatment later today," Forge said. Kade heard the hesitation in his voice but wasn't sure how to read it.

"Good work, General," he said. "Anything from Xavier?"

"Nothing so far."

Kade looked out over the water, deep in thought. "I'll head to the engineering rig next, to check with Pedro and try to get through, check on their status."

"Didn't you say you were going to see Alton off to school?" Woody said.

"Oh, bugger, that's right," Kade said. He had promised to take Alton to school, even though Tia volunteered to handle it. It would do them all good.

"Meet me at the engineering rig later today, General," Kade said. He looked out over the arsenal one last time and then left the *Osprey* with his four guards. Their fishing boat motored away toward the trading post rig as the first civilians showed up to receive their weapons.

A gunshot cracked, making Kade flinch. Zuni had a shield in front of the king so fast, he didn't realize what had happened.

Dakota had taken his hands off the wheel and had a sword pointed at Woody.

"I'm sorry!" Woody shouted. He held a pistol in the air. "I didn't mean to!"

"Crikey, ya dickwit," Beau said.

Dakota lowered the sword and reached out for the pistol.

"Give him the gun," Kade said.

Woody handed it to Dakota, who ejected the magazine, unchambered the round, and handed it back to Woody in less than two seconds with the admonishment "Gun no a toy."

"I guess I should just be court jester," Woody said with a sigh.

"You'll learn. Just be careful in the meantime, mate," Kade said.

The boat motored up to the trading post rig. Dakota pulled alongside the pier, and Woody jumped out with Beau to tie them up. Zuni led the way across the docks. Today they weren't packed with people bringing items to barter or sell. Most everyone was headed out to the *Osprey* for weapons.

At the top of the rig were a few parents who had just dropped their kids off at school. Zuni kept a close eye on every face. He seemed to look at one longer than the others. Tia.

She stood with Alton, Phyl, and Katherine in front of the school.

"Cowboy King!" Alton shouted.

He came running over.

"Hey, pal, you excited for school?" Kade asked.

"Seriously? Spending all day with dumb bullies—I'd rather be out on a boat, fishin'."

"I know, but school is important."

"Why?"

"Because to survive, we have to be a community, and a community needs engineers, doctors, farmers, sailors, and—"

"Hell Divers," Phyl said. "Like my daddy and brother were."

Katherine gazed at the ground.

"There are many important, respectable jobs that require bravery," Kade said.

"Like the tattooed metal men?" Alton asked. "They always look at me like I'm a bug and they want to squash me." He jerked his little chin at Zuni and Dakota.

"They are here to protect you," Kade said. "And you'll grow. I was small at your age, too."

"You *were*?" Alton asked.

"Oh, yeah. A real runt."

Alton shrugged. "I just want Michael to come back in the airship, and the old king to return on the *Sea Wolf*. When are they all coming back?"

"I don't know, could be a while, pal."

"Oh, poop, I'm sick of waiting."

"Time will fly, don't worry," Kade said. "Now, go inside and pay attention. I want you to report on what you learned today, and every day."

The other kids shuffled through the open doors, moping much like Alton. Some of them were only six and seven years old. It would be a long time before they filled the crucial jobs that kept the islands functioning.

"Go on, now," Kade said.

Alton looked up at him.

"What if the other kids still think I hurt Oliver and Nez?" he asked.

"They won't," Kade said.

"Phyl will have your back," Katherine said.

"Anyone gives you a hard time, you tell me," Phyl said, punching her palm with her fist.

"Hey, Kade," Woody said.

"One second, mate," Kade replied.

"Come on, kids," Katherine said. She herded Alton and Phyl toward the doors while Kade hung back and watched. He had a ton of respect for Katherine and understood her pain from losing not only her partner but her son as well.

Alton turned back and waved one last time before entering the building, and Kade turned to leave. Tia followed him away from the school.

"Ready to head to the engineering rig?" Woody asked.

"Yeah," Kade said. The sea breeze whispered through the rooftop gardens as they crossed. Tia ran to catch up.

"You see that?" she said. "We did that."

The rows of crops she pointed at were from the seeds the divers had found back in Australia. Green leaves and stems were already poking out of the ground. The morning farming crew tended to the crops—a dozen workers, all wearing brown suits and sun hats.

"I got an idea," she said. "I know how we can train without an airship."

"What?" Kade replied.

"We could use hot-air balloons for divers to jump and land on ships," she said.

"Kade," Woody said. "Over there."

Kade stopped and looked across the field where Woody was staring.

On the other side of the crops, a man stood wearing a hood and a pair of sunglasses. He ducked away before Kade could get a good look, but it looked as if he was holding a crossbow.

Dakota and Zuni had stopped up ahead, not far from the stairs that would take them back down to the boat. Neither of them had seen the unexplained man in a hood.

It was probably nothing anyway—just a curious onlooker. Kade was starting to get used to the stares.

Voices came from the stairwell where Dakota and Zuni were waiting. They moved out of the way to let Commander Slayer and Sergeant Blackburn through.

"Duty calls again," Tia said.

"Can we talk later?" Kade asked.

"Yeah, sure, let me know when you *aren't* busy."

"Soon. I'm sorry, but thank you for looking after Alton. It means the world to me, Tia."

She bowed slightly, then waved to Zuni. Kade thought he heard her say something about seeing him tonight.

The guard gave an acknowledging nod. It was clear he and Tia were seeing each other now, and equally clear to Kade there was nothing he could do about it.

Not nothing, he thought.

This wasn't the best time or place, but Kade couldn't hold back. Zuni had walked over, and it was just the two of them at the edge of the pumpkin patch.

"Break her heart, and we're going to have problems," Kade said quietly.

"Sir?"

Zuni halted, but Kade kept walking. Over his shoulder, he said, "I'm a Hell Diver, which means two things: I'm half-cracked and I have eyes in the back of my head."

Kade went to Slayer for what he feared would be bigger problems than Zuni breaking Tia's heart.

"General Forge located Gran Jefe," Slayer revealed. "He's drunk again but sobering up."

Kade had wanted to ignore the hard decision on what to do with Gran Jefe, but he knew he couldn't avoid it, not after the Cazador warrior's bold statements at the council meeting.

It was time to face the truth that something must be done with the warrior.

And Kade had something else he must face: that Xavier and Magnolia were not bringing the airship back from Rio. Hell, they might not return at all. He thought of that as he looked out at the rows of crops sprouted from the new seed stock.

Without an airship, the islands would be isolated. Cut off. There could be no future without Hell Divers and some sort of aircraft.

"Tell General Forge to bring Gran Jefe to the engineering rig," Kade said. "And I want you there as well. I've got something to announce."

TWELVE

"Magnolia, do you copy?" X asked. He checked his HUD for her beacon. She wasn't far from his location in the port of Grenada.

The faint, muffled sound of Magnolia's voice surged in his ear. She was still alive, waiting with Miles. And X was still trying to come up with a plan to get himself out of this cruise ship.

By a stroke of pure luck, he and Jo-Jo had kicked up through a hole in the overhead just as the leviathan's calves came out to feed.

That hole had opened to a portion of the ship that stood above water. But there was no way out. They were trapped inside a compartment some two hundred feet long. It was filled with industrial kitchen equipment once used to prepare fancy meals for vacationers. Most of it was unrecognizable due to rust and rot, though the walk-in cooler looked almost as if it still functioned.

X had been exploring for a way out, but there didn't seem to be one besides the way they came in. He had blocked it off the best he could, stacking a table and a stove against the hatch that opened to that part of the compartment—just in case the beasts somehow had a way to move about on land.

Out here in the wastes, who knew what was possible? He felt better having the area blocked off.

Glowing yellow light bled from the rusted edges of the hatch. Whistles and moans from the hungry calves resonated through the ship.

Another moan came from behind X. He went back to Jo-Jo, who lay on the deck, under a mess table. She had gotten banged up while trapped in the mouth of the leviathan and had cuts on her back and both legs. The leviathan's acidic vomit had also burned off some of the fur.

X had sustained his own injuries. He bent down to examine his right boot and a section of his suit left exposed under the armor. He had sealed it off when they first escaped, but a cut on his shin was already red with infection.

"Hang in there, girl," X said. He bent down and opened his med kit. "We're gonna get out of here, and don't you worry."

Jo-Jo let out what sounded like a purr. He applied some ointment on her cuts while listening to the calves pound on the hatch with their long prehensile arms. The barricade rattled but didn't topple.

He had to find a way out of this hellhole.

Under the table, Jo-Jo curled up, taking shallow breaths. The animal was in survival mode, with her hackles spiking up. Even a born denizen of the toxic wastes had a limit to how much she could take.

X racked his mind for anything that might help them get out of the ship. He looked down at his armor. The nuclear battery unit at his chest could be detonated if rigged properly. It was how Hell Diver Alexander Corey had sacrificed himself back in Rio to save the other divers.

If X could rig it up, it would blow a massive opening in the hull, but it would also likely kill him and Jo-Jo. And if he should somehow survive the blast, he wouldn't last long without the life-support system that depended on the battery.

He had his blaster, but shotgun shells and flares were useless against plate steel, and he certainly couldn't use them in the water.

"Wait a second," he muttered.

He pulled out the weapon and broke it open. A flare was loaded in the top chamber above the two shotgun shells. He had more vacuum-sealed flares on his duty belt.

X visualized his plan of firing a flare into one of the exposed arms of the calves. It would likely retreat back into the water, where the flare would continue to burn, and with a little luck, the ensuing chaos would allow them a few moments to dive back down and swim out the way they had come.

If the adult monster had gone, they would have a chance of reaching the surface. If it hadn't, then this was indeed the end of their journey.

It was a gamble. They could end up inside the beast again.

He flipped the break shut and holstered the weapon. The main problem was going to be getting Jo-Jo to follow his lead. But he had a plan for that too.

X went to a bin of hardware he had seen earlier, and pulled up a lightweight chain with welded links. He brought it back to Jo-Jo. She glared at it, then pulled back.

"I'm not going to hurt you," he said soothingly. "This is the only way back to Mags and Miles. You want to see Miles again, right?"

She grunted.

He bent down with a carabiner and clipped the chain to the collar she still wore. Then he clipped the other end to his duty belt.

Next, he pulled out the blaster again. Jo-Jo studied the weapon with a dubious air.

"It's the best I got," X said. "You ready?"

Jo-Jo knuckle-walked over to him.

"Go time," X said.

He pulled the table down, then moved the stove away from the hatch.

He motioned Jo-Jo back, and she hovered behind him in a crouched position. X grabbed the hatch, blaster in hand. He pulled it open and stepped back, raising the weapon. It wasn't hard to find a target. A calf whipped a half-dozen arms out of the water in the hole midway down the compartment.

He pulled the trigger, firing a flare under one of the arms. A garish red glow bloomed across the compartment, and the beast let out a high-pitched whistle as it retreated.

"Now!" X yelled.

He switched the selector to shotgun and fired once, then again, into the pool of water.

The whistling came again—direct hits, by the sound of it.

He started to jump in but felt resistance on the chain.

"Come on!" he shouted at Jo-Jo.

She hesitated, but he gave another hard pull and she followed. X holstered the weapon and jumped in, and down they went. It took X a moment to get his bearings. When he saw the red streak from the flare, he turned in the opposite direction.

Together, he and Jo-Jo found the exit and swam out the way they had come. X stared into the darkness but didn't see any glowing monster from the pits of hell.

"Thank the Octopus Lords!" he yelled.

Jo-Jo was first out from under the ship. She pulled up, and X kicked after her noticing something moving deeper in the water beyond the ship. His heart skipped when the grotesque, barnacled hide of the leviathan emerged. For some reason, it wasn't glowing—perhaps on purpose, to conceal its presence.

It worked.

By the time X turned, the beast had opened its mouth, sucking him back in. He tried to kick away, but the force was inexorably pulling both him and Jo-Jo to their doom.

There was nothing he could do.

Actually, there is one thing…

Jo-Jo didn't have to die too.

X pressed the gate on the carabiner to unclip the chain from his duty belt. With only a second to decide, he would set the monkey free. But in that split instant, the animal pulled on it, jerking X away from the gaping maw. Kicking as hard as he could, he felt the jaws come crashing together behind him.

Still kicking madly, he closed his eyes and prepared to be smashed between the rigid rows of whalebone. This time, his body would be mashed into chunks that would catch in the baleen before being swallowed into the hatch he was trapped in before.

"No way!" X yelled. He put everything he had into his legs and feet, thumping through the water, just as the mouth closed behind him. A rush of water pushed X toward the surface.

Jo-Jo continued to pull him away with a surprising fierceness. Hoping they had gained some room, X risked a glance over his shoulder, seeing the oil-drum-size eyeballs staring at him and the colossal maw opening a second time, just ten feet behind him.

"Oh, hell no!" X yelled.

He kicked with Jo-Jo toward the surface, breaking through the choppy waves. Jo-Jo hauled him over to the hull of the ship. She climbed up on the tilting deck, grabbed X, and practically tossed him up onto the rusted hull.

The glowing leviathan surfaced, arms whipping back and forth. X and Jo-Jo were already climbing through a hole above the waterline. This time, they entered a section of the hull with several gaping ruptures.

Arms shot through two of them, feeling about for X and Jo-Jo. They took a right down a passage filled with decaying life vests and ropes, running deeper into the ship for safety from those grasping arms.

X bumped on his comms, waiting for a respite in the monster's whistling. When it finally faded away, he yelled, "Mags! Mags, we shook the big ugly bastard! We're free!"

* * * * *

Maniacal cackling followed Layla deeper into the caves. She whipped around with her rifle, trying to pinpoint the location, but the noise echoed over and over in the rocky tunnel. She switched off her helmet lights and went dark, using only night vision. Not that it would matter much. Chances were, whatever creature was out there had adapted to see down here. Or it would have the sensory acuity to find her by scent, or perhaps echolocation as the Sirens did.

She crouched with her rifle, scarcely daring to move. Afraid to try another transmission to Michael. Afraid to do *anything*, really.

The hair on her neck stood up, but not from fear. It was like an electric charge. Her HUD flickered, the data spooling out in a jumbled mess.

What the hell was happening?

The mad cackling came again, then faded away. It didn't come again.

Not long after entering, Layla had fled into the connecting tunnel to escape the electrically charged fog and the beast lurking within it. Now she waited, hearing only the drip of water somewhere nearby. Not from the waterfall, whose roar she could no longer hear.

The caves protected her from the electrically charged fog but not from the creature that was following her.

She turned her helmet lights back on and crept deeper into the blackness. The ceiling in the passage seemed to get lower, forcing her to crouch down. Steel support beams held up the ceiling, their paint long since chipped away over the years in the subterranean dampness.

This was not a natural cave formation. Someone had built this hidden annex under the mountain, maybe after the war, maybe before it. The underground passages she had discovered were rough and jagged, indicating it was a hasty excavation. From the looks of it, the builders had blown the cave out with explosives. This was definitely not like the properly shored tunnels she had explored in ITC facilities. Whoever carved these passages out of the rock was either looking for resources or trying to hide.

But the deeper Layla trekked, the more it felt like the latter. There was no evidence of mining activity. No abandoned tools, worn-out bits, or ore carts.

She wondered whether, if she kept going, she might find a bunker. Maybe there were still people down here. Or maybe she would stumble into the lair of whatever was making that horrifying laughter.

The thought chilled her.

Layla shouldered her rifle as she approached a bend in the tunnel. She listened for footsteps or scrabbling claws. Hearing nothing besides the drip of water, she moved around the corner. The corridor had metal conduit runs on both walls and the ceiling.

Brass sprinkler heads jutted from a rusted overhead pipe. She played the light down the tunnel, couldn't see the end. Layla hesitated after a few steps. Maybe this led to a bunker, maybe to the nest of some alien beast, or maybe it led to a different way topside, above the fog.

Having gone this far, she decided to keep going rather than retrace her steps and face the unknown laughing creature. Filled with a dash of hope, she pushed on, faster now. The cackling had stopped, but there was a new noise ahead—a whooshing of some sort, almost like thousands of birds beating their wings. Twenty or so paces in, she came to a blast door—a bunker after all.

And that bunker door was ajar.

She raked her light over a large wheel handle. After approaching slowly, she stopped in front of the door to listen. The whooshing sound was coming from the other side. The opening was wide enough that she could squeeze through, barely. She angled her body to try to see what was on the other side.

Her HUD flickered again, then shut off completely. Her helmet lights went off too, plunging her in darkness.

Senses on high alert, Layla backed away from the door, her finger moving to the trigger, ready to squeeze off a burst. She waited for the suit to power back on.

It didn't.

The whooshing, flapping noise continued, but there was another sound as well now: a *click-clack, click-clack*. Something was stalking her, and she could *hear* it coming from behind.

Her heart pounded in her ears as she reached down and felt the switch for the battery-powered tactical light on her rifle.

She backed quietly toward the door, aiming her rifle the way she had come, waiting to turn on the light.

Click-clack . . .

The sound was closer.

Another few seconds passed. She held her breath in her chest, waiting to twist the knob on the tac light. When she couldn't stand it anymore, she pushed the button, sending a spear of light down the rocky passage. The beam captured a pair of glowing green eyes at the other end.

They stood still, then bolted toward her at breakneck speed. In the glow of her light came a thin, oddly distorted humanlike figure running with arms outstretched. Abruptly, it vanished. Then it came again before dimming like a hologram that had lost power.

Layla fired her laser rifle. The bolt vanished into darkness. She squeezed off another blast, but again the creature, person, or whatever the hell it was shifted away.

Electricity flashed across the hallway. Her HUD flickered back on, then off again. She aimed one last time at the head and fired.

A twisted smile crossed the face of a man with wild brown hair and dark eyes. He let out the same cackle again.

She held the rifle steady and fired again. The man vanished before the bolts could wipe the insane grin off his face.

Layla squeezed through the blast door and put her shoulder against it.

The laughing came again, louder, *crazier*. With all her might, she pushed the blast door shut. It made an audible thud. Then, panting, she put her back against it.

The tac light from her rifle flickered across the ground. She raised the weapon, and the beam hit a wall of stacked wood crates and, beyond it, some big mining equipment: a skid loader, a bulldozer, three old motorcycles, and an ATV.

The maniacal cackling continued outside the door. She stepped away from it to explore what appeared to be some sort of vehicle bay. She had to find a way out of here. This couldn't be the only way in and out.

She shined her light against the opposite wall and gasped at the sight of a mounted head with antlers.

Layla almost shot the damned thing, but it wasn't moving. And it wasn't alone. She swept her light over a wall lined with the taxidermied heads of deer and other animals. A boar with fearsome tusks, a snarling bear. Dust covered their glossy eyes and matted fur.

The laughing seemed to retreat, fading some but still out there. Then it stopped altogether.

Silence filled the bunker. She combed over the rest of the

space and found three doors. Between the first two was a wall of open lockers. Keeping her rifle up, she explored them and found boxes of shotgun shells and bullets of various common calibers. Even a few 50 mm grenade projectiles.

She found the launcher a few lockers down. The weapon had a wood stock and a web strap. She slung it over her back, then carefully loaded the grenades into a bandolier as an idea seeded in her mind. Who knew if any of this ammo was good? She wasn't going to leave it all here, and if she couldn't find an exit, she might have to blast her way out of this mountain.

The laughing came again, but it didn't seem to be coming from the hallway. She glanced up at the ceiling.

Was it above her now?

She went to the next door and opened it to a supply room lined with shelves. Unlike the lockers, these were mostly empty. Scattered along the floor were rusted cans and rotten boxes of MREs. Even in this temperate subterranean climate, none of it would be edible. She searched a shelf of medical supplies and scavenged a roll of gauze and some medical tape.

Then she left the room and went to the next door. It opened to a hallway with stairs. She passed it by and went to the last room. Three rows of troughs under hanging lights filled the space, which was probably a hundred feet long and fifty wide. Dirt and leaf mold lined the troughs—all that remained of the plants that must have grown under these lights centuries ago.

Layla hurried out into the hallway and took the stairs up to another level with more doors. The deranged laughter was harder to hear now, but the crazed man, creature, or hybrid remained somewhere out there.

The first room was a living space with four empty bunks, neatly made. Bookshelves and an Old World TV covered one wall. There was also a desk with a chair tucked under it. Finding nothing of value, she left and tried the next door, halting right after she pushed it open to an office.

The remains of a man were slumped in a chair. Wispy hair made a border around the moon roof in the back of his skull. One day, centuries ago, it all became too much, and he ended it.

She looked over the shelves of books, and a journal caught her attention. Pulling it out, she opened it and began to read, trying to ignore the laughing that echoed all around her.

Day 29

All of our preparations paid off. The radiation is minor inside the tunnels, and so far we have had no problems with the water supply. I think it's okay to say we're safe down here. My wife called me crazy. She said the end would never come. We still don't know what happened, only that we were lucky to be at our cabin when the bombs began to fall.

All the money I spent on supplies, equipment, and building this place was money well spent. Kelly and I will be dead long before it's safe to go back outside, but our two sons just might live to see a day where they can walk on the surface again. This place gives them a chance.

Marcus

Layla flipped ahead to day 363. Reading about how his wife, Kelly, and sons, Trav and Jon, were depressed. *I'm doing everything I can to keep our spirits up, but our first crop is failing, and I fear I can't save it. We don't have enough dried and canned food to last us forever.*

As she read, a scene of horror unfolded on the pages. Two crop failures in a row. Radiation seeping in. A party of raiders that showed up on the cameras.

She didn't need to go on to understand what had happened. The family had starved, and Marcus killed himself—probably after his wife and sons.

Another shudder went through her. If they didn't get the water, this could be her family's fate too. But before she could worry about that, she had to find a way out, past the crazed being that haunted this place.

Turning to leave the room, she found a picture frame on the floor, near the corpse's rotted boot. She picked it up and removed the broken glass from a picture of Marcus, Kelly, Trav, and Jon.

She brushed off the dust and stared in shock at Marcus. He bore a striking resemblance to the maniacal laughing creature she had seen in the hallway.

Was it one of their sons? That seemed to be the only explanation.

Ghosts weren't real. So how had that thing shape-shifted?

There had to be an explanation, and there had to be a way to kill whatever was stalking her . . .

THIRTEEN

Zuni and Dakota stood guard outside the control center on the engineering rig. Inside, Kade listened to static from a bank of radios. Pedro sat trying to get a radio transmission through with the best equipment they had available. Signal boosters were attached to towers rising hundreds of feet into the air. If they were going to get through to X and Mags, this was their best shot.

"*Sea Wolf*, do you copy?"

Kade tried not to listen as he stared at the maps spread out across the table. Sitting around the table with him were Beau, Woody, and Imulah, plotting the coordinates he gave them. Slayer and Blackburn were at a smaller table, reading through Cazador logs, some from centuries ago.

Lot of ground to cover, Kade thought.

He surveyed the maps of North and South America, also Hawaii. They had marked the locations of all Cazador raids over the years—the documented ones, anyway. There were also plenty of freelance sorties during periods of peace in the Cazador history, when warriors headed out in boats as pirates and not as part of the military expeditions.

Somewhere out there, Kade knew there was an airship. The people of the *Hive* had discovered *Deliverance* at the Hilltop Bastion. There had to be more airships in storage somewhere…

"King Kade," Pedro said. He took off his headset and shook his head solemnly. "I can't get anything through to Xavier," he said.

"It could be interference from the storms," Beau said.

Blackburn glanced down, clearly not buying it.

"I fear that something bad has occurred on their journey," Imulah said.

Kade feared the same. Something had likely happened to Xavier and Magnolia on their voyage to Rio.

This was all the more reason he had to start the search for another airship. They had to find a way to get back into the sky.

You don't have many eggs left, and the few you do have are all in the same basket.

He had made up his mind. They would launch a mission to look for an airship, and they would begin a new round of Hell Diver training.

Kade walked over to the windows as Pedro turned back to the radio.

Outside the control center, wind turbines on the engineering rig churned, cutting through the air and feeding hundreds of batteries. If the Vanguard Islands had a beating heart, it was this place—not the farms, not the fishing trawlers.

These were the machines keeping the blood flowing.

And it wasn't just the batteries or the windmills, or the oil the rig produced. They also had their helium reserves here from when the *Hive* was restored. Soon, those tanks would be put to use by tethering small lighter-than-air platforms over ships and rigs, for the Hell Divers to jump from. He was excited to tell Tia, for it was her idea that had made this possible. But first, he had to explain it all to General Forge.

He would be here soon.

Kade went back to the maps.

"We must have faith in X," Imulah said.

"Yes, and we must also have a backup plan," Kade said. He hovered over the maps, glancing at South America. The entire Atlantic coast had marks where Cazador raiders had plundered cities. It seemed impossible they had never discovered an airship.

"Imulah, you're sure no aircraft were ever discovered at any of these locations?" he asked.

The scribe scratched his beard. "I scoured the archives for King Xavier, and did again recently, sir. Nothing in them indicates any airships were located."

Imulah lowered his finger to a spot in the former state of Georgia, in North America.

"El Pulpo documented wreckage of an airship outside the city of Savannah, but it was not much more than burned aluminum," he said. "He referred to it as a 'sky horse.' I located other mentions of sky horses in previous raiding documents from decades and even a century ago, but those seem to be not about airships but about airplanes, all of which were destroyed."

"I see," Kade said.

"I have no evidence of Cazador raids at the following ITC facilities." Imulah put a thin yellow tag over Buenos Aires in Argentina, Santiago in Chile, and Lima in Peru.

"Those are considerable distances."

"Precisely why they have not been raided."

"There's nothing closer?"

"North America, but my guess is that the *Hive*, *Ares*, and perhaps even your former ship *Victory* have already raided those locations."

The scribe was likely right again.

A knock came on the door, and Slayer got up to let Zuni in.

"Sir, General Forge has arrived with a squad and Gran Jefe," reported the praetorian guard.

Kade looked out the viewport to see a heavily armed complement of six Cazadores with General Forge. Gran Jefe stood in the middle of the phalanx, wearing green fatigues and a leather vest. The imposing warrior wiped snot from his pierced nostrils. He turned his bloodshot eyes up at the command center.

Those eyes had likely looked into Ada's right before Gran Jefe cut through her rope only moments before Kade arrived at the scene, whereupon the hulking Cazador lied to him about what happened.

Anger tore at his heart as Kade pictured her falling to her death right before Jo-Jo's eyes. No wonder the animal had twice tried to kill Gran Jefe.

Kade couldn't deny the rage he felt now thinking about Ada. But he had to remind himself that plenty of Cazadores felt the same when she dropped a container filled with their comrades into the ocean.

"Slayer, tell Forge to come up, but leave Gran Jefe down there," Kade said.

"Yes, sir," Slayer said.

"What ya gonna do with him?" Beau asked.

"Depends," Kade said.

Forge entered the room a few moments later. He took off his helmet and set it on the table. "Our prisoner is responding well to treatment and is able to move his feet," he said.

"Good," Kade said.

Forge looked down at the maps, then to Kade.

"What's all this?" asked the general.

"Part of my plan to protect the islands," Kade replied. "I've done my best to prepare for the Knights of the Coral Castle and to make sure our people are fed, but there's something else we need to plan for."

He looked down at the map of Rio de Janeiro.

"If Xavier and Magnolia don't find Michael and the airship, we're going to be restricted in our travels by the sea itself," Kade said. "Having lost radio contact with the *Sea Wolf*, I must assume the worst and have decided to launch a new mission."

"The Immortal will return," Forge said. "We must give him time. The journey is long and hard."

"I hope so, but suppose he doesn't. What if we never see that airship again?"

Kade walked around the table, looking at all the marked locations for the tenth time.

"El Pulpo and King Xavier both knew we had to secure new resources or this place would never survive," he said. "We went to Panama to try and do that, then to Australia to search for the Coral Castle, which we now know exists. There must be other places out there too, but without an airship, we're all but stranded here."

Forge lifted his chin as if to reply, but Kade pushed on.

"We have to take the skies back," he said. "And we need Hell Divers. It's the only way to secure our future."

"Sir—"

"Let me finish," Kade said. "I'm authorizing a mission with scouts to search for an airship at the locations Imulah has noted on the map."

Forge went to look at all three tags, then quickly looked up.

"Sir, we need every warrior, every ship, every spear here to defend the islands," the general said. "The fuel, manpower, and ammunition it will take to mount one of those raids is something we can't afford to risk right now."

There was anger in his voice.

"King Xavier asked me to stay here and defend the islands," he said. "To do that, I need every weapon at my disposal. You are the king now, and you have my wholehearted allegiance, but you should consider his order."

Kade trod carefully. He didn't want to sound arrogant.

"While I agree that the bulk of our forces should remain here, we can afford to send out a few scouts," Kade said. "In fact, our very future may well depend on it."

"King Kade, the Cazador empire existed for two and a half centuries without an airship before your people came."

"Right—by eating each other," Woody said.

Forge shot the man behind Kade a glare.

"We did what we had to do, and we will again if these knights come," said the general.

"Things have changed significantly," Kade cut in. "Our fleet is down to a single warship. We will also look for ships and boats on this expedition, General, to replenish what's been lost."

Forge looked away from Woody.

"The seeds now growing on the rooftops came here by way of Hell Divers and an airship," Kade said. "We would all soon be starving if it weren't for them—"

"Ninety percent of my military is dead because of an airship and sky people, which include Hell Divers." Forge checked his angry tone with a short pause. "King Xavier did what he thought was best by expanding, and I supported it because I believed in him. However, to risk more lives and precious resources to find something that likely doesn't exist is a strategic error that I won't support."

Imulah stepped up, cleared his throat. "King Kade, I agree with the general. If we had some sort of intelligence about an airship location, then perhaps, but right now we have nothing. It's like a needle in a haystack, as they used to say."

Kade could see his people already turning against him. They didn't believe what he believed. Part of being a leader was listening to your advisers and admitting when you were wrong.

But Kade didn't think he was wrong—he was convinced this was the only way to save the islands in the long term.

"A needle that we can *find*," Slayer said. "We're Cazadores. Don't forget that, Imulah."

Forge and Imulah both stared at the Barracuda leader.

Even Kade was surprised to hear the vote of confidence.

"I volunteer to lead this mission with Blackburn," Slayer said. "We just need a single boat and supplies for the trip."

"You're both combat ready?" Kade asked.

Blackburn stiffened his body, or did his best. The soldier had clearly been working hard to minimize his injuries from the fight with Charmer. Not that it was unusual for injured fighters to be redeployed—they didn't have the luxury of R and R while they convalesced.

"Yes, we are both combat ready," Slayer replied without looking at Blackburn.

"You're my top commander, and Blackburn is one of my best fighters," Forge said. "I need you both here."

Everyone waited on Kade for his decision. He felt the weight of the words as he uttered them.

"A single boat, two men, and a civilian crew," he said. "That's all I'm asking for, General."

"I've given my counsel, King Kade. If we are finished here, Gran Jefe is on the deck below with my guards. And Charmer still draws breath. When is this trial by combat? I volunteer to face him in the Sky Arena and get that sorry chapter of our history over with."

"I'll deal with Gran Jefe in a moment," Kade said. "As for Charmer, if you want to be his challenger, then by all means, *yes*, General."

Forge picked up his helmet, bowed slightly, and left. The door slammed behind him.

"Not your biggest fan," Woody whispered.

Things seemed to be getting worse between Kade and his highest-ranking soldier. He had to find a way to fix things before they broke beyond repair.

"Pedro, keep trying X, and contact me the moment you reach him," Kade said.

"Yes, sir."

"Beau, Woody, Slayer, Blackburn, let's go," Kade said.

Imulah stayed behind to stow the maps in their tubes. Kade opened the door to the upper platform, which looked down over the deck. Dakota and Zuni had left their guard post and were on the deck with Forge below.

Kade started down the rusted stairs to the lower decks, where Gran Jefe waited with the six guards. This was something he had been dreading for the past few days. But it had to be done.

"Sergeant Jorge Mata!" he called out.

The soldiers on the deck all turned and looked up at Kade. Then they slowly fanned out around Gran Jefe.

General Forge held a crossbow behind him.

"Go to the king and watch your tongue," Forge said to Gran Jefe.

The big warrior strode out onto the deck with Forge following. Kade descended the stairs, preparing himself mentally for what was about to happen.

Woody and Beau, unaware of Kade's plans, strode up behind Gran Jefe. By design, Slayer and Blackburn were equally in the dark.

"Stay here," Kade ordered them all.

Dakota and Zuni walked over. Each held an assault rifle.

"Halt," Forge said.

Gran Jefe stopped four feet from Kade. He pulled his pants up over his gut.

"*Su Majestad*," he said.

He reeked of body odor, but Kade didn't smell any booze on him today.

"King Xavier forgave you for killing Ada," Kade said. "He forgave you once again for testing him below the decks of the *Frog* against the water bug."

Gran Jefe glanced around him, curious. Kade saw the exact moment that curiosity turned to the look of an animal as it realized it was about to be slaughtered.

"I kill Jamal for this place," Gran Jefe said through clenched teeth. "I spill my *own* blood."

"Yes. You have also disobeyed many orders, to the point you can't be trusted. You've had many chances."

General Forge walked over to stand just behind Kade. He raised his crossbow, aiming it at Gran Jefe.

"You had one last chance," Kade said.

Gran Jefe raised his chin, clearly having accepted his fate. He gave a nod so subtle that Kade almost missed it. That nod, it seemed, wasn't recognition of his fate, but an acknowledgment to Forge.

Kade saw that the crossbow in his peripheral vision was no longer aimed at Gran Jefe. It was aimed at the side of Kade's head.

"King Kade!" Gran Jefe shouted. With surprising speed, he charged like a rampaging beast of the wastes, nostrils flaring and enraged eyes pinned on Kade. Those eyes went to General Forge as Gran Jefe lowered his shoulder and plowed into him. He lifted Forge off his feet and slammed him to the deck with a crunch. In an instant, he had the knife unsheathed from Forge's belt and at the man's throat.

Drawing his Monster Hunter, Kade pointed at the sky and fired a blast.

"Drop it!" Kade shouted.

The report's echoes faded away, and Jefe slowly turned, the blade still pressed to Forge's throat. The other soldiers fanned out, all of them surrounding Gran Jefe.

Kade turned to Dakota and Zuni, who had Woody and Beau facedown on the deck.

"It's okay," Kade said. "You can let them up."

He turned back to Gran Jefe.

"He want me to kill you, Cowboy King," said the Cazador. "He find me on the rig, try to hire me as you say."

Kade glanced over to General Forge, staring at him as he lay there.

"I slit his throat, if you say," Gran Jefe said.

"No," Kade said. "Let him up."

Gran Jefe cocked his head slightly in confusion, but the knife didn't budge. Slayer and the other soldiers inched closer.

"I ordered General Forge to approach you as a final test," Kade said. "It was the only way to know if I can trust you."

He motioned for Gran Jefe to pull the knife away.

"Let him up now," Kade said. "You earned my trust."

"Crikey," Beau said. "You *planned* that?"

"I about blew Dakota's head off," Woody said.

Dakota laughed. "Check gun," he said. "Only brass in magazine. No bullets."

Kade had planned that too, making sure his friends had their magazines swapped out when they weren't looking.

"It was a test for you two as well," he said. "Next time, make sure you have ammo."

Woody laughed, but Beau was not amused.

"You could have gotten our biscuits blown off, or worse," he said.

"But I didn't," Kade said.

Gran Jefe eased the knife away, and Kade reached down to help Forge up. Forge hesitated a moment, then took his hand.

Kade yanked him up. He held on to the general's hand for a moment.

"You're right; we can't risk more men to find an airship," Kade said. "Not right now."

"I'm glad you agree, King Kade," said the general. "There are no aircraft anywhere close to us, or we would know. If that changes, I will fully support a raid to find an airship and bring it back."

"Rooftop," Gran Jefe said.

Kade looked over to see the big man pointing at the horizon.

"What?" Kade asked.

"Rooftop, enemy ship."

"The airship that makes up the top of the capitol tower," Imulah said.

"No," Gran Jefe grunted.

He walked over and asked for the notepad that Imulah had clutched under his arm. The scribe didn't hand it over.

"*Dámelo*," Gran Jefe said. "Give."

Kade nodded, and Imulah reluctantly handed the pad over. Gran Jefe took a pen and scribbled out something that Alton might have drawn.

"Enemy ship," Gran Jefe said with a grin. He pointed to Kade. "Sky horse."

Kade recognized the helicopter from the Coral Castle that Bulldozer had crashed on the rooftop.

"What about it?" Kade asked.

"We use."

"It's destroyed," Kade said. "*Destruído*."

"No, no," Gran Jefe said. "*Más* sky horses in wastes."

"Not according to the scrolls," Imulah said.

"Then the stupid scrolls are wrong," Gran Jefe said. "*Equiv-ocados.*"

Imulah raised a brow.

"How so?" Kade asked.

"My first raid as Barracuda warrior," Gran Jefe said with a pound to his chest. "I see sky horses."

"Why isn't it documented?"

"Because I'm the only survivor left."

"Is this possible?" Kade asked Imulah.

"Of course. Many missions were either doomed or not properly accounted for," said the scribe. "And there are those that weren't officially approved by the Cazador military."

"Even if they were there ten years ago, they might not be anymore," Forge said.

"I go back," Gran Jefe said with a snort. "If sky horses still there, I find them for you, Cowboy King."

FOURTEEN

"Layla, do you copy?" Michael said into the comms.

Static fired back.

He crouched on a mossy bluff overlooking the valley. He had roped down into the hills above the DZ where Layla had landed, near the stream. The strange red fog was lighter here and seemed to be concentrated along the stream and Crabtree Falls.

He tried Layla again, but nothing was getting through.

With his pistol drawn, he kept hiking into the forest to find a path above the waterfall. Blue flashes bloomed in pockets of the carmine murk rolling across the valley.

He kept his distance, as Timothy had advised. The AI was definitely correct in his theory about something creating the electricity. The flashes seemed to originate in the same general area each time.

Michael kept moving with his gun held out in front. Crabtree Falls wasn't far. He could hear it in the distance, although he couldn't see it through the fog.

He trekked along the dense mutant trees, using his helmet lights to guide him. The fog had created a disturbance that messed with his electronics, shutting down his digital map and night vision—pretty much everything but his battery pack and headlamps.

And Layla was surely experiencing the same things out there. He had to find her fast.

"Layla, if you can hear me, I'm coming," he said into his comm.

Pistol out in front, he trekked across the soggy moss-carpeted soil. The reddish fog tendriled up the slope below, reaching out like ghostly fingers.

He pushed onward, not stopping until he had gotten to the top of the bluff. Crabtree Falls flowed over the side, crashing into the stream below. Michael crouched at the edge, pistol pointed downward. The beams from his helmet hit the pool and the shore where the disturbing monopod track had followed Layla.

The drone they had lost was in shallow water near the rocky shore. The fog swirled around the edges but didn't venture out into the misty spray over the water.

Michael holstered his pistol and dropped the rope slung over his shoulder. He ran it around the base of a tree and tossed both ends over the falls. It was slick, mossy rock, and he would need to be extra cautious with only one arm.

He ran the rope through his rappel device, gave a tug, and started backing down over the edge of the rock. Some twenty feet down, he heard something that stopped him.

A faint cackling noise carried over the cascading water.

Not so much cackling as mad laughter. It sounded almost human, like someone deranged.

Michael looked over his shoulder and rappelled quickly down the rope.

About halfway, he slipped and spun with the rope, braking at once to keep from slipping. Facing outward, he looked a hundred feet above him and spotted the beetle-shaped craft in the wake of a lightning flash. A tube dangled below its belly, ready to suck up the precious water.

Michael turned to face the slope. Only twenty feet to go now…

Only ten feet from the bottom, he slid again. He instinctively reached out with his foreshortened, handless arm, the stump sliding along a mossy boulder. With nothing but the rope to stop him, that foot and leg slipped down the rock.

His braking hand lost the rappel line, and for a moment he felt weightless, as in the first second of a dive. Then his guts tightened and he was falling. His arm windmilled but found nothing.

He landed on his back with a loud *whump,* and the wind burst from his lungs.

Michael tried to move, but he didn't know how badly he was hurt. He sucked in a breath, then another. A fleeting view of the world returned, vanished again. He felt his hair prickle along his body. As he lay there taking physical inventory, blue light arced outward.

Realizing that it was coming from the electrical charge in the fog, he pushed onto his side.

Michael reached to his holster and fished out the pistol with his shaking hand.

A hysterical laugh answered his movement. It seemed to be coming from *inside* the fog.

Closing one eye, he centered the pistol on the bright arcs sizzling through the red curtain. Filaments of blue spiderwebbed outward, and with them came the fog, slowly creeping around the edge of the pool. It snaked closer and closer.

Michael roved the barrel back and forth, waiting for a shot.

As the electrical charges closed in, so did the fog.

Within the red haze, a ghostly shape appeared. He stared at an almost human-looking form for a second before pulling the trigger. He heard the blast, then the ping of the shell casing on a rock, but there was no cry of pain from his target. Just that crazed cackle.

He fired again, then once more, but the bullets seemed to have no effect. The gibbering creature kept coming and kept *laughing*.

As it drew closer, the electrical charges seemed to come from the ground and then rise up through this manic being. Michael glimpsed a sand-colored ball moving on the ground, leaving a rounded furrow about the size of the track he had seen earlier.

He adjusted his aim just as the face of a man came into focus. He looked to be fifty to sixty years old, with a long chin and pointy nose. But there was something odd about his skin…

Michael fired at the device on the ground that was somehow projecting the image.

The first shot missed, but the second hit. Sparks shot out, and a whirring noise sounded. The cackling man turned abruptly and vanished into the fog.

Michael lay there a moment to gather himself. He released the magazine—still five cartridges left—and clicked it back into the weapon.

After a few moments, the shock of the fall lessened and he managed to sit up, groaning in pain. Nothing seemed broken, but he hurt everywhere.

The mad laughter pealed again on the opposite shore of the pool. Michael pushed up onto his feet, staggering.

The insane cackle turned into a taunting snicker. The noise seemed to come from all directions. Electrical charges bloomed as the fog rolled in his direction.

He backed away toward the falls, stopping beside the roaring water.

He dared not proceed. The pool was charged. If he stepped in…

Carmine flashes came from all around the pool, encroaching

on the waterfall and the ground he stood on. With nowhere to go, he was about to fry no matter what.

Not like this…

The grinning man emerged again on the bank of rocks to Michael's left, but this time he wasn't laughing. His eyes narrowed on Michael.

"Stay back," Michael called out. "I'm not here to hurt you."

All at once, more ghostly figures emerged from the fog, all of them laughing maniacally.

"Tin, get down!"

He didn't have time to look for his wife's voice. He dropped to the ground, and a thump sounded overhead. The explosion that followed sent bits of rock and soil raining down on him.

Another explosion shook the ground as Michael looked up. Then another. The blasts hit on the opposite shore, where those laughing faces flickered in and out. His ears rang.

He didn't even hear Layla as she ran over and helped him to his feet. Then she raised her grenade launcher and fired off another projectile.

Her mouth made the shapes of words that Michael couldn't hear. But somehow, he could hear laughing. No longer many voices, it was just one now, coming from a single figure alone in the fog.

"Stop!" the man cried.

"Fire," Michael said. "Kill him, Layla."

"Wait!" The man held his hands up. "I was just playing a game. I would never hurt you."

The fog was already dissipating around the smoking craters, but it clung to the lunatic standing fifty feet away, across the pool of water. A burst of electricity shot out of the fog swirling around his gaunt form.

"I won't touch you… I can't," said the man.

"Don't trust it," Layla said. "Get ready to hit your booster."

She pulled another grenade from the bandolier and loaded it on the grenade launcher.

Michael reached over his shoulder, hesitated.

"It?" he asked.

"That's not a man," she said. "It's an AI of a man who once lived here. His family died, he died, and this is what remains."

Michael understood. He recalled a time when Timothy Pepper also went haywire. The AI had lost his family, just like this guy.

"I've been alone for two hundred and forty-five years!" he shouted. "Please, take me with you."

Michael felt empathy for the AI. But it wasn't a man, and they couldn't trust the program, which clearly had more than a few screws loose.

The comm channel suddenly came to life.

"Commander Everhart, do you copy?" Timothy asked.

"Copy," Michael said.

"Sir, the electrical charges are dissipating."

"I know," Michael said.

The fog receded in several spots where the holoports were generating the different images of this AI.

"Back up!" Layla said. She walked forward with the grenade launcher aimed at the final holographic image in the fog. "Back up or I'll blow the last holo-port!"

The man suddenly looked down, bowing his head.

"Go, Tin," she said.

"You first," he replied.

"I'm covering us, just in case he tries to electrocute us."

"Back up!" Michael yelled.

The man did as instructed, head still bowed.

Michael reached over his shoulder and hit his booster. The balloon fired out of the cannister, filling with helium from the attached lines and yanking him off his feet. Layla kept her grenade launcher aimed at the AI, then punched her booster.

The man looked up as they rose into the sky.

"Wait!" he called out. "Finish me!"

"Leave him," Michael said.

"No, please! Immortality is a curse—you have to end this cycle, I'm begging you!"

Layla looked over at Michael, who nodded after a beat. She aimed the launcher and pulled the trigger. The explosion boomed below them, smoke swirling away from the impact crater. When it faded away, the AI was gone, this time forever.

He was right: immortality was a curse.

"Timothy, lower the hose," Michael said. "Time to get what we came here for."

*　*　*　*　*

"X!" Magnolia shouted into the comm.

Miles chased her down to the shore, his bark drowned out by the leviathan's high-frequency whistle. She couldn't hear anything over the channel either, if X should try to respond. But he was likely too busy staying alive.

Whatever he had done had enraged the monster. The marina lit up as the glowing beast careened through the underwater graveyard of boats, smashing hulls, splintering masts. The tentacular arms writhed up out of the water.

Magnolia looked for X and Jo-Jo in the chop of the bay. According to the beacon still active on her HUD, they were out there and hunkered down; she just couldn't tell exactly where. She raised her laser rifle, searching with the scope for heat signatures among the half-sunken remains of ships.

A half-dozen white images, all underwater, flickered when

she scanned a cruise ship. It took her a beat to realize this was the leviathan's den, where the babies lived.

Another moment passed before she realized this was where X and Jo-Jo were hiding.

"X!" Magnolia shouted into the comms again.

After the shrieking beast crashed back into the bay, sending up a minor tsunami in the harbor, she heard huffing and puffing in the respite. The arms shot back out, snaking across the deck of the ship. It knew where X and Jo-Jo were, and it was only a matter of time before it had them again.

She had to do something to distract the leviathan. Cradling her rifle, she ran down the rocky shore, weaving between wrecked boats. The bow of a container ship had carved a trench in the shore ahead, pushing up a hill of dirt and rocks. If she could get up there, she could see the cruise ship better.

Magnolia waved for Miles to follow her back up to the road. The dog barked viciously, as if aware that X was in danger.

"We're gonna get him out!" Magnolia shouted.

The animal took off after her, toward the slope on the beach. Her boots slid in the loose dirt, and she fell near the top. She pushed herself up and looked around.

The container ship's bow rail jutted onto the shoulder of the road, and an anchor with a thick chain had fallen off, crushing the asphalt. She moved around it and trained her rifle on the port side of the cruise ship, where the baby monsters nested.

The creatures were now on the move, squirming through the broken hull and into the bay. Though much smaller than their parent, they were still the size of large mutated sharks.

She propped her rifle on the rail and aimed at the head of the next beast leaving the den. Just as it emerged, she pulled the trigger. The laser bolt hissed into the water, through the deformed head.

Steam rose off the water as the dead creature drifted down. Two others tried to get out, but laser bursts maimed them and they retreated to their nest.

A low-pitched clicking came from across the bay. Magnolia glanced up from her sights to see the body of the adult leviathan sliding backward into the water. Eyes the size of an Old World car flitted in her direction.

Her heart thumped. She had its attention now.

The mammoth sea creature let out another series of low-pitched clicks in what had to be communication to its babies. Then came a high-frequency whistle.

Magnolia backed away from the rail. She didn't think the beast could walk on land, but those arms had some reach, and she didn't want to be standing on this bluff when it arrived.

She retreated a few feet from the road, but Miles stayed, barking madly until she pulled him away by his collar. She ducked behind a rusted automobile and hunkered there with Miles.

"X, do you copy?" Magnolia said into her comm link.

It took a beat, but his exhausted voice replied, "Yeah, copy."

"What's your twenty?"

"Slide," he panted. "We're at the top of a slide."

"Slide?"

"The pool deck. Look there!"

She stood with her scope trained on the top deck of the cruise ship, which had ancient swimming pools filled with dark water. Towering water slides, some twisted and mangled, came into focus. At the top of one, she saw two heat signatures.

"I see you. Bought you some time to swim ashore," she said. "I'll cover you."

X didn't move right away. Jo-Jo didn't seem to want to go down the way they had come up to the slide.

"Go!" she said. "While you can!"

He finally turned to Jo-Jo and coaxed the monkey into the slide. Down they went, vanishing from view.

"Over here, asshole!" Magnolia shouted. She fired a bolt at the monster swimming toward the container ship. It was about a thousand feet away now. The lasers didn't have any obvious effect on the immense creature. It charged at the bluff, its whale-like head glowing just under the surface.

Those eyes searched the beach for her, and she ducked back behind the car with Miles. The dog was barking, but in the opposite direction.

She turned just as a shadow swooped down.

"Oh, fuck!" she whispered.

The Siren's wings flared, the frayed tips catching as its muscular legs thrust clawed feet right at her chest. There was no time to bring up her rifle, or to do much of anything besides curse.

The creature hit her in the chest, slamming her into the side of the rusted car. She dropped her rifle from the impact. The claws scraped against her armor as the beast tried to lift her stunned body off the ground.

Miles leaped, only to be knocked away by the knobby elbow of a wing. Then both wings closed around Magnolia, and darkness enveloped her in the leathery cocoon.

She tried to move her arms, but the muscular beast had her. Teeth cracked against the top of her helmet. Unable to break through, the beast twisted Magnolia's head back and forth so hard, it felt as if her neck would snap.

A distant whistle rose over the beast's snarling. She heard another noise too. Barking. As the Siren clamped down on her helmet again, she saw blue daylight through the frayed wing. That wing suddenly peeled back.

The creature immediately let go of her head, and she hit the pavement. Miles had somehow shaken off his helmet and mask and was ripping away at the Siren's wing.

The monster's other wing unwrapped itself from Magnolia and smacked Miles with its horny elbow. Still, the animal held on, tearing skin. The Siren shrieked in pain.

It lunged toward Miles, its jaw-full of needle-sharp teeth yawning closer... when its face exploded. In that same moment, the report of a blaster registered in Magnolia's awareness.

Blood spotted her visor as the eyeless beast fell beside her, its brains on display.

"You okay?" X yelled.

He jogged over, dripping wet. Behind him, a bleeding, whimpering Jo-Jo knuckle-walked with a limp. Miles bolted over to X, tail wagging under his suit.

"Mags!" X called out.

"I'm okay," she said, waving him off.

Squatting down, X got the helmet back on his dog.

Magnolia finally managed to sit. Grabbing the car, she pulled herself up. Fifty yards off in the bay, the leviathan's glowing limbs probed the water.

"You sure you're okay?" X asked.

Magnolia checked the deep grooves the Siren's claws had left in her armor. Her wrist computer confirmed suit integrity was still at 100 percent. She was lucky, but X was charmed.

"How... how did you escape?" she asked.

"I'll tell you later. Let's get back to the boat. Where is it?" X asked.

Magnolia pointed into the jungle. From the bay came another ethereal whistle. The leviathan lifted the limp, pale forms of its two dead young out of the water and let out another long, sad clicking noise.

"Come on," X said.

Magnolia limped away, leaving the monster to mourn its dead offspring. Miles led the way, glancing over his shoulder every few steps to check on his companions.

Jo-Jo was moving slowly and stopped several times.

"Almost there," X said. "Come on, girl, we're gonna get you some medicine to make you feel better."

Jo-Jo pushed on.

Soon, they got to where Magnolia had beached the *Sea Wolf*. She turned to make sure they weren't being followed, then ran to the boat.

X helped Jo-Jo up on the deck, then Miles. Magnolia checked their six one last time before climbing up on the deck. They all went to the lower deck, shutting the hatch behind them. When the tide came in, they could work on getting the boat off the beach. Right now it was time for some rest.

Magnolia leaned back against the hatch and gave a long sigh.

"Did that really just happen?" she asked.

X pulled out a medical kit and bent down to Jo-Jo.

"It happened," he said. "We're all damned lucky."

"That will go down as one of the top monster scenes in your epic biography," Magnolia said. "I think the book has earned its title."

"Title?"

"*The Immortal*, what else?"

X finished wrapping a bandage around Jo-Jo's leg. "Whatever. Let's just get to Rio," he said. "We're still a long way from Michael and his family."

FIFTEEN
TEN YEARS AGO . . .

Gran Jefe pulled on the oars of the skiff, his heart pounding like a war drum. This was his first raid with the Barracudas. They were headed toward a city called Port Arthur, in the former state of Texas. Thanks to Gran Jefe's fighting skills and bravery, Lieutenant Rhino had personally attached him to the Barracudas after a routine scavenging mission turned up survivors in the wastes. The mission had gone from scavenging to a full-on raid, with no idea what awaited them on land.

This was Gran Jefe's opportunity to gain a reputation for more than being a fearless killer. He planned on bringing home treasure, ammunition, medicine. And he would find something for Jada. He had only just met her, but she had ignited a raging fire in him that no other girl had ever sparked.

As he rowed, he pictured her tan, freckled face.

He would make her a queen like those married to el Pulpo, decked out in their white dresses, gold bracelets, and ruby earrings.

He would be a great general someday.

A glance over his shoulder told him the skiff was nearing

the mouth of Sabine Pass, where the Sabine River emptied into the Gulf of Mexico. Just east of the river, on the Louisiana side, was the Sabine Pass Lighthouse. Gran Jefe could see its beacon sweeping through the darkness now. He felt the adrenaline coursing through him as he dug deep with the oars, matching the strokes of Whale, Wendig, and Fuego. In the bow stood the great Rhino, gazing out at the shore through the visor of his spiked armet.

Rumor had it this was only fifty miles south of the place where Rhino and his people were discovered and captured years ago. Ironic in that he was now returning to conquer more survivors.

On their flanks were two more skiffs, crewed by Cazador raiders in thick armor. Snaking hoses connected their helmets to breathing packs and scrubbers.

The stim Gran Jefe had taken on the transport ship was kicking in. Combined with the adrenaline already flooding his system from preraid jitters, he felt more alive than he had in years.

On the horizon, the beacon from the lighthouse that had drawn out the survivors flashed.

"Listen up!" Rhino bellowed in Spanish. "The lighthouse in this sector brought two rats out of the ground."

Gran Jefe marveled at the irony. Once, Rhino himself had been one of those rats, taken by the Cazadores on a raid and completely assimilated into their warrior society.

"Our job is to find their nest, plunder it, and claim it all for the king!" Rhino shouted.

"*¡Por el Pulpo!*" the warriors chorused.

Gran Jefe shouted in unison with the others. In his peripheral vision, he noticed the skiff on their left pulling ahead. He couldn't let them beat the Barracudas to shore.

"*¡Más fuerza!*" he shouted, and dug his oars a little deeper.

The other soldiers laughed.

"*Cálmate, muchacho*," Fuego said, adding that there would still be plenty to eat when they got ashore.

I'm not a kid. I'm not a kid.

Gran Jefe let that become his mantra as he hauled on his oars. The skiff went faster, pushing closer to the boat on their left.

"Don't waste your energy, squid dick!" Wendig shouted. "It's not a race!"

Most of the men laughed at their female comrade's choice of words.

"*¡Silencio!*" Rhino yelled. "Prepare to beach!"

The laughing and chatter died on the gusting wind as the most esteemed commander in the Cazador military spoke. Gran Jefe pulled with less vigor and caught his breath. The skiff hit the surf a moment later, rising up, then nosing down.

"*¡Fuera!*" Rhino roared.

The Barracudas hopped over the side. Gran Jefe stood in waist-deep water. Grabbing the boat, he pushed it up toward the beach. Within seconds, the other warriors were pulling weapons from their oilskin bags.

Whale heaved the Minigun out, and Fuego grabbed his flamethrower. Wendig pulled the charging handle on her assault rifle. Gran Jefe did the same thing, pausing to fix his bayonet on the end.

"Time to go fishing," Wendig said.

"Fuego, on point," Rhino said.

The big man swung his flamethrower up in front of them and trekked up the beach. Gran Jefe followed, scanning the mounds of rubble and debris for hostiles lying in ambush.

Lightning burst over the shore, illuminating the ruined structures that were once homes and businesses, now nothing more than piles of debris. The nuke that hit Houston had burned in this direction, but this was probably the result of tsunamis and hurricanes over the years.

The only fully upright structures were three offshore oil rigs that were under construction in port before the war. The same type that the Cazadores had made their homes at the Metal Islands. Nature had not spared the rusted monstrosities here. Twisted beams hung off the rigs, swaying in the breeze, and some levels had collapsed onto those below.

"Looks like Whale sat on that one," Wendig said with a chuckle.

A few laughs followed, but Rhino was all business.

Nature had reclaimed much of the area beyond the rigs, turning it into a dense jungle of brush, palms, and saplings. Fuego stopped ahead, then waved Wendig over. She crouched to examine the mud.

They had found tracks that led into a densely weeded area. It would be impassable in their bulky armor.

Gran Jefe moved up to look at a pair of footprints left by fleeing humans. They were much smaller than the large boots the warriors wore.

Wendig stepped back to give Fuego a clear line of fire. He unleashed an arc of flame, and the growth withered back, forming a sort of doorway into the thicket. Rhino hacked away the still-burning tendrils.

Gran Jefe followed them, with Wendig just ahead and Whale on rear guard. The team moved with cautious haste to be the first to claim the bounties. The caution was out of fear—not of other humans but of the monsters that lurked in these places. Many kinds of beasts prowled these regions, including the eyeless mutant humanoids that screeched in alien electronic voices.

He had already slain four of the monsters on other raids. This time he hoped to face one of the huge beasts with an external skeleton. They could crush a man's head in one paw. What the

Cazadores called *el rey demonio*, the demon king, or sometimes, simply *bone beast*.

Rhino finished cutting through the burning limbs and motioned for Gran Jefe. Excited, Jefe charged through the opening in the thicket. Coming out the other side, he found a vast swamp.

The chirp and hum of insects made a loud cacophony as flies the size of birds chased smaller prey through the air. The Cazadores knew to avoid the swamps, for the monsters that lived in the toxic water weren't worth the fight. From man-eating snakes to frogs with poison that could kill the hardest warrior in minutes.

"Can't wait to die, can ya, Jorge?" Wendig asked.

Gran Jefe ignored her and continued on point along a low ridge that snaked between the stagnant ponds. Bright spears of light from the other teams' flashlights flicked and flitted in the distance, but Rhino called out for Gran Jefe to stop.

"*¿Qué pasa?*" Gran Jefe asked. He hunched down and scanned the swamp. The tail beam and rotor of a sky horse jutted from the mud. Seeing nothing, he lowered his rifle and motioned for the all clear.

"Okay," Rhino said.

Fuego took a step back.

"The Octopus Lords are excited to accept you as an offering," he said in Spanish.

Whale chuckled.

Cheeks warming, Gran Jefe fumed but said nothing. He would show them. He would prove himself a worthy hunter by taking point and leading them through the area.

Rifle up, he set off along the ridge, keeping his distance from the water. He watched the surface for any movement but saw nothing there or along the muddy banks.

Just ahead, a cluster of moss-covered boulders blocked

the way through a weedy area. Thorny, twisted limbs of bushes formed an effective barrier between many of them. Nothing that Fuego's flamethrower couldn't handle.

Gran Jefe turned to motion for help but found all the warriors looking at him. They hadn't moved a foot since his last scan.

Was this some sort of joke? If so, it was getting old.

A guttural roar behind him startled him, and the ground began to rise under his boots. He jumped back, bringing up his assault rifle as caked mud broke off the gray flesh of a gigantic harelipped beast. It had flippers for arms and a bottle-shaped body that tapered to a paddle tail.

He thrust his bayonet into the whiskered face, and it reared back, howling.

Gran Jefe pulled the weapon back and dived to the side as its tail slapped the mud. He glanced up as the other boulders began to move and shuffle about.

He had been so wary of the water, he never took the boulders for what they were: the thick, moss-covered hides of mutant beasts. The creatures dislodged from the mud, clambered down the hill, and splashed into the water.

But the beast in front of Gran Jefe was enraged. It bounded toward him as he rolled and tried to push himself up. The cleft upper lip snarled, and the toothy jaw snapped. He fell on his back, scrabbling away as the creature came at him, roaring and snorting.

"Down!" shouted Fuego.

Flames blasted over Gran Jefe. He rolled facedown and buried his head in the mud. Heat warmed his back. The ground shook, but the noise of the stampede seemed to be fading.

He opened his eyes. It took a beat, but he realized that what he heard now wasn't the angry retreating beast—it was the sound of laughter.

Rhino walked over and crouched down to him.

"*Manatí,*" he said in Spanish. "*Son herbívoros.*"

"What the hell does that mean?" Gran Jefe asked. He pushed himself up and turned as the burning monster fell into the water.

"It means it eats plants, and not interested in a squid dick," Wendig said.

Gran Jefe grunted.

The Barracudas kept walking, all except Rhino. He stood there, slapped Gran Jefe on the back, and said, "You look in the wrong place again, and the next beast might eat meat."

Then he was gone, leaving Gran Jefe to ponder his mistake. He cursed under his breath.

Rhino laughed for the first time Gran Jefe could remember. "Use *all* your senses," he said in Spanish.

After securing his rifle, Gran Jefe hurried after the team. The beams from the other squads were more distant now—nothing but faint points of light in the blackness. By the time the Barracudas caught up, they had reached a barrier of dense forest. The footprints of the human rats they were pursuing led into the dense woods.

Rhino gave the signal to advance, moving the squads into the drooping canopy of dense, low trees. Gran Jefe looked from the barbed limbs with tear-shaped leaves to the ground.

The path sloped downward, into a valley. At a clearing between two thick trunks, Rhino pulled out his cutlass and hacked through vines blocking the way. Several swift strokes peeled the foliage back to reveal a deep excavation area with three distinct levels. Each level had entrances to mine tunnels, several of which appeared to be partially collapsed.

Steel bones of heavy equipment jutted up from a field of weeds at the bottom of the dig site. The earth-moving equipment and oil-extraction rigs were in disrepair, along with the outbuildings. A single flatbed trailer was visible through the vegetation.

This was exactly the kind of place where a human population could have survived over the centuries.

Wendig followed the tracks to a tunnel in the dirt wall and pointed it out to Rhino.

Using hand signals, Rhino positioned one squad here at the clearing, then requested a second to join the Barracudas on the dirt path into the site. The warriors jogged down onto the winding trail toward the entrance of the mine tunnel. Thick support timbers had been added over the years.

Fuego was first into the entrance, which was wide enough for the largest mining vehicles.

The pilot flame on the end of Fuego's flamethrower barrel gave a feeble light as the warriors started into the tunnel.

Two gates hung across the corridor. One was bent open. Behind them, the rusted hull of a four-door truck blocked the way. Behind this stood a Jersey wall of concrete road barriers.

Fuego ducked under the bent vehicle gate and started around the truck. Rhino and Wendig followed, then Gran Jefe. The warriors pushed into the darkness, guided by the tactical beams on their weapons.

The tunnel ended at an industrial-size freight elevator shaft without a car. The shaft was wide and tall enough to transport mining equipment.

Fuego stepped up close, angling his helmet down for a look.

Rhino turned to Wendig. "Strap up and ride a cable down," he said in Spanish.

Gran Jefe stepped up to volunteer, but Rhino hesitated, and Wendig shook her head. "You really do have a death wish, don't ya, squiddo?"

It was time to prove he wasn't a kid. Time to become the man Jada would want to marry.

"I won't let you down, Lieutenant," Gran Jefe said in polite Spanish. "I will use my senses."

Rhino nodded.

Wendig grunted and handed Gran Jefe a cable rider from their gear. He took the device and went over to the edge of the shaft. He reached out to the closest cable, gave it a tug, and felt the cold rush of adrenaline in his fingertips when he almost stumbled.

Fuego grabbed him by the shoulder plate to hold him steady while he attached the cable.

"Good luck," Rhino said.

Gran Jefe nodded and started down into the darkness on the ancient cable. The noise echoed as he picked up speed. Luminescent numbers on the wall of the shaft flashed by in the glow of his helmet light: *20... 19... 18...*

He looked from the numbers down to his boots, searching for the bottom. At the tenth-floor mark, he noticed something below.

"*¡Mierda!*" he growled.

He had only seconds to brake as the roof of the freight elevator car rose up to meet his boots. He pulled on the lever, and the cable rider jerked to a stop.

He opened his eyes. The roof of the elevator car was five feet below him. He lowered himself the rest of the way, planting his boots on the roof. It seemed stable enough. The roof hatch was open. He looked inside.

Something was on the floor of the car. It looked like sticks of stovewood. He unclipped from the cable and bent down to check it out.

What he found was an elevator car full of human bones, including skulls. The elevator door was open into a corridor.

He turned on his short-range radio and reported his finding to Rhino, who ordered him to keep going.

Gran Jefe unclipped from the cable and swung down into the car, crushing bones under his boots. He picked one up. It had gnaw marks.

He swung up his assault rifle at the open doorway of floor 9. A trail of bones led into the darkness. Lining the path were suitcases, luggage, and clothing.

He started down the corridor, heart thumping. Over his years as a Cazador *asaltante*, he had seen his share of *cosas horrorosas*, but this macabre scene gave him the creeps.

The tunnel came out at an open pair of sliding doors on tracks. Each was easily fifteen feet in length. He raked his light across the room beyond. Tarps covered a dozen pieces of equipment some twelve feet high and wide, and thirty feet long.

Rifle up, he walked between the bulky tarped-off objects. On the other side were several doorways, and a wide hallway with a high ceiling. He started toward it, then noticed the muddy tracks. Two pairs, both human. They led to one of the doors on his right. Following them, he found a stairwell with the door propped open.

These people had taken the elevator down from the surface, apparently. He went back to the larger passage and followed the footprints. Blocking the way was a door some two feet ajar.

The tracks went inside.

Gran Jefe checked the opening—too narrow to squeeze through. He hated slinging his rifle, but he had to wedge himself against the jamb. He pushed with every fiber of muscle and sinew. Metal shrieked, and he held his breath, waiting for an answer to the noise.

But there was only the distant sound of dripping water. Moving inside the gap, he found himself standing on a bridge overlooking an enormous dark chamber.

He raked his lights up over the concrete walls marked with

safety signs and arrows pointing upward. None of the signs were legible, but someone had engraved biohazard symbols into them.

Gran Jefe stood on the bridge and peered over the mangled rail to the bottom, a hundred feet below. *Or maybe not,* he realized when a ripple moved across the surface. That wasn't the bottom. It was murky, yellowish water, and something in it had just moved.

He crossed the bridge toward an open door. A scratching noise came from the other side, giving Gran Jefe just enough time to duck a poleax that whipped through the air. The wielder then thrust the pike at Gran Jefe's helmet.

As Gran Jefe fell back and brought up his rifle, the light on the end captured the tumorous face of a half-naked man gripping the medieval-looking weapon. Growths hung like clusters of grapes from his forehead, drooping over an eye swollen shut.

The hideous assailant slashed with the axe edge. It skittered off Gran Jefe's chest rig, and he nearly fell backward onto the bridge over the chamber. His attacker lunged, snarling.

Gran Jefe moved to the side, grabbed the shaft of the weapon and a fistful of hair, and hefted the man up into the air. Swinging him over the rail, he let go. A muffled scream echoed, ending in a splash.

Gran Jefe picked up his rifle and aimed it over the railing. Bubbles rose to the surface. These didn't look like air bubbles. This was some sort of a chemical bath.

He doubted that the attacker would resurface, but waited a couple of minutes to be sure. Then he went back to the stairwell and listened.

He heard something in the distance. Coughing, maybe?

With his flashlight dimmed, Gran Jefe crept down the stairs, testing each step.

The coughing grew louder, interspersed with what sounded

like voices. Around the next landing, he saw the flicker of fires at the bottom. Then shadows in the glow—human-looking shadows.

Gran Jefe stared out upon a sprawling room lit here and there by small fires in steel barrels. The flames illuminated an underground city with multiple floors. On each of them, filthy half-naked people moved between tents and shacks. There didn't seem to be enough shelters for everyone. Some people lay under blankets or sat with their backs against walls. He took in the sight so he could report to Rhino.

A central assembly line flanked by large machines dominated the space. One section of the belt was still being used. Six people stood around it, hacking a large hunk of meat splayed out over the wide belt.

Moving closer for a better look, Gran Jefe saw a flipper and the paddle tail of a manatee. The people were butchering the carcass and tossing the pieces into buckets.

The faces and limbs of the butchers were covered in filthy bandages.

The radio in his helmet flickered with a request from Rhino for a sitrep. Gran Jefe squelched the comm line, fearing it would attract attention.

He stayed in the darkness of the stairwell, surveying the underground city from a distance and looking for anything that they might be able to plunder. From the looks of it, these people, if you could call them that, didn't have much. And they all appeared to be sick—not the best for eating.

Having seen enough to make his report, Gran Jefe returned to the stairwell, where he saw a glow. At first, he thought it was his squad mates, but this wasn't the bright white of flashlights; this was something else—something *blue*.

Half a flight above him, a glowing man suddenly emerged. He wore a red flight suit with a logo sporting two anchors. Under his arm, he held a helmet with the same logo and white letters that read *US Coast Guard.*

He raised his hands and spoke in English.

Gran Jefe could make out only snippets, including the word *intruder.*

He charged with his rifle, thrusting the bayonet into the man's chest. But instead of finding the resistance of flesh and bone, Gran Jefe crashed into the wall of the stairwell.

"No English?" the figure said. "*¿Habla español?*"

By now, the shrieks of the tumorous people back in the subterranean city resonated into the stairwell. They had heard him crash into the wall, or perhaps the guard he killed was now missing.

"*Hay que moverse,*" said the man, who looked none the worse for Gran Jefe's bayonet thrust. "You better move. The occupants of this facility don't like strangers."

The glowing person vanished, then emerged a few stairs farther up.

What was this dark magic?

Heart hammering, Gran Jefe ran up the stairs to the top.

"*Mata, ¿qué pasó?*" Rhino asked over the comms.

"*¡Hostiles!*" he huffed back. "*¡Muy hostiles!*"

Gran Jefe raced across the bridge where he had encountered the first enemy, when the strange glowing ghost appeared again.

"There are one hundred and forty-four, if you would like a precise number," he said. "They have lived here for two hundred and thirty years after this location was discovered and retrofitted by a Coast Guard rescue team."

Gran Jefe ran harder, pounding across the bridge to the open doors. Shrieks burst from the top of the stairwell he had just abandoned. He glanced over his shoulder at the flood of damaged humans pouring out the open door.

Gran Jefe shouldered his rifle and fired a burst. In the front of the pack, a woman's head exploded.

"You don't have enough bullets," said the glowing man. "I would run."

Gran Jefe fired again and again, dropping the diseased freaks left and right. But they kept coming, wielding cleavers, javelins, and all sorts of clubs and cudgels.

"*Mata!*" Rhino said. "*Wendig is on her way.*"

"No. Send her back. I'm coming up!"

Lowering his rifle, Gran Jefe ran right through the ghost pilot, or whatever the hell he was supposed to be. With the raving mutants screaming behind him, he took off at a dead run, or the closest he would ever get to one under the weight of his armor.

He ran back through the room with the tarps. One had fallen to the ground, exposing the cockpit of a helicopter.

"I see you found one of my Jayhawks," the ghost called out. "If you would be so kind as to cover that back up, I plan on flying her again someday."

"Who the hell's *that*?" Wendig shouted in Spanish. She was in the center of the room, her rifle trained on Gran Jefe, or so it seemed. The glowing man was right behind him.

"*¡Vámonos!*" Gran Jefe yelled. "We have to get out of here!"

The throng of crazed humans piled into the room behind them as he grabbed Wendig by a shoulder pad, pushing her toward the exit. They raced back to the elevator shaft and climbed up through the roof of the car.

It took him two attempts to clip the cable rider to his belt. Wendig fired down into the car, where two of the cretinous humans pawed up at them. He reached out.

"Grab me! We're going up!"

She jumped onto him without hesitation, and he clipped her belt to his and activated the rider. They jerked upward, climbing as the creatures stormed, shrieking and howling, into the elevator below.

"I got you, kid," Gran Jefe said. "Don't worry."

*   *   *   *   *

"Interesting story," Kade said. "But that was no ghost. That man was an AI, like Timothy Pepper, and my guess is, he can fly those Jayhawks."

Gran Jefe shrugged.

Kade and Imulah had an ancient, stained map of Texas rolled out on the table at the capitol tower. They had moved Gran Jefe here from the engineering rig hours ago, after the test.

Gran Jefe was still reeling from the ruse that King Kade had designed with General Forge to test his loyalty. But he understood. It had to be done.

Deep down, past the anger, he was just happy to be alive.

Not everyone seemed to trust him fully just yet, though.

Dakota and Zuni watched Gran Jefe from the corners of the room. Slayer and Blackburn had shot him plenty of glances too, as had Pedro, Woody, and Beau. Lieutenant Wynn was also here, looking uneasy. Then there was General Forge, who didn't like that Kade had spared Gran Jefe. But he would prove himself again, just as he had on that mission to Texas.

Perhaps someday, he would be *General* Mata.

"It must be some sort of old mining facility," Imulah said. "From my first observations, it's not marked on any of our maps."

"Keep searching," Kade said. He looked up to Gran Jefe. "Do you remember how many of those helicopters were down there?" he asked.

"Two," Gran Jefe said. He had told the story the best he could remember it, embellishing only a few parts.

"Imulah, look up anything we can find on these Jayhawks in the archives," Kade said. "And see if you can find any better maps of Texas."

"Yes, sir."

"Did you see a way to get them out of this facility?" Forge asked.

"*Sí, es posible,*" Gran Jefe said. "If you have truck. Tunnels *muy grandes*, elevator *más grande.*"

"Under the noses of those hideous creatures? Didn't you say there were hundreds?" Slayer asked.

Gran Jefe nodded. "*Pero sin fusiles*—no guns."

"Why run, then? Why not kill them all?" Kade asked.

"Disease," Gran Jefe said.

Kade had a hard time understanding until Forge cut in.

"The risk of bringing disease back is not worth whatever is inside that facility," the general explained. "It still isn't."

"I agree," Kade said. "But maybe there is a way to sneak them out without any exposure."

Forge looked dubious but said nothing. Gran Jefe had a feeling it didn't matter. The king wanted the sky horses.

"I get them out," Gran Jefe volunteered. "I go with Slayer and Blackburn."

Kade thought on it, then nodded. Gran Jefe wondered if this had been part of his plan all along. Test the big Cazador's loyalty and then assign him to a dangerous mission if he passed. The new king was a smooth operator. Calculating, much as X had been.

"Perhaps, if this mission is a success, we can use the sky ship to search for King X and Magnolia if they are still missing," Imulah said. "Sending a search party by air is much faster than by sea."

Pedro exchanged a glance with Kade, but Kade shook his head. Gran Jefe wasn't sure what that was all about, but he wondered if Kade was planning on sending out a search party.

Gran Jefe hoped X and Mags were still alive. It was a perilous journey, especially in such a small boat. But that wasn't his concern. He had his own mission to focus on, and a son to make proud someday.

"Say we can get the Jayhawks out but this AI can't fly," Forge said. "Then what?"

Kade looked at Woody and Beau, who loitered in a corner, talking quietly.

"I might have a way to get at least one of them out," Kade said.

Gran Jefe didn't like the idea of going out there with one of those weak men. From what he could tell, they had sat on their asses ever since they were rescued from the machine camp. But General Forge would likely be pleased if sky people went on this mission. He wanted them to have more skin in the game, especially with the Cazador army shrinking by the day.

"Woody, get over here," Kade said.

The former pilot of the airship *Victory* walked over.

"What's up?" Woody said.

"How would you feel about flying again?" Kade asked.

Woody bit the inside of his lip.

"Flying what, exactly?" he asked.

Kade explained the location of the Jayhawks and the dangerous situation surrounding them.

"It won't be easy, but I believe those two aircraft could help secure the future of our home," he said. "For the Hell Divers, for the military, and for rescue missions."

"Let me get this straight," Woody said to Kade. He nodded at Gran Jefe. "You want me to go out with this guy and his friends, to a place where hundreds of sick feral humans have built a nest. You want us to sneak in, pull out two helicopters—which I've never flown, mind you—and then find a way to get them back to the islands. That about it?"

"Yes," Kade said.

Woody stroked the end of his mustache, then chuckled. "Tell ya what, if this big lug and his friends can get the choppers out of there, I'll find a way to fly one, and I'll train someone else to fly the other," he said. "Least I can do for everything I've been given."

Kade glanced to Forge, who gave a grudging nod of approval.

"It's settled, then," Kade said. "We'll send a boat with an APC and trailers. Zuni, this is the land you came from, yes?"

The guard nodded. "I was a child when I left with my people in the back of a Cazador boat, but I remember the terrain."

"I'd like you to accompany Slayer, Blackburn, Gran Jefe, and Woody on this mission."

"Yes, sir," Zuni said with a salute.

Gran Jefe had a feeling Tia wasn't going to be happy about that. But Zuni knew as well as Gran Jefe that *mission* always came before *relationship*. For without missions, there was nothing.

"Get ready," Kade said. "You'll leave as soon as possible."

SIXTEEN

"She's down there, sir," Dakota said.

Kade stood at the top of the Sky Arena, looking down on the field where countless Cazador warriors and slaves had met a grisly end. He had agreed to let General Forge slay Charmer in this very place. Soon, Forge would gut him in front of a screaming crowd. And Kade would watch with satisfaction. He wasn't a violent man, but some people deserved to die.

He shook away thoughts of vengeance and started down the stairs.

In the moonlit arena, a single figure stood in the sand. The trim profile and dreadlocked hair could only be Tia's. She stood looking at the two rattan baskets and tanks of helium and other supplies that Kade had delivered here to surprise her.

There were a hundred unpleasant things Kade had to do, and telling Tia about Operation Jayhawk was at the top of the list. He hoped that putting her in charge of relaunching Hell Diver training would make up for his taking Zuni away—something she would no doubt see as a personal attack on their relationship.

He made his way down to the recessed floor of the arena.

"Tia."

She turned as he strode across the sand.

"Hey," she said. "You actually listened to my idea, Kade. I'm impressed. Thank you."

"It's stage one of getting Hell Divers back into the sky." He took a moment to look over the neatly stacked tanks. "I'm actually here to tell you about stage two of that objective," he said.

"Did X and Mags find the airship?"

"I'm afraid we still haven't been able to reach X or Mags," Kade said. He gave a little sigh. "Everything I'm about to tell you is confidential, Tia."

"Okay."

"I'm serious. No one can know."

"Okay, swear on my dad, I won't tell anyone."

Kade remembered his promise to look after Tia when Raph died. He had done his best over the years.

"I'm launching a mission to search for aircraft, based on recent intel," Kade said.

"A new airship?"

"No, two helicopters that can be used to transport Hell Divers."

"That's pretty cool."

"There's something else. The birds are located in the same area where Zuni was born and kidnapped by Cazadores. I need him there."

Tia stared at him and said nothing at first. There was no way she could have known, though. Zuni had been on duty since Kade ordered the launch of the mission.

"I know you're going to say no, but please, Kade, let me go with," she said.

"Out of the question," he said. "I'm telling you because I want you to understand why Zuni has to go."

She clenched her jaw.

"He'll be okay," Kade said. "This is what he's trained to do."

"You're sending Zuni away because you don't want me to be with him. Just admit it, Kade. He lived there as a kid—probably won't even remember."

"He's the best scout we have left, and his skills should be used for something better than watching over my wrinkly old biscuit."

She let out a huff. "You still think I'm just a kid who can't make decisions for herself? You think you have to protect me, but you don't, Kade. Alton's a kid; he needs to be watched after to stay out of trouble. I can take care of myself."

"You're a woman now, and I'm proud of the woman you've become." Kade reached out to her, but she pulled away.

"You're not my dad, no matter how hard you try," Tia said.

She walked away and crouched down to one of the baskets.

Kade didn't follow. Better just to leave her alone for now. True, she wasn't his daughter, but he knew her the way any parent would know their child. And right now she needed space.

He left the Sky Arena with Dakota, heading back up to where Beau and Woody waited. He had a backpack slung over his shoulder with the gear he was taking on the mission to Texas.

"How'd she take it?" Beau asked.

"Not great," Kade said. He glanced at Woody and his pack. "You ready?"

"Ready as I'm gonna be," he said with a smile.

They boarded a runabout with Dakota for the next stop of the night—the oil rig that the Cazadores had long ago transformed into an enclosed dry dock for their ships and boats.

When the boat coasted up to the dock, Captain Tiger was waiting with a proud smile on his face.

"Welcome, King Kade," he said, waving eagerly. "Please follow me. The mechanics are almost finished."

Five militia guards escorted the young captain along with Kade, Woody, Beau, and Dakota to a platform overlooking the interior of the enclosed boathouse. Several boats were up on hoists.

"Which one's my ride?" Woody asked.

"Look down," Tiger said. "On the water."

There, moored against the interior dock, floated the former research yacht that el Pulpo had transformed into a transport vessel.

Five mechanics and three engineers were wrapping up their welding and electrical work on the transport craft. Normally, a hundred men and women would be swarming all over the yacht, but only these eight had been authorized. Like the five militia soldiers with Wynn, all were sworn to secrecy.

Kade had decided to keep the mission a secret from all but a select group of trusted confidants. Tonight, Operation Jayhawk would launch. Cazador mechanics were finishing last-minute improvements. One man carefully painted *Angry 'Cuda* in red letters.

The former research yacht was two hundred feet from stern to bow. The front end had two levels of cabins, and aft of these was 150 feet of unobstructed deck—room enough for two Jayhawk helicopters. The Cazadores were preparing to transfer an APC by crane from the rig's cargo-loading deck to the *Angry 'Cuda*. Two flatbed trailers would then be craned over, each to be towed by the APC to extract the helicopters at the target site in Texas.

Armor plating covered much of the hull, including the command center, which had retractable metal shutters on the windows. Bullet dents from past battles marred the metal here and there.

An engineer was at the top of the bridge, working on the long-range radio-signal booster that would keep the boat in contact with the islands. It was identical to the booster that X and Magnolia had aboard the *Sea Wolf*.

Kade tried not to think about them either, but it was hard not to while Pedro worked full-time trying to reach them.

"You have planned for that," he'd said. "Trust the plan."

"This way," Tiger said. He took a ladder to the lower decks. At the midlevel, a bridge took them to the deck of the *Angry 'Cuda*.

Forge spoke to Slayer in the bow while Blackburn, Zuni, and Gran Jefe stowed crates that were coming in by the crane load. They came to attention as Kade entered.

"Almost loaded," Forge said. "Just waiting on the APC and the trailers."

The crane set down another net of boxes, and the operator swung the boom back over to the deck on the rig.

"You sure you're good with this?" Kade asked Woody.

His old friend smiled again. "I spent the past year in the sun, enjoying this paradise and afraid to do anything that might get me killed," he said. "It's time for me to do somethin', and if this is what we need to survive into the future, I'm set to go, mate."

Kade reached out and shook Woody's hand. "Be careful out there, and come home."

"You got it, King Kade," he said.

They embraced.

Beau also hugged his friend and patted his back.

"I'll be fine," Woody said. "This can't be any worse than the machine camp."

Kade hoped his friend was right.

He addressed the Barracudas. "Listen up. I stand before you today wishing I could be standing *among* you. For this mission you're about to embark on, in my view, is one of the most important in the history of this place."

Kade understood that not everyone believed in his vision, but he was convinced this was the only way to save the islands.

"We bring back sky horses," Gran Jefe said, slapping his chest armor.

"The Barracudas won't let you down, sir," Slayer said.

Blackburn gave a stern nod. Zuni saluted respectfully, no sign of anger or discontent in his gaze. He was a soldier and had grown up following orders.

As they returned to their tasks, Kade walked with Beau and Dakota back over the gangway with General Forge.

"Wait," Gran Jefe said.

The big man walked over. He reached into the magazine carrier over his chest armor and pulled out a small box.

"*Por favor*, King Kade," he said. "I need ... help."

He handed the box over, and Kade opened it to see the fat diamond set in a gold ring.

"You give to my boy if I no come home," Gran Jefe said.

"Your boy? I didn't know you had a son," Kade replied.

"Yes, the secret is out." He grinned. "Maybe someday he can be proud of me."

Kade took the box. "I'll hold on to it until you return."

"*Gracias*, King Kade."

Tiger motioned to the king. "Sir, I have something to show you."

He followed Tiger across the platform to a section of the rig that was closed off by a hatch. The captain unlocked it and turned on a light. In this enclosed chamber, six of el Pulpo's former war boats were raised on chain hoists, in various stages of repair.

"Our mechanics will continue the work tomorrow," Tiger said. "For now, this is everything we've been able to salvage."

"And the boat I asked for?" Kade asked.

Tiger pointed across the enclosed boathouse, to a long craft with four gleaming outboard motors. "The deck will be lifted and a hidden compartment added inside."

"Good," Kade said.

"Is this the boat you're sending the knight home in?"

Kade shook his head. "I have other plans for this boat."

"Okay, sir, I'll have it complete as soon as possible."

"Thank you, Captain."

Tiger closed the hatch, and Kade walked back to a raised mezzanine with Beau and Dakota to watch the *Angry 'Cuda*'s final preparations. Forge had returned to the deck to double-check the boat. When he finished, he joined Kade at the top to watch the launch.

"Everything is good, King Kade," he said. "Ready on your mark."

"Proceed with the launch," Kade said.

Forge gave the orders with a whistle.

The engines fired up, rumbling, smoke drifting away from the stern as the repurposed research vessel slowly motored forward.

In the bridge, Slayer piloted the vessel toward the massive doors at water level, which were now parting.

They were using the cover of darkness to leave the marina, but the chug of the motors would no doubt attract attention on this rig and others.

Woody stood in the bow, raising a hand up to Kade and Beau.

"Good luck!" Beau shouted down.

Kade simply raised a hand to his friend, hoping this would not be the last time.

"Let's hope this works," Kade said.

"If anyone can pull this mission off, it's the Barracudas," Forge said. "They are the best we have left, but they could use some luck."

*   *   *   *   *

"Water reserves are ninety-eight percent and holding," Timothy said. "The leaks have been fixed and the pipes are stable."

Michael stood in the command center of the airship, going over the data with the AI Timothy's holographic form. Almost two days had passed since they escaped from Mount Mitchell with their precious cargo of water. They were now twenty thousand feet above the North Atlantic Ocean.

The airship's hull juddered and shook in heavy weather. Michael looked up at the bridge's white overhead. Victor was at a station a few feet away, watching the radar. He had taken an interest in how the ship was piloted. But some of that, Michael guessed, was boredom. There wasn't much else to do right now but worry about the storms.

Michael tried not to think about losing Steve, but the downtime brought up all the grief he had yet to face.

Almost a week after Steve's death, it was time to honor his sacrifice now that the ship was stable and water reserves in place. Michael finished going over the recent reports before making the announcement.

"I'm going to check on Layla and see if she's ready for the ceremony," he said.

"Okay," Victor said.

"Very well, sir," Timothy said.

Michael got up and walked to his living quarters. Not wanting to disturb Layla or Bray if they were resting, he pressed his ear to the hatch.

"*Grrrrrrr,*" Bray said on the other side.

Smiling, Michael twisted the latch and went inside. Layla was on the bed with their son in her lap, reading a book with a lion on its cover.

"Daddy," Bray said, reaching up.

Michael bent down and scooped the boy up one armed.

"How's it going?" Layla asked.

"Everything's good at the moment," Michael said. "We're two

days out from the Canary Islands, as long as we don't hit more bad weather."

Layla looked hesitant, as if she wanted to say something, but she simply nodded. She had dark circles under her eyes, but aside from fatigue and being shaken up from the dive, she was fine.

Standing up, she turned to a page with the image of an owl.

"Bray, what's an owl say?" she asked.

"*Ooooo, ooooo,*" Bray said, mimicking the sound that Layla and Michael had taught him.

She flipped to the next page. "How about a dog?"

"*Woof, woof.*"

Layla and Michael both chuckled, which set the boy to laughing. These were the moments that drove Michael to keep fighting through the loss, hardship, and pain. For their son's future.

They could experience this joy thanks to the sacrifices others had made—people like Steve.

"You ready to give Steve a send-off?" Michael asked.

"Almost," Layla said. "I just need to change Bray."

"Okay, I'll be right back."

Michael left the room and went to the open hatch down the hall, where Steve had slept. There wasn't much, since he had been wearing almost everything he brought on the ship during their captivity. But there was one thing—a bandanna.

Picking it up, Michael tucked it into his pocket and closed the hatch. He went to the closest comm speaker and tapped the button.

"Timothy, Victor, we're heading to the launch bay for the ceremony," he said.

Michael went back to his quarters and waited for Layla. In a few minutes, she opened the hatch with Bray in her arms. She wore officer's dress whites that matched Michael's. The uniforms had been kept in storage.

Bray had on red pants with a white T-shirt that Layla had packed with her when she came to rescue Michael.

"Ready?" she asked.

"Yeah," Michael said.

Bray reached out, and Michael took his son in his arm. Side by side with his wife, Michael walked down the corridor. They passed under the recently painted images that passengers had drawn to celebrate the end of Captain Leon Jordan's tyrannical rule.

A green pasture with grazing livestock. The churning rapids of a roaring river and waterfall. Brick row houses on a street of colorful trees in autumn.

These were the pictures that reminded them of what once had been, and gave them hope for what might still be.

"Car," Bray said, pointing to a painting of a street busy with vehicles.

"Yes, car," Layla said. "What's that?"

She pointed to a mural of blue sky with fluffy white clouds and a bright-yellow sun.

"Ska … ska," Bray tried to say.

"Sky," Layla said.

He gave her a toothy grin. He had cut another molar over the past few days, which had made him a bit grumpier than normal. Today, though, he seemed happy.

The launch bay was just ahead, and Victor waited outside the hatches. Timothy flickered to life, wearing a white suit. He straightened his bow tie.

Victor wore clean, loose-fitting yellow coveralls that he seemed to like. He had shaved his square jaw and buzzed off his dark curls.

He pushed open the door to the launch bay, and Michael carried Bray inside the shadowy room. The hoses that had sucked up the water were still here, stacked in neat coils.

Michael walked toward the row of lockers that Hell Divers had used over the years. Over the past two and a half centuries, hundreds of men and women had stored their gear and good-luck charms here. Bray pointed at the different faded stickers of Hell Diver teams.

Raptor. Phoenix. Angel. Wolf. Wrangler.

"Nay-y-y-y," Bray said, reaching toward the picture of a horse with a mounted cowboy. He reared his small head back and yelled, "*Ha-wooooo!*" after pointing at the wolf.

The boy was really getting his animal sounds down.

Michael stopped in front of the locker that Steve had used, and handed Bray off to Layla. Victor and Timothy stepped up.

"Tonight, we honor Steve Schwarzer," Michael said. "Steve was a great man. One of the best I've known. He would have given the shirt off his back to someone in need. In the end, he gave something even dearer—his life."

Michael reached into his pocket and pulled out the bandanna. Steve had used it often to wipe the sweat from his brow—a casual act that spoke to his hard work in everything he did.

"Steve was a bladesmith," Michael said. "He made weapons of war but was a man of peace and justice. He was good with his hands and could fix pretty much anything, from a toy boat to this airship.

"We honor Steve tonight," Michael went on, "and remember his perennial smile and his positive attitude. He was always eager to help."

Michael sniffled, then exhaled.

"Thank you, Steve. I'll never forget you." He opened the locker and placed the bandanna inside.

"Wait," Victor said.

Michael turned as the warrior limped over, grimacing in pain.

"I didn't know Steve like you," Victor said. "But I think he would want you to keep that. For good luck."

"Victor's right," Layla said.

The airship rumbled and shook from a lightning strike. The thunder came a second later.

Bray whimpered.

"It's okay," Layla said.

"Everything good?" Michael asked Timothy.

The AI blinked in and out a few times, then solidified. "Yes. Actually, the strike hit very close to the panels that Steve helped you repair."

"From beyond the grave," Layla whispered. "See, he's saying he wants you to keep the bandanna for good luck."

Michael slipped the faded cloth into his pocket. He would take all the luck he could get.

SEVENTEEN

"X, get up!" Magnolia yelled over the boat's PA system. The message crackled right next to X's ear in his bunk. He shot up, smacking his head on the bulkhead.

"Son of a damn…"

Miles barked, wagging his tail as X swung his legs over the edge and put his feet on the cold deck.

"X!" Magnolia yelled again.

He pushed the button on the speaker. "What?" he grumbled. "What is it now?"

"We're almost to Guanabara Bay!"

X grabbed his wrist computer off the pile of clothes on the deck. It was almost noon. He had slept way too long—and not for the first time since they escaped Grenada. Getting the boat off the beach had consumed the rest of his energy, and he had fallen sick during the efforts. Now he was fighting off a viral sinus infection on top of all the normal aches and pains.

"I'm awake," he said into the comm. "I'll be up there shortly."

The smell of fish drifted out of the kitchen. After dressing in his suit and armor, X went there to find Jo-Jo resting under a blanket on the deck, two fish skeletons picked nearly clean in her hands. She had slept for much of the journey, and her bandaged wounds were healing nicely. Some of that had to do with the fact that her body was meant to survive, maybe not in the mouth of a leviathan, but pretty much anywhere else. Like Miles, Jo-Jo could withstand higher levels of radiation than a normal animal. Or human.

"How you feeling, girl?" X asked the monkey.

She glanced up with tired saucer eyes, bloodshot and swollen around the edges. X bent down to give her a gentle rub on her head.

Miles wanted one too and nudged up next to X.

"Don't get jealous, boy," he said, rubbing the dog.

Feeling achy, X went over to the small kitchen and mixed Cazador vitamin powder into a bottle of water. He shook it up and took a long swig, then blew his nose into a rag. Both he and Magnolia had been exposed to their fair share of not just radiation but also chemical toxins, in Australia and on this journey as well.

"X, let's go!" Mags said over the comm system again.

"I'm coming," he said. Not that he wasn't excited. He was thrilled to finally be arriving at the Old World port, but he had a feeling in his gut that it wasn't going to be easy to find Michael and the airship. Tin wasn't stupid and wouldn't have the ship hovering in plain sight after what happened.

X went to the aft hatch with Miles following. Jo-Jo shook off her blanket and also got up. He wouldn't waste his breath telling the animals to sit still, instead opening the hatch to let them onto the afterdeck.

Wind gusted against X, hitting him with light rain. He went to a bucket of fish they had caught, and tossed another to Jo-Jo. She caught it in one paw and bit it in half. X climbed the ladder to the command center, where Magnolia was at the helm.

"You see anything yet?" he asked.

She pointed with her chin at the viewports. Lightning cleaved the horizon, but there was still no sign of land.

"The map shows we're about a mile from the port," Magnolia said.

X alternated between the viewports onto the afterdeck, checking on Miles and Jo-Jo. The animals seemed content, but it wasn't exactly safe down there, even with razor wire wrapped around the rail.

Especially with it wrapped around the rail, X thought. In rough seas, the monkey and dog could get snarled in it. Fortunately, the ocean was about as calm as it ever got.

"Stop worrying," Magnolia said. "They need some fresh air."

"You call this fresh?" X asked.

He joined her at the helm as they entered the mouth of Guanabara Bay. X checked the sonar for any enemy craft, or worrisome sea creatures that might be lurking in the dark waters. The leviathan was still fresh in his mind.

"Seems like I was just here," Magnolia said. "I even remember where I beached the boat last time."

She was on a mission with General Santiago, Lieutenant Alejo, and other Cazador warriors who, only months before that trip, had been her captors and mortal enemies. X had remained back at the islands under the protection of Rhino, only to fall into the trap of a Cazador ambush that cost Rhino his life.

And now they had returned here because of another ambush—this time by the very people Michael had saved.

X reached up to his throbbing head as his achy body shivered from a momentary chill. He was pretty sure he had spiked a fever. There was no denying he wasn't at his best. But he didn't have time to be sick. Michael and his family were out there somewhere, and he was going to find them.

X scanned the horizon for his first look at the ruined city and forested peaks beyond as Magnolia guided them into the bay. He saw a chain of lightning flashes over the port, and masts and bowsprits of small craft sticking out of the water.

The catamaran carved through the chop of the bay, toward a thin mist drifting over the surface. A storm lingered over the peaks on the horizon. In the afterglow, mutant jungles grew up through the remains of the city, as X had seen so many other times in the tropics.

He searched the sky for an airship.

"You see anything?" he asked.

"No," Magnolia said.

X waited another minute before turning to the hatch. "I'm taking Miles and Jo-Jo inside," he said. "I'll be right back."

"Okay, I got this."

X left the command center and went to the afterdeck. Miles greeted him at the bottom of the ladder. Jo-Jo was at the rail, staring out over the mist-covered bay.

"Come on," X said. The animals followed him into the main cabin, where he motioned for them to sit. Based on her condition, X didn't know if Jo-Jo was in any shape to make the trek to the bunker that Pedro and his people once called home. But if he left her here, she would find a way to break out and escape.

Maybe you should let her go…

X had considered releasing the monkey into the wild. She had the instincts to survive. But what kind of life would that be, with neither her own kind nor any humans to love her?

No, for now he was going to take care of her the best he could. That meant bringing her with him to the bunker.

X popped open the crate of extra hazard gear and got out Miles's suit and mask. He helped the dog into his gear, then went over to check Jo-Jo's bandages. A few needed changing—no easy feat when the animal didn't like to be treated. Facing a mutant beast in the wastes or fighting Gran Jefe was no problem, but putting on a new bandage seemed to scare the creature beyond reason.

"It's okay," X said. He crouched in front of the creature. She was gentle at heart, and he could see why Ada had loved her so much. The animal had saved his life, and he owed it to her to make sure she was okay.

Gently he unraveled a bandage over her right calf. She whimpered and reached down to the wound. The bark-like scab had cracked in half. X dabbed away the pus and applied antiseptic ointment.

"It's okay," he said. "I'm not going to hurt you. This will help you."

She seemed to understand and looked away as he wrapped the new bandage around her leg. Then he went to work on the next one. A message blared on the comms just as he was putting the first-aid supplies back into the crate.

"X, better get up here," Magnolia said. *"I see something."*

He motioned for Miles and Jo-Jo to stay, then hurried back outside. The fog had lifted, and he could see the rubble-strewn shore from the port side. He climbed the ladder, heart pounding in anticipation as he opened the hatch.

"What?" he asked.

"There's something up there," Magnolia said.

"The airship?"

"Up *there*," Magnolia said, pointing toward a granite bluff. "The statue of the Old World god."

X brought up his binos, following her pointing finger to what appeared to be flames. In the glow, he saw the ancient statue with one outstretched arm, the other missing.

"Are those flames?" Magnolia asked.

"Yes," X said.

"Maybe from lightning or something?"

X kept the binos on the statue. The fires seemed to be surrounding it.

"I don't think so," he said.

"Then what?"

"I think someone lit it," X said. "I just hope it was Tin."

*　　*　　*　　*　　*

Not even a full day at sea, and Gran Jefe was more than ready to see land again. He had grown up on ships and boats and spent many of his younger years on them, training to be a raider. But this vessel was a far cry from one of the massive warships el Pulpo had deployed to the wastes in search of treasure and slaves.

This boat was a research yacht that the Cazadores had discovered a century ago. Forge had selected it for its long open deck, which would accommodate both Jayhawk helicopters.

Gran Jefe sat in the cargo bay eating canned fish and thinking of the past. But he wasn't thinking about glory days. He was thinking about Jada and what could have been. If he was correct, the night he had fathered Pablo was the same night they had split for good.

It had to be, because that was their first night together in the almost six months since Jada gave Gran Jefe the boot for fooling around. It wasn't unusual for Cazadores to have several wives—hell, Blackburn had three. But that was an arrangement, and not every woman was okay with it.

If only he could go back and make things right. He would have given up all the women, booze, and treasure to be with Jada and Pablo. To be a family. Something Gran Jefe never had and didn't know anything about.

He shoveled the rest of the fish into his mouth, ran his finger around the inside of the jar, and licked it. Across the cargo hold, Blackburn was playing a hand of cards with Zuni and Woody. They spoke quietly together in English, talking about their lives. He was still learning the language, and it was hard to understand when he couldn't see their lips move.

"We tried to fight back against the machines once," Woody said.

Blackburn glanced up from his two cards. "You *fought* them?"

"Not me." There was guilt in his voice. "Kade did. He lost his whole family in the crash—all three boys and his wife. That changed him. After that, he didn't care about dying."

Gran Jefe thought about those words. In a different way, he could relate. Knowing that he had a son had changed his entire perspective. He loved the boy and didn't even know him.

Oddly, knowing that he was a father made Gran Jefe fear death for the first time—partly because if he died, he would never know his son. Staying alive was something Gran Jefe had never really worried about, until now. But it was the only way to keep his son safe.

This mission was immensely important. The cowboy king was right—to have any hope of surviving, they needed aircraft.

Gran Jefe also believed what both el Pulpo and King Xavier had believed: that they needed outside resources to keep the islands running. With their outposts all wiped out, they could use aircraft with Hell Divers to help them restock.

"Want in?" Blackburn asked.

"Nah," Gran Jefe said. He got up and told them he was going to check in with Slayer. Really, he just wanted out of the cramped compartments, even if it meant getting wet.

He went to the stairs and opened the hatch that led astern. To his surprise, there was no rain. Still, he pulled his hoodie up to protect his face from the wind. The APC was there, with a dozer blade mounted to the front. Two flatbed trailers with new tires flanked the armored vehicle.

Gran Jefe remembered the feeling of anticipation the first time he was on a ship with other men and women, ready to embark on an adventure into the wastes. All the new recruits were hot to claim their treasure and take their first monster kills.

Or die trying.

Gran Jefe had many memories of glory, and before he met Pablo, those were the best memories in his life. Now there was something that dwarfed even the bone beast kills.

He had made something good in this world.

Maybe, if he was lucky, he would someday have a conversation with his boy. Until that day, his job was to protect him. From afar or near, it didn't matter.

Gran Jefe took the ladder up to the bridge. Slayer was slouched in a chair, watching a monitor.

"¿Qué pasa?" he asked.

"Nada, nada."

Gran Jefe switched to English. "I come to see how far."

"From Texas?"

"Yes."

"Another day, maybe a bit longer. We've made good time. Weather's been decent."

Gran Jefe stepped up to the two viewports. The yacht's lights speared through the darkness off the starboard bow, hitting the waves that seemed to roll forever.

"Want me to take watch?" he asked.

"Nah, I'll cover the rest of my shift," Slayer said. "Go get some sleep. We're all gonna need it when we get there."

Gran Jefe grunted. He was sick of trying to sleep. On this craft in sloppy seas, it was impossible.

"Jorge," Slayer said.

Gran Jefe walked to the hatch, then turned.

"This place we're going," Slayer said. "You think it's possible we can get past those mutated humans or whatever they are?"

"Yes."

"What makes you so sure?"

"'Cause we must."

Slayer scratched the stubble on his chin. The answer seemed to satisfy him.

Gran Jefe left the bridge and climbed back down to the deck, returning to the stern. Not wanting to go right to sleep, he moved out among the tarp-covered boxes on the other side of the APC. He stood looking out over the ocean, again thinking of what awaited him.

A grunting came over the whistling wind.

Gran Jefe didn't think much of it, but it came again. He turned to his left. One of the tarps was moving.

What in the name of the Octopus Lords was this?

He reached for his rifle, but he had left it below. Not wanting to make any noise by calling out for help, he walked quietly over to a mounted speargun and pried it free. Then he approached the rustling tarp, preparing to skewer whatever beast had found its way up onto the deck and into their supplies. Seeing a boot under the tarp, he drew back the spear and peeled the canvas away to reveal a prone human...

It was a Hell Diver.

"Wait!" the woman yelped.

He stepped back, brandishing the spear. It was Tia.

Gran Jefe couldn't help but chuckle. He turned to the command center and yelled, "*¡Teniente!*"

When he turned back to Tia, she was struggling to get up.

"Here, take hand," Gran Jefe said.

"So you can throw me over?" she snapped.

"Ha! Zuni kill me twice for that." Gran Jefe laughed again, but Tia didn't seem amused.

"What's going on down there?" Slayer shouted. He stood on an upper deck, shining a flashlight down.

Gran Jefe didn't know how to answer in English.

"We have company," he called back up in Spanish. "Zuni's girlfriend!"

The hatch to the lower decks opened, and Blackburn and Woody hurried out. Zuni stumbled out wearing only a pair of pants and shoes.

"Crikey, Tia! What you doing here?" Woody asked. "Kade's gonna be bloody pissed!"

Zuni nudged his way through the others. "Tia," he said. "You shouldn't be here. I told you—"

"I'm sick of being told what to do," she said. "I'm capable. I can help."

Gran Jefe couldn't help being reminded of Jada. She had the same passionate can-do attitude. He had no doubt Tia was a strong young woman—after all, she had survived Brisbane. But where they were going, they would face something even worse than mutant beasts.

"God damn it," Slayer grumbled. "Get her inside. I'll figure out what to do with her later."

EIGHTEEN

Kade finished going over a briefing in his office with Imulah at the capitol tower and tucked the papers away. Beau was nearby, cleaning his newly issued pistol. Staying busy seemed to help him keep his mind off his grief, but at odd moments Kade would find him staring into space. It would be a long, painful road ahead for the man, who had done everything he could to keep his sons alive.

A knock came on the door, and Kade looked up from the desk as General Forge stepped inside, carrying his red-plumed helmet under his arm.

"Sir, Dr. Huff has informed me that our prisoner is up and walking around," he said. "The boat to take him to the Coral Castle is ready to deploy on your orders, along with the tracking device."

"Excellent news," Kade replied. He stood and rubbed the bony upper part of his nose. "And what about the greenhorn divers?" he asked. "Have we tracked them all down?"

"All of them except for one. Tia is unaccounted for."

Kade was not surprised. She had been mad as hell at being left behind on Operation Jayhawk. He thought back to their conversation in the Sky Arena. At the time, he had considered having

Imulah follow Tia but decided that would just make her angrier. Now he wished he had.

"Imulah, get your people to track her down," Kade said.

The scribe stood and shuffled his papers.

"I already did, sir," Forge said.

"And?" Kade asked.

"Before you met with her in the Sky Arena, she was last seen at the trading post. After that, no one's seen her."

Kade's eyes narrowed.

"Imulah, find out what she bought or bartered there," he said.

"Yes, Your Majesty," Imulah said.

The scribe hurried out of the office, moving faster than he had in days.

Forge cleared his throat. "Sir, I have to ask, when will I face Charmer in the Sky Arena?"

Beau looked over at Kade.

"Tomorrow night," Kade said.

"Excellent. I'll make the arrangements."

"First, I want you to bring Gaz to the rooftop," Kade said. "I want to show him something before we send him back to the Coral Castle."

Forge nodded, then left Kade inside the office with just Beau. He took a deep breath, trying to remain calm about Tia.

"Don't worry, I'll bet she's fine," Beau said. "Probably doesn't want to be found."

"Yeah, I was thinking the same thing, but I can't help wondering if something happened to her."

"No need to chuck a wobbly, there, Kade. You're doing too good a job to entertain negative thoughts."

"Thanks, mate, but it doesn't feel that way."

"Just look at all you've done in a week. The school's reopened. People have food. There's been relative peace since Donovan…

You've launched missions, including one to Panama to watch for the knights, and one to Texas to bring back the helicopters."

He clapped Kade on the back. Those were just the things Beau knew about.

"Let's go see Lucky," Kade said. He grabbed a backpack, and they left the office. Dakota waited in the hall, a spear in one hand, shield slung over his light armor.

"To the rooftop," Kade said.

Dakota led the way. "You're really going to let this knight see the sun?" he said quietly.

"Yes, and I'm going to show him what he showed me back at the Coral Castle," Kade said. "I'm going to show him how we live. That we aren't monsters."

"Speaking of monsters, Charmer's gonna get his tomorrow?"

"Unless he can somehow best General Forge in combat," Kade said.

"I almost feel bad for Carl. Almost." Dakota shook his head.

They walked up an interior stairwell, and Dakota opened the door, letting in the bright sun.

Forge was already topside with two Cazador soldiers, Lieutenant Wynn, and their prisoner, Lucky. He wore a blue jumpsuit and had his hands cuffed in front of him.

"Release him," Kade said.

Lucky turned, squinting in the sunlight that he had seen only once before in all his life.

A guard unlocked the cuffs.

"Amazing to see you standing," Kade said.

Lucky raised a hand to shield his eyes from the sun. When they lit on Kade, a grin cracked his face.

"Leave us," Kade said to the guards.

They stepped away to give the two men space.

"I have you to thank," Lucky said. "I honestly didn't think I'd walk again."

"Want to go for a stroll?" Kade asked.

Lucky smiled wider and gazed out over the rooftop, still shielding his eyes from the dazzling sun as he took in the view. The crops, the forest, and the guns. Kade wanted him to see those as well, to see what would await his people if they came here.

They set off toward the forest in the midafternoon heat.

"This place is paradise hidden in the wastes," Kade said. "Many men and women have died fighting for it. It has made a few go insane, including my old captain, Rolo."

"I can see why," Lucky said.

Kade stopped at a tree and picked a ripe orange. He used his knife to cut into the rind. Peeling off the skin, he handed it to Lucky.

"Go ahead," he said.

Lucky bit gingerly into the fruit, as if unsure just what it was. His eyes lit up at the taste.

"Not bad, eh?" Kade asked.

Dakota followed at a distance, watching Lucky's every move. So far, it was just two men having a conversation.

The knight wasn't a fool, though. He had to know that Kade was up to something. And Kade also understood that they weren't friends.

Kade's people had struck first, unknowingly poking a hornets' nest. The knights had every right to respond, but Kade had a plan to mitigate any future conflict.

He stopped at the edge of the forest, overlooking the distant rigs.

"There's enough for both our peoples," he said. "We can be allies; we can set up a trading partnership. Your seaweed and seafood for our fruit and vegetables."

"So that's what this is all about? You want to be mates now?" Lucky wiped the juice off his mustache.

"Allies," Kade said. "You saved my life, and I've saved yours. But that doesn't matter. What matters is the lives of all the people out there, on my side and yours."

"Sounds nice." Lucky eyed the soldiers trailing them. "But we both know there isn't enough for both our peoples. Not after the radiation from that nuke destroyed our food supply."

Kade recalled the irradiated crabs at the Coral Castle market.

"We have seeds that we can give you," he said. "I saw the underground labs; I'm sure you can find a way to get them to grow."

Lucky faced Kade. "I'll take these ideas to the Forerunner, and I'll do my best to convince him you are a peaceful man."

"What's he got planned?" Kade couldn't hold in the question. "If it's war, we're ready. You see that."

"I already told you, I don't know."

The trace of anger in his voice surprised Kade.

The knight looked over his shoulder as if worried about eavesdroppers. He lowered his voice.

"You don't know what the Forerunner is capable of," Lucky said. "I don't know what is planned, but if it's war, I highly recommend surrendering at once."

"That will never happen," Kade said. "These people are fighters. You know this."

"Yes, I do."

"Then you know it's not possible."

"Then they will die, along with many of my people."

Kade searched the man's eyes. "I believe that you and I can help change that. Promise me you will try."

Lucky nodded. "You have my word, mate."

They shook hands.

Kade turned back to signal for Dakota and Beau, and Lucky reached out and grabbed his arm.

"Wait," he said.

"Yeah?" Kade waited for more.

Lucky's mouth moved, but he said nothing. He kept his grip on Kade's arm for another second, holding his gaze. In his eyes, Kade saw something he hadn't seen in the knight before: raw fear.

"What?" Kade asked. "What is it?"

Beau and Dakota hurried over to see what was going on. Lucky finally let go of Kade.

"It's nothing," Lucky said with a shake of his head.

"You're sure?" Kade asked.

Lucky nodded.

Kade looked back to Beau. "Return our friend to his quarters."

"He no *amigo*, King Kade," Dakota said. "He taste *la naranja*. That will change a man."

Beau guided the knight back into the building while Kade stood and stared out at the horizon. Lucky definitely wanted to say something, but what? What the bloody hell was he hiding?

"King Kade," said a voice.

Imulah walked at a brisk pace, grimacing from his still-healing belly wound. He had news, and Kade braced for something bad.

"Sir, I have information on Tia," Imulah said. He stopped and raised his clipboard. "I was able to track down her purchases at the trading post."

He turned to a new page.

"She bought a heavy-duty coat, a pound of dried fish, and some dates," Imulah read. "Also, two Old World books and a flashlight."

Beau returned as the scribe talked.

"It's Tia," Kade explained. "Imulah has some info on what she bought at the trading post. Read it again, Imulah."

Imulah traced with his finger from the top of the page.

"What the hell would she need that shit for?" Beau asked. "It's like she was planning on being bored and cold."

"Fishing trawler?" Kade asked.

"But why?"

"Imulah, do you have a full roster of boats and ships that have embarked since Tia was last seen?"

The scribe opened to another page, but before he could start reading it, Kade reached out. "Here, let me see."

He scanned the entries: militia patrol boats, a Jet Ski squad, fishing trawlers, and . . .

"Holy shit," he said.

According to Imulah's note, someone had discovered a motorized raft afloat in the ocean, out of gas.

The scene played out in his mind. When the *Angry 'Cuda* set off as discreetly as possible from the enclosed marina, Tia had stolen the raft and pulled parallel to the yacht, matching its speed. It would then be an easy lob with a grappling iron on a rope with knots, to the rail on the bottom deck. Then, hauling on the knotted rope, fit, agile Tia would have walked her feet up the yacht's hull and vanished aboard with no one the wiser. Meanwhile, the raft would have kept going, eventually exhausting its fuel supply, while she stowed away on the *Angry 'Cuda*.

If that was even possible. Chances were, she had landed in the ocean and drowned, or was now drifting out to sea.

"God damn it," Kade grumbled. He pulled out his radio. "Pedro, do you copy?"

"Copy, King Kade," came the reply.

"I need you to contact the *Angry 'Cuda*," he said. "Ask them to search the vessel for Tia."

"Copy that," Pedro said.

Kade held the radio and turned toward the horizon. His heart rate ticked up when his handheld showed a message.

"Sir, I'm getting interference right now," Pedro said.

"Keep trying," Kade said.

"Yes, sir."

Kade closed his eyes. He had screwed up telling Tia about the mission. Maybe he should have just held Zuni back. But none of that mattered now. What was done was done, and he could only hope she had somehow made it onto that vessel and that the Barracudas would protect her in the wastes.

"There's something else," Imulah said.

Kade tensed for more trouble.

"Charmer told the guards he's ready to confess to his crimes—with conditions," the scribe said.

Kade scratched his five-o'clock shadow, trying to suss out whatever trickery Charmer had up his sleeve now. But no matter, if he wanted to confess, Kade wouldn't say no.

"Thank you, Imulah," he said.

"Should we change the plans for combat at the Sky Arena?" Imulah asked.

Beau looked to Kade, clearly wanting to speak his mind.

"No," Kade said. "Charmer can confess all he wants. His time for redemption has come and gone."

*   *   *   *   *

Michael was up before dawn in his jumpsuit and Hell Diver armor. They would arrive at the Canary Islands in two hours, and he wanted to be ready. Not that he could have slept anyway.

The airship had traveled through a storm during the night, rattling in some of the worst turbulence Michael had experienced in years. Thanks to Timothy, they had made it through the brunt of it unscathed.

"Well done, Pepper," Michael said.

"Thank you, sir," replied the AI. He joined Michael in front of the digital map showing their location over the Atlantic Ocean. The green dot representing the airship inched toward their destination.

The bridge hatch creaked open, and Victor clomped down the stairs to the first level, grinning.

"Good morning," Michael said.

"Yes, yes, it is!" Victor said. "I never thought I would see home again."

Michael had sat down with him several times on the journey to go over exactly where home had been. The city of boats was located in the bay of the destroyed port of Arrecife.

According to Victor, the bay had drained after a tsunami formed a wall blocking off most of it during the war. The hulls of the broken-down, stranded ships, like the one Victor was born in, had become home to survivors there.

"We had defenses on those walls," Victor said, "but the pirates had better weapons. Not many of us made it out when they broke through."

Michael was banking on those pirates being long gone. If they were like the Cazadores, they raided a location and moved on, rarely settling anywhere. But he had to worry about hostiles having taken root there.

"Timothy, the first thing we do is a life scan for any animal bigger than a dog," Michael commanded. "I also want to do some flyovers to make sure there aren't any moving ships down there. Map a course."

"Working on it, Commander."

Victor went up to the digital map that Michael was studying.

"Let's again go over the location you fled to with Ton and the other refugees after the attack," Michael said. "Maybe you'll remember something else."

"Jameos del Agua," Victor said. "Here."

He pointed at the former resort on Lanzarote, one of the islands making up the chain. They had already gone over the blueprints that the archives had on the former Center of Art, Culture, and Tourism, created by a man named César Manrique. According to that data, the volcanic tunnel and caverns had been home to a resort with an underground concert hall and salt lake.

"I don't remember exactly how to get there in the tunnels, so I will need to explore," Victor said.

"Okay, no worries. We'll do it together," Michael said.

The hatch to the bridge opened again. Michael turned to find Layla walking down, dressed in a black suit with Bray in her arms.

"Daddy," Bray said. Layla carried him down the bridge. He reached out and pointed to Victor. "Uncle Vic."

Victor smiled from ear to ear. He was becoming a big part of the boy's life, and Michael was delighted to see it. Bray needed more than just his parents and his AI friend, Pepper.

"Good morning, little fella," Timothy said.

"Hiiii," Bray said, waving.

"Are we close?" Layla asked.

"Yes, very," Timothy replied. "We're thirty-two minutes from la Gomera. I plan to do a full sweep of the islands forming the archipelago before we head to Lanzarote."

Layla sat while Bray ran around, pointing and laughing at the different banks of monitors and equipment.

"Are you all ready?" Timothy asked. "If so, I will start our descent."

Michael exchanged a glance with his wife, both of them eager.

There were bound to be dangers ahead, but they had escaped

the evil tendrils of Charmer, had managed to fix the airship and fill the water tanks, and had a fresh start ahead of them.

Michael checked with Victor.

"Let's go," he said.

"Okay," Michael said. "Take us down."

"Preparing for descent," Timothy said.

Michael helped Layla buckle Bray in. They gave him a cup of dried peas to munch on to keep him distracted. He stuffed a handful into his mouth, crunching them between his little square teeth.

The airship groaned as it descended from twenty thousand feet and entered the storm clouds. They hit a pocket of turbulence almost immediately. The hull rattled. Bray stopped crunching his peas and looked over to Layla, who gave him a reassuring nod.

"It's okay, sweetie," she said.

"You're fine," Michael added. "Everything's going to be okay."

Bray whimpered as the shaking intensified. Lightning blasted the exterior panels on the port side, and even Layla flinched.

"Pepper, report," Michael said.

Timothy flickered twice before responding. "Shields holding steady, sir. Scans revealing no evidence of radiation. This does appear to be a green zone."

Michael nodded at the good news. He would take it.

Layla reached over and put a hand on Bray as he began to babble-cry. He looked at her and then Michael in turn for assurance.

"It's okay, bud," Michael said.

"We go see my home," Victor said. "The place I was born."

Bray tilted his head slightly, then stuffed another fistful of dried peas into his mouth. The airship rumbled down to ten thousand feet, and by eight thousand, the ship seemed to be through the worst of it.

"Looking good, definitely a green zone," Timothy said. "Preparing to lift viewport shields."

The metal shutters rose away from the glass viewports at the helm, revealing the dark and swirling storm. Clouds drifted lazily past as the airship angled downward.

At two thousand feet, the view lightened. A scrim of cloud parted, and the ocean filled the green-hued field of the night-vision optics. The first island emerged on the horizon: el Hierro.

Timothy worked to relay images onto a digital screen, showing an unremarkable hunk of land in the ocean. It was hard to make out anything down there, but Michael didn't see anything to indicate the presence of animal life new or old. No towns. No buildings. Not even ruins.

"The sea must have taken it back," Michael said.

"Tsunamis," Layla said.

"Initiating life scans," said Timothy.

The sensors on the airship's belly activated, and a digital monitor relayed the results. So far, nothing on land.

No sign of boats or ships on the water either.

All Michael could see were the waves crashing against the shore. But if he could see down there, it was possible someone on the surface could see them. He wanted to tell Timothy to be careful, but the AI always knew exactly what he was doing.

They flew between la Palma and la Gomera next, where they finally saw some sign of past human habitation. Brick and stone debris clung to bluffs and hillsides.

From what he could see, nothing had been repaired.

The search continued to the largest island in the chain, Tenerife. The ship passed over Mount Teide's dead forest, whose valleys, ravines, and streams had, according to the archives, been home to a variety of native wildlife.

"Closing in on Santa Cruz de Tenerife," Timothy said.

"Or what's left of it," Layla said.

An image of a city obliterated by nature spread across the screen. The coast was gone, and with it the buildings that had once towered over the port where ships from around the world came with tourists and trade.

Death—it's all death, Michael thought to himself.

On the one hand, he was glad they wouldn't have to deal with pirates or potentially hostile locals. On the other, it was hard to visualize how his family could survive in such a dark, desolate place.

He looked over to Bray, still munching on his peas and oblivious to all else. Layla gave Michael a smile, sensing his concern.

"It's gonna be okay," she said.

"Life scans negative," Timothy said. "Proceeding to Gran Canaria and Fuerteventura."

Those two islands showed the same results of destroyed civilization.

Finally, they carved northeast toward Lanzarote.

The final island's western shore came online. And with it, more images of destruction. Timothy flew along the coast, heading south and wrapping around the base of the island to come up on the port city of Arrecife.

From the sky, they could see the wall of rock and rubble that had formed the barrier around the port. Victor unbuckled his harness and got out of his seat for a view. He walked over to study the remains of boats in the dry harbor.

"There," he said, pointing to one. "That is where Ton and I come from."

He stared for a long moment.

"Welcome home, my friend," Michael said.

Victor turned with a cautious smile.

"Life scans are negative," Timothy reported.

The smile on Victor's face faded. Perhaps he had held on to the hope that some of his people were still here.

"Shall I continue to the location of the bunker?" Timothy said.

"Yes," Michael said.

The airship pulled away from the port, heading north to the eastern tip of the island. Clouds drifted by, blocking the view out the ports. The dark sky had turned a bruised purple.

Michael thought nothing of it until Layla said, "What's that?"

"Stand by," Timothy said.

The ship drifted through the eastern sky, toward the edge of the island. Beyond the island, the next landmass was the western coast of Morocco, over fifty miles away.

As they flew east, a fiery glow cut through the purplish cloud bank.

"I'm detecting a break in the weather patterns," Timothy announced.

"A break . . ." Michael started to say before his jaw dropped at a sight he had never expected.

Dazzling golden sun broke through the cloud cover on the horizon, spreading over an enormous patch of ocean.

"Sun!" Bray said, pointing.

"Yes, sweetheart," Layla replied.

"I never see this before," Victor said with surprise. "Never the sun here."

Michael didn't know what to say at first. It was almost too hard to believe that this was real. But his eyes weren't being deceived. The sun shone through a growing gap in the storms, lighting up the clear blue ocean below.

"Maybe it's a random event," Michael said.

The ship slowed as they approached the island's northwest tip.

"Life scans are all coming back negative," Timothy said. "Should I start the descent?"

"No, hold here for a moment," Michael said.

The airship halted above the surf, with a view of both shore and ocean. For a moment, it seemed the opening in the storm was widening, the rays reaching out.

Michael kept watching this miracle.

But like most miracles in the wastes, it didn't last.

Just as quickly as the rays had emerged, they began to dim. The storm clouds closed from all directions, choking out the sunlight until darkness swallowed the horizon.

Michael looked over at Layla, their son, and then Victor.

"What are you thinking, Tin?" Layla asked.

"At first, I was thinking we might not need to live in a bunker," Michael said. "That we could plant our seeds down there, assuming the soil is fertile."

"I don't think this is random, sir," Timothy said. "I think the sun may shine here often."

"Only one way to find out: by diving down, exploring, and doing tests," Layla said.

"I'll get ready," Michael said.

"No." Victor stood up and tapped his chest. "I go this time. I dive so humanity survives."

NINETEEN

A light rain fell over Rio, though the fire at the base of the Old World deity's statue continued to burn.

"I don't like this," Magnolia said.

She moved over to the broken-out windows of an apartment in the largest building still standing—a thirty-story high-rise ten blocks from the marina where they had moored the *Sea Wolf*.

X played his binos over the statue.

"It just looks like a fire to me," he grumbled.

"Just one? Why one, and why there of all places?" Magnolia asked. "That makes no sense."

"I don't know, Mags. Lightning maybe, or some sort of underground gas pipe…"

"After all this time?"

"Who the hell knows? I don't see anyone up there, and I really doubt Michael would light it. It could be a trap, like when the Cazadores used a lighthouse to help them catch Sirens for the stewpot."

"Has it occurred to you that someone *lit* it?"

"Yes, but like I said, I don't see anyone."

"Maybe we should split up," Magnolia said. "One of us goes to check out the fire up there, while the other goes to the bunker."

"Hell no," X said.

He coughed, his lungs crackling. Magnolia didn't like the sound of that. He wasn't well. Maybe they shouldn't be going out at all right now. Maybe they should have stayed on the catamaran.

Jo-Jo wasn't in the best shape to be out here either. The monkey hung back in the apartment with Miles.

"We proceed to the bunker," X said. "*Together.*"

He unslung his rifle, coughed, and went back into the living room. He gave his thigh a slap, and Jo-Jo limped after him, her legs freshly dressed with new bandages. X had spent a lot of time making sure she wasn't in pain. But it seemed he was taking his own health for granted.

If anyone could understand, it was Magnolia. Not long ago, they had arrived at Panama, where she hoped to find Rodger. She was a mess back then, physically and mentally. The raw pain of finding his ashes still ate at her heart. But she took comfort in the prospect of finding Michael and Layla here.

Magnolia stood at the window a moment, staring, hoping this wasn't a mistake. All she could do was follow X and try to keep them safe. She hurried after them, moving into the stairwell.

Halfway down the long stairwell, X broke into a violent coughing fit. The rattle in his lungs was louder this time.

"Maybe you should rest a bit," Magnolia suggested.

"I'll rest when I'm finally dead."

Magnolia wanted to tell him he wasn't immortal, but to what avail? He was every bit as bullheaded as she.

She held in a sigh and followed him all the way to the lobby. Destroyed furniture littered the decomposing parquet floor. A few bones were scattered in the debris. This building was one of the better preserved, but the mutant jungle had reclaimed most of the city.

Two feet of standing water filled the broken floor in front of what were once large sliding glass doors to a terrace outside. Some broken stone planters were still there, their contents long since washed away by storms.

X slogged out into the water and stopped just inside. "Okay, which way now?"

Magnolia had the map Pedro had given them in a waterproof case. Already turned around, she double-checked the building location and then the street. It didn't help that the road signs were rusted to nothing. And it wasn't easy following Pedro's markings. He had gone over it with her several times before they left, but it was different when you were actually in the wild.

"Mags," X said.

"Hold on," she said.

Jo-Jo suddenly growled as she knuckle-walked outside. Miles joined her.

X went on guard, raising his rifle in the direction the monkey was keying on—their right. Magnolia checked the map one last time, then pointed that way. "We got eight more blocks to go in that direction, assuming we don't run into any major obstacles."

Moving down the sloping city blocks, it was hard to see what lay ahead. She worried about landslides, sinkholes, and collapses that had occurred since Pedro and his people were rescued from the city years ago.

"Stay alert," X said. "Eyes up."

Magnolia looked up to the mounds of rubble lining the street. Vines clung to the cracked exterior of a fallen building. Beautiful, deadly flower petals the size of his chest armor hung from open windows.

She noticed a ten-foot-tall carnivorous plant growing in a

park across the street, the bulbous head closed. This wasn't the first she had seen over the years, and she knew to stay well out of striking distance. The thing was big enough to swallow Miles whole. It could also twitch off an arm or a leg, poisoning you in the process. And like a snake, this plant would then go to work ingesting the rest of its prey without waiting for it to die.

Ahead, X hugged the scree of exfoliated concrete that had slid over the sidewalk and into the road. Miles kept up with X while Jo-Jo stuck close to Magnolia. She liked having the beast close to her, especially out in the open.

The center of the street had burst open, and a tree with a snaking trunk thicker than Gran Jefe had risen through it toward the stormy sky. Branches laden with some sort of bright-yellow fruit drooped from twisted limbs.

X passed right under them, then swept up around the rusted-out shell of an armored personnel carrier, turned on its side. Just ahead of it were two trucks, corroded down to their frames.

Magnolia followed X around the vehicles. He crouched behind the second truck to look out over the next intersection. Jo-Jo stared with her wide eyes at a four-story building at the end of the block. A tree grew out of its right side. Its branches drooped over the street, blocking the view.

The monkey bared its canines. Miles also seemed agitated.

"Mags, see if you can get a better look at that structure," X said. "Over there. I'll cover you."

He pointed toward a mound of debris that offered a decent view of the block to their right. She turned toward it, paused when X said, "Be careful, Mags."

Nodding, she dashed across the street, searching for the best way up the rubble of the collapsed structure. Several cracked concrete slabs remained intact, so she used those to get her two-thirds of the way up.

She was high enough to look around. Crouching behind a pile of bricks, she brought up her rifle scope. Switching to infrared, she zoomed in on the building that had Jo-Jo and Miles so spooked.

Sure enough, a dozen signatures showed through a window on the fourth floor—the wiry, muscular shapes of Sirens, packed together in a single room. Youngsters moved among them.

It was a den, and there were probably more.

Magnolia pulled out the map again, using the vantage point to look for an alternate route. In all directions, she saw the same unremarkable piles of what were once restaurants, bars, hotels, banks, and grocery stores.

For a fleeting moment, she pictured what this place had looked like. Full of vibrant colors, the sun blazing down on pedestrians carrying bags of groceries or merchandise. People talking on phones, sitting on benches. Cars and trucks motoring down the street on a sunny day.

All of that vanished when she noticed something three blocks to the north. Tendrils of smoke curled into the air. She zoomed her scope in on a flicker of flame and quickly lost sight.

She caught a glimpse of the smoke again. It was definitely moving. Panning the scope eastward, she searched for the fire burning around the statue. It was still there, winking like a star in the sky.

Turning back to the north, she located the smoke again. The cloud seemed to be wafting down another block. She glanced at her map and saw that they could avoid the strange cloud and make to the bunker by a route two streets up.

She picked her way back down the loose scree.

"Well?" X asked.

"Siren nest in that building," she said. "I saw smoke a few blocks north."

"Smoke? Maybe there are firewalkers here, like…" He reached

out to Magnolia. "I'm sorry," he said. "Didn't mean to remind you of Rodger."

"It's fine. Let's get moving before those Sirens detect us."

She took point. Miles and Jo-Jo followed her, with X on rear guard. Keeping to the edge of the road, Magnolia used what cover she could find. Mostly rotted vehicles, but then something that looked like a food stand from the trading post on the *Hive*. She ducked behind a plastic sign depicting fish tacos.

Rising up, she looked over the rusted grill that had once cooked street food.

The next street was blocked by a collapsed railroad bridge. Cars lay strewn across the road, along with part of the rail. She found a raised section and crouch-walked underneath, scraping her helmet along the underside. As if in answer, an ethereal Siren wail floated on the air behind them.

She turned to X. He was looking the way they had come.

"Go," he said.

Magnolia kept going to the other side and ducked out from under the collapsed bridge. She stood and saw, a few blocks away, a Siren taking to the air, flapping up and up.

Crouching, she motioned for Miles. The dog trotted under the broken bridge, with X following, then Jo-Jo. By the time they were all safely under the elevated concrete slab, two more Sirens had gotten airborne.

Magnolia and X raised their weapons, but the beasts were flying away from them. As more tendrils of smoke rose up from the streets, Magnolia could see what they were searching for.

One of the Sirens dived, right into a jet of flames that shot up from the ground.

"What the..." Magnolia whispered.

"Come on," X said.

"Wait..."

"No. Move. *Now.*" X got up and started down the road. "Which way?" he asked.

"Left, I think," Magnolia said.

Around the next corner, half the road had been swallowed by a sinkhole on the right side. They went left, advancing down another rubble-strewn road. A bus, cut in half, blocked their view.

Keeping low, X led the way. He abruptly motioned for Magnolia and the animals to take cover. Two jets of fire shot into the sky from an adjacent road. Four Sirens flapped away from the flames, heading right overhead.

"Burn 'em all!" came a muffled shout.

"Tin," X said. He started to raise his voice, but Magnolia grabbed him.

"Wait," she said.

The voice was human, but it didn't sound like Michael or Steve or Victor. This was a deeper voice. Odd, almost machinelike.

Keeping down, they moved over to the bus and took shelter inside the rusted shell. The Sirens screeched their electronic discords, circling over three city blocks.

A burning shape suddenly came hurtling down from the sky and crashed on the ruined roadway. The smoldering body of a Siren lay not twenty feet from the bus. Miles whined, and Jo-Jo growled.

"We need to get out of here," Magnolia said.

X remained standing, staring through a broken window until she shook him by his shoulder plate.

"X, come on," she said.

Jo-Jo grunted in a low, scared voice and hunkered down. Miles backed away too, tail down, still whining.

Magnolia and X both crouched, watching the smoke tendril out behind the dead Siren, into the intersection. A thick curtain of the smoke moved out into the street.

X had his rifle aimed in that direction, using the window as support.

"Something's moving out there," he whispered.

Magnolia brought up her scope and switched to infrared. Inside the dark cloud, a single heat signature flickered to life. It was probably too big to be a human.

"You got to be kiddin'," X whispered.

Lifting her head from the scope, Magnolia pulled down her night-vision optics. In the green-hued field of view, she saw the exposed skull of a bone beast emerge from the smoke. Next came the eyeless, bloodied face of a Siren. Then another mutilated skull of a Siren. All of them leering down from pikes held aloft.

Carrying that pole was a massive man in a hooded red robe. It was the biggest man she had ever seen—even bigger than the late General Rhino.

A breathing mask covered most of his face, the cords snaking into a long gray beard that hung over his chest.

Two more people followed the giant, each of them wearing red robes with some sort of symbol in the center. These people had red helmets with two round filters mounted on the sides, and spiked crowns.

She zoomed in on the logo—a pentagram with the image of a goat's head in the middle. Five small markings she couldn't make out surrounded the head.

Both men carried flamethrowers, while their leader and two others carried pikes with the mounted heads.

"Who are these freaks?" Magnolia whispered.

"No idea, but I don't want to find out," X said. "I'll lead them away with Miles. You go to the bunker with Jo-Jo."

"But, X, you said not to split—"

"Don't argue, Mags. We're trapped in this bus."

There was no time to protest even if she wanted to. The

five men continued to advance and would be within visual range any second.

"Find Tin and his family," X said. "I'll take care of these weirdos."

*   *   *   *   *

Gran Jefe stood at the helm of the *Angry 'Cuda*. On the digital map, they were nearing the mouth of the Sabine River, where it dumped into the Gulf of Mexico. On the Louisiana side of the river, to the right, was the Sabine Pass Lighthouse.

He tapped the intercom to indicate that they were nearing their destination.

Within the next few minutes, Zuni, Slayer, Blackburn, Beau, and Tia all climbed up into the command center.

"Have a seat," Slayer said, motioning toward the table.

Gran Jefe remained at the wheel, watching the waves in the masthead light, as the others sat around the table behind him.

"To start, Tia, you're staying with the boat," Slayer said.

"What!" she protested.

"Tia, now's not the time," Woody said.

"I came to help. I'm not going to sit out. I've been on missions before."

"No like this one," Gran Jefe chimed in.

"A bunch of human freaks don't scare me," Tia said. "They can't be any worse than monsters."

"There are hundreds of them and five of us," Slayer said.

"Six, and that's exactly the reason I should be coming."

"They are diseased, Tia," Woody said. "You don't want to be anywhere near them."

Zuni had yet to say a word, but Gran Jefe could tell that the praetorian guard wanted to speak up. From what Gran Jefe had seen, he cared deeply for Tia. They had remained separate belowdecks for the last leg of the trip, but there were a few times when Slayer and Blackburn were topside that the two sweethearts found time to talk quietly.

"I've been to Brisbane, which is far worse than where we're going," Tia said. "Right, Jorge?"

Gran Jefe looked over his shoulder and saw Slayer glaring at him. That told him the commander didn't want his commentary. Certainly not his opinions. All it took was that glare. He was a by-the-book kind of soldier.

"We've already got one greenhorn on this mission with Woody," Slayer said. "My job is to protect him, and I don't need to be looking out for you too."

"You don't have to protect me," Tia said.

"Sir, I will watch out for her," Zuni said.

"That's exactly what I'm worried about," Slayer replied. "I need you focused on the mission, not on your girlfriend."

"Girlfriend?" Tia asked.

Gran Jefe chuckled, drawing another glare from Slayer.

"Commander, all due respect," Woody said.

"Oh, now you've got an opinion too?" Slayer asked.

"I was just gonna say—"

"Your job is not to say. Your job is to fly the choppers when I get them out, got it?"

Woody nodded.

"And you," Slayer said to Tia. "You were never authorized to come on this mission. In fact, King Kade is not happy that you're here. I finally got a message through to him, and—"

"He's not my dad, and you're not my boss," Tia said. "I'm a Hell Diver."

"A cocky girl is what you are," Slayer said.

"So I've been told."

"Did you have orders to come here?"

She raised her chin.

"You broke the Hell Divers' code by your irresponsible actions." He grunted. "You certainly aren't one of us. Way I see it, that makes you a civilian, and if you keep mouthing off, you'll be a civilian sitting in the brig on short rations."

"You can't lock me up."

"Watch me. Cocky gets people killed out here, and I'll handcuff you before I let that happen." Shaking his head, Slayer said, "Since I can't lock you in this ship and trust that you'll stay, I'm going to lock you in the APC and bring you with us."

Tia held his gaze for a long moment.

"You will follow my orders out there, or you'll spend the mission in handcuffs," he said. "Do you understand?"

"Yeah, I got you."

"I want to hear an 'Aye, aye, sir'!"

"Aye, aye, sir," she murmured, all the cockiness gone.

"All done?" Gran Jefe asked. "We almost there."

Slayer looked out at the distant outline of land. "Lights out," he ordered. "If we can see the shore, those mutants can see us."

Gran Jefe switched off the exterior lights and piloted the boat in darkness. He would have to make do with the blue glow from the constant lightning strikes. As they drew closer to the surf line, his gaze jumped back and forth between the choppy surface and the depth gauge.

Brilliant flashes of lightning illuminated the southeastern corner of the former state of Texas. They motored around it, leaving the Gulf of Mexico and entering the Sabine Pass. On the eastern shore of the river stood the missile-shaped lighthouse that el Pulpo had activated ten years ago. It was dormant now, the light long since dead.

Gran Jefe thought of Pablo. What would the boy think of such a sight? Maybe someday he would be able to share this story.

For now, he had to focus on surviving, which meant getting the boat safely to shore in the darkness. Behind him, the others had finished suiting up.

Slayer and Blackburn checked Woody's suit. The sky pilot was clearly nervous as they cinched light armor down over his suit: chest rig, elbow pads, wrist and shin guards. Stuff to protect him in a fall, but nothing that would do much against a monster.

"Relax," Slayer said.

"You think I'm nervous or something?" Woody said with a grin. "What gave it away?"

"The fact you've taken four shits," Blackburn said.

Slayer finished tightening Woody's chest rig down and gave him a pat on the chest.

"You're good to go," he said. "Blackburn, his weapon."

Blackburn handed Slayer a shotgun.

"You just point and shoot, but make sure you got a good grip on the front stock, like this. Otherwise, it'll jump," Slayer said as he held the weapon.

"Got it," Woody said. He reached out and grabbed it by the barrel.

"Careful, man, damn," Slayer said.

"Sorry." Woody turned the shotgun upside down. "Where's the clip?"

Slayer stared for a beat, probably waiting for the joke.

"First of all, it's called a magazine," Slayer said. "Second, it takes shells."

"Christ," Tia said. "You sure you want to give him that? At least I know which end to shoot from."

Slayer bent down to fish a bandolier of shotgun shells out of an ammo crate, then started thumbing in the shells.

"After you fire one, you pump in the next," he explained.

"This weapon holds six. Once those are gone, you got to load more, just like this."

"Yeah, understood—load like that, add more when I'm done, and don't blow your biscuits off," Woody said.

"Just point it away from us, okay?"

"Bloody hell, man, do you think I'm an idiot?"

"Where we're going, I'm not taking any chances," said Slayer. He handed Woody the loaded weapon, hitting him in the chest. "Don't fuck around out there."

Gran Jefe pushed the boat through a patch of knobbly purple weeds growing out of the water. The depth meter chirped a warning, and he trimmed up the motors slightly.

He eased off the gas as they swung into the wide inlet, entering a channel that opened into a large marina. Two oil rigs, mangled by forces he couldn't begin to imagine, still stood in the water where they had been built before the war.

"That looks like the rigs we live on," Tia said.

In the center of the harbor, a moss-covered bulk three times the size of their boat protruded above the surface. A lightning bolt showed it to be the hull of a sunken ship.

Gran Jefe pulled to starboard and looked out the left viewport at the hull of the ancient vessel.

"Over there," Blackburn said, pointing to an old boat ramp.

Gran Jefe brought the boat about, then put the throttle in reverse and backed toward the concrete ramp.

Blackburn and Slayer both left the cabin and went astern to fire up the APC.

"Zuni, watch," Gran Jefe said.

The young soldier went to the back viewports to guide them in.

Gran Jefe eased up on the throttle, slowing the boat's approach.

"Okay, good... good... stop," Zuni said.

With a flip of a switch, Gran Jefe turned off the engine, stopping the propellers. He left the wheel and went to the back windows. Slayer and Blackburn had unchained the APC and were hooking it to one of the trailers.

Gran Jefe scanned the terrain beyond the marina for any sign of the mutant humans. Clanking came from the stern as Slayer climbed back into the APC and started down the metal loading ramp, into the water with the first trailer.

Blackburn led the way up the shore, guiding him with his hands up the concrete boat ramp. As soon as Slayer had the trailer up the ramp, Blackburn unhooked it. Slayer backed the APC into the water and up the loading ramp to the stern.

They repeated the process with the second trailer.

Gran Jefe had returned to the helm to start the boat's engines and pull away when he heard shouting.

"What's that?" Tia asked.

Zuni grabbed his rifle as Gran Jefe turned back to the window. Down on the ramp, Blackburn scrambled away from a huge gray beast that flopped down a muddy embankment to the left of the ramp.

Gran Jefe knew this animal.

The manatee had to be nine hundred pounds. But despite the size, it could move.

The animal waddled toward them, roaring as Blackburn fell to his bum on the ramp in front of the APC and trailers. Slayer hopped out and ran to help Blackburn. The creature galumphed toward them, letting out a roar.

"What is that thing?" Woody shouted.

Zuni opened the hatch and went outside with his rifle.

"Go! Go help," Tia said.

It took Gran Jefe a beat to realize that she was talking to him.

Woody too was urging him to go with Zuni. For the moment, all Gran Jefe could do was chuckle.

"Why are you laughing?" Tia asked.

"Monster no eat meat."

"You sure about that?" Woody asked.

"*Sí, sí.* The beast eats … *¿Cómo se dice?* … weeds and grass and shit."

Tia headed outside with Zuni, but Gran Jefe blocked her way.

"Stay," he said. Then he went outside and put his hand on Zuni's rifle before he could fire a shot.

"No shoot," he said.

Slayer and Blackburn retreated down the ramp to the water. The manatee followed them, slapping the ground. Blackburn fell again, this time into the water.

The beast charged, slamming into Slayer and knocking him to the ground. That wiped the grin off Gran Jefe's face. He pulled out his hatchet, raising it in the air and shouting. The creature roared and snapped the air as both Blackburn and Slayer backed into the water.

Slayer had his rifle out now, apparently more worried about being eaten than alerting the locals with a gunshot.

"No shoot," Gran Jefe said again. "I got it."

He hopped off the boat into the water. Then he waded over to the two men. He grabbed Blackburn by the shoulder pads and moved him out of the way. Slayer backed up, rifle still shouldered.

The monster rose up on the bottom of the boat ramp, towering above Gran Jefe. A memory of his last visit here popped into his head. That was years ago, when he was a very different man.

He had feared this animal. But that was all it was, just a dumb beast.

Now there was only one thing he feared: not seeing his son again.

The creature roared louder.

"Kill it," Slayer ordered.

Gran Jefe considered hacking at the beast with his axe but decided against it. He sheathed the weapon over his shoulder.

"What are you doing, Mata?" Slayer practically yelled.

The manatee slapped the bottom of the ramp in front of Gran Jefe, lowering its face and roaring. Clearly an attempt to tell the Cazadores it was the king of these wastes.

"Not anymore," Gran Jefe grunted.

He strode forward and threw an uppercut, connecting right under the jaw. The creature let out a yelp that ended in a grunt. Then it slumped onto the concrete ramp.

Gran Jefe turned back to the other Barracudas. All three had their weapons aimed at the creature.

"No worry," Gran Jefe said. "*Es herbívoro*. No eat us."

TWENTY

City blocks of buildings loomed above X and Miles. They were over two miles away from Magnolia and Jo-Jo now, trying to lead the human hunters away from the location of the bunker.

Miles stopped with X as he tried to catch his breath, his lungs burning from the strenuous exercise. He took a minute to scan ahead too, just to be sure they weren't being flanked by more of these robed men.

The gray high-rises in this section of the city had survived the tsunamis by being out of reach. Some of the reinforced concrete exteriors had peeled away, exposing the steel beneath.

X looked over his shoulder at the smoke billowing away from the city blocks. Even through their filters, they could pick up the scent of burning flesh from the roasted Sirens. The three hunters who had torched them were at least a mile away by now. That was a good thing, because his cough was getting worse and his muscles and joints were aching. He decided to head inside a ruined storefront to look for something to ease his ailments. It wasn't just a cough now but also a headache and chills.

This wasn't the best place to try to rest, though. There could be more hostiles out there. And they probably had transportation as well. A boat. Vehicles. Even an airship...

X scanned the flashing clouds for any sign of an airship. It was a long shot but not impossible for another ship to exist. Captain Ash had always told him it was just the *Hive* and *Ares*, before *Ares* went down, but maybe she was wrong. Certainly, there were feral humans out there, like the ones Kade and other dive teams described.

But the people X had just seen were not feral, and there was a reason they were here, of all places.

X kept walking through a former playground, past broken seesaws and swings with missing seats in the waist-high weeds. The red blades were harmless here, but plenty of other mutant bushes and vines posed a lethal threat.

Moving fast but cautiously, X guided Miles through the area, looking for a suitable high-rise or bluff to get a view over the city. That way, maybe he could figure out how many hostiles they were dealing with and get a better look at those odd fires around the one-armed god statue.

And with every step, the question: Who were these robed men with the pentagram design? Could this be a Cazador offshoot that had left the Metal Islands back during the time of the skinwalkers? Or perhaps survivors from a Cazador outpost...

But that voice he had heard spoke unaccented English.

This had to be a different group. But why come here?

To hunt the local mutants, maybe? The guy did have some heads on a pike. That wasn't the first time X had seen something like that in the wastes. Hell, back in Australia, heads mounted on pikes came with the territory.

He just needed to make sure *his* didn't end up on one.

As he stalked through the weeds, an idea finally took shape. What if these people had heard the same SOS that brought Michael here years ago to rescue Pedro and his people?

That had to be it, which meant these freaks could already have found Michael and his family. They could even be waiting for Magnolia.

X motioned for Miles to follow him into a building. Once he was safely inside, he bumped on the comms.

"Mags, do you copy?"

The response came a beat later. *"Yes, I'm at the bunker. But, X…"*

His heart sank. "Just say it straight up."

"I don't think they're here," Magnolia said. *"I'm exploring the facility, but so far, nothing."*

X sighed hard, in equal parts relief and despair. She hadn't walked into a trap with Jo-Jo, but Michael wasn't where they'd hoped to find him.

If he isn't here, he's somewhere else…

Until he either embraced them or found their dead remains, he would keep looking.

"There's still a bit more to search," Magnolia said. "I'll get back to you soon. What's your position?"

"I'm trying to get a visual."

"Copy that, but be careful."

"Yeah… you too, Mags."

He bumped the comm off and erupted into a cough. Lowering his helmet, he tried to muffle the noise. A drink from his helmet straw wet his sore throat.

Back into the road he went, heading up the sloped streets. He was closing in on the granite spire with the statue of the Old World god. He hadn't planned on heading up there, but there was nothing else in the area to give him a good look around.

If he could hike up there discreetly, he would have the best view of the entire city.

"Okay, Miles, ready for a little trek?"

X and the dog walked through the city. The closer they got to the bluff, the more X could see how thoroughly nature had reclaimed this section. What few buildings remained were covered by a dense canopy.

Miles sniffed his way into a parking lot blanketed with purple and blue flowers. Spikes some three feet tall sported petals fused into a keel. The sight was breathtakingly beautiful, but X knew not to get suckered by that beauty.

He guided Miles around the spikes of flowers. The buildings beyond separated them from the base of the bluff and, with luck, a trail up. Yellow ivy plants hung from the brick and stone structures that were once houses and apartments. In the hillside above the buildings, red banana leaves drooped from thick branches.

Unable to rely on the lightning flashes alone and unable to use his flashlight for fear of being seen, X donned his night-vision optics. By the time they got to the base of the bluff, he was starting to feel light headed.

The burn in his lungs returned, and he let out a cough. It passed more quickly this time, and he took another long pull from the straw.

Closing his eyes, he took a long, deep breath to relax. Then he looked up at the jungle-clad rock above them. There was the sparkle of flames at the crest. If there was a path up, it wasn't visible from here.

He wanted to look for it, but his lungs didn't agree. After another coughing fit, he unslung his pack and pulled out his med kit. He downed a pain pill with some water, then got out some food for himself and Miles.

The dog was hungry and took a big bite as soon as X pulled his mask off. Wagging his tail, Miles took a second bite, then abruptly went rigid.

"What is it, boy?" X whispered.

He grabbed his rifle and aimed it back the way they had come, searching for movement in the silent jungle. He didn't see anything, but something caught his ear.

A distant voice.

Lowering his rifle, he put the mask back on Miles one handed, as he had practiced. Then he slung his pack, picked up his rifle, and hurried with Miles toward the sound of people talking. It seemed to be coming from somewhere above them.

Following the base of the bluff, X saw flames in the jungle not far above them. Three torches were slowly working their way downhill.

X took Miles over to the trunk of an enormous tree, then scoped the area with his rifle. After a few minutes' wait, he saw men in robes in the glow of their torches. But they weren't on foot. All three sat in saddles on horseback.

"Not horses," X whispered. These beasts had humps on their backs, and long, curved necks. He remembered seeing an animal like this in a book as a kid. It was called a caramel. No, that wasn't right. *Camel*, he remembered. The domesticated animals stored water in those humps. X lost sight of them as the path led away.

He took a second to weigh his options, then decided to find the trail access. At least he would have a way to the top.

With Miles behind him, he moved warily through the jungle until he came to a road. Based on the burned vegetation, these men had cleared it with their flamethrowers.

X spotted the riders already moving into the city. He waited a few more minutes before bumping on the comms.

"Mags, do you copy?"

White noise crackled in his helmet.

"Mags," he tried again.

Shouting broke over the silence, followed by the electronic wail of a Siren. Liquid fire, from the band of hunters X could no longer see, shot into the sky. Two bright arcs of the flame chased a pair of flapping monsters.

"X," Magnolia said over the channel, followed by a garbled string of syllables he couldn't make out.

"Mags."

There was a faint response, but he couldn't pick out the words. He pulled up her beacon location on his HUD and saw that she was still at the bunker.

"Mags, there's three more men," he said. "All on camelback, heading into the city. Watch your six."

"Copy," she replied. Or so it sounded to X.

Miles moved past him, looking up the winding path along the bluff, then turning for orders. X decided to follow it for now. He patted his thigh, and the dog went ahead, following the two-toed footprints of the camels.

X did his best to keep to the side of the path, to mask his and Miles's tracks.

As they neared the top of the mountain, X was out of breath, but the medicine had helped his cough.

Crouching, he looked out over the city, to the marina where the *Sea Wolf* was hidden. The path he and Magnolia had taken into the city wasn't hard to find, which meant these people could potentially discover their boat.

X checked his rifle and magazine, drank water, and then proceeded up the last section of the path. It wound between a dense section of trees and into a parking lot. In that lot was something he hadn't expected: four small black tents and one larger one. There was also a trailer the color of charcoal, hitched to a rusted semi. Two motorbikes were parked on their kickstands.

Based on the number of tents, there were maybe ten men and four or five camels.

Keeping hidden in the jungle, X scoped out the vine-laden

trees beyond the lot. Above those, a staircase festooned with red vines led to the top of the granite bluff, where the one-armed god watched over the city.

He kept to the tree line, away from the path carving up to the fires. Camel dung littered the stone pathway, but there were also splotches of blood—lots of blood. As he emerged from the jungle below the statue, he saw the source of the gore.

Sprawled on the ground among five burning pentagrams were several headless carcasses. Sirens. A bone beast. Some of the bodies were burned too badly to be identifiable as human or anything else.

The thought made him shudder. What if Michael and his family were among these bodies?

No, X thought. *They aren't here.* But he had to be sure.

He signaled Miles to stay put. The dog protested but kept himself hidden in a thicket of giant ferns. X ventured out to the path that led up to the statue. Looking down the long flight of stairs to the parking lot, he saw nothing. But he didn't trust his eyes alone.

Crouching, he listened for several minutes before finally going over to the burned carcasses. The bone beast was easily recognizable, but the Sirens could have been humans except for their clawed hands and feet. Walking around the base of the statue, examining everything, he came to a tiny burned body, curled up in a fetal position.

His heart sank.

Bending down, he opened the clenched fist to reveal tiny claws. It was a relief to see the infant wasn't human, though he still felt empathy. Normally, he didn't have a lot of feelings for beasts, but seeing an infant Siren did appeal to the soft side he had for the young, whether it was puppies or kids or, apparently monsters.

He had almost made a full circuit around the statue when

he heard Miles grunting from the jungle, trying to warn him of a threat.

Standing, X spotted torches flickering up the pathway toward their location. He ducked back down behind the part of the statue facing the bay. There wasn't time to make a run for it and join his dog. He gestured for Miles to stay put.

Voices drifted up from below. English.

And they were coming this way.

He sneaked a glance, seeing six torches and a purple banner with that image of a pentagram around a goat's head. The man holding it lumbered up toward the statue. In the open space on the back side, he thrust the butt of the banner's staff into a base that held it upright.

Five men in red robes took up position at a wall in front of him. Two of them carried flamethrowers. The other three were armed with holstered pistols and some sort of harpoon gun.

Reaching up, the leader pulled his crimson hood down, exposing the back of his head. If X wanted, he could have blown it right off with a laser bolt. There was no doubt in his mind these people were evil. But right now they weren't threatening him or Miles.

If they did, then he wouldn't hesitate to engage.

"We came here to purge these ruins of the demonic hordes," the man boomed, "and to offer the heretics hoping for rescue a chance to join our great journey."

"We serve the Dark Lord," the other five men began to chant. "We serve you, Crixus."

Their leader, apparently named Crixus, held up both arms. His robe sagged away from muscular arms covered in bulging veins. Tubes snaked out of ports in his arms to disappear under his robe.

"The almighty Dark Lord is not pleased with our offerings!" he roared. "We are the instruments of his wrath, who thirst for new souls to feed the great journey. We must convert heretics and bring more blood offerings of infidels!"

He turned toward the statue, but his face remained in shadow.

X ducked down again, heart pounding as he gripped his rifle and waited for the flames that would incinerate his body like the smoldering carcasses around him.

"For years, we have traversed the world to fulfill the vision of the great one—the Dark Lord, the almighty Satan," Crixus said. "To convert the heretics who once worshipped this false god before us. From the Great Wall of Cathay through the deserts of the Middle East, to the shores of our homeland in Egypt, and now here…"

The colossal man turned back to his followers.

"There are heretics hiding like rats in these ruins!" Crixus yelled. "I can smell their vile stench as easily as I can smell rotting guts!"

X held in a breath. Had they seen him or Magnolia?

Holding the air in his wheezing, sickly lungs made them burn. And suddenly, X was holding back a cough. The huge man in front of the statue lowered one arm but pointed the other out over the city.

"Go. Find them!" he bellowed.

X lowered his helmet and let the cough go, trying to sync it with the speaker's booming voice. Then he sank down into the undergrowth and crawled away from the burning pentagram poles toward the edge of the bluff. Another cough threatened to explode from his lungs. His ears popped from the sensation as he tried to hold it back.

"Father!" yelled an adolescent voice.

Other voices followed in the distance. X stole another glance as he muffled the cough that he could no longer hold back. More robed warriors were chasing a child in a snug black suit with a leather vest and a grayish helmet. Crixus looked in their direction, then turned abruptly toward X.

He must have heard the cough.

X scrambled for cover, but there was nothing out here besides rocks and the long plummet over the bluff. He got to the edge and glanced over his shoulder. Miles was out of sight—hiding, he hoped.

In the glow of the flames, X watched the robed figures approaching. There were more than he had counted earlier—twelve plus Crixus and this boy. With no other choice, X swung his legs over the side of the bluff and found a narrow ledge of rock. He bent down and looked over the side at a vertical drop of maybe two thousand feet—a long way down without a chute.

Wind whistled against his armor.

He faced the bluff and, with his back to the marina, eased his body over the ledge. Holding on with his one hand to use, he dared not look down as he felt about for a new foothold. Another cough was building in his chest as the footsteps came closer, crunching rocks above him.

X clenched his throat, but there was nothing he could do. Seconds later, the cough erupted, rattling from deep in his lungs.

The footsteps stopped—all of them at once.

They had heard him.

He couldn't reach down to his blaster without taking his only hand off the rock. So he hugged the wall and hoped no one would see him if they looked over the edge. For a moment, he regretted climbing down here and not blowing their heads off when he had the chance. Then he remembered the flamethrowers.

A footstep crunched so close, dust and grit sifted down over the bluff. Seconds passed. A minute. X could hear labored breathing above him. Then came a heavy grunt, like that of a bone beast.

A softer grunt followed, mimicking the first.

The child, X realized.

"Can you smell them?" Crixus asked.

"Yes, Father."

"Good, Lucca. You're turning into a wolf, but your hunt has not yet started."

A howl made X flinch—definitely from the child. It lasted a few seconds.

"Now, come, Lucca," Crixus said. "You must stay with the others until your time comes."

The footsteps finally crunched away.

X sighed in relief. But the feeling was short lived. He still had to cross the city with Miles and link up with Magnolia and Jo-Jo, before this cult of devil-worshipping warriors hunted them all down.

TWENTY-ONE

Kade had much on his mind this morning. So much uncertainty. No word from the Barracudas other than to say that Tia was on the boat. That was a huge relief, but it didn't mean she was safe.

He had yet to hear anything more from the *Sea Wolf*, and there was no word from the scouts in Panama.

There wasn't much he could do to control any of those missions, but he could control something else.

At dawn, Kade went with Dakota and Beau to the radio room in the capitol tower. Imulah and Pedro were already there.

"You're all set," Pedro said.

The mic was connected to all audio circuits, enabling him to transmit to every single rig, ship, and boat. Today he would start delivering a daily address to every soul out there.

The idea had come from a tactic Kade once read about when he was a younger man. He couldn't remember the former president's name, but there was a leader in the United States who would give the citizens "fireside chats" on the radio.

Being able to reach everyone, from the fisherman on a trawler out at sea, to the homemaker raising a family on one of the rigs, to the militia soldier standing watch, was a great way for Kade to communicate with those he served.

Today he had a special guest for his announcement.

The door opened with Lieutenant Wynn and General Forge entering. Behind them stood Charmer, head down, skin burned pink by the sun, both arms in casts. Shivering, he fixed his single eye on Kade. It flitted over to Pedro, who was once beaten down by guards under Charmer's orders.

Pedro had every right to want to do the same thing back to Charmer, but the honorable man from Rio stood stiffly without a shred of emotion in his hard features.

Charmer, on the other hand, looked like a kid who lost his dog in a storm.

"I'm told you want to confess," Kade said.

"Yes," Charmer replied softly. "With specific conditions laid out."

"Of course you do, but the time to negotiate ended when you lied to Donovan and the others," Kade said.

Charmer shrugged. "Then I don't confess."

"You have no supporters left, Carl." Kade leaned forward. "I don't need your confession anymore. The people want your head, and General Forge is happy to take it tonight in the Sky Arena."

Charmer cocked the brow over his empty socket.

"Just hear me out, Kade," he said. "I can still be of service."

"*King* Kade," Forge growled.

"Yes, King Kade," Charmer said.

"*Service?* This should be rich," Kade said.

"Yes, I wish to be helpful, to do something for the future of our people and make up for Captain Rolo's sins. To do that, I'd like a boat with supplies to head to a Cazador territory. An island or former outpost—somewhere I can do something for the future of the Vanguard Islands."

Kade laughed at that.

"Let me get this straight," he said when he finished chuckling. "You want me to provide a boat and supplies to send you somewhere that you can... *help*?"

Charmer nodded eagerly. Apparently, the man had lost his damned mind.

"Think of it as exiling me, like what X did to Ada," Charmer said. "Was my crime so different from hers?"

"Uh, you had a kid beaten to death."

Charmer scoffed. "Jamal was never supposed to do that. The bloody brute got carried away."

"So you admit it?"

"I admit nothing until you grant my request."

"You want to help?"

"Yes, King Kade, I swear it." Charmer stepped forward, only to have Forge grab him by his shoulders and yank him backward.

"Ouch!" Charmer shouted. "For God's sake, King Kade, can you please call off your dogs? We can all be civilized."

Kade grabbed him by the throat and said, "You listen to me, you slippery bastard. You're going to admit all this over that mic right there," he said. "If you do a convincing job, then maybe I will allow you to help the islands in a way that I see fit."

Charmer glanced up, lips quivering as if he wasn't sure how to respond.

"Like a job here?" he finally asked.

Kade let go of the captive's throat and pointed to the mic.

"Okay, okay, I'll do it," Charmer said.

Kade went to the chair and took a seat in front of the mic. He flipped the all-comms switch and pulled the transmitter up to his mouth.

"Good morning, this is your king, Kade Long," he said. "As you all know, I am the new steward of the crown—a duty I am honored to carry out. In the coming days, I will be transmitting each morning to connect with you about a range of topics."

He paused slightly.

"Today, I want to start by assuring you that we have seen no sign of any hostile forces that you may have heard about. We will continue to monitor the situation and stand ready to meet anyone who threatens our home."

Kade looked back to Charmer.

"Next, in the interest of settling the disputes between all people here, I have Carl Lex here to shed light on the horrible violence between the sky peoples."

He motioned for Forge to let Charmer go.

"Don't fuck it up," Kade whispered.

Charmer took a seat and leaned forward. He hesitated, then brought the mic to his cracked lips.

"My friends, this is Carl Lex," he said in a voice reminiscent of his old charming tone. "As King Kade mentioned, I'm here to speak to you and admit a crime I committed while serving King Rolo. It was not Michael Everhart who killed Oliver and his son, but rather Jamal, who was ordered to beat Oliver. Jamal took it too far, and for that I am sorry. I'm also sorry for my lies. I only meant to serve the islands and the people here in a way that would keep our home safe from internal and external threats."

Charmer paused, then added, "I have sworn to serve the islands as King Kade sees fit."

He stood up.

And just like that, the islands now knew the real truth—truth that could have saved many lives. But maybe, just maybe, Charmer could still save lives.

An idea bloomed in Kade's mind as he sat back down at the mic.

"This bloody chapter of our history is now closed," he said. "We must move on as one people. When I lived in the sky, it took everyone to keep our ship in the air. The same is true here. A vanguard is effective only if everyone moves in the same direction. Stay steady with me, hold the line, and the future will be bright. Thank you, and I will talk to you all again very soon."

Kade turned off the mic and stood.

"How'd I do?" Charmer said, smiling.

To him, this was still one big game.

"Take him to the marina," Kade said.

"What!" Forge thundered. "You're just going to let him *go* now? After all he just admitted to?"

"The king is a man of his word," Charmer said with a broadening grin.

Wynn pulled him away, leaving Forge glaring at Kade.

"Trust me, General," he said. "I've realized that Charmer can be more important to us alive than dead. I'll show you how, shortly."

Forge snorted and followed Kade out of the room along with Beau and Dakota. They took the elevator down to the piers, passing the cage that had been Charmer's lodgings ever since the brief civil war. The piers below bustled with activity—sailors arriving with supplies, and fishermen heading out to sea.

Kade took the side door into the enclosed marina. He went to the yacht they were preparing for Lucky to take back to the Coral Castle. It was almost ready to go. All it needed was the knight, and . . .

"Here's the boat you requested," Kade said.

Charmer walked slowly over, suspicious at first. Then a smile began to form on his face.

"Sir," Forge said as he stepped up next to Kade.

"Please trust me, General," Kade whispered back.

Charmer turned with a wide grin. "Thank you, Kade—er, King Kade. Thank you for giving me a second chance."

He bowed and held up his casts like a thankful beggar who had just been given a gold coin. "You're a good man," Charmer said. "A *great* man."

Kade thought harder about what he was about to do. Sending Charmer with Lucky as an offering to the Forerunner seemed a good idea. With Rolo dead, Charmer was the next best thing.

But that last line about Kade being a great man stuck with him. Just days ago, Charmer had screamed that Kade was evil, a murderer.

If Lucky should manage to get them to the Coral Castle, Kade couldn't trust Charmer to tell the truth. But Kade had a plan for that as well.

He reached into his vest and pulled out a magnetic tape cartridge.

"You will be taking this with you to the Coral Castle," Kade said.

"To the *what*?" Charmer said. His brows knitted in confusion.

"You said you want to be of service. Well, this is how you're going to do it," Kade said. "I'm sending our prisoner back home, and you're going with him."

"Wait…"

"This tape is a confession, not just by you but also by Captain Rolo," Kade said.

Charmer shook his head. "They will kill me! They will torture me!"

Kade gestured to Forge. "Would you rather face the general in the Sky Arena?"

"You're a cunning bastard, Kade," Charmer said. He exhaled long and then reached out for the tape, but Kade pulled it back.

"You think I trust you to hang on to this?" Kade laughed. "I'll be giving this to Lucky."

"And what makes you think the snake won't strangle him in his sleep?" Forge asked. "Sending Charmer along threatens the very mission."

"Not if he's in a cage."

"Please, no," Charmer begged. "I don't deserve it!"

"Did Eevi?" Kade asked. "Did Michael?"

Charmer backed away, glancing about him like a trapped beast.

"How about Donovan? Did he deserve to be killed because he believed your lies?" Kade asked. "Did Oliver, or his *little boy*?"

In his mind's eye, Kade saw Donovan fall with an axe buried in his chest. He thought of the macabre scene where Oliver and Nez were found.

Heat rushed through Kade as fury gripped his heart. The rage spread to his limbs, as it had on the piers when he almost killed Charmer then. This time, Alton wasn't here. Or Tia, or anyone who could have talked Kade down.

Reaching down, he swiftly drew his sword.

"Wait," Charmer said, stepping back. "You swore…"

"I swore I'd find a way for you to serve the islands," Kade said. "That's what I'm going to do."

Charmer held up his arms in an X as the sword swung down. The blade broke through the top cast, crunching into bone.

Charmer howled in agony.

He went down on his knees, screeching as blood flowed over the casts.

Kade hesitated for a moment to look Charmer in the eye.

"No!" Charmer screamed.

Kade brought his blade down on the side of Charmer's neck, cutting deep into flesh, bone, and gristle.

Charmer reached up to clutch the spurting wound after Kade pried the blade free.

Gripping the sword in both hands, he brought it above his head.

"*Wait…!*" Charmer croaked.

Kade swung down, cutting through Charmer's fingers and severing his head in the same stroke. His body crumpled to the deck, and the head rolled lopsided to a stop against his side.

Silence filled the enclosed marina as Kade sheathed his sword. He expected to feel some sort of relief now that Charmer was dead, but there was no time for that.

Kade picked up the severed head and stuffed the tape cassette into its mouth.

"No more lies," he said. "From now on, only truth."

Grabbing a fistful of blond curls, he handed the head out. Forge, who never seemed fazed by violence, hesitated.

"Box this up and prepare it for shipment with Lucky to the Coral Castle," Kade ordered.

"And the body?" Forge asked.

Kade considered hanging it from the piers for all to see, but Alton and the other kids didn't need to look at that.

"Feed it to the Octopus Lords," Kade said.

*   *   *   *   *

"Victor, do you copy?" Michael said into the comm link.

Static crackled from the speakers.

He looked out the viewports of the bridge and saw only darkness. It was two hours after sunset, but there was no sign of the moon. Perhaps the sunshine they had seen earlier was just a fluke.

The airship now hovered in the cloud cover over the ruined resort where Victor had fled years ago. Three hours ago, he had dived to the surface of Lanzarote. From the bridge of the airship, Michael and Layla had watched him walk up the shore to Jameos del Agua.

The radio crackled, and a message from Victor broke through. *"Chief, do you copy?"*

"Copy," Michael said.

"I've reached the property and am preparing to enter."

"You see any recent activity?"

"No, nothing."

"Copy. Be careful," Michael said.

He looked up to the second level on the bridge. Layla stood looking down, with Bray at her side. The boy hugged a book against his chest.

"Daddy, book," he said.

"Yes, but I can't read it to you right now, pal," Michael said.

He turned back to the monitors and watched the beacon's slow advance.

"He must be entering the tunnels," Timothy said.

Minutes passed. Fifteen. Then thirty.

Bray became increasingly bored. He threw his book down and started to run around the top deck of the bridge with his hands up.

At first, Michael thought it was funny, but then Bray decided he wasn't happy anymore. He wailed when Layla picked him up and tried to quiet him down.

The boy was going to be two soon, and now that he could walk, there was much to explore.

Michael looked out the viewports. Soon, if all went to plan, he would have plenty of space down there to do all the moving and exploring he wanted.

Another fifteen minutes passed with no word from Victor.

Layla brought Bray down to the radio equipment. "I'm going to put this little stinker to bed."

"Okay," Michael said. Normally, he wasn't relieved to put his son down, but tonight he needed some calm. "Night, little man."

"Nigh nigh," Bray said.

Michael watched them go up the stairs. Bray wanted to do it on his own, but Layla held his hand on the way up.

"Sir," Timothy said.

The hatch closed, and Michael turned back to the map and screen.

"Yeah, what is it?" he asked.

Then he saw it. The beacon on the map was gone.

Michael leaned down. "What happened?" he asked.

"I … I don't know."

Michael stared at the digital map, his heart racing. "Is it a glitch?" he asked.

"I don't believe so, sir," Timothy replied.

"Run a life scan," Michael said. He rushed over to the two monitors that relayed vital data from the sensors under the airship.

"Stand by," said the AI.

Michael watched the screen as the sensors swept over the landscape where Victor had just been. Several minutes passed, each one adding to the icy knot forming in his stomach.

"Inconclusive, sir," Timothy said. "We're too high for an accurate reading."

"Shit, shit, shit, this is—"

"What's wrong?" Layla asked, reentering the bridge. Michael bit the inside of his lip, unsure how to tell her what had just happened.

"Tell me," she insisted. "Did something happe—"

"His beacon went off a few minutes ago," Michael said.

"It just *went off*?"

"Yes," Timothy said.

"We have to do something," Layla said.

"If he's gone, what *can* we do?" Michael asked.

"Go look for him."

"That would be unwise, I'm afraid," Timothy said. "If someone, or something, is down there, they'll be looking for you."

Michael felt the icy ball start to melt in a wave of heat. It wasn't fear. It was anger.

He had lost Steve. Now he was going to lose Victor?

No, that wasn't going to happen.

"I could lower the ship," Timothy suggested. "We have the cover of darkness in our favor."

Michael exchanged a nod with his wife.

"Wait. If we're lowering through the clouds, we should strap Bray," Layla said.

Michael nodded. "Stand by, Timothy."

She returned a few minutes later with a babbling Bray. He looked bright eyed and clearly had not fallen asleep yet.

"Strap in," Michael said.

He helped Layla and Bray into their seats, then remained standing.

"Prepare for descent," Timothy said.

The bow dipped, the ship groaning as it began to lower. Clouds rushed over the viewports, as if they were flying through smoke. The altitude clicked down, down... Michael didn't like it, but this was the safest way to run a life scan for Victor.

A second later, the airship broke through the cloud cover for a view of the dark ocean. Bray pointed at the viewport.

"Wah-wah," he said.

The waves crashed against a rocky shore. A road ran along the shore, partly covered by an overhang to protect vehicles from falling rocks. Over the street rose tiered bluffs covered in hanging vegetation. Built along those cliffs were dilapidated structures, also covered in the same luxuriant growth.

It was easy to see what took Victor so long after the dive. He had landed several miles off course and had to hike to Jameos del Agua.

The airship came lower, heading over the open stretch of

brown rocks and sporadic green flora. There was little cover in an area devoid of buildings and trees.

"Nothing on the radar for ships, vehicles, or aircraft," Timothy said.

"Copy, take us lower," Michael said.

The airship dropped down to just over a thousand feet.

"Entering life-scan range," Timothy announced. "Stand by."

The sensors under the ship activated, sweeping over the desolate terrain. Michael alternated his gaze between the screen and the viewports.

"Prepare for visual image of target location," Timothy said.

Michael could already see it on the horizon. The boxy white structures stood out like bones in the otherwise unremarkable terrain. Stone walls surrounded the facility built over the volcanic tunnels that Victor had entered.

"All animal life scans negative," Timothy reported.

Michael ran a hand through his hair. He looked back to Layla and Bray.

The airship hovered over the facility, running scans on the surface.

"Nothing, sir," Timothy concluded.

"Do another pass," Michael said.

The thrusters fired, taking them toward the sea to turn around. Michael felt the deep dread of losing yet another friend. It never got easier. He was still mourning the deaths of X, Mags, and everyone else back in Brisbane. Layla was devastated too, and although they were together, he couldn't help but feel an emptiness inside.

The airship flew out over the water and had begun to turn when a monitor beeped.

Michael went to the life-scanning equipment screens.

"I have a hit," Timothy said.

"Where?" Michael asked.

"Bringing up location onscreen."

The reading was coming from the shoreline to the northeast, some three-quarters of a mile from their location. From what Michael could tell, it was in the middle of a steep bluff. Perhaps a climber, or someone inside a cave?

"How many life-forms?" Michael asked.

"Just one, sir, and judging by the size, I believe it to be human."

"Get us within visual distance, but be careful," Michael said.

"Yes, sir."

The airship swung northeast, flying toward a chain of rocky crags over the shore. Michael watched the monitor relaying images from the bow cameras. They drilled in on the bluffs. The shore had eroded away from the sea, like gums around rotten teeth.

Openings in the rock revealed caves and tunnels. The airship closed in on the tunnel where the life-form was detected. Layla unbuckled herself and Bray and joined Michael.

"Wait," Michael said.

In his mind's eye, he pictured a defector or a hostile soldier firing a missile into their ship.

"Scan for explosives," he said.

"I already did, sir. No explosives detected," Timothy replied.

Michael relaxed slightly as his wife and son came up to him.

"Closing in on visual," Timothy said.

The airship whirred lower, toward the bluff.

"Front beams," Michael said.

"Activating," Timothy replied.

The powerful rays blasted from the bow, illuminating the vertical walls of the cliffs a hundred yards ahead. Michael went to the viewports for a look.

"Contact identified," Timothy announced. "Relaying to monitor in three, two, one..."

There was no need to look at the monitor. Michael had a

view of the half-naked man crouched in the mouth of a cave. The man held a hand over his face, shielding his eyes from the bright glow of the beams.

Michael wondered if they had perhaps discovered a feral human. Perhaps someone who had murdered Victor. The person stood, revealing a bandage around his lean and muscular midsection. It was then Michael realized this *was* Victor.

The cameras relayed a better view on the main screen. The warrior had removed his suit and most of his clothing, which explained his beacon turning off.

"Victor!" Layla said, clapping.

"Uncle," Bray said. He mimicked his mother, clapping his hands.

Michael still couldn't believe his eyes, but there was no mistaking it. Victor waved up at them with both arms, squinting into the glow.

"Can you get us down there?" Michael asked.

"I think so," Timothy said.

"Good, angle us in and I'll throw a rope down to him."

Michael dashed out of the command center, running through the airship. By the time he got to the launch bay, the ship was rising up over the bluffs.

He secured his helmet and then tapped the button to open the launch-bay door. Wind blasted in, pushing back on his armor. Holding on to a handle, he glanced down to see that the ship was directly over the rock ridge.

"In position," Timothy announced over the comms.

"Lowering cable," Michael said.

Tapping the controls for the robotic arm that stretched out of the open launch bay, Michael dropped the cable down into the darkness. He could just begin to make out the structures of the resort through his night-vision optics.

Rocky, bare terrain stretched between the cliff and the

buildings. There were plenty of places for hostiles to hide down there, and the airship was low enough to be vulnerable.

"Timothy, do another scan," he said into his comm.

"All scans are negative for animal life other than Victor," replied the AI.

Michael relaxed a degree and focused on getting his friend back up to the ship. The cable reached the cave entrance, and Victor already had a harness on.

"Ready?" Michael shouted down.

"Yes!" Victor called up.

The winch clanked, pulling Victor toward the ship. He was looking out over the ocean and pointing at something on the horizon. There, Michael noticed a white light.

*Moon*light.

The rays spread over the water miles away. The cloud cover had broken again, and for that one instant, it felt like being back at the Vanguard Islands.

A minute later, Victor was at the open launch-bay door. Michael stepped back and tapped the control panel. The robotic arm retracted into the launch bay, swinging Victor inside.

"I'm sorry," Victor said. "I'm very sorry, Chief."

"What for?" Michael asked, helping Victor out of the harness. He wrapped his good arm around the shivering man.

Layla entered the launch bay with Bray.

"Get him a blanket!" Michael called out.

The hologram of Timothy came to life, spreading its glow across the dimly lit room. Michael left Victor for a moment while he secured the launch-bay doors.

"Get us out of here," Michael said.

"On it, sir," Timothy said.

The airship lifted back into the sky, toward the storms and safety.

Teeth chattering, Victor stared at Michael with sad eyes.

"It's all gone," he said. "The bunker is…"

"Take it easy," Michael said.

Layla jogged over with a blanket and wrapped it around Victor.

"I'm sorry," Victor repeated. "Tunnels all flooded. I take off armor, suit, and I swim down. I almost drown, but I find my way up."

"It's flooded?" Michael asked.

Victor nodded. "I think all of bunker gone. I'm so sorry. So very sorry. We come for nothing."

Michael looked out the launch-bay viewports at the moon-lit sea.

"Not for nothing," he said, patting Victor on the shoulder and showing him the view. "This place might still be habitable for us after all."

TWENTY-TWO

"That blade doesn't work for shit," Slayer said. "We should have brought a bulldozer."

"Better—you got Gran Jefe," Zuni said.

Gran Jefe grinned at that as he bent down and put his shoulder against the concrete Jersey barrier. A very long time ago, someone had placed a dozen of them here. They were too heavy to shove aside with the APC without damaging both blade and vehicle.

Sweat dripped down his head as he looked out over the fields of tall weeds and mounds of debris. His gut told him they were being watched. He got the feeling when they reached the first roadblock back near the port, but all infrared scans had come back negative.

He scanned the rubble of buildings in the small coastal town. A former gas station was one of the only structures remaining, with a red awning that had collapsed over the pumps and a row of electric charging stations.

It was a crappy place to be stranded, but there was no other option than clearing the road. It was the only way to get to the target with the APC and two trailers.

Slayer stood in the turret with a belt-fed light machine gun, watching for hostiles. Inside, Woody and Tia waited with Blackburn, who guarded them from themselves as much as from any monsters out there. In Gran Jefe's mind, Tia was just as dangerous as the inexperienced pilot. She couldn't be trusted with orders.

With a loud grunt, Gran Jefe toppled a Jersey barrier into the ditch, splashing up a wave of muddy water. Zuni pushed vainly against another concrete barrier, his boots sliding on the wet road.

"I help, *amigo*," Gran Jefe said. He put his shoulder into it, and the two of them heaved it over.

"Okay, that's it," Slayer called out. "Get back in the APC. We can plow through the rest."

Slayer slid down into the vehicle to take the wheel as Zuni climbed in on the passenger side. Gran Jefe climbed into the turret and tapped the roof, ready to roll.

The APC grumbled back to life, hauling the two trailers in tandem. Gran Jefe gripped the light machine gun in the turret, ready to fire at anything attracted by the noise. The convoy rolled forward, picking up speed on the old highway. This was a different route from the one he had taken with the Barracudas ten years ago, but it would lead to the same location.

They drove out of the ghost town, heading deeper into the blasted terrain. The swamps wouldn't be far now. He scanned for the dense forest where he remembered the mining facility's location.

There wasn't much out here—mostly razed buildings all but consumed by weeds and bushes. A crater came into view on the right side of the road. From this vantage, he could tell that it was man made. But this wasn't from mining; it was from a bomb.

Gran Jefe put a hand on his growling gut.

"You okay up there?" Tia asked. "I got some protein bars."

"No," Gran Jefe said. "*Todo bien.*"

He kept his focus on the road. Four more craters lay just beyond the cracked asphalt. Odd that someone would waste bombs out here where there was nothing to destroy. Then he saw the next crater as the headlights hit what should have been a bridge.

It was gone, and in the blast, much of the bank had slid into the canal. The APC stopped, and Slayer hopped out.

"You see a way across, Mata?" he asked.

Gran Jefe scanned the fractured walls of the canal but didn't see a way to get the trailers across anywhere near their position. The banks had caved into the water in both directions. Fields of high weeds blocked any view beyond the crater.

"No," he called back.

"That's some shit luck," Slayer said. He walked over to the edge, peering over the side into the stagnant water. "How far are we from the target?"

"Two miles," Blackburn said.

"Mata, see if you can find a way across this."

Gran Jefe climbed out of the turret and dropped to the ground.

"Zuni, go with him," Slayer said.

The back door opened, and the warrior hopped out.

"Don't even think about it," Slayer said as Tia tried to scoot out.

Gran Jefe shut the door and set off with Zuni, who didn't look back. He seemed to be trying to do his professional best but was embarrassed that Tia had come along for him. Although the military turned a blind eye to the bending of various rules, one thing they didn't budge on was the banning of relationships between soldiers. They couldn't very well have lovers dashing about trying to save one another from monsters or other threats. In the wastes, a romantic relationship was a unit killer.

Gran Jefe was all for this rule. Of all the women he had been with over the years, none were Cazador soldiers at the time.

Zuni started down the slope of the riverbank. Gran Jefe jogged to catch up, unslinging his rifle on the fly. The steep bank was a ten-foot mudslide down to the dark water. Maybe the APC alone could get across here, but the trailers made it impossible.

Gran Jefe splashed into water that came up to his knees. Zuni went down the left side of the canal, keeping near the bank. They sloshed along for a few minutes.

"I know what you're thinking," Zuni said. "I didn't tell her about this mission."

"I no think *nada*," Gran Jefe said.

Zuni turned in the water. "She should not have come; I told her that."

This time Gran Jefe stopped and turned to the young Hell Diver. "You push all love out of *corazón*," he said, tapping Zuni in the chest. "You make heart hard, survive, then go home and love. No room for love in wastes."

Zuni kept going toward the wall of the crater. Water fell in a narrow cataract to the stream.

Gran Jefe slung his rifle and climbed up onto the muddy bank for a look. Weeds blew in the wind. Beyond them, he heard the buzz of insects over what looked like marshland. In the other direction, the APC and trailers were out of view, but Gran Jefe did see a way across where the canal was only a few feet wide and two feet deep.

If they could drive through the field to this location, it was possible to get to the other side—if they could just hack away some of the growth.

"Make self useful," Gran Jefe said. He pulled out a machete and handed it to Zuni. "Make door."

"Where are you going?"

"Take shit," Gran Jefe said.

"We have a dozer blade. Why do I need to cut this down?"

"'Cause I say so."

Gran Jefe wandered out into the weeds to do his business behind a tree. The buzzing of insects grew louder, and he swatted a fat green fly away from his helmet.

He was going to have to make this quick or risk getting bitten on the ass.

Moving around the tree, he looked out over the marsh and beyond, where a cloud of insects flew over a muddy field. He started the process of removing his armor, then paused when he realized what the bugs were feeding on.

"*¡Santa mierda!*" Gran Jefe breathed.

The insects buzzed over some fifty corpses rotting in the mud. Some of the bodies were picked down to bones and gristle. Others, more recently dead, were bloated near to bursting.

He dressed, hastily cinched his armor down, grabbed his rifle, and hurried back to Zuni.

"The others are on their way," Zuni said, handing the machete back to Gran Jefe.

Gran Jefe must have looked a sight, because then Zuni asked, "You okay?"

"I find something," Gran Jefe said, tilting his head toward the marsh.

The APC slowed to a stop, and Slayer hopped out.

"Looks like we can make it," he said.

"Wait, wait, come see . . ." Gran Jefe took a breath. "I find bodies. *Muertos*."

"Human?" Slayer asked.

"*Sí*, come, I show you."

Slayer ordered Zuni to stay with the APC.

Tia opened the door, and Woody peeked out with her.

"What's wrong?" he asked.

"Get back in the truck," Slayer said.

He followed Gran Jefe back to the edge of the marsh. They stopped a few feet from the water.

"It's a graveyard," he said.

"Less for us to kill, I guess," Slayer said. "Come on."

They made their way back to the vehicle.

"Zuni, take the turret," Slayer said. "Mata, you're up front with me."

Blackburn hopped out at shotgun and jumped in the back with Woody and Tia while Zuni climbed into the turret.

Tia leaned forward. "What did you find out there?"

Slayer ignored her, putting the truck into gear and pushing down on the gas. The trailers bumped up and down behind them as they drove down into the shallow canal and splashed into the water, wheels churning through the mud.

Slayer gave it some gas, and the APC rolled up the other side, pulling the first trailer up. The second trailer, however, got stuck, jolting the chain of vehicles to a stop.

"Shit," Slayer muttered. He looked in the rearview mirror, then mashed the pedal. "Come on, damn it."

He rocked the APC up, then down, then up, and the second trailer finally got up the bank. Slayer kept going, out into the field before cutting through back to the road. Minutes later, they were on the other side of the crater and back on track. A few raindrops smacked the windshield.

Steam came off the hood from the overworked engine as the rain lanced down. Gran Jefe searched the roadsides for hostiles as they neared the target.

"Almost there," Slayer said.

Lightning illuminated a dense tree line ahead. He put on the brakes as they approached the dark forest.

"Get ready," he said.

The little light that the storms provided retreated as the convoy rolled under the forest canopy. Slayer drove slowly through the nearly pitch-black terrain, relying entirely on night-vision optics.

Gran Jefe hated using his, but he turned them on.

He would have missed the sign if Zuni hadn't pounded on the rooftop and pointed it out. Slayer stopped, and Gran Jefe got out to check the sign. Sure enough, an old road peeled off from the main path.

Gran Jefe got back in the APC, and it crawled through the dense woods. It wasn't long before the road ended at a drop-off that was difficult to make out.

Again Slayer slowed, and Gran Jefe got out. He walked down the road and saw the tiered levels of the mine.

They had arrived.

Lightning flashed over the site, and he shut off his optics. In the blue glow, he could see the very tunnel he had entered a decade ago. It looked different. A scree slope of debris had poured out of the mouth.

Slayer pulled up after Gran Jefe waved them forward. Getting back into the APC, he heaved a breath. "This it?" Slayer asked.

"*Sí, pero* we have *un problema*," Gran Jefe said. He pointed through the windshield at the entrance he had once used to access the mine, now sealed off from a cave-in.

"That's the entrance you used to access the elevator?" Slayer asked.

"What's wrong?" Tia asked.

Both she and Woody tried to see through the rain-streaked windshield.

"We'll have to find another way in or clear that debris," Slayer said.

Gran Jefe nodded and started to get out again, but the commander grabbed his arm.

"No, Mata. You sit here with Tia and Woody. Don't move from this position. I'll go check this out with Blackburn and look for an alternate entrance first. Zuni will stay in the turret and cover us."

Gran Jefe looked at Woody and then Tia, thinking this had to be a joke.

"Before you say a word, don't," Slayer said. "I want you here, Mata."

Before Gran Jefe could say anything, the commander got out of the truck and quietly shut the door. He walked down the road with Blackburn, neither of them looking back.

"You going to tell us what you found in those marshes?" Woody asked.

"No," Gran Jefe said.

"Sounds like it could be a good story. I was hoping to have several to take back with me."

"*Shhh.*"

"Someone's pissed about getting left behind," Woody said.

"*¡Silencio!*" Gran Jefe snapped. Then he glared at Tia. "You quiet too."

Gran Jefe opened the door and stepped outside. He couldn't sit in there another moment with those two.

Lightning split the horizon in a brilliant blue wave that flashed over the mine site. Gran Jefe walked down the road to look at the three levels of the ancient excavation. Slayer and Blackburn had already reached the scree pile plugging the mouth of the mine.

They checked it out, then moved on, looking for another way in.

Standing guard, Gran Jefe thought of Pablo. The boy had no idea that places like this existed, or what the Old World had looked like. At Pablo's young age, Gran Jefe had always wondered what lay beyond the rigs.

Since then, he had come to answer that question. Beyond the rigs lay nothing less than hell on earth.

Now it was his job to protect Pablo from places like this, and from people like those living inside the tunnels.

A distant clicking noise hit his ear. Gran Jefe turned back toward the truck. Zuni rotated in the turret, apparently hearing the same noise. He trained the machine gun on the forest to the left of the truck.

Gran Jefe moved back to the vehicle. The clicking came again, along with a low hiss. Then a grunt.

Something was out there.

Tia opened the door. "Hey, I got to pee," she said.

Loud clicking answered her. The sound devolved into a rattle, then back into a clicking. Tia had frozen, staring off into the forest.

Gran Jefe motioned her back into the truck. She obeyed and slowly shut the door as Gran Jefe walked that way, eyes flitting rapidly, attuned to any movement. He considered sending a transmission to Slayer and Blackburn but decided to keep radio silence until whatever was making the odd noises appeared.

The noises came again a moment later—a combination of rattling, clicking, and hissing. It reminded Gran Jefe of a kind of snake he had encountered on raids before. Of all the mutant creatures in the wastes, he hated snakes the most.

Motion in the forest caught his eye. A hunched figure darted between trees. He followed it with his rifle barrel, but with his flashlight off, it was impossible to get a good look from this distance, even with night vision active.

The creature stopped at the edge of the road about twenty feet away and clicked again. It behaved as if the noise was some sort of scanner.

Maybe an echolocation device, like what the Sirens used, Gran Jefe thought.

He shut off his night vision and waited for the next lightning flash. When it came, he tensed up at the abomination of nature that it captured in the glow. The thing had been human, but its naked flesh was covered in tumorous growths. Some looked like brown or black bark, while others appeared to be orange and red scales.

He remembered that the feral humans had been sick when he was here last. Now it seemed that sickness had spread, somehow transforming what had been a man or woman into a warty, eyeless monster.

Zuni rotated the turret again with a loud clanking of gears and cogs.

The creature hopped over a fallen log, into the middle of the road, and bounced a little, as if it were fitted with springs. It tilted its scaly head and peered in their direction.

It seemed this creature had locked on to their location.

Gran Jefe prepared to squeeze the trigger. He could blast the thing to pieces if he wanted, but that would only draw other diseased creatures to their location.

A loud cracking noise rang out across the mine behind him.

The creature jerked in that direction, tilting its head once more. Then it took off, dropping to all four legs and bounding away at an amazing speed.

Gran Jefe followed it with his gun barrel until it had vanished into the forest. He lowered his rifle and looked up to Zuni.

"Stay, and no let them out of truck," Gran Jefe commanded. He hurried back to the edge of the overlook and saw the creature sliding down a slope to the second level. It followed two sets of footprints.

He had to warn the other Barracudas.

"Slayer, do you copy?" he said into his comm.

"Copy," Slayer replied.

Gran Jefe related what he had just seen.

"Stay put, Mata," Slayer said. *"We'll be back soon."*

Gran Jefe stayed another minute, scanning for the creature. The minute became five. At ten, he turned back to the APC.

Zuni was still in the turret, looking in his direction.

On the short walk back, Gran Jefe saw movement in the forest on the right. He had only a second to raise his rifle as a figure leaped out of the woods and clambered up the side of the truck.

"Zuni!" Gran Jefe cried in alarm.

Zuni tried to turn around in the turret, but the beast grabbed him.

Gran Jefe had his rifle up, trying to get a shot. He cursed as the creature hauled Zuni out of the turret and to the ground on the far side of the truck.

Lowering his rifle, Gran Jefe ran toward the truck, flinching at the sound of a gunshot. Screams followed the blast, then an odd gurgling noise.

Gran Jefe raised his rifle again and darted around the truck.

When he got there, the humanoid abomination lay in a puddle of mud, with gray and white tissue protruding from the blown-open skull. Woody stood over the creature with his shotgun.

Zuni was standing up, Tia by his side.

"I got it," Woody said incredulously. "I freaking got it."

"You okay?" Tia asked Zuni.

He nodded. "You?"

"The bloody hell is this thing?" Woody asked, bending down to the puddle of blood.

Gran Jefe, worried about infection, pulled him back.

Hearing footfalls behind him, he whirled with his rifle up to find Slayer and Blackburn approaching.

"What happened?" Slayer asked, slowing as he approached the carcass.

"I killed it," Woody said. He laughed. "I freaking nailed it, man, blew its ugly head off!"

"Looks like you got your story," Tia said.

Slayer told Blackburn and Gran Jefe to make a perimeter. Then he knelt to examine the creature.

"It was human, I think." He looked over at Gran Jefe. "You said they were sick when you came here."

The big Cazador nodded. "*Sí, pero* no look like it. These much sicker."

Slayer got back up. "Get back in the truck, and get ready to dig."

"Dig?" Tia asked.

"The only way inside is the cave-in. We're gonna have to try and clear it out."

"Won't that be dangerous?" Woody asked. "What if the tunnel's completely collapsed?"

Slayer didn't say another word. They all climbed back into the truck, Gran Jefe taking the turret. As the engine turned over, clicking and rattling sounded in the distance.

Gran Jefe swept the light machine gun over the forest, but this sounded closer.

Puzzled, he looked down at the monster with the sheared-off skull. Tendrils on the ruined head still wriggled, glowing red.

"*That thing no* muerto," he said over the comm.

Slayer got out to look.

"Want me to shoot?" Gran Jefe asked.

"No, I'll handle it."

Slayer got back in and backed up. The tires crunched over the deformed body.

Slayer shifted gears and drove the APC over it again. The first trailer thumped over it, then the second. A wide swath of blood streaked behind the left tires as the trailers rolled on.

In the turret, Gran Jefe tried to look in every direction at all times. This monster reminded him of what awaited them in the mines. Whatever these things were, they had changed in the past decade. And for the first time in years, he felt a trickle of something he hardly recognized.

Fear.

TWENTY-THREE

X had hugged the rock bluff for what seemed an hour before finally climbing back up. Miles trotted over to him as soon as he stepped into the forest. Five guards had remained at the camp where X assumed that the boy Lucca was sheltering.

The thought had crossed his mind to try to kill the men and kidnap the boy as collateral for safe passage out of the city, but he couldn't risk it. Nor did he really want to try. Lucca was seven or eight, about the same age Tin had been when X was separated from him.

Children were innocent, no matter how evil their parents were. And Crixus seemed to be a real asshole based on what X had seen so far. After all, he did *worship* the Old World devil. That alone meant there had to be some screws loose in his head— and evil in his heart.

X wouldn't hesitate to kill the man if he got him in his sights again.

Miles guided them back to the trail. Halfway down, X could see the procession of warriors with torches marching through the streets.

He had to warn Magnolia and tried multiple times, but the short-range radio wasn't working. Once he reached the city, he selected a ten-floor building that had somehow been spared from the tsunamis and bombs, to try to get a signal.

Climbing the dozen stairs didn't help his burning lungs or aching back. Miles too seemed to be slowing down. The once-agile dog had suffered injuries on the missions to Panama and Australia. Coming here hadn't given him much chance to recover.

"We can rest soon, okay, boy?" X said. "Just a little farther until we get back to Magnolia. Then we'll go find Michael and his family."

Miles wagged his tail under his suit, but X couldn't help feeling that he was lying to the dog about the second part. He knew now that Michael wasn't in Rio and maybe never had been. That meant he could be anywhere in the world. And if X had to guess, it was far away from the Vanguard Islands.

He tried not to think about that and to focus on the present—on saving those he could. He went into the burned-out remains of a condo, moving cautiously to the missing window for a sprawling view of the ruins all the way to the marina. With his chin, he bumped on the comms. "Mags, do you copy?"

Static crackled back.

He raised his wrist computer, tapping it to bring up the digital map with her position. The green beacon was on the move. The location was four blocks west of where she had entered the bunker, which told him she had abandoned it.

"Mags," he tried again. "Mags, answer me."

White noise hissed in his ear. He cursed and slapped the concrete wall. Dust sifted down. He felt a wave of light-headedness and stepped back lest he tumble over the side.

Miles whined behind him, sensing that something was off with his handler. X retreated to the kitchen island, where he unslung his bag and left it on the counter. A toppled stool lay in the ashes. He pulled it upright and sat.

A check of his wrist computer showed his temperature at 102 degrees. His head throbbed with a growing pressure.

He was sick; there was no denying that.

What he needed was something to get him through this mission. He rifled through his pack for his stim pills. He had used a few to stay awake on the journey here.

Finally, he found them and swallowed one with a slug of water. Miles watched quietly until X leaned down and removed his mask so he could drink. As soon as it was off, X noticed that his black nose was cracked and dry.

He looked at X with his blue eyes, but where there was once an electric spark, X saw the same thing that greeted him when he looked in the mirror: fatigue and a hint of sadness.

A memory of the first day they spent together, in the bunker beneath the ITC facility in Hades, entered his thoughts. Miles, just a puppy, was full of life and joy, amused and happy with the simplest things: tossing him a ball; rubbing his belly. He was glad just to shadow X through the corridors on their daily routine of pruning plants, picking fruit, and checking the traps for the Sirens that lurked in the darkness.

So much had happened since then. Adventures. Battles. Losses. Too many to count.

X pulled the small plastic bowl from his bag, set it in front of Miles, and poured water into it. While Miles lapped it up, X found some healing ointment and gently massaged it into his dry, cracked nose.

The comms crackled.

"X, do you copy?"

"Mags," X replied.

He shot to his feet. The dog watched him curiously as X moved over to the missing windows.

"Mags, I copy. Can you hear me?"

"Yes, we're heading your way," she said. *"I'm sorry, X, but Michael and his family aren't here. I found no—"*

"Hold your position, Mags. Those freaks we saw earlier—they're hunting us and they know we're out here."

There was a pause. *"Okay, I'll find a place to hunker down."*

"Good. I'll head your way. Get somewhere high. If they find you, you shoot and you run."

"Got it."

X hurried back to Miles and put on his mask. After packing up their gear, he led the way to the stairwell. The stim was already kicking in. He felt a rush of warmth, and the pain in his chest and head suddenly seemed manageable.

Hearing from Magnolia had certainly helped, even though it was with news he already knew: Michael wasn't here.

Miles followed X down the stairs to the fifth floor. They stopped for a few moments to rest. X coughed a few times, but his lungs already felt better. By the time they got to the bottom floor, he felt twenty years younger.

He wasn't going to waste it.

With a glance to his wrist computer, he memorized the route to Magnolia. Her beacon was idle again. Fifteen blocks east—less than two miles.

Good. Stay put. I'm coming, Mags.

Rifle barrel resting on his prosthetic arm, he moved out the open doorway to clear the street outside. The hostiles were nowhere in view, and he didn't hear them either. He motioned for Miles to follow.

They moved quickly the first few blocks, but on the third and fourth, Miles started to slow. By the fifth, he was trotting behind X and favoring his near hind foot.

X looked out toward the marina, wondering if he should drop his dearest friend off at the *Sea Wolf*, then go in and extract Magnolia and Jo-Jo.

No, he couldn't risk it—too dangerous.

He wanted to be with the dog, and if it meant he had to carry him, he would. A few more minutes of rest, and X flashed a hand signal to his dog. They stalked through the darkness—Miles relying on his eyes, and X on his night-vision optics.

The distant shriek of a monster stopped them at the edge of a crater. X mounted a ridge of dirt and rock with a view over the section of city that the earth had swallowed.

A tongue of flame jetted into the sky across the crater's rim. He brought up his scope and zoomed in on three robed men advancing between two buildings, torching a section of broken windows with their flamethrowers.

Gunfire cracked. A Siren's wail penetrated through the din. But this wasn't an enraged shriek or a hunting call; this was the sorrowful cry of a beast in mourning.

These men weren't killing for survival. They were killing as offerings to some malicious Dark Lord. X knew the insane man wouldn't hesitate to do the same to Miles and Jo-Jo. And that sort of person could incite X to violence.

"Come on, boy," he said.

They took off around the edge of the crater. The animal seemed to be doing better now, with no discernible limp in his gait.

X, meanwhile, was starting to feel the stim's effects wear off. The headache was returning, and he felt a faint tickle in his throat.

He glanced to his wrist monitor, seeing it was just a few more minutes until he would reach Magnolia. She had holed up in a building three blocks away, in the opposite direction of the freaks.

He made it another block before the comms crackled.

"X, I've got eyes on a guy riding a beast. Is that a horse?"

"It's a camel. You got eyes on anyone else?"

There was a slight pause. *"Negative, just the one hostile,"* she replied. *"I can take him out easy, just say the word."*

X thought on it, decided against it. "Hold fire for now. We might be able to get out of here unseen."

"Copy that. I'll wait for you."

"Almost there, Mags. Stay low."

X kept going with Miles by his side. Having him there helped him forget the pain. It always did. This was just one of countless times they had ventured into danger with injuries or illness.

"You got this, X, you got this," he muttered. He ran through the rubble-strewn landscape, sighting from the humps of collapsed towers, skirting sinkholes and unsteady rubble. Miles too seemed energized by this new momentum.

A block and a half later, the comms crackled with a message from Magnolia.

"X, I've got two hostiles in view—scratch that, three," she said. *"Two mounted on camels and armed with rifles. The third is on the ground and has a sniper rifle."*

X digested the information quickly. This was just one squad of at least three, maybe four, out there. If they were to take these men down, they would have to do it fast and then get back to the boat.

"Sight up the sniper," X replied. "If they make a move toward your position, take him out first."

"Copy that. Got him in my sights."

X hurried down the road, toward the five-story apartment building with a cracked concrete exterior where Magnolia had taken shelter. Two burned vehicles lay on their sides just shy of the next intersection. When he got there, X crouched behind the shell of a panel truck, trying to catch his breath. Through the broken windows, he could see the two camels lumbering down the connecting street on the left.

He scanned the area. Looking for more hostiles and seeing none, he darted into the road with Miles. They entered the lobby of an old bank, glass crunching under their boots and booties.

X found a stairwell and directed Miles into it. They weren't even to the first floor when the radio crackled again.

"They're coming right for me," Magnolia said. *"I think they know we're here."*

Voices called out on the street X had just left.

He cursed under his breath, turned, and crept back down the stairs with Miles behind him. Propping the rifle up on his prosthetic arm, X crouch-walked through the lobby. Seeing no other option, he gave the kill order.

"Take out that sniper in ten seconds. I'll mop the rest up down here," he said quietly. "As soon as the bodies hit the ground, get down here and we make a run for the boat, understood?"

"Copy that," Magnolia said.

He stopped at the side of the door, signaling Miles to stay put. Using debris piles for cover and concealment, X counted the seconds down and started toward the three hostiles advancing toward Magnolia's building on the left side of the road. The closest camel and rider were two hundred feet ahead—not an easy shot, but he had plenty of charge in the laser rifle.

On the count of eight, he went down on one knee and prepared to fire.

Nine…

Crack! Crack! Crack!

The robed man with the sniper rifle crumpled to the ground in front of the camels, his robe catching fire from the laser.

"Infidel!" yelled the mounted rider on the lead camel. He

raised his rifle, only to be pounded by a flurry of laser bolts that hit his chest with short, hissing smacks.

The man slumped out of the saddle as the beast let out a loud bellow and took off at a lope.

X ran toward the second rider, firing as he moved. The bolts hit the camel in the hindquarters, shearing off a leg. It crashed to the ground, pinning the screaming man beneath it.

"You better be moving, Mags," X said into the comms.

He ran over to the pinned rider. The man raised a hand in a futile involuntary attempt to shield his face.

"Sorry, bub," X said. He fired a bolt that flashed through the hand and into the visor, spattering the pavement with gore.

The camel let out a groaning sound, and X put it out of its misery with a bolt to the head. The second rider, his boot caught in a stirrup, was being dragged in a circle over some very rough terrain. Judging by the streak of blood on the road, he was as dead as he was going to get. But the animal's high-pitched bleat might as well be a dinner bell for all the monsters in the city.

It turned toward X, its bleat turning into a rumbling roar. He feinted as the camel charged, then hit it in the jaw with his prosthetic elbow. The beast went down like a Siren on fire.

Another groan came from farther down the road. To X's surprise, the sniper was still moving. The weapon was on the concrete, out of reach, but seeing X, the guy went for a holstered pistol.

X pulled out his hatchet and went over as the man struggled to draw the gun.

"No, no, please!" he shouted.

X hurled the hatchet, hitting him square in the helmet visor. He plucked it out, then turned toward the building.

"X!" Mags shouted.

She burst out of an open door with Jo-Jo at her heels.

"Run!" she shouted.

Assuming that they were being flanked, X looked behind him, but he didn't see any movement. He felt something, though. A rhythmic vibration under his boots, as if something truly immense were trotting down the road.

The vibration turned into a rumbling. He looked at the door Magnolia and Jo-Jo had just come flying through. Zigzagging cracks ran up the concrete wall of the building. Dust and grit sifted down.

On the second floor, a wall exploded outward, pieces of concrete and metal raining to the road.

Not a dinosaur, but close enough.

A bone beast emerged in the opening. Its red eyes angled downward, found X. It raised its bone-covered arms and let out a guttural roar.

X took a step back, nearly stumbling as Magnolia and Jo-Jo sprinted past him.

"Move it, old man!" Magnolia shouted.

He didn't need to hear it twice. He took off after them, back toward the bank, where Miles was standing outside, barking.

A quake shook the road when the bone beast jumped down. The monster must have been using the structure to nest or hibernate or whatever the hell it did when not busy ripping things in half.

That roar rose to a pitch and volume that made X cup his ears.

Magnolia ran farther ahead with Jo-Jo. X ran harder, lungs burning.

"X, come on!" Magnolia shouted. She stopped ahead, brought up her rifle, and fired a burst. The shots found their target but seemed only to further enrage the beast.

Something sailed past X and slammed into the charred metal skin of a truck just ahead of him. It rolled on the ground and lay still. The long-lashed eyes of a camel stared up at him.

X looked over his shoulder at the bone beast chasing them with a man's limp body held in its glowing fist.

"X, watch out!" Magnolia shouted.

A rumble filled his ears, this one mechanical in nature.

An engine...

X had only a second to turn, right into blinding headlights. He reached up to shield his eyes from the bright glare.

"Move your ass!" Magnolia yelled.

She fired her laser rifle at a vehicle speeding toward him. He moved at the last second, but the front grille clipped him in the shoulder and sent him skidding across the ground.

He managed to look up as the truck stopped. Robed soldiers jumped out the back, firing some sort of electrical weapons at Magnolia.

"No," X stammered.

She went down and lay jerking on the ground. Miles nudged at her as Jo-Jo charged, then buttonhooked as a blast from a flamethrower caught her left side.

She howled in pain and took off screeching.

X tried to get up but was too stunned. The ground rumbled under him as the bone beast advanced from the other direction. He watched Miles pace between X and Magnolia, who had stopped twitching where she lay.

"Run, boy," X said. "Go help Jo-Jo!"

Miles barked, then took off, following the monkey into the rubble.

A wave of fire blasted over X, heating him in his suit. He managed to roll onto his side as the two robed men aimed their weapons at the bone beast. It had stopped in the middle of the street, twisted the corpse in two, and tossed the upper half at the men. Then it roared and strode off.

The two robed men watched it go, holding their position.

Another pair of boots walked over, right in front of X. He looked up to see the gray beard and muscular arms of Crixus.

The man tilted his head at X, like a scientist examining some creature new to science.

"This one is a woman," said someone behind Crixus. "Haven't seen one of them in a long time."

"What do you want us to do about their animals?" asked another. "They ran off into the buildings."

"Leave them—we've lost too many of our own," Crixus said with a heavy grunt. "You will pay for that, infidel."

Crouching, he grabbed X's helmet in both hands and squeezed in on the sides. Unable to move, X stared into the soulless gaze of this man who seemed intent on popping his head like a pimple.

The man's strength was remarkable, and X prepared to have his head crushed in. He felt a crack, as if his skull were on the verge of imploding. At least it would be quick…

Red encroached on his vision—blood, perhaps from breaking vessels in his eyes. He watched as they dragged Magnolia away.

X let out a groan of pain.

"Let… her… go!" he screamed.

The pain increased … then lessened as Crixus let go of his helmet.

X blinked, trying to see clearly. He tried to hold his head up, but it fell, the chin bar hitting the concrete.

"Too easy, old man," Crixus said. "I'll let Lucca deal with you."

X went limp as two men grabbed him by the armpits and feet. They carried him away with Magnolia. She wasn't moving, but the beacon on his HUD said she was alive.

They both still had air in their lungs, but X knew he had to come up with a plan soon or their heads would soon be on a pike with the others.

TWENTY-FOUR

"Good news, sir," Imulah said. "I just got a dove with this note from Pedro."

Kade got up from the desk in the library at the capitol tower, where maps were spread out across the tables. Beau and Dakota were here with him tonight, along with Lieutenant Wynn.

Imulah handed Kade the note, and he unfolded it under the glow of a burning candle. His heart filled with relief as he read the short message.

The Barracudas had arrived in Texas. Slayer had confirmed that they were heading to the target.

Kade looked at his watch. Ten days had passed since Lucky activated the beacon. It would take three weeks minimum for the Forerunner to reach the islands by sea—at least, according to Kade's numbers. So far, the scouts in Panama had seen no activity in the canal.

That meant he still had time to get the helicopters back here. And he had left the best warriors in charge of that mission. If all went to plan, they would be back at the Vanguard Islands with the aircraft and have time to spare before the Forerunner could arrive.

But if the Forerunner was already on his way, then it was too late to send Lucky back to the Coral Castle. The only way that could work was if the knights got a late start.

They might never come, Kade thought.

No matter, it was finally time to send Lucky off.

"Let's go," he said.

Dakota, Beau, Imulah, and Wynn followed him out of the library. Kade led the way down a stairwell to the enclosed port. At the bottom, Dakota opened the door. Of all the boats on lifts, one had been lowered to the water—a small yacht with a single cabin.

General Forge and two of his guards stood on the dock with Lucky, who wore a hooded sweatshirt with the hood up.

"Leave us, please," Kade said.

Forge motioned for the two men to follow him. Everyone walked away, leaving Kade alone with the knight.

"This is it, mate," Kade said. "You're going home."

Lucky raised a brow under his hood, as if he still couldn't believe it. He had a patchy beard growing in on his hard face.

"I can't thank you enough for what you've done for me," he said.

"The only thanks I want is for you to take my message to the Forerunner." Kade stepped up to Lucky so they were face to face.

"We both have a choice. We can be allies and set up a trading network. Or…" Kade stared into his eyes. "Or we can be enemies. You've seen a small piece of our territory, and our military might. You know that if the Forerunner comes, the fighting will claim many innocent lives on both sides."

"The choice isn't up to me, King Kade, but I'll do my best to persuade the Forerunner to consider your proposal."

Kade pulled from his vest a folded map.

"I trust you will be able to find your way home," he said. "We have outfitted you with provisions, gasoline, and batteries, but it's a long trip—over a third of the way around the world."

"I can handle it," Lucky said.

Kade took his hand. "I hope to see you again someday," he said.

Lucky held his grip for a long few seconds. It was as if he wanted to say something again, just like back on the rooftop when he had first seen the orange trees. But the moment passed, and he let go a moment later.

He walked over the gangplank to the yacht and turned.

"I have a hunch we'll see each other again," Lucky said. He went into the cabin.

Kade followed him. "I forgot something," he said.

He squeezed past Lucky in the open hatch, into the cabin. On the deck, between two captain's chairs, was an aluminum box that would accommodate a Hell Diver's helmet. Kade picked it up and handed it to Lucky.

"What's this?" he asked.

"Open it."

Lucky cocked the metal lid open to behold four plump oranges neatly stuffed around the glassy one-eyed stare of Charmer's head. Some men might have tossed it, dropped it, or yelped in alarm, but Lucky just looked up at Kade with a stern gaze.

"Take that to your Forerunner as a gift from me," Kade said. "That's the head of the last traitor to nearly destroy us. In his mouth is a tape with his and Rolo's confessions."

Kade recalled what the Forerunner had said about the Cazadores and their brutality. It was true, and instead of trying to hide it, Kade had decided to use that brutality to his advantage by showing the knights just how brutal his people could be with this offering.

Perhaps this would make the Forerunner think twice before attacking.

"The fruit is a taste of what a trading partnership could bring between our people," Kade said. "We can have it all, my friend."

He left Lucky holding the aluminum box in the cabin. The boat roared to life as he stepped out onto the pier. Kade nodded to the guard at the end of the marina, and the door cracked open to a moon-dappled sea.

It was a long journey, but the knight was a sailor, and Kade trusted that he would make it home. With this last mission deployed, he climbed the stairs to the Sky Arena with Beau and Dakota. The two hot-air balloons were being prepped to lift a platform constructed by the Cazadores, just as Tia had envisioned.

Kade thought of her, hoping she would listen to Slayer. He should have known better than to tell her about the mission. She should be here with the twenty-five new divers.

"I tried to talk Roman out of it, but you can guess how that went," Beau said.

His son was one of the new volunteers.

Kade had no answer to that, but he would lend his support if this was the route Roman decided on. "I'll make sure your boy gets the best training, even if that means I train him myself."

"Thank you, my friend, thank you," Beau said.

Kade felt his friend's pain. They shared a bond that only a parent who had lost a child could understand.

"All hail King Kade!" Sofia shouted. She stood at the front of the group, leaning on a crutch.

The divers all turned and stood at attention in front of Kade.

"At ease, everyone," he said.

He walked over and inspected the line with Sofia. She briefed him while crutching alongside.

Two of the greenhorns were from the ITC *Malenkov*. Valery "Chester" Malevsky seemed to be the most promising of the crop. The young man with a buzzed head and bright-blue eyes was intelligent and fit. They had almost selected him for the mission to Brisbane before deciding that he wasn't combat ready.

Then there was Slava Baganov. While Chester was a fair shot, Slava could put an arrow in a gull on the wing. But unlike Chester, who was a natural in the sky, Slava was about as graceful in the air as a tuna flopping on a boat deck.

Watching Slava dive before the Brisbane mission had been painful. He hadn't even come close to landing on the deck of the *Osprey* during their first training dive, almost drowning before a rescue boat could get to him.

Roman, from the airship *Victory*, was here along with a twenty-year-old named Hugh that Kade hardly knew. At only five feet, six inches, Hugh had to be one of the shortest male Hell Divers in history. But what he lacked in height he made up for in lean muscle built by manual labor at the machine camp and then as a laborer on oil rig 14 after he was brought here.

At the end of the line of recruits was someone Kade had not expected to see. Yejun, who had lived on the *Osprey* for years on his own, was standing stiff as a board, with a pair of goggles over his eyes. On his wrist, he wore the language translator that made communicating easier.

He held it up and spoke into it. "King Kade, I'm here to volunteer as a Hell Diver. Perhaps one day, we will return to my people's country."

Kade wasn't going to turn the kid down. He was young and green, but he wanted to be of help. And they needed all they could get.

"Okay, listen up, mates," Kade said. "You may all be wondering why you're here when we don't have an airship. That won't always be the case, and when it changes, we must be ready."

He scrutinized the young faces in front of him, remembering others that were no longer here. Johnny and Raph from *Victory*, and then Arlo, Edgar, Ada, and so many others Kade had served with over the past year.

There was strength in the faces of the men and women standing before him, but there was also fear. To Kade, it was a good sign. Lack of fear was what got people killed, or made them do stupid things as Tia had.

He pushed her from his mind.

"You've all met Commander Sofia Walters," Kade announced. "She will be the lead instructor. I will also help out while I can."

He walked in front of the line, taking time to look into each face.

"You all have heard about the Knights of the Coral Castle and their leader, known as the Forerunner. We still don't know if they will come and attack us, come in peace, or not come at all, but we must be ready, and that means by both sea and sky."

Several of the greenhorns exchanged glances.

"Your training will consist of diving, shooting, and hand-to-hand combat," he said. "You will learn how to use your gear for trips to the wastes, and how to survive and come back from those trips."

Kade put one hand on his sword hilt and the other on the pistol grip of the Monster Hunter. "Becoming an expert on your weaponry is as important as learning how to dive," he said. "The day may come when it will save your life."

He looked up at the sky. A few lazy wisps of cloud drifted past a brilliant platinum moon. This was a perfect night to dive.

"Ignite the burners," he said. "We're going up."

Kade was the first aboard. The platform was light—nylon cloth stretched over aluminum ribs. A railing with a gate provided some safety for the divers, who were also clipped in with carabiners. Cascade lines suspended the diving platform beneath the two balloons.

The balloon envelopes began to inflate with air heated by the burners, and up they rose, lifting the frame and rising away from the Sky Arena.

It was hard not to admire the gorgeous view.

"This is why we dive," he said. "This is our home—a place where you will raise your families and, we hope, grow old. That all depends on you."

The pilots of the hot-air balloons sounded their horns, indicating they were in position. Kade unclipped his harness and walked over to the lever that served as a gate. He lifted it and stood at the edge, looking down at the ocean.

Two thousand feet below them, the *Osprey* was anchored, ready to intercept them.

He turned toward the divers.

"I can't be with you for every dive, but I'll sure as bloody hell try," Kade said. "Mark my words. We dive so humanity survives!"

Kade fell backward and rolled into a stable falling position, arms and legs bent at right angles. For the first few seconds, there was the feeling of weightlessness, then the rush that came with his body adjusting to the wind and to plummeting toward the ocean at an accelerating rate of speed.

This being a low-altitude jump, he had little time to take in the view, but he managed to sight up a single boat below him. The yacht. Two Jet Skis flanked it as Lucky piloted it southwest, toward the Panama Canal.

Kade hoped Lucky would make it back home in one piece, and hoped even more that he could persuade the Forerunner to agree to a peace.

Former king Xavier had taught Kade something invaluable: try mightily for peace while preparing for war.

All missions were now launched, all plans set in motion. There was nothing to do but prepare and wait.

The water yawned up at Kade, and he pulled his chute. The canopy fired, the lines snapping taut and jerking him back up into the sky, or so it felt. He hung beneath the canopy, looking out over the sparkling ocean and the distant rigs.

Something about diving again reminded him of a time when things weren't so complicated. When his objective was to survive and bring needed parts back to the airship. Most of those missions were in green zones, and everyone came back.

He had never thought he would miss diving, but in some ways it was much easier than being king. Being king was a burden that ate at his insides. Never in his life had he been responsible for so many people's welfare. The sight of the glowing rigs arrayed below was a slap-in-the-face reminder of that.

As he prepared to land on the deck of the *Osprey*, he heard a voice calling out from the capitol tower. He pulled the right toggle and turned toward the shouts coming from one of the most important people left in his life.

"Go, Cowboy King!" Alton yelled from a balcony.

Kade couldn't help but grin. The kid always made him laugh, and right now, with so much at stake, laughing felt good.

*   *   *   *   *

"Preparing for descent," Michael said into his comm.

"Copy that," Layla replied.

Victor, wearing light armor, stood ahead of Michael with a laser rifle cradled over his chest. It was an hour before dawn, and the airship had lowered them back over the bluffs. The two men had roped down to the beach.

The goal was to find a way into the bunker, or an area that wasn't completely flooded, and also to recover the armor Victor had left behind. Michael wasn't too worried about that. He was more concerned about the structural integrity of these catacombs. If they were flooded, they were in danger of collapse.

He had prepared for everything he could think of, and carried a pack full of items to keep them safe. Timothy had uploaded to Michael's wrist computer a new scanner program that would test for all sorts of toxins in the air, soil, and water.

Michael activated the computer scanners and looked up at the dark sky. Twenty thousand feet up, the airship hid above the storms, with Layla and Bray safely inside.

They had passed the biggest test yet: getting here.

"Okay, let's go," Michael said.

Victor shouldered his rifle and started into the mine tunnel, running his tac light over the walls. Paintings, drawn by ancient residents who must have lived here after the war, depicted cities with people strolling on sidewalks. Cars passing them by. Forests with deer, rabbits, a bear. Snowcapped mountains. Crystalline lakes and rivers. The beach full of sunbathers. Surfers in the waves, and boats out beyond.

Another section showed something that made Michael pause.

Missiles streaked across blue skies. Bombs exploded in cities, blotting out the azure sky with dark mushroom clouds.

Craters where those cities had been, and the electrical storms raging over the ruined planet.

The walls told the story of what happened to the world.

Victor came to a fork in the tunnel system, looked left, then right, and went right.

"Wait," Michael said. He pulled out one of the glow sticks that they often used on dives in confusing conditions. Plucking off the cap, he scratched *X1* on the wall.

"Smart idea," Victor said.

Michael followed him down the next tunnel, which had both smooth and grooved walls. A machine had made this one. In front of Victor, the passage widened. His light hit a rusted fence, its bent gate hanging loosely ajar. A chain lay in a pile on the ground. In the end link was a lock with the key still inside.

"Do you remember this place at all?" Michael asked.

"Not really," Victor replied. "I remember many tunnels, but all above the main bunker. Bunker now underwater."

He held open the gate for Michael, who raised his computer for another scan. Still no toxins and no radiation. This was indeed a green zone.

The corridor opened into a chamber. Right away, Michael could see that it was also flooded.

Whether this was from natural causes or by design—that was the real question. He looked for evidence of the latter—explosive residue, implements, newly fallen rocks. He found nothing to sway his opinion one way or the other.

The pool of water appeared to cover an area the size of the water-treatment center on the airship. Michael did a life scan with his computer and detected multiple smaller biological entities. They were too small for the airship scanners to pick up, but not for his scanner.

"Hold up," he said to Victor. "I've got hits on my computer."

Victor pointed his rifle at the water and inched up toward the edge with Michael. His helmet lights, combined with the tac light on the rifle barrel, illuminated the pool. Small blue creatures, all about the size of a shoe, darted away from the light.

"Fish," Michael said.

Something skittered away from a rock, into the water. Michael's light revealed dozens of crabs the size of his hand, with their pincers up as they clambered away to hide.

The two men circuited the pool and found another tunnel access. Again Victor led the way. Crab shells and claws littered the ground. It looked like old debris left by some animal that had fed on them.

Michael looked for tracks but saw nothing in the long passage. A downed metal fence with a twisted gate lay on the ground ahead.

Victor walked over the panels, moving cautiously into the junction and scanning both ways. He gave the all clear. The right side of the passage ended in a pile of rubble from a cave-in.

This time, Michael found charred debris. Someone had intentionally blown these passages.

But why? That was the question he had to figure out.

He turned left, where the corridor ran farther than he could see with his light. After leaving another mark on the wall, he followed Victor.

Ten steps in, Michael's computer went haywire. Halting, he raised it while Victor crouched with his rifle pointed into the darkness. The lights speared into another chamber, where the sensors seemed to be picking something up inside.

Michael checked the screen, but the sensors were coming back with an inconclusive reading. It meant one of two things: whatever lay ahead wasn't in the database Timothy had uploaded, or the sensors were messed up.

With a nod, Michael gave Victor the green light to proceed. They followed the passage toward the sounds of dripping water. Their lights played over the walls, ceiling, and floor as more crab shells crunched under their boots.

There was life down here; they knew this much. How big and dangerous was another question.

The path of pincer claws and crab carapaces led to another cavern. Here, water dripped from a hundred stalactites in an arrhythmic cacophony.

Victor played his light over the rocky ceiling, seeing more of the rocks that looked like dirty icicles. The men passed under them, into another cave with vaulted ceilings and thousands more stalactites.

NICHOLAS SANSBURY SMITH |

Their lights captured a carpet of green moss and ferns grow-ing throughout the room. Some of the ferns were waist high with arching red fronds. Clusters of nettle flowers sporting pink petals grew along a creek that meandered through the cavern.

But how could this ecosystem exist without light?

Michael checked his scanner. This was indeed what had set off the sensors. Looking up, he saw the answer to his question. There was a narrow gap in the rocky ceiling—further confirma-tion that the sunlight wasn't random, that it was regular enough to allow photosynthesis.

A trickle of waterfall slid down the rocky walls on the left side, forming a freshet that ran through the dark but apparently vibrant ecosystem.

He followed the running stream to a small crack in the rock wall. Through the gap, he glimpsed the ocean, and heard the distant white noise of the surf.

"Over here," Victor said.

He trekked along the central rivulet toward a slick hump of boulder. On the other side, he was mildly surprised to find an all-terrain vehicle, sitting on rims with rotted tires. Michael rushed over to find crates toppled on the ground next to the vehicle. Inside were cracked glass jars and plastic bottles. Several jugs lay near the stream.

Michael crouched down with the same testing kit Layla had used at Mount Mitchell. He took a sample of water, then plugged it into the scanner.

"Do you know where we are?" he asked.

Victor shook his head. "I never see this place."

Michael put the kit away, stood, and checked his computer. The temperature was sixty-five degrees with high humidity. There was no trace of radiation.

"I find something," Victor said. He shined his light on a

doorway in the cave wall across the chamber. Ancient stairs provided some traction down the slippery rock. A rail hung loose in parts where the rusted bolts had given way.

Michael followed Victor cautiously down the steps. The sounds of running, dripping, trickling water filled their ears as it flowed downward, seeking sea level. Sure enough, the crashing of waves greeted them at the bottom of the stairs.

Victor walked out into a cave that opened onto the beach. Pools of water left behind from the last high tide formed little ecosystems in the mouth of the long rock corridor. Crabs sidled across the ground, fleeing in all directions.

"Over there," Victor said, pointing at an elevated platform. A rusted ladder hung down from the crooked metal overhang.

He started to climb up while Michael waited at the bottom. The platform creaked under Victor's weight. At the top, he disappeared into a doorway.

A moment later, Victor's voice called out, "Chief, come look."

Michael swung up onto the ladder and climbed up to a steel platform anchored into the rock. His helmet lights chased shadows in the connecting cavern. Stacks of lobster pots, piles of nets, an anchor, and an old steamer trunk lay strewn about the passage.

Victor had already moved past all that and was crouched next to a corpse holding a speargun. Michael walked over.

Two more corpses lay facedown in the tunnel. An arm and a leg—just bone and sinew—lay a few feet away from the bodies. Victor leaned down to examine the skulls, which were broken in many places, like eggshells. A crab pincer snapped at his finger as he reached down.

He turned to look at Michael, a tear falling behind his visor. It didn't need to be said: these were three of his friends.

"I'm sorry," Michael said.

Victor got up and continued down the corridor, but Michael

didn't see a fourth body. He remembered specifically that four people had stayed behind when Ton and Victor embarked with friends on a boat to American shores.

More items were strewn about: empty jugs, cans, discarded clothing, rotted sleeping bags, packs. The corridor ended at another cave-in.

It was obvious that these people had flooded and destroyed the tunnels to keep out some threat. Probably the same pirates who had raided Victor's home.

In the end, though, the hostiles had found them.

He turned back to the bodies. Years had passed since they were killed, though any evidence beyond that had been picked clean by the crabs.

Michael went over to Victor and put a hand on his shoulder. "I'm sorry about your friends."

"Thank you. I was hoping, just maybe…"

The fourth was still out there somewhere, but they might never learn that person's fate.

"I have one thing left to check out," Michael said.

Victor followed him back to the steel platform secured to the rock. They took the ladder and followed the inlet back to the beach. Waves pushed tan windblown froth up onto the sand. A dirt path wound up the rocky shore to the top of the bluffs.

Michael took it to the top, where he crouched again with his testing kit for a soil sample. While he waited for the results, he stood at the edge of the cliff, looking out over the water.

The sun would be coming up soon, and he wondered if it would once again break through the storms. Victor held security, looking out over the unremarkable rocky terrain and clusters of barb-leafed plants.

Beeping came from Michael's wrist computer with the results from all tests.

No toxins present.

He looked out over the fields. Was it really possible to grow crops here? Could the water really support life?

Only time would tell.

"Layla, do you copy?" he said.

"Copy, Michael. What did you find?"

"The scan results all came back good. I'm sending them to you now, but we found something else. Bodies. Three of them. Murdered years ago."

There was a pause. *"Any sign of recent activity?"*

"No, I think it's safe to say the culprits are long gone."

"And the bunker?"

"From what we've seen so far, all underwater."

"Are the caves habitable?"

"It seems they could be, but we'd need to do some work." He sighed. "It's not what we thought—"

"No," Layla replied. *"It's better. There's fish and crabs, clean water, the soil is toxin-free according to your scans, which I'm looking over now, and we might even get sun every once in a while."*

He looked up at the sky, unable to see the airship but smiling at his family all the same.

"Timothy, bring the ship down," Michael said. "It's time for Bray to see our new home."

TWENTY-FIVE

Gran Jefe picked up a dry-rotted wooden beam that had once propped up the entrance to the mine. He dragged it from the debris blocking the entrance. The APC and trailers were behind them, ready to extract the two Jayhawks stored deep underground. But the birds weren't going anywhere until they could clear the rubble.

Beams from the APC illuminated the excavation site, where Gran Jefe worked with Slayer to lift away chunks of rock scree while Zuni shoveled the dirt aside. They couldn't use the blade on the APC for fear of causing an even worse cave-in.

Blackburn was in the turret of the APC, watching for hostiles. Woody and Tia were inside the cabin, watching through the windows.

Gran Jefe heaved the beam onto the muddy pile and paused to scan the terrain for more of the clicking diseased humanoids that had attacked them earlier. Seeing nothing, he went back to the debris pile. Most of the big beams of wood and steel shoring were moved out of the way, leaving just loose dirt and rocks blocking the entrance.

"Mata," Slayer said.

Gran Jefe turned around to see that his two comrades had finally exposed the entrance to the mine. Zuni crouched down for a view through the opening in the mound.

"I see a way," he said. "Looks like the shaft is still good."

"Finally," Gran Jefe said. Sweat stinging his eyes, he stepped back and took a drink from his water bottle.

Slayer got down on his belly with a flashlight.

"It looks stable," he reported. "If we can dig out the rest, we should be able to get the rig and trailers in and come out with the helos."

The door to the APC opened, and Tia and Woody hopped out.

"Did I say to get out of the truck?" Slayer asked.

"Oh, you're serious," Woody said. "You want us to stay inside for the entire mission?"

Slayer stared at him.

"I'm not worthless, ya know, mate," Woody said. He held up the shotgun. "I killed that bloody freak."

"Yeah, and I said thanks," Slayer said. "Now, get back in the truck until I tell you to get out!"

For the next hour, Gran Jefe worked with Zuni and Slayer to clear away more dirt and rock. Finally, they had an opening big enough for a man to squeeze through.

Slayer took a look, then glanced back at the APC. "We can probably plow through the rest, but before we make that kind of noise, I want to make sure those birds are really there."

"I go this time," Gran Jefe said.

"I'm coming with you," Slayer said. "Blackburn, you stay on the LMG and blast anything that moves. Zuni, stay here with him."

Gran Jefe felt a hand on his shoulder as he checked his rifle.

"We go in quiet," Slayer said. "Don't shoot anything unless you have no other choice, understood?"

"Sí, teniente."

"Question," Woody said. He was halfway inside the APC and holding the door open. "Am I allowed one?"

"What?" Slayer asked.

"You guys stop to think what might have brought that tunnel entrance down but not the shaft behind it? That tells me it was some*one* and not some*thing*."

Slayer didn't answer.

"What if it's someone trying to do us a favor by keeping us out?" Woody said.

"Or maybe someone doesn't want us stealing whatever's down there," Slayer said. "Either way, we have a mission, so get back in the God damn truck."

"Best of luck to you, mate."

Gran Jefe checked yet again to make sure he had a round chambered. It was habit. Next, he did the same with his pistol. He was also equipped with his double-bitted axe in a strap over his shoulder, two sheathed knives on his duty belt, a smaller blade in each boot, and a pair of grenades hanging from his magazine carrier.

"Let's hope the beast we killed is the last of the infected humanoids, but we proceed like it isn't," Slayer said. "I think they use sound to hunt. You understand what that means, right?"

"That maybe Zuni should be going instead of the big lug," Blackburn said with a chuckle.

"Mata's going with me," Slayer said.

Zuni got back into the APC while Blackburn kept the LMG trained on the entrance. Gran Jefe flattened his body as best he could and started through the muddy doorway. In the green hue of his night-vision goggles, the walls of the shaft came into focus. It was just as he remembered it, down to the fence and the abandoned truck.

Slayer moved ahead, slightly hunched, rifle butt firmly against his shoulder.

Gran Jefe followed, trying to keep his footfalls quiet. The path was covered in a thin layer of dust and grit. Nothing had come this way recently.

Maybe the diseased abomination Woody had blasted topside was the last of these feral humanoids. Perhaps the fungal infestation had killed the rest of them off. There sure were plenty of corpses back in the marsh.

Or maybe the beasts were using another route to get in and out of the underground city. Gran Jefe would find out soon enough.

He joined Slayer at the open elevator shaft. The car was only a few floors below them.

That was the one difference—a decade ago, the car had been lower in the shaft. Now it seemed to be between floors.

"Good news," Gran Jefe whispered.

"Why?" Slayer replied.

Frustrated with trying to say it in English, Gran Jefe switched to Spanish, saying he remembered the car being farther down, which meant that there was still power to the installation.

Slayer shined his flashlight down on an access door in the wall ten feet above the car. "We rope down the shaft to the access door, then find a way to open that and get inside the facility," Slayer said.

"Okay," Gran Jefe said. It was a good idea to go on foot. Taking the elevator freight car would alert whatever creatures might be prowling down here. If they could rope down, then get that door open, they could get inside and find the choppers, power up the elevator, and send down the car.

The sheer racket of doing all that was bound to draw attention, making a fight inevitable if there were beasts living inside the shafts still.

They roped down to the roof of the car, landing as quietly as they could on the top. Gran Jefe looked through the open access door, seeing the broken bones below. Slayer motioned to join him against the wall, right below the access door. Then he pointed at the ground. At first, Gran Jefe didn't understand.

"*Yo no soy perro.* Gran Jefe… not dog."

"Just do it, Mata," Slayer said. Grumbling in two languages, Gran Jefe got down on all fours. Slayer got on his back and reached up. Grabbing the ten-inch ledge for the access door, the commander hauled himself up as Gran Jefe gave him a boost. Slayer looked down from the ledge.

"I got to open it more," he said.

While waiting on Slayer, Gran Jefe went to the elevator access hatch and looked down into the car for evidence of any recent kills. All the bones on the floor looked as though they had been there awhile, and a few in one corner had grown some sort of furry black mold.

He heard clunking and scrabbling above, where Slayer was wedging open the door. Slayer unholstered his pistol and aimed it inside, then bent down and dropped a rope to Gran Jefe. Gran Jefe threw a loop in it, stepped up into the loop, grabbed the ledge, and, with an assist from Slayer, hauled himself up and over.

Slayer started to talk, but a rapid clicking silenced him.

Slayer swapped his pistol for his rifle while Gran Jefe also unslung his rifle, trying to determine the location of the clicking. The noise echoed and faded away.

Slayer motioned to continue inside the open space beyond the access door. They entered a stairwell and moved down to the next landing, where a rusted sign indicated this was floor 19.

"You said in the briefing the Jayhawks are on floor ten," Slayer said.

Gran Jefe thought on it but he couldn't remember exactly.

"*Sí,*" he replied.

Slayer kept moving down the narrow stairwell. A few floors down, something cracked under his boot. He shined his flashlight down on a human femur. More bones littered the stairs at floor 15.

The two men picked their way between the remains, trying not to make too much clatter as they headed down. A body on the next landing seemed to be the source of the bones. A cracked skull, half a rib cage, and a spinal column were all that remained of a person who had been literally torn to pieces.

At floor 12, they found an open door, which Slayer checked out with his light. All that Gran Jefe could see was another mine tunnel.

At floor 10, the stairwell door was completely gone. Slayer stepped back for Gran Jefe to take a look.

"This it?" he asked.

Gran Jefe raked his light back and forth over a wide tunnel. He thought back ten years, getting off that elevator and walking into a chamber with large sliding doors. But this wasn't it. Two hulking bulldozers with rusted blades were the only things here.

"No," he said.

"You said floor ten, right?" Slayer asked.

"*Sí, pero no.* I mistake it."

"Or someone already took the—"

More clicking. But this sounded slightly different from what they heard in the elevator shaft. To Gran Jefe it seemed more mechanical than biological.

Slayer waited until it stopped.

"Keep going," he said.

Gran Jefe hoped he was wrong about the floor, hoped they hadn't come all this way for nothing. Down the two men went, to the next landing, marked 9. The door was locked, and Slayer got out his picks again.

Distant noises reverberated through the facility. Coming from above and below, it seemed. It was impossible to tell where the noise originated. Gran Jefe aimed his rifle up the way they had come, suddenly feeling anxious. Was something flanking them?

"Got it," Slayer said.

The door clicked ajar. Gran Jefe shifted his rifle, and when Slayer opened it he strode inside, tac light on.

He moved into another chamber with two sliding doors half-open in its far wall. Beyond, he could see the open elevator shaft that he had entered through ten years ago.

As he turned, he saw what they had come here for. Relief filled him at the sight of two helicopters, still half-draped in tarps.

Slayer followed him into the large space, sweeping his light over the machines. He suddenly held up a fist. Gran Jefe halted, scanning for whatever had the commander spooked.

Slayer pointed at the other end of the room. There, another, smaller door led to the railed bridge where, a decade ago, Gran Jefe had nearly lost his head to a diseased humanoid wielding a poleax. He looked down over the railing, to the vat of yellow liquid where his attacker had sunk without a trace.

Lumpy forms lay on the floor. He didn't remember seeing those.

Gran Jefe started toward them. Through the open door, his tac light illuminated dust particles that wafted like snowflakes in the still air. They seemed to be coming from above.

Slayer walked with him, pointing his light at a layer of dark-gray ash that covered the ground near the door. The beam went to the lumps on the floor. As the two men drew closer, the strange clumps took on the appearance of dead coral. Brown fan-shaped growths had formed little colonies on the metal, in six distinct locations.

Both beams picked out a railing with a hard, bark-like fungus growing on the metal. The concrete wall was encrusted by the same sort of growth, its frayed edges reaching out like fingers.

"What in the devil is this?" Slayer whispered.

Gran Jefe centered his light on a raised hump of the strange fungus that had an arm protruding. The beam hit a face half-consumed by a growth with brain-like convolutions. A closed eyelid and part of the mouth were the only recognizable external features.

He located two more of the infested humans. Then four. After a few seconds, he counted ten.

Gran Jefe moved his light back to the fungal clusters on the bridge as the realization set in.

Those too were people. Or once had been.

Slayer took another step forward, crunching a small bone on the ground. Gran Jefe froze at the string of clicks that answered the noise.

Red glows suddenly lit up the bridge, running up the wall of the silo like strands of decorative lights. Tendrils with barbed ends flickered back and forth as they searched for the source of the noise.

"Don't move," Slayer whispered.

Gran Jefe resisted the urge to raise his rifle.

Hearing a clank behind them, he turned to see the sliding doors closing. A bright blue light washed over Slayer and Gran Jefe. They both whirled to face the Coast Guard pilot AI that Gran Jefe had encountered a decade ago.

"I would run if I were you," it said. "In ten seconds, those doors will close."

A loud roaring burst across the bridge as the disfigured humanoid creatures popped up, standing on fungus-covered limbs. Their bodies creaked like trees in a high wind.

Gran Jefe raised his rifle, but Slayer yanked on his shoulder plate.

"Run!" he said. "To the doors!"

He turned and started toward the sliding doors, already at half their earlier gap. The two men raced past the pair of tarp-shrouded helicopters, guttural shrieks and hissing right on their heels. Gran Jefe could hear the pounding of fungus-encased feet and hands crunching, squishing, creaking in a macabre chorus behind them.

The doors narrowed, closer to entombing them inside.

Slayer pulled ahead, his boots crunching over bones. Their lights danced across the floor, making it almost impossible to see where they were going.

"Hurry!" yelled the AI.

The hologram flickered on the other side of the doors, waving at them. Slayer made it through, and Gran Jefe was just about there when he slipped, falling hard to the ground ten feet from the door. Bullets zipped over his head, bursting a face deformed by fan-shaped growths.

"Come on!" Slayer yelled.

Head spinning, Gran Jefe pushed at the ground. He managed to get up and stumble sideways toward doors that could cut him in half. When he paused, Slayer reached out and yanked him through, then raised his rifle and fired a burst. Pulp and gore followed Gran Jefe through the gap. Something slapped to the ground beside him.

He lay on his back, panting, listening to the creatures pound on the other side.

"Mata," Slayer said, reaching down to help him up. "You good?"

"*Pues, sí...*" Gran Jefe took the offered hand and got up. Then he saw what had landed by his side: a still-twitching arm covered in bark, dark blood pooling beneath it. "*¡Hijoeputa!*" he shrieked.

After scrambling away, Gran Jefe pushed himself up, right in front of the pilot's glowing hologram.

"Oh, it's you again," said the AI. "I must say, I'm surprised to see you came back after all this time."

"We came for the aircraft," Slayer said.

"The Jayhawks," replied the AI.

"Yes."

The pilot looked from Slayer to a still-panting Gran Jefe before moving in front of the door. Standing in front of it, he folded his arms over his chest.

"If you want to leave with my aircraft, you'll need more bullets," he said. "But I can help you if you agree to help me."

TWENTY-SIX

"Mags," X said quietly.

He sat with his back against the wall of a truck bed, his hand bound to his prosthetic arm. His ankles were tied with rope. Magnolia was also bound and still unconscious. Their captors drove them out of the city, to the winding path up the bluff, where the fires burned around the broken statue of the Old World god.

A robed warrior covered them with the laser rifle that Magnolia had dropped when they shot her with a stun gun. The man had his back to them now and was staring out over the jungle.

The second guard, wearing a spiked helmet like his comrade's, stood inside a swivel turret on the cab of the truck, holding a mounted flamethrower. He kept glancing back at Magnolia—*only* at Magnolia.

It was obvious these men hadn't seen a woman in a very long time.

Miles and Jo-Jo had escaped, for now. X hoped they would stay well away. They were lucky to be alive still, and lucky these men hadn't chased them.

X was also lucky to have sustained only minor injuries when

the truck hit him in the shoulder. His armor had another dent to go with all the others. His neck hurt, and his ribs too, but the true source of his misery was the fever.

"Mags," he said, a little louder this time.

He leaned down and watched until satisfied that her back was moving rhythmically up and down.

Maybe that wasn't so lucky...

They would no doubt kill X, probably sacrifice him to this Dark Lord. But not Mags. Not right away, at least. These lowlifes were going to have fun with her.

Things were bad, but X had gotten out of worse situations than this. Some of them replayed in his mind as the truck jolted along on the bumpy path.

Ninety-six dives. Ten years wandering the wastes with Miles. Cancer. War with el Pulpo, then with the skinwalkers. Fighting countless monsters in the wastes: radiation-emitting beasts, giant water bugs, Sirens, bone beasts, and even finding himself in the mouth of a leviathan. Traveling to Panama, Australia, Rio... But he didn't yet know how he would escape this situation alive with Magnolia, Miles, and Jo-Jo.

He tried to stifle a cough. Mags stirred, raised her head.

The guard turned with a flashlight that he then pointed at her.

"Ah..." she moaned.

"Take it easy," X said. "You're okay."

"Where... where are we?" she asked.

The man stood and stomped. X held on to Magnolia as the vehicle slid to a stop. One of the front doors opened. Boots crunched toward the back of the truck. Their hulking leader, Crixus, came into view.

"She's awake," said the guard.

Crixus climbed up into the truck bed, the tires sagging under his weight. Magnolia kicked at him as he leaned down. In a crouch, he lifted up his mask to reveal a youthful, clean-shaven face with catlike green eyes over a freckled, well-formed nose.

X had expected to see a monster, but many would consider this man handsome. That might change soon if X could get his arms free.

Crixus reached out with a finger, running it along her helmet as she tried to pull away.

"Don't be afraid," he said. "You're safe now. You will have redemption."

"Don't touch her," X said.

The man turned to X, focusing those piercing green eyes on him.

"You touch her, and you will regret it," X said. "I promise you that."

Crixus patted his belly. "Soon, you will be in here," he said. "And your woman will be beneath me."

"I'm warning you," X said.

Crixus laughed, deep and hard.

"Do you know who I am?" he asked. "I am Crixus, the God of the Wastes, and I've crushed many men like you in my lifetime. Watched them burn and then feasted on their hearts."

"Do you know who he is?" Magnolia asked. She jerked her helmet toward X.

"No, and I don't know who you are yet either," Crixus said.

"I'm Magnolia, and this is the Immortal, Xavier."

"Immortal." Crixus laughed hard again. "We shall see about that…"

He put his mask back on and stood, peering down at them for another moment. Then he jumped down onto the dirt, and seconds later they were moving again.

The path wound in switchbacks up toward the crest of the bluff. The fires around the statue seemed brighter now.

X had a feeling that soon he would be fed to those flames. He sat up straight, trying to get his hand free without being seen. The rope was tight, but he managed to saw the prosthesis back and forth, trying to fray the thick fibers enough that he might pull the metal arm free. He couldn't do anything about his ankles right now, but if he could get his arms free, maybe he would have a chance.

Magnolia was also upright now and scooted over next to him, leaning against the cab of the truck.

The guard watched their every move but said nothing.

X felt the clock ticking down as the truck thumped up the rocky road. On the summit, his fate awaited him at the feet of their Old World god.

There had to be a way out of this, and he had to find it fast. He was sick and feeling worse by the minute. But if he could just free his hand and prosthetic arm, maybe he could take the laser rifle and kill all these sickos.

"Where's Miles and Jo-Jo?" Magnolia whispered.

"They got away," X replied softly. He coughed, his chest rattling.

"You're worse?"

He nodded.

"Shit," Magnolia whispered. "We need a plan. You got any ideas?"

"Not just yet."

The truck kept going, and every minute that passed, X felt his body weakening. He thought back to one of the most painful times of his life, when the *Hive* had left him behind in Hades. He had made it back to the ground with a gut wound, freezing cold, with no food, shelter, or weapons.

And he had survived. Found a place to camp, found food. Fought the monsters. Saved Miles. For ten years, they had scraped out an existence. This was just another roadblock he had to navigate.

You can do this, he thought. *You have to.*

As the truck pulled into the parking lot below the statue, he felt a new sense of energy and strength.

The guard put the back gate down and reached for Magnolia.

"Don't touch me!" she shouted.

She got up, but the man still grabbed her. Squirming, she fought as he handed her to Crixus, who waited in the dirt.

"Let me go!" she yelled. "Let me go or I'll have your pricks on a pike along with your heads!"

X used the distraction to work on his hand some more. He sawed back and forth with the prosthesis against the rope, fraying apart one fiber at a time, working the edges until it loosened enough… Mustering every atom of strength, he pulled, suppressing the urge to cry out in pain.

The hand slid free.

The guard who had handed Magnolia off turned toward him. X kept both hands behind his back and waited for the man to reach down. The moment he did, X smashed him in the visor with a metal fist, then grabbed the arm with the laser rifle.

He yanked it free and was about to vaporize the man in the turret when he felt a hand on his duty belt. The next instant, he was yanked backward, right over the side of the truck bed. Landing in the dirt with a thud, he peered up at the masked face of Crixus.

Grabbing X by the neck, the beast raised him off the ground with one hand and held him a foot in the air, his bound ankles and feet kicking away.

He squeezed hard, and once again the world turned a dim, dark red. X knew he didn't have long. The man had almost crushed his skull before; he would crush his windpipe and not break a sweat.

X reached up to free himself, but it was useless.

"Stop!" Magnolia shouted. "We'll do what you want!"

"Oh, I agree," Crixus growled.

He tossed his captive away like a rag doll. X hit the dirt again, this time on his side, with a thump that knocked the air from his lungs. Still, he pushed himself up and searched for a weapon. A rock—anything.

"No!" Magnolia shouted. "Leave him alone!"

Crixus strode over and cocked one leg to kick him in the stomach, but X rolled away on his back. He scooped up a fistful of dirt and tossed it up at Crixus's mask.

X got up and swung with his prosthetic arm just as an electric jolt hit him in the side. He jerked and crumpled to the ground.

"Who fired that?" Crixus roared.

On his side, X had a view of the guard who had fired the Taser at him. The man lowered the weapon. "I did . . . I'm sorry . . ." he started to say.

Crixus raised a hand to the truck. X glanced up as the soldier in the turret swung the spout of the flamethrower around to the robed guard. A wave of flame squirted out, enveloping the man. He screamed, arms flailing as if he might fly. Then, somehow, he managed to run to the edge of the cliff, where he leaped over the side.

X lay there in agony, knowing he had missed his chance to save Magnolia. And still he pushed at the ground again, fell back down, and pushed himself up once more.

Crixus walked over and bent down. "You're strong, old man, I give you that," he said. "You will be a good offering for the Dark Lord."

He stood and beckoned Magnolia to him.

"Take her to my tent," he said. "String up this 'immortal' and prepare the sacrifice."

Two guards rushed over to X and picked him up as another dragged a screaming Magnolia away.

"No!" she shouted. "I'll kill every one of you!"

*   *   *   *   *

A brilliant silver disk of moon blazed in the sky over the trading post rig, capturing the crowds of people who had come for the festivities marking the Wolf Moon.

Kade was exhausted but had promised Alton he would show up for the Cazador celebration. And celebrating they were.

A band of six Cazadores played on an elevated platform centered in the deck, surrounded by dozens of vendor stalls. The men wore fancy charro suits, and the women were dressed in vibrant reds and yellows. Armed with violins, a trumpet, guitars, and drums, the band produced lively, upbeat music that kept the growing crowd energized.

At least a hundred people in the audience were dancing and singing along to a song about love and heartbreak. Hundreds more had packed onto the large deck, and many more were sitting at long tables, enjoying grilled fish and alcoholic drinks. Others stood around, talking and laughing.

From Kade's count, there had to be over five hundred people down there.

Four militia soldiers and a pair of Cazador warriors, all armed with assault rifles, lingered on the elevated platforms. They wouldn't be able to do much if violence broke out, and the fact that nearly everyone had a weapon didn't help matters.

So far, everyone seemed to be enjoying themselves. But the night was young, and there was plenty of wine and shine to consume.

Kade remained in the shadows, under an awning on an upper

deck with his small entourage. Beau, Dakota, Imulah, Pedro, and Wynn had joined him and were now listening to a briefing from General Forge.

No word from Texas. No word from Rio. And no updates from the scouts in Panama.

Kade again had to remind himself of the positive. No updates from the scouts was a good thing. It meant they had yet to see any sign of the knights. That meant he had plenty of time for X to return, and the last he heard, Tia was alive and well. It was a huge relief and a desperately needed win.

Things are going to be okay. Relax.

He pulled out the handheld tablet that showed the beacon for Lucky. His boat was already fifty miles to the south, making good time. But he had a long way to go before reaching the Coral Castle.

"Cowboy King!" shouted a voice.

Kade moved out and looked over the railing, down to Alton. The boy had found him somehow. Katherine and Phyl were right behind him.

"You coming down here, or what?" Alton asked. "You got to see the tuna they caught today. It's like a dinosaur!"

"Not that big, but pretty big," Phyl said.

"Take a break," Katherine said. "Come join us."

"Come on!" Alton yelled, waving.

Kade nodded. "I'll be down shortly."

"Go ahead and enjoy yourself, King Kade," Forge said. "I'll keep the watch."

Kade hesitated, but Beau gave him a nudge. "You need a break, mate," he said. "Let's go have a drink, just like old times."

That did sound good to Kade. He left the platform and took a stairwell down to the middle deck, where Dakota and Lieutenant Wynn walked by his side.

Curious eyes found Kade the moment he stepped onto

the deck. Cazadores, sky people, and survivors rescued from around the world were down here, all of them gawking at the newest leader of the Vanguard Islands.

Alton ran over with a huge grin on his face. "Follow me," he said, tugging on Kade's hand.

Katherine and Phyl hurried after them.

"Slow down, pal," Kade said.

Dakota held up his shield as they joined the crowd of civilians. Most people weren't paying attention to Kade and were watching the band with a drink in their hand. The crowd swallowed them as they made their way inside, where the bouquet of body odor, booze, and piss was strong. This was the scent of the islands and wasn't all that different from the machine camp, or even the airship when Kade lived there.

Cramped corridors, lack of resources for hygiene, and bad plumbing seemed to be universal. At least there was open air here. And a beautiful moon.

Kade looked up to admire it. The glow spread over the smiling faces of people who had managed to forget their sorrows for a little while and celebrate life.

"Be right back," Beau said. He walked to a stand with a barrel of wine resting on a wooden ledge. A bartender carefully poured with a lever, filling each glass with precisely the same volume of dark red wine.

Kade kept going with Katherine, Phyl, Alton, and the guards. A new scent greeted them as the group made their way around the back end of the crowd to an area of open grills.

"There!" Alton yelled. He pointed to a table staffed by a Cazador chef with a narrow, sharp blade. He delicately sliced sashimi cuts from large tuna filets. The head was on one end of the table, and the tail on the other. Another chef was cooking up the steaks at a nearby grill.

Customers stood in a line ten deep, awaiting their turn to purchase the high-quality fish.

Kade recalled the market at the Coral Castle, where the woman had learned that her catch was radiated. He thought of Lucky and how the knight had brought him to see his sister.

"Crikey!" Alton said. "I'd love to catch one of those. Maybe I will have my own boat someday—a trawler, or a catamaran like Michael took me on."

He looked away from Phyl, who was fingering through a purse of coins that Katherine had given her to buy some food with.

"Have you heard from Michael yet?" Alton asked. "Or King X? What about Tia? How come she vanished? Where's she been?"

Beau called out, creating a good distraction from the questions that Kade didn't want to answer publicly.

"Here ya go," Beau said. He caught up, carrying three glasses of wine. "Katherine?" he asked.

"Yes, please," she said.

Kade also took a glass. "Thanks," he said.

"Uh-huh," Beau said. He took a long gulp and wiped his mouth.

It was good to see him kicking back, but Kade also knew that the wine was just a temporary palliative for the pain of losing Cooper.

Katherine lifted her glass to Kade.

"Cheers, King Kade," she said.

"To the islands, our home," he replied with a raised glass. As they touched, he said, "Please, call me Kade."

She nodded and took a drink.

Kade did the same, savoring the warmth. He watched Alton and Phyl bring back two platters of sashimi, bought with the coins Katherine had given them.

"Want to try it?" Alton asked. He held the plate up to Kade.

Kade liked his food cooked, but picked up a thin piece. It

was actually much better than he expected. He reached into his pocket and pulled out a few coins for the kids.

"Get as much as you like," he said.

"Thank you, Your Majesty," Alton said with a bow. He laughed with Phyl as they raced back to the line.

"They're becoming pretty good friends," Katherine said.

"I'm really happy to see that."

"She really misses her older brother. Having Alton around helps. Helps me too. I miss Trey so much."

"I'm sorry. I miss my…" Kade let his words trail off. He felt a dagger buried in his chest when he thought of his family.

"Can I ask about Tia?" Katherine said. "I know you can't tell me where she is, but is she okay?"

Kade nodded, although he couldn't swear it was true. As far as he knew, she was safe.

"She should be back in a week," he said.

"Okay," Katherine said.

"I'm sorry she didn't say anything before leaving; she didn't tell me either. It wasn't right to leave you to take sole care of Alton."

"It's fine. I really don't mind. When Layla gave me the note about taking care of Alton, I didn't think twice about it. Like I said, I'm glad he's with us."

"He's lucky to have you."

"Lucky to have you too," Katherine said. "He really looks up to you."

The kids returned a minute later with more sashimi. Kade took a few more pieces, savoring them again. In no time, his drink was gone and he had another in his hand. For the first time since his return from Australia, he felt relaxed.

But as soon as his mind deviated from the present, he felt the dread of things happening beyond the boundary of light and dark. The chances of all the missions going well were remote. He had to accept that not everyone was coming back home. Hell, it was possible that Lucky might not survive his trip to the Coral Castle.

The crowd suddenly went wild, stomping the deck and clapping to a new song. A woman playing a violin came down off the bandstand to mingle with the crowd, along with a male guitarist. They sang together in Spanish—something about *la luna* and *el amor*. Kade was still not good with the language, but he was determined to become fluent. A king must be able to understand all his people.

Alton took Phyl by the hand and led her out with the dancers. Both of them were laughing.

Kade smiled as he watched them. The resilience of children amazed him. Here they both were, playing and dancing without a care in the world despite all their losses.

Seeing that resilience and innocence made Kade realize more and more the importance of his job to keep them both safe. To keep *all* the children safe. They deserved a better future than the one their ancestors had left for them.

The violinist and guitarist came together, back to back, energizing the crowd. Their clapping and stomping made the deck shudder. A gunshot cracked, and Dakota moved in front of Kade.

Some of the dancers dived to the floor, others fled, and most just stood where they were. It took a moment to see the shooter, a drunken Cazador man whose pistol was quickly wrested away by two militia guards.

"I shoot moon!" the man yelled.

"What a dummy," Alton said.

He walked off the dance floor with Phyl. Panting, he wiped the sweat from his forehead.

"That band's really good," he said. "Too bad I don't know what they're singing about."

Another song kicked off, and this time Alton hesitated when Phyl pulled on his hand.

"Why don't you two dance?" Alton asked.

Kade looked around, not sure who the boy was referring to until Alton grabbed him by the arm. He then grabbed Katherine by the arm and pulled them together.

"You should both have *way* more fun," Alton said. "You look like a couple of mopes."

Katherine and Kade locked eyes.

Somewhere deep down, he considered it. And there in his mind's eye was the image of his dead wife. He pulled away from Alton.

"Maybe some other time," he said.

"Yes," Katherine said. "Another time, perhaps."

She held his gaze, and in it he saw the same guilt he felt. She too had lost her life partner.

"Don't be so boring. You are the cowboy—" Alton said. His eyes went behind Kade.

At the sound of boots and creaking armor, he turned to see General Forge with three soldiers.

"Sir, please come with us," he said.

"Is something wrong?" Katherine asked.

"I need to talk to the king," Forge said.

"If you'll excuse me," Kade said.

He walked away with the soldiers, Beau, Wynn, and Dakota keeping pace. They didn't stop until they got to a private hallway off the deck, away from curious eyes and ears.

"What's wrong now?" Kade asked.

"The scouts in Panama," Forge said. "They've spotted ships."

Even though Kade was prepared for the news, it still struck a note of dread. "What kind of ships?"

"Naval vessels, sir," Forge said.

Kade felt his heart sink now. He looked over his shoulder. Katherine was still back there with Alton and Phyl, all of them waiting for him.

"I'll be right back," he said.

Kade went over to them, trying to remain calm.

"I'm sorry, guys, but I have to get back to work," he said.

"Noooo," Alton said. "You pretty much just got here."

"I know. I'm sorry, pal. I'll make it up to you."

Alton frowned and folded his arms over his chest.

"Everything okay?" Katherine asked.

"Yes," Kade replied.

He realized how easy it had been to lie to her, and wondered if this was the start of something.

"Enjoy yourselves," Kade said.

He nodded at Katherine, and again she held his gaze. It was obvious she wanted him to stay as well. But there was no more time to relax. And no room or time for a new relationship.

He still hoped for peace as he kept preparing for war.

TWENTY-SEVEN

"No men, no monsters, just us," Michael whispered.

"I like it here," Layla said.

She walked beside him with Bray in a harness. They were in a long cavern, Victor walking just ahead. The boy loved it and was pointing at rocks, seashells, sand crabs—just about everything he saw. He didn't even seem to mind the hazard suit they had him in, or the mask to protect his lungs from any toxins their sensors might have missed so far. The boy had pawed at the mask obsessively when they first put it on him back on the airship. But as soon as they lowered down, he had so much to see, he quite forgot it.

His big, alert eyes flitted from one new sight to the next, taking it all in. For the child, this was a whole new world.

Victor led the way back out to the cave's mouth, overlooking the beach. Purple sunset streaked the horizon.

"Beautiful," Layla said.

"What do you think of your new home?" Michael asked.

"Home, home." The boy pointed at the sky, where the airship hung above the clouds. Soon it would come back down to retrieve Layla and Bray while Michael and Victor continued to explore.

"This is going to be our home now," Layla said.

Michael gazed out at the warm purple glow. He had been hesitant to believe the sun would come out again, but he was here now, staring right at it.

Michael was also reluctant to believe this place was habitable, but after searching the tunnels for the better part of a day, he believed it to be as safe as the surface could ever be.

There was zero evidence of anyone being inside these caves in recent years. Even the pirates who had likely killed the three members of Victor's old group seemed to have quit the area. And whatever happened to the fourth member, they might never know.

Michael listened to the waves slap against the rocks below. He loved that sound.

If only X could have seen this place.

Or his father, or Aaron, or Steve, or the countless divers who had only ever seen a world of darkness inhabited by monsters.

It seemed that more places across the planet were starting to recover from the war. Places where the sun peeked through and the land supported life again.

He raised his wrist computer—radiation here was nonexistent. The rich volcanic soil was free of toxins, sea life was abundant, and the temperature was a balmy sixty-eight degrees. With the water on the airship, the crops on the farm, and the fish in the sea, this place would support them indefinitely.

"Come and see where we're going to live," Michael said.

They took another passage to a cavern Victor and Michael had discovered during their forays. There were no supplies inside, but they would soon get the tour of four different living spaces.

Conduits snaking across the rock ceiling had powered light bulbs over two centuries ago. Most of the bulbs were broken or missing, but Michael thought he might be able to get the system back up and running with spare parts from the airship.

He followed Victor, Layla, and Bray to a steel door at the end of the passage. Beyond it was a communal space—a wooden table, three chairs, and a bookshelf. Trash and discarded jugs and buckets littered the smooth rock floor. Four more rooms jutted off the main space. Two had doors of eight-inch steel plate. The doors to the other two rooms lay on the stone floor. It was hard to tell whether they had fallen naturally or been ripped off, but there was no evidence of claw marks, which eased Michael's fears of something still lurking out there undetected.

Layla carried Bray to check out the bedrooms while Michael followed his nose to a foot-square hole in the floor. Several empty buckets with darkly caked rims lay scattered about.

A rusted metal sink was mounted against a wall with yellowed plastic tubes sticking out the bottom. It would take some work, but he planned on piping in water for the sink and installing a shit can with spare parts from the airship.

The biggest question was what to do with the ship. They could leave it drifting above the clouds indefinitely with Timothy at the helm, but that risked an accident, be it mechanical or weather related. Bringing it down and landing on the surface was probably riskier.

They would make a decision soon, but first they had a lot of work to do, to make this place habitable.

Michael went back into the communal space and found Layla in one of the bedrooms with Bray. Filthy blankets lay crumpled on the floor.

"We could paint the walls," Layla said. "Bring in some lights; make this less of a dungeon."

"No," Bray said. "No."

Michael laughed. The boy was saying a lot of that lately.

Bray reached out, and Michael took him in his one arm, hefting him up as they continued the tour.

"We make this nice," Victor said. "Too bad Steve not here to help us."

"He would have liked it here too," Michael said quietly.

"Steve would be glad we made it, and so would X," Layla said.

Michael shook away the grief from all his losses. "We better get you two back to the airship."

"Already?" Layla said.

"Yeah, until Victor and I can clean this place up and secure it, that's the safest place for you to be."

"I can help clean it up with Bray in the carrier."

"There's still some tests to run." Michael pointed at the black fuzz growing in the bathroom. "I need to get rid of that and check for anything else that might be a health risk, especially for Bray."

"He's got his mask on, and his suit."

Michael thought on it. He could have Timothy lower the airship to drop off some supplies, but this place was not yet in livable condition.

"Pepper," Michael said into his comm link. "Do you copy, Pepper?"

Static crackled for a beat before the smooth voice of the AI answered.

"Copy, Chief. How may I be of assistance?"

"Do another sweep of the area: life scans, everything. If it's clear, lower the ship back down."

"On it, sir."

Michael motioned for Layla to follow him with Bray and Victor. They traversed the tunnel and ended up back at the mouth of the cave. To the gentle slap of waves on sand, Victor stepped out with his rifle and watched the shore.

The moon peeked through the breaking cloud cover, spreading its glow over the ocean to the east. Michael lifted Bray one armed from the harness.

"I'm going to teach you to fish," he said.

Victor said, "Ton and I used to chase crabs at night. Very fun. Good eat too."

"Never had crab before," Layla said.

"Almost sweet, like fruit, but meat."

"Sounds kind of gross," Layla said, putting her hand around Michael's shoulder, "but I learned a long time ago not to be a picky eater."

The hum of the airship drew their eyes skyward as the big beetle-shaped vessel descended from the clouds, facing out to sea.

Timothy maneuvered it in front of the cave entrance and extended a lift gate down. His hologram flickered to life just inside the airship's cargo hold, where stacks of cleaning supplies awaited transfer. Victor was the first one on the lift gate, with Layla staying back while Michael carried Bray.

"No, no!" Bray said, shaking his head. He squirmed and arched his back, trying to get free from Michael's grip.

"Come on, Tin," Layla said behind them. "Let's go back and clean this place up together."

"Sir," Timothy said.

"What is it?" Michael asked, still wrestling Bray.

"I would highly advise that we all go back up into the sky for now," said the AI.

"Why? What's wrong?" Layla asked.

She quick-stepped onto the lift gate and into the cargo hold. As soon as she was inside, the hatch closed behind them.

"Pepper, what's going on?" Michael asked.

Timothy fiddled with his bow tie, clearly nervous.

"On my scan, I didn't pick up any life-forms, but I did see a light," he said.

"Where?"

"At the port of Arrecife."

"The old boat city where Victor was born?" Michael asked.

Victor stepped over, looking tense.

"You're sure it was a light?" Layla asked. "Like something using electrical power?"

Timothy shook his head. "Inconclusive on what produced the glow, but there's something down there."

Michael put Bray down on the cargo hold's deck, and the boy yelled louder.

"Hold on, bud," Michael said.

Bray reached for Michael to pick him up, but Michael stared at Timothy. For the first time today, he felt a real stab of fear that this place wasn't as safe as it seemed.

It seemed that something, or someone, was down there.

"Take us up," Michael said. "We stay in the sky until we figure out what's making the light."

*　*　*　*　*

The humanoid beasts on the other side of the sliding doors had tired of pounding and slamming against them. But Gran Jefe could hear their raspy breathing.

Several hours had passed since they woke the nest of fungally infested humans. They had been on the comms with Sergeant Blackburn, but Slayer refused to talk to the resident AI beyond telling it what they came here for.

Although the holographic pilot had vanished, Gran Jefe could sense it. He thought they should try to engage the intelligent machine, but he wasn't going to press it with Slayer.

For now, they were waiting for the monsters to return to their hibernation-like state and give the men an opportunity to get topside.

Gran Jefe's stomach growled, and a hiss came from the other side of the door. Slayer shot him a look.

"*Lo siento*," Gran Jefe whispered.

"Your plan to wait them out won't work, I'm afraid."

The pilot's hologram reappeared before Slayer.

"I can help you. In fact, I already did by sealing those beasts out." The translucent blue form walked closer. "Approximately twenty of the infested remain in this facility. If you want out of here, you *will* need my assistance."

"Why should we trust you?" Gran Jefe asked.

"Well, you don't have much of a choice, now, do you?" The AI paused as if to let the fact sink in. "Trust is built on communication, so let me start. My name is Frank Tannenbaum. What are yours?"

Gran Jefe stood but didn't speak, deciding it best to defer to Slayer.

"It's been a decade since I last met a normal human. Ironically, that was you," Frank said to Gran Jefe.

Gran Jefe ignored him.

"You know, I could open that door," said Frank.

Slayer finally broke his silence. "So you're gonna threaten us?"

"Not a threat. I'm trying to explain to you, I am not your enemy." Frank gave a friendly smile. "I can help you get the Jayhawks out of here, and I can fly them anywhere you want. The batteries are the most advanced of their kind. With two recharges, you could circumnavigate the globe!"

Static broke over the comms.

"*Slayer, come in,*" said Blackburn over the team channel.

"Copy," Slayer said.

"*What's your status?*"

"Brainstorming a way to get these choppers out."

"Easy," said Frank. "I send the elevator up, you bring down the armored vehicle that I can see with one of my cameras, and you kill the infested humans with that machine gun. There are only five hostiles in the chamber," he said. "The other fifteen are on various floors of this facility. Eliminate the first five, and you should be able to seal off the doors to prevent others from flanking you."

"Not bad," Gran Jefe said.

Slayer seemed to think for a moment. He then shrugged and said, "You fuck us, and I will find a way to pull your circuits or whatever the hell keeps you glowing."

"I will not 'fuck you,'" Frank said. "You have my word."

"Yeah, your kind probably said that right before they nuked the world."

"I had nothing to do with that."

Slayer nodded. "Send the elevator down."

"Only if you agree to take me with you when you leave," Frank said.

"And how do we do that?"

"There's a power source on floor five. You can eject my hard drives and insert me into the Jayhawks."

"How many hostiles on that level?"

"Three."

Slayer looked to Gran Jefe, who gave a shrug.

"Okay, you got a deal."

"Trust is a two-way street, friends," Frank said.

"¿Qué?" Gran Jefe asked.

"We must trust each other," said the AI.

"Ah, sí, sí." Gran Jefe pounded his chest plate.

"You have my word too," Slayer said.

As the elevator car jolted to life, Gran Jefe moved away from the door and the clicking monsters behind it.

Slayer switched the comms back on. "We're coming up in the elevator. Stand by."

Gran Jefe followed the commander to the elevator doors, and when the rattling car arrived, Frank joined them inside.

"I've waited so long for this day," said the AI. "I honestly can't believe I'm leaving."

"Yeah, well, better hope we can kill all those creatures," Slayer said. He motioned to Gran Jefe. "You're best on the LMG. I want you on it as soon as we get through the tunnel."

Gran Jefe liked that plan. Knock out the last of the debris, bring the APC down in the elevator, open the doors, and eradicate the monsters with the light machine gun and some covering fire.

The elevator clanked to the top a moment later. Gran Jefe opened the lift gate and stepped out with Slayer. Frank stayed in the elevator car as they walked through the mine shaft back the way they had entered hours earlier. A light rain fell outside the man-size gap they had made, turning the freshly dug earth to mud. The two Barracudas squeezed through the narrow opening and walked out to the waiting APC.

Slayer waited until they were in the vehicle before he spoke to Blackburn.

"We got a problem," he said. "Two, actually."

Slayer explained about the twenty humanoids infected with the fungal growths, and the AI pilot that seemed to believe the Jayhawks belonged to it.

"I don't trust it," he said at the end.

"I'll never trust an AI," Woody said. "But I gotta ask, he was a pilot?"

"It," Slayer clarified. "*It* was a pilot. Now it's a machine."

"Did you ask if he can fly the Jayhawks?"

"It claims it can, but that's why you're here."

Woody looked unsure. "I . . . I can maybe fly one, but there are two."

"Yeah, and we'll take them back to the boat and then the islands, where you'll learn and train someone else."

"Wait, wait, let me get this straight. You brought me out here *why*, exactly?"

"You're here because King Kade wanted you here," Slayer said.

"Yeah, okay. So what's the bloody plan, mates?"

"We're gonna push aside the rest of this debris with the blade and drive in with one trailer," Slayer said. He crouched in the back of the APC, opening an ammunition crate. "Zuni will head to the fifth level with Blackburn on a mission the AI thinks is to remove the hard drives."

Slayer held up an EMP grenade.

"We're gonna destroy it?" Woody asked.

Zuni took the grenade from Slayer.

"You'll go in with Blackburn," Slayer said. "Kill those little clicking bastards, and toss the grenade to destroy the hard drives and system. Meanwhile, I'll drive the APC in with the first trailer, and Gran Jefe will kill the critters that are in the chamber with the Jayhawks."

"We'll need to make two trips," Woody said. "Trailers won't both fit in the elevator with the choppers."

"No shit."

Woody frowned. "Sorry, mate. Just sayin'."

"Just listen close, because we can't afford any screwups," said Slayer.

Nods all around.

"Okay, go time." Slayer opened the back gate and hopped out with his rifle up. He went with Zuni to unhitch one of the trailers while Gran Jefe climbed up into the turret. By the time he had the LMG in his hands, the APC was purring. They drove away from the second trailer.

"Hold on!" Slayer yelled.

He mashed the pedal and hit the muddy debris with the blade, pushing it aside. Then he backed up and hit it again, pushing more mud away.

After a few runs, he drove over the remaining hump, into the wide tunnel with the trailer in tow. Frank remained inside the elevator, standing at parade rest.

Gran Jefe felt an uncharacteristic chill. To him, the AI wasn't a machine; it was a man's ghost. A man who lived in the Old World, like Timothy Pepper on the airship.

Gran Jefe caught himself wondering whether Frank had a family. That made him think of Jada and Pablo. This would be a story he could tell his son someday. If he survived.

He rocked the LMG on its pivot. There were still twenty ghastly little humanoids inside these tunnels, and they wouldn't be easy to kill.

Slayer backed the trailer into the elevator. Then he unhitched the trailer, pulled the APC forward, and backed it in, parallel to the trailer. The car groaned under the weight.

"It'll hold," Frank called out.

Blackburn and Zuni lowered the slatted gate.

"Okay, here we go," Frank said.

The elevator jerked, rattled, and started down. They heard a disconcerting grinding noise on the way down, but the car held. Gran Jefe didn't like it, but he had to trust the AI on this.

A jolt rocked the carriage. It jerked to a stop at floor 15, where Zuni and Blackburn got out of the vehicle. They moved cautiously over to Frank.

"These two men will be coming with you to remove your hard drives," Slayer said.

Frank nodded to each of them in turn. "Nice to meet you," he said. "I am grateful for your assistance. Please be advised, there are three hostiles inside the main mechanical room where my drives are located, and two others in the connecting hallway. Fortunately, according to my cameras, they are hibernating."

The hologram went to the door of the car.

"Wait," Slayer said.

"Yes?"

"If we haven't already disturbed the creatures, it's vital we attack at the same time."

"I agree."

"Then wait for my order to take Zuni and Blackburn into the mechanical room. You'll open the doors on floor nine at the same moment, understood?"

"Yes."

"Good."

Zuni raised a hand, then nodded toward the back of the APC, where Tia was undoubtedly looking out the window. The gate opened, and Gran Jefe swung the machine gun around into the connecting tunnel.

Blackburn and Zuni strode in with their rifles up, tac lights on. Slayer got out, closed the gate, and got back in.

Down the overladen car went.

Moments later, it stopped at floor 9. Slayer got out again and opened the gate, and there were the tunnel and the massive doors sealing off two Jayhawk helicopters.

This was the moment of truth.

Gran Jefe checked the machine-gun belt yet again as Slayer steered into the wide passage.

"Blackburn, report," Slayer said.

"In position," Blackburn replied.

"Copy. Stand by."

Slayer called up to Gran Jefe, "Ready, Mata?"

"*Sí, sí, listo,*" Gran Jefe said.

"Okay, Frank, open it up!" Slayer yelled.

The massive doors groaned apart. Slayer turned on the head-lights, illuminating an infested humanoid that raised bark-like wings to cover a yellow eye.

The creature could have been from the very pits of hell. And Gran Jefe was about to send it back there.

"Die," he grunted.

Chunks of gore, bone shrapnel, and fungal mycelium flew through the air. Pieces caromed off the hood of the APC as Gran Jefe rotated the barrel, aiming at the next beast as it scrambled on all fours, wispy hair and clothing whipping behind its tumor-ous body.

The creature was ten feet away, with a smaller monster right behind it.

Gran Jefe fired a burst into the leader, taking off an arm. As the creature tumbled, its comrade hurdled the sliding beast and kept running. Gran Jefe led this faster creature a little more with the gun barrel.

The next burst blew the fungus-encrusted body apart.

"Watch the Jayhawks!" Frank yelled over the din of gunfire.

He needn't have bothered—Gran Jefe was ever mindful of the machines they had come to extract. He put the iron sights on another creature running with bark-covered hands outstretched. Both hands flew off as it reached up into the stream of gunfire that then erased its face in a spray of gore.

The final two monsters darted into the shadows, but Gran Jefe managed to maim one with shots to the legs. The creature slid behind one of the helicopters while the other darted out the open door, to the bridge. Gran Jefe rotated the gun turret, ready to fire if it reemerged.

Then he tapped the roof of the truck. In the same moment, the comms fired with a message to Blackburn and Zuni to advance.

Gran Jefe played the machine gun's muzzle this way and

that, scanning for additional hostiles that might come sprinting through the open door across the chamber.

Distant shrieking resonated, audible over the rumbling APC. Gunshots cracked in response.

"Engaging hostiles," Blackburn confirmed on the comms.

Slayer stopped the vehicle and got out. "Cover me, Mata."

He went around the side of the helicopter where the wounded beast was hiding. Gran Jefe kept the LMG aimed at the door to the bridge.

Slayer fired two shots, then ran over to close the door.

"¡Vuelve!" Gran Jefe shouted.

He fired to Slayer's left as a creature bounded toward the open door. The bullets caught it in the torso, blowing it backward.

Slayer grabbed the door and pushed it shut, securing the lock.

"Blackburn, sitrep," he called over the team channel.

"All hostiles eliminated," Blackburn replied.

Frank walked over, smiling and holding a glowing translucent helmet.

"Proceed with second phase," Slayer said over the comms.

"Copy that," Blackburn said.

Gran Jefe felt bad for the AI, but this was the right move.

The hologram flickered, the smile dimming, and then the entire body vanished.

A beat passed before Blackburn confirmed the job was done.

"Get down here," Slayer replied over the comms. "Ride the cables."

He began pulling the tarps away from the two Jayhawks. Gran Jefe swept the ceiling for any vents or other ways into the chamber.

The rear hatch of the APC opened, and Tia called out.

"Let us help," she said. "Faster we get them loaded up, the faster we go home."

Slayer looked over his shoulder to Gran Jefe.

"Is it all clear?" he asked.

Gran Jefe nodded. He didn't hear any hissing or clicking now. But he stayed on edge.

Tia and Woody hopped out of the truck and went over with Slayer to uncover the first Jayhawk. The tarps fell by the side, revealing the ancient helicopter. Aside from a bit of dust, it looked to be in pristine shape.

"Bloody gorgeous machine," Woody said.

"Tia, back the trailer over here," Slayer said. "You can do that, right?"

"Yeah, I've driven a few times," she replied not so confidently.

Woody stayed with Slayer, his shotgun cradled across his chest.

As Tia went back to the truck, a scream rang out. Gran Jefe swung the turret around as a loud clatter issued from the elevator car. Agonized cries followed the noise, which seemed to come from above the freight elevator.

Had Blackburn and Zuni fallen somehow?

Tia turned toward the shaft and walked a few steps. Then a hologram flickered to life before her.

Gran Jefe instinctively swung the machine gun around at the AI, knowing full well that firing would do nothing. The hologram gave him an admonishing look.

"I thought we were going to trust one another," it said. "You destroying my hard drives was not the way to build trust, so I waited until your men were lowering to activate an electrical pulse on the cables."

"You son of a bitch!" Slayer shouted.

"There's still time to make an agreement," Frank said. "You might even be able to save Zuni from his injuries, though Blackburn appears to have perished in the fall."

"Zuni!" Tia shouted.

She ran toward the agonized moans coming from atop the elevator car.

"Tia, get back here!" Slayer shouted.

He bolted after her, yelling for Gran Jefe to cover them.

The clicking of humanoid monsters answered the cries, as if they could sense the sudden weakness in the Barracudas.

A whirring noise drew Gran Jefe back to the helicopter, where Woody now stood. The sky horse turned on its wheels. There was only a second to warn the man when the tail rotor began to whir.

Woody turned, right into the pale-gray disk that was four steel blades spinning too fast to see.

One second he was there; the next, he was a falling headless body and a poof of pink mist.

Frank shook his head. "Shame I had to do that, but I fear it's the only way you will uphold your side of the deal," said the AI. "If you ever want to fly those birds, you need to take me with you."

TWENTY-EIGHT

"Where are you from?" Lucca asked.

Magnolia ignored the eight-year-old boy standing inside the entrance to her domed tent. She looked around him, to the communal tent in the center of the large habitat. Gold lamps with red shades gave the space a warm glow. A carved-wood desk rested on an Old World hand-woven rug.

"Did you hear me?" Lucca said. "I asked where you're from."

She glanced over to him but didn't respond. Behind her back, her hands chafed in vain against the handcuffs, although she had no good idea what she would do if she got free. They had stripped her down to her diving suit, taking all her armor, weapons, and gear.

There was one idea in her mind: grab the boy by the neck and threaten to snap it if she didn't get safe passage for her and X.

The odds of success were small, but it was all she could think of right now.

"We're from across the ocean—a place called Egypt," Lucca said. "Have you heard of it? There are great buildings there. Pyramids."

Magnolia recalled seeing one of those in a book many years

ago. The structures were unlike any she had encountered on dives in all her years. Built by an ancient civilization that worshipped a whole slew of gods.

"Yes," she finally replied.

He seemed to like that and took a step closer.

"Are you from this place?" Lucca asked. "I overheard that my father saw your boat, a catamaran. It can't be just the two of you and your pets."

He took two more steps, his shadow enveloping Magnolia.

"I would enjoy knowing more about your people and your home," Lucca said. "Are you nomads? I've met a few before. They are in the other tent."

Magnolia fiddled with her handcuffs, wincing as the metal dug into her wrist.

"Don't be afraid," Lucca said. "My father has selected you for the great dark journey."

Magnolia finally glanced up at the young boy. He had an innocent enough face, with high cheekbones, dark-brown eyes, and curly brown hair that fell to his shoulders.

He grinned, revealing the gaps from several missing baby teeth.

"I won't hurt you," he said. "I would love to be friends. I haven't seen a girl for a long time, not since my mom died."

"I'm not your friend," Magnolia said.

"Not yet, but you will be. You'll see, we'll become good friends. I promise."

He turned and stiffened at the sound of a tent unzipping.

"Lucca, I told you to stay out of here."

Crixus ducked under the awning of the tent, wearing a sleeveless tunic that showed off his muscular arms and shoulders. He stood there a moment, studying her with those strange green eyes. She avoided his gaze, focusing instead on the weird-looking ports in his forearms, just below the elbows.

"I'm sorry, Father. I wanted to talk to her," Lucca said.

Crixus snorted. "Go get ready for the ceremony, and make it fast."

The boy backed hurriedly out of the room, bowing slightly. Crixus left Magnolia but quickly returned, holding a white item of clothing that unfolded into a dress.

"Put this on," he said.

He held it out to her, looking her body up and down where she stood. She backed away as he came closer, breathing through the slits where his nose had once been.

"I'm going to unlock your cuffs and let you dress."

He reached out his hand and brushed her cheek with his rough, calloused fingers. She bridled and looked him in the eyes.

"I'm not putting that on, you freak," Magnolia said. "You may as well kill me, because I'm not playing any part in whatever fucked-up drama you're into."

He let out a low growl as he pulled his hand back. For an instant, Magnolia thought he was going to hit her. But then he grabbed her by her upper arm, squeezing with bruising force. He pulled her toward him till their faces were mere inches apart.

"You will do... what... I ask," he grunted.

Magnolia winced but held his gaze, her glare masking any fear. He would be hard pressed to hurt her worse than she had already been hurt. Not after losing almost everyone she held dear.

Her mind drifted to Rodger and finding his ash remains back at Outpost Gateway.

Her anger intensified, and she snarled at Crixus. "You think you scare me?" she said. "You think there's anything you can do to me that I haven't already been through?"

Crixus licked his lips and came within an inch of her mouth, his fetid breath filling her nostrils.

"You might not fear death, but I promise I can do things to your friend that you've never seen before," he said.

He let go of her upper arm, and she turned away.

"I can make it quick, or I can take my time picking away his flesh," Crixus said. He opened a pouch on his belt and pulled out a small vial. "My scientists have created many potions over the years. Do you know what this one does?"

He turned the bottle in his hand, sloshing the fluid inside.

"This is potent enough to paralyze the bone-covered beasts you awoke out there," he said. "I give it to your friend, and he will be paralyzed. But just because he won't be able to move doesn't mean he won't be able to *feel*... He will feel everything. In fact, his nerves will be even more sensitized to the pain I inflict."

He shook the vial again.

"Put the dress on and come outside for the ceremony," he said. "We sacrifice your friend swiftly or slowly, your choice."

"Don't kill him," Magnolia said. "I'll do what you want."

Crixus reached out to her face. This time, she didn't pull away, but let him stroke her cheek with his rough fingertips.

"You'll do what I want regardless, including telling me where you're from, who your people are, and whatever else I care to know," he said. "Tonight, your friend will be sacrificed to the Dark Lord, and nothing you can do will stop that. All you control is his suffering—and, of course, your own."

He pulled his hand away and put the vial back into his pouch. Then he pulled out a key.

"Turn around."

She complied, and as he unlocked her cuffs, she considered going for his eyes. But what if she missed? It was too great a risk.

She decided to obey his commands for now and wait for

a better chance. Miles and Jo-Jo were still out there, and if she knew Miles, he would come for X. But what could one dog do?

Unless Jo-Jo helped. Then again, Magnolia wasn't sure what the monkey could do. First off, she was injured. Second, she wasn't intelligent enough to devise some master plan to save them.

Crixus took the cuffs off and stepped back. He watched Magnolia pick up the dress. She turned her back to him and slipped out of her suit. She thought of Rodger again, the last man who had seen her like this. She pictured his smile, his kind words of adoration that made her feel so beautiful.

She still hadn't dealt with the pain of losing him. Grief was easily buried when you were fighting for your life. Anger was getting the upper hand, trying to force her into a fight she couldn't win.

Don't, Mags. Be smart. Take your time…

The voice in her head was Rodger's. It calmed her down just as Crixus drew near.

She could feel his hot breath on her back.

Magnolia slipped into the dress, then turned around.

"The Dark Lord will be pleased," Crixus said with a hint of a demented grin. He held out his hand. "Come with me."

She took his hand, suppressing the urge to rip into his neck with her teeth. He led Magnolia into a connecting tent that contained racks of swords, spears, and axes. But it wasn't just weapons here.

Glass jars contained human heads, and burned skulls graced a wood bookshelf.

"You say you meet many evil men," Crixus said. "I have as well." He indicated the first skull on the top shelf.

"A man from Japan," he said. "Leader of a mountain tribe." Next he pointed to a skull with the top missing.

"A witch from France thought she could defeat me with black magic," Crixus said.

He tapped his foot against the bottom shelf, rocking a head inside a glass case. "A nomad in the former state of California."

"I get the point," Magnolia said. "You must have once had a huge army."

"And many slaves, which you will soon be seeing."

Crixus stepped away and took Magnolia into an immaculate room where two men in robes waited. They gave her a mask with filters and sprayed her down with something that made her exposed skin tingle.

"You want me to go out there dressed like this?" she asked.

"You can wear these." Lucca walked into the room with a pair of sandals in his hand.

"You've got to be kidding me," Magnolia said.

"You'll do as I say, lady," Lucca demanded in a deep voice.

Lady, Magnolia thought. She no longer felt bad for this kid, who didn't seem as innocent as he had earlier.

She slid the sandals on and waited while Crixus and his son dressed in black suits. A guard helped them into black chest armor.

Lucca bent down to fasten shin guards and elbow pads. Crixus didn't use any. Maybe they couldn't find any big enough to cover his tree-trunk legs and arms, Magnolia thought.

Crixus ordered a guard to open the tent door. He unzipped it and stepped out, raising a beckoning arm to Magnolia. She walked out into the cracked parking lot.

Two camels stood in hazard suits, with goggles shielding their eyes. She did a quick scan—two guards outside with scope-mounted rifles.

She looked up at the flames surrounding the broken statue on the bluff. X was up there somewhere, and she was running out of time to save him.

As the little procession wound up the stairs between two abandoned buildings, Magnolia searched the jungle for Miles and

Jo-Jo. Maybe they could somehow create enough of a distraction for her to get hold of a weapon.

A guard with a flamethrower stood on the stairs above them. He turned and led the way up to the base of the statue, where four more robed warriors waited, all armed with assault rifles.

Coughing drew her eyes to the ground behind them, where a naked man lay curled up in a fetal position. His face was covered, but the scars on his body told Magnolia exactly who this was. Xavier Rodriguez. The Immortal.

He looked like a weak, sick old man.

This wasn't his first time to be taken hostage. Both el Pulpo and his son Horn, the leader of the skinwalkers, had captured X. But back then X had fight in him.

Now there wasn't much left in his frail, ailing body.

X glanced up with bloodshot eyes, strands of hair falling over his scarred face.

"Mags," he mumbled.

She had never seen him look so weak.

"Will the Dark Lord really accept this pitiful offering, Father?" Lucca asked.

Magnolia resisted the urge to slap the words from his mouth.

Her heart pounded. There had to be a way to save X, but how? There was nowhere to run.

Wait, she thought.

Maybe that was the answer. Running and threatening to throw herself off the bluff unless they spared him. Or grabbing Lucca and threatening to toss him over?

Any hope of that ended when five of her robed captors formed a pentagonal perimeter around her. They bowed their heads and began to hum.

Crixus held up his arms.

"The Dark Lord has blessed us tonight," he boomed. "Tonight, the Dark Lord has given us a queen!"

Oh, hell no, Magnolia thought.

"To thank the Dark Lord for this gift, we offer up a soldier of the wastelands," Crixus said, pointing to X. "His people have called him a king and an Immortal, but we know that only you, great Dark Lord, are either of those things."

X pushed himself up, and Magnolia could see his muscles trembling in the glow of the fires burning around the statue. He spat and fell forward, face first in the dust.

Crixus grunted. "He doesn't look like much, but I pray his soul is suitable, great Dark Lord."

"Please, stop," Magnolia said. "He's more useful to the Dark Lord alive than dead."

Crixus looked over at her, tilting his head slightly as if in consideration.

A hundred things went through her mind, including offering up the location of the Vanguard Islands in exchange for his life, but she knew she couldn't do that.

Tears broke from her blurring eyes and ran down her grimy cheeks as she tried to come up with something, anything, to save the most important person left in her world.

"Mags," X said. "Find Miles, watch out for him…"

"No," Magnolia said. She turned to Crixus. "Don't do this! I'll do everything you want, anything you desire."

Crixus stared at her, then nodded to the soldier with the flamethrower. He raised the barrel with its tiny blue flame flickering off the end. He pointed it at X.

"No!" Magnolia shouted. "Stop—"

Barking rose over her voice.

Crixus raised his hand, and all the guards fell into a defensive position, with their rifles pointed out over the jungle below.

The barking came again, from a different location this time. The man with the flamethrower stepped away from X and angled the weapon toward the jungle on the right side of the path to the parking lot.

Magnolia scanned the foliage around them but saw nothing moving in the dense growth.

"Miles," X grumbled. "Get out of here, boy."

He pushed himself up using his prosthetic limb, staring at Magnolia with a look of pure agony in his bloodshot eyes. Legs bound, he made only a step before stumbling. Then he reared his head back and yelled, "Run, boy!"

Crixus looked back to the guard with the flamethrower and gave another nod. The man squirted a bright stripe of fire into the jungle.

"No, you sorry fucks!" X yelled. He got up, standing naked in the darkness, yelling, "I'll kill you all! I'll fucking rip your hearts out and stuff them down your throats!"

He took another step and fell to his knees.

"Burn him," Crixus said.

The man with the flamethrower swung the barrel around to X. Magnolia lunged, blocking the soldier for a moment before Crixus grabbed her.

"It will all be over soon," he said, dragging her back.

"Stop! Stop!" she wailed, squirming in his grip. Crixus finally pulled her away, giving the flamethrower operator a clear shot.

Blood erupted from the side of the man's helmet. He fell sideways, shooting flames into the sky.

Crixus shoved Magnolia to the ground. Then he motioned for Lucca to run for cover. The boy got down behind a stone a few feet from Magnolia.

Cracking gunfire came from the jungle, but she saw no muzzle flash.

Was it Michael and Layla? Had they been here after all?

The robed warriors spread out, kneeling and searching for a target. One of the men went down from a round to his chest. The others looked to Crixus.

"Fire!" he roared. "Slay the heretics!"

One by one, his guards went down, bullets piercing their hearts and heads. Crixus grabbed a fallen guard's assault rifle and fired into the jungle, draining the magazine in seconds. He tossed the weapon away, then hunched down and scooped up the flamethrower.

Bullets slammed into his armor. A round hit him in the calf, but he remained standing.

"Father!" Lucca yelled. The boy tried to get up, but Magnolia bolted over and grabbed him. He fought to get free as Crixus unleashed a curtain of fire into the jungle.

Two of his remaining soldiers fired from cover. Magnolia finally spotted the flash from beside a tree about two hundred feet away. Another muzzle flickered from over a rock to the left.

More bullets slammed into Crixus.

He bled from holes in his arms, legs, and chest armor.

And yet, he seemed unfazed.

Crouching down behind a low wall of stone, he pulled a vial from one of his pouches and injected it into the port in his arm.

The howl Crixus let out didn't sound human.

Another howl, which was anything but human, answered from the jungle.

Crixus got up and looked over as Jo-Jo jumped into the air, fists up. Once again she seemed to coalesce from the shadows, just as she had when she caught Charmer by surprise on the *Frog*. The fists came down on Crixus's helmet, knocking him to the ground.

Jo-Jo raised one arm but kept the other by her side. Magnolia could see the skin burned raw from the flamethrower blast back in the city.

Lucca tried to buck Magnolia off him, but she put him in an arm bar and dragged him over to X, who was on his butt, trying to unknot the ropes around his ankles. Miles darted over, helmetless, going straight for the ropes.

"Let me go!" Lucca howled.

Magnolia tightened the arm bar and watched Jo-Jo battle the boy's father. His helmet had come off, and with it his breathing mask.

Jo-Jo bit at his face, but he punched her in the jaw, knocking her backward. Then he waded in, throwing punches to the burned flesh on her arm and side. She howled in agony and cocked a fist, which he grabbed.

She swiped with her other paw, but he caught that too. Then he began stretching both her arms. Jo-Jo tried to snap at his face, but he headbutted her in the nose.

Motion came from the left. Magnolia had been so fixated on the fight, she didn't see that X had freed himself. He walked over, still naked, a shotgun in his hands. He walked up behind Crixus and put the muzzle against the base of his skull.

Magnolia turned the wailing Lucca away from what was coming.

"Give the Dark Lord my regards," X said.

The shotgun blast took off the top of Crixus's head. Jo-Jo fell to the ground as the monstrous warrior released her. He stood there for a moment, then toppled to the side, sending up a puff of dust and gore that slopped out of his skull.

"Father!" Lucca shouted.

Magnolia finally released him and let him run to his fallen dad. Scanning the area, she realized that all the guards were dead. Still, she picked up an assault rifle and held it at the ready.

X bent down to check on Jo-Jo.

"King Xavier!" shouted a voice.

Magnolia looked to the jungle. Two heavily armored Caza-dores came striding out of the dense forest holding sniper rifles. One stood guard near the stairs as the other walked over to X.

Shivering, he stood there staring at the man who had saved them.

But this was no man, Magnolia soon saw. Not even a very big woman.

It was Corporal Valeria.

TWENTY-NINE

A knock came on the doors of the council chamber.

"See who it is," Kade said.

He looked up from a map of the Vanguard Islands spread out on the war table. General Forge, across the table from him, was in charge of the overall battle strategy. On his flanks were Lieutenant Wynn, assisting with the defense of the rigs, and newly promoted Captain Tiger, who had tactical command of the remaining naval fleet.

Part of Kade couldn't help but wonder if the twenty-two-year-old man was experienced enough, but he wasn't much younger than Michael Everhart. The lad even looked a bit like Michael, with his long hair tied behind his head.

The four men had worked through the night and into the early morning after learning of enemy ships spotted in Panama.

"Sir, Pedro is here to see you," Beau said.

Kade waved him in.

Dakota pulled back his spear and stepped aside, and Pedro entered the chamber. He practically ran down the aisle between the pews, stopping at the table.

Kade prepared himself for bad news, but then he saw Pedro smile.

"I have . . . a message, sir," he panted. "Corporal Valeria has located Xavier and Magnolia."

Kade let out a sigh of relief. Wynn and Forge nodded at each other, and Tiger grinned.

"And the airship?" Kade asked.

"Not there, unfortunately," Pedro said. "Xavier and Magnolia plan to return to the islands to help with the defenses."

"I knew the Immortal would return," Forge said. "He will help fend off these knights if they dare invade."

Kade nodded, but deep down he knew that even with the Immortal, there would be severe bloodshed if the Forerunner and his knights came under the banner of war. Not only that, but there was no way X could get back to the islands in time.

"I'm glad to hear they're alive," Kade said. "Have you been able to reach the Barracudas again?"

Pedro shook his head.

"Okay," Kade said. "I'll take the good news. Let's get some rest and come back at dawn for a meeting with everyone else."

"Sir, it *is* dawn," Pedro said. He stepped over to the shuttered windows behind the elevated throne and let in the first golden rays of light, which crawled quickly across the chamber floor.

"The others will be here soon," Forge said. "Would you like to delay?"

Kade was exhausted, but he wasn't slowing down now.

He went back to the Vanguard map spread out over the war table. On it, each rig was represented by a metal replica. Wood replicas stood for the major ships and large boats in the fleet.

They had spent the night agonizing over how to deploy their remaining troops and what to do with civilians. Kade's heart sank as he looked at the maps. The Vanguard Islands comprised twenty-one rigs—far too many to defend with so few trained soldiers. They didn't have enough boats either.

The *Frog*, their last warship, was still being repaired from the damage sustained in the battle with the Wave Runners and Charmer's confederates. Four of the twelve war boats were ready for battle, but the others remained inside the mechanical rig, where Cazador teams worked around the clock to get them ready.

Kade raised his wrist computer. He had a new countdown—five days. That was the time he believed they had before these ships would arrive. It wasn't enough, but if the Barracudas could get the choppers, they could fly at least one of them back in time. That would give them the aerial advantage.

"Sir, the council and guests have arrived," Beau called out from the door.

"Bring them in," Kade said.

Imulah and the other invitees for the meeting filtered in over the next few minutes. Seeing them reminded Kade just how desperately low they were on personnel.

Martino waddled in wearing a white tunic with gold cuffs. Sofia crutched in, along with a few new Hell Divers who had shown promise during training. Roman, Slava, Chester, and Hugh would be the next team, if all went to plan. And Kade had an idea that made them more valuable than any Cazador soldier.

Once everyone had gathered, Dakota and Beau shut and locked the doors.

"I called you here tonight with dire news," Kade announced, "but first, good news. Xavier Rodriguez and Commander Magnolia Katib are on their way back to the islands. A team I deployed located them in Rio."

Smiles broke out everywhere.

Sofia gave a happy sigh. "Thank God," she said.

Kade didn't let the news sink in for long before moving to the bad.

"Last night, we received a transmission from our scouts in Panama," he said. "They detected two large ships in the Panama Canal. Both are civilian craft, but make no mistake, I believe they sail for war."

All sense of relief vanished. Hushed voices broke out behind Kade, including a question from Martino.

"You know for certain these are the Forerunner's vessels?" he asked.

"Yes, they're marked with a trident," Kade replied. "The logo of the Knights of the Coral Castle."

More hushed conversations broke out.

"Over the past week, I've worked with General Forge to put together a defensive plan in case our fears should become reality," he said. "But what happens next depends on all of you."

Kade walked between the pew of Hell Divers and the war table.

"Three days ago, I deployed the Barracudas to Texas, on a mission to extract two helicopters and deliver them to us," he said. "These will be the machines that take you into the skies if that mission is successful."

"When will we know?" Sofia asked.

"Soon, I hope," Kade said. "In the meantime, I want the divers to continue their training."

The greenhorns around Sofia all wore the same fearless gazes, but Kade could see the fear in their body language. He didn't blame them. He turned to Martino.

"The Vanguard navy will need all your vessels for the defenses," Kade said. "Tiger has been promoted to captain and will need every seaworthy craft he can get."

Martino didn't look happy about it, but he gave a slight nod.

"General Forge and I have decided to move the children to the capitol rig, where we can best defend them," Kade said. "We will start doing that over the next few days. The rest of the rigs will be consolidated so that every able person can defend them."

Nods all around.

"Any questions?" Kade asked.

His eyes swept the room.

"Okay, let's get moving," he said. "Sofia, Forge, Tiger, Wynn, please stay behind."

Beau and Dakota went to the doors to see everyone out. As soon as the door shut, Kade planted his palms on the table and looked at Forge.

"Will it be enough?" he asked.

Forge nodded sternly. "If those boats come for war, they will be destroyed with everyone aboard, down to the last soul."

Kade studied the maps, the rig replicas, and the tiny ships and boats. He had done everything he could do to secure this territory, to make any invasion so painful to the enemy that they must withdraw or perish.

But in his heart, he hoped there was still time to negotiate a peace.

"The war boat I asked for," Kade said to Wynn.

"It's almost complete, sir. Should be finished by this evening."

Kade had planned on stowing a bomb under a dorsal hatch on the armored boat that Captain Tiger had prepared for him. If negotiations went south, Kade planned on driving it out to meet any hostile forces and negotiating. If the negotiations didn't work, he would end this. Even if it meant his own demise.

But now he had other plans, involving the Jayhawks.

He stood and paced, massaging his forehead.

"If the choppers arrive in time, I'll head out on one with Woody to these ships that we've spotted going through the

Panama Canal," Kade said. "I will offer the Forerunner a peace treaty. If the answer is no, then I will offer them a bomb that I plan to stow on this war boat Captain Tiger has outfitted."

"And if the choppers don't make it in time?" Sofia asked.

"Then I will deliver the same message—or the same fate—by sea," Kade said.

Everyone at the table remained silent.

"There's still hope," Kade said. "We must proceed with optimism."

Several nods acknowledged this, but Kade saw the fatigue in these faces. Everyone was sick of fighting. And everyone feared losing more of their loved ones.

"Okay, we all have jobs to do," Kade said. "Let's get 'em done."

As the chamber emptied, he stepped out onto the balcony, pushing open the doors to the blazing morning sun. Leaning with his hands on the rail, he looked out to sea. And as he had done so many times before, he wondered what the Forerunner was planning.

Holding up his wrist computer, he activated the display that showed Lucky's location with the tracker on board.

He stared at it for a long moment.

That couldn't be right. The coordinates were the same as the last time he had checked.

Something was wrong.

Engine troubles, a storm, sea monsters... His head spun with possibilities.

Nothing really made sense. If the boat had gone down, they would have lost the signal. He turned back to the chamber, weighing whether to send out another boat. But they needed every single vessel that would float.

Another idea took shape in his mind.

If the Jayhawks got here soon, there was still a chance to

pick up Lucky off the boat in the Caribbean. Maybe Kade could somehow persuade Lucky to give up the location of the Coral Castle. The information could be vitally important in negotiations with the Forerunner. Or perhaps in an outright threat. A threat based on a lie…

Yes. Kade would spin the lie that they had deployed forces on helicopters and boats to destroy the Coral Castle. It was a threat of mutually assured destruction that Kade hoped would deter the Forerunner.

"No, that sounds crazy," he muttered. He knew that desperation could compromise his reason.

He felt an uncharacteristic flash of anger. At first, it was aimed at Lucky, but this wasn't Lucky's fault. Rolo was responsible for their plight. If the old bastard hadn't dropped the nuke, none of this would have happened.

Kade's anger grew. All his plans were unraveling as fast as he could hatch them.

The only hope now was to find Lucky and somehow get him to give up the Coral Castle's location. Then use the information in a bluff to avoid bloodshed. If the Forerunner did sniff out his lie, well, then Kade would be ready for that.

*   *   *   *   *

Gran Jefe walked between the two Jayhawks parked on the afterdeck of the *Angry 'Cuda*. They partially shielded him from the lancing rain. Thunder boomed just seconds after lightning arcs split the horizon.

A violent storm was moving into the area, stirring up the water. Waves generated by the intense winds pounded the shore. It was a miracle they had gotten both helicopters on the boat before the surf picked up.

Slayer stood in the stern of the boat, near the APC with its mud-caked blade. He crouched in front of Blackburn's corpse. The sergeant had broken his neck in the fall down the elevator shaft. Zuni was damned lucky to have survived. He was below-decks resting, with Tia looking after him.

Gran Jefe put a hand on the commander's shoulder plate.

"*Lo siento*," he said.

Slayer slowly rose up. "We have to destroy the AI," he growled.

Pulling his hand away, Gran Jefe looked back toward the cabin. Frank was on a platform, watching them both, helmet in hand.

"We need the *hombre fantasma*—the ghost man—to fly the sky horse for cowboy king," Gran Jefe said.

"I don't fucking care," Slayer said. "Someone can learn. That machine is a murderer."

He glanced up with bloodshot eyes.

Gran Jefe almost didn't believe it.

For the first time in his career, he saw tears streaking down the lieutenant's face. Blackburn had been his best friend and one of the last living Barracuda soldiers. They had survived the blood-sucking sea monster together on the submarine, and countless other battles against daunting odds. Losing him now—to an AI, no less—seemed unfair.

Blue light spread across the dimly lit cabin.

Not a good time, Gran Jefe thought.

Slayer shot up and swung a fist right through the holographic figure.

"If I could rip your face off, I would, you son of a bitch!" he shouted.

Frank stared, then politely bowed and said, "I understand you're upset, Commander, but you made a deal; then you tried to murder me. Right now I'd be more concerned with getting out of here before the storm makes sea travel impossible."

"Get the fuck out of my sight, you soulless holographic shit-bag," Slayer growled.

The AI backed up a step.

"We're leaving, Mata," Slayer said. "Go let Tia know and check on Zuni; then meet me in the cabin."

He strode off, leaving Gran Jefe with Frank.

"You seem like a reasonable man," said the AI. "Perhaps you can explain my skills to your leader when we get to wherever it is we're going—which, come to think of it, is where, exactly?"

Gran Jefe shrugged.

He traversed the deck, moving carefully between the two choppers. The rain had washed off most of Woody's blood and brains, but little lumps of gore were still plastered to the hull of a Jayhawk near the back blades. Gran Jefe didn't want to end up like that.

He turned back to Frank and raised his hand, palm out. It was an odd gesture, trying to be nice to another man for fear of what he might do. But Frank wasn't even a man.

"*Adiós,*" Gran Jefe said.

He went to a hatch that led into the dark compartment belowdecks. A ladder took him down into a puddle of water at the bottom, splashing past the crew quarters and the galley. The next hatch was sickbay, and it was closed.

"*Hola,*" he said, knocking.

"Come in," Tia said.

He opened the hatch and stepped in to find her by Zuni's side. He lay in a bed, both legs elevated and his arm in a sling. He managed to turn his head ever so slightly to look at Gran Jefe. One eye was swollen shut.

He wouldn't be fighting anytime soon, or doing much of anything with Tia, for that matter.

She turned to look at Gran Jefe with rage in her eyes.

"What are we going to do with that freak machine?" she snarled.

"Not up to me," Gran Jefe said. "Ask commander. We leave now, I come to tell you. Better strap Zuni in. Could be, how do you say…"

"Rocky," Tia said.

"*Sí*. Could be rocky."

The engines started up as he stood there.

"That thing killed Woody," Tia said. "It will kill us all if it gets the chance."

Gran Jefe nodded. "Maybe, *pero* I don't make orders."

He nodded at Zuni, then left the quarters, shutting the hatch behind him. By the time he got outside, the yacht had pulled away from Texas and was chugging out to the Gulf. A scan of the deck told him Frank was gone for the moment.

Gran Jefe took the ladder up to the bridge, where Slayer had taken off his helmet, revealing his recently buzzed head and heavily stubbled face. He was a young man in his thirties, but the grays were gaining ground.

"How's Zuni?" he asked without turning.

"Hurt, but he strong. He will survive. *Pero no* …" Gran Jefe made a suggestive hip thrust. "Not that for a while."

Normally, Slayer might have laughed, but he hardly acknowledged the comment. He looked past Gran Jefe to the radio equipment.

"Try and get a transmission through to King Kade," he said. "Let him know about the choppers and that we're on our way back."

"And Woody?"

Slayer hesitated. "He needs to know what happened."

"*¿Todo? All* of what happened?"

A nod.

Gran Jefe nodded back. He went to the radio transmitter, took a seat, and turned on the channel they had used to contact the Vanguard Islands. Then he took his helmet off and pulled the mic up to his lips.

"Pedro," Gran Jefe said. "Pedro, you copy?"

White noise hissed from the speakers.

Wave after wave slammed against the port bow as the yacht motored into the Gulf of Mexico. With each crest, they went up, then down, then wallowed to starboard. Gran Jefe could already feel his empty stomach getting queasy.

"Pedro," Gran Jefe repeated. "Pedro, you copy?"

Static crackled, filling the cabin.

Gran Jefe looked over at Slayer, who just kept staring blankly out at the whitecaps, holding the wheel and checking the navigation equipment now and again.

On the third attempt to raise the Vanguard Islands, Gran Jefe shook his head and took his hand off the dial.

"Try again later," Slayer said. "The storm is probably messing with the signal booster."

Gran Jefe settled into his chair and folded his arms over his chest. He dozed off at some point, because he awoke to Slayer asking him to try the radio again.

Reaching back to the mic, he renewed his efforts.

"Pedro, you copy?" he said.

Only static crackled through the cabin.

In a burst of anger, Slayer pounded the wheel with his palm. He stomped the deck, then kicked the bulkhead next to the navigation equipment.

Gran Jefe looked out the viewport for Frank, or whatever else had upset Slayer. This was another first for him with the commander. Back at the APC, he had shown actual tenderness toward Blackburn's body.

Now he was displaying something equally rare: rage. Normally, Slayer took everything in stride, remaining his professional and, at times, brutal self. But every man had a breaking point.

"You want to kill us too?" he yelled. "Come on!"

Slayer took his other hand off the wheel and stripped off the rest of his chest rig. He dropped it on the floor with a clank. The boat swerved as a wave slapped up over the port bow.

Gran Jefe got out of his seat but didn't approach or say anything else to Slayer.

"The ocean! The land! Men! Monsters! Fucking *holograms*!" he yelled. "Everything wants us dead! There is no peace in this world! Nothing but destruction, death, ripped-apart families!"

Gran Jefe couldn't tell which was louder: Slayer or the screaming wind outside.

The boat jolted hard from a wave hitting them broadside. Gran Jefe considered doing something now. If he didn't, they could capsize.

"Sir, do you want me to . . ." Gran Jefe used his hands to mimic steering.

Static crackled over the radio.

"Angry 'Cuda, *come in,*" said a faint voice.

Slayer shook his head, as if by doing so he might exorcise some demon that had taken him over.

"Take the wheel, Mata," he said, stepping back from the helm.

"*Hailing the* Angry 'Cuda, *come in, come in. This is King Kade, do you copy?*"

Slayer brought the mic up to his mouth. "Copy you, sir, this is Slayer."

"*Great to hear your voice, Commander,*" Kade grunted back. "*What's your status?*"

Slayer looked to Gran Jefe before replying.

"We've got the Jayhawks, sir—both of them. But we took casualties . . ."

Static obliterated Kade's next words.

"Blackburn was killed, and Woody didn't make it either—I'm sorry, sir," Slayer said. "Zuni was also severely injured."

Another round of white noise resonated through the cabin.

"What about the AI?" Kade replied, his voice cracking.

"We have it on board," Slayer said. "It claims to be able to fly both helicopters, but I would highly advise against trusting it."

"After the machine camp, I understand the feeling, but we need it."

"Sir, there's something you need to know."

Slayer lowered its voice and explained what happened after the EMP attack. Gran Jefe feared that Frank was listening, but at this point, it didn't matter. There was no trust between them to lose.

Another long moment passed before Kade responded. *"We have two ships bearing the trident logo heading our way, Commander. That AI killed one of your best friends and mine, but at this point, the enemy of my enemy is my friend."*

Gran Jefe felt the old battle itch as he digested the news. Two large ships, heading toward his home—toward Pablo and Jada.

"Commander, you are to return here on the Angry 'Cuda *with Tia, Zuni, and one of the helicopters,"* Kade said. *"Gran Jefe will go with the AI to coordinates I will patch through shortly. These coordinates are the location for the stalled boat I sent Lucky home on. Something's happened out there and I need him."*

Gran Jefe and Slayer exchanged a glance.

"I believe that the knight is our best advantage in the case of war," Kade said. *"We must find him, because he and only he knows the location of the Coral Castle."*

"You think he'll just give up the location of his home and won't sniff out your plan?" Slayer asked.

"That's why I'm sending Gran Jefe," Kade said. *"Mata, you do what you have to, but keep him alive and get the location out of him. Leave the rest to me."*

"Comprendo, Cowboy King," Gran Jefe replied. "I understand."

THIRTY

"I'll go by myself, Chief," Victor said.

"It's better we go together," Michael said.

"Michael's right," Layla said. She helped him fasten his armored wrist guard. They needed to figure out the source of the light in the port of Arrecife. Michael hoped it was nothing more than a light connected to solar panels. That would explain its activation now that the sun was starting to shine over this area.

"There ya go," Layla said, cinching down the wrist guard.

"Thanks," Michael said.

"Up, up," Bray said. He reached out with both hands, but Michael had to ignore his son, much as he hated to.

"Daddy's got a mission," Layla said, scooping Bray up in her arms. She turned him so he could watch as Michael checked his duty belt: holstered pistol and two extra magazines, knife, flashlight, two flares, and eight shotgun shells. Tonight, he was going light. No pack—nothing but his belt, his armor, and the blaster on his thigh.

At midnight, he and Victor finished their preparations in the launch bay of the airship.

"We're in position," Timothy said.

His hologram illuminated the gear the two men would use on the mission. A four-person black raft with a small electric motor sat near the launch doors, ready to lower to the ocean on the cable pulley system.

"Is everything set for launch?" Timothy asked.

"Yes," Victor said.

Michael nodded. He kissed the top of Bray's head, then kissed Layla on her lips.

"Don't worry," he said. "We'll be back down there listening to the waves in no time."

"Fishing too?" she asked.

"Fishhhh," Bray said.

"Yes, little guy," Michael said.

"I'll help," Layla said. "I like fishing."

She smiled at Michael. Soon, they would be doing just that as a family.

"Okay, Pepper, take us down," Michael said.

Layla and Bray left to strap in to their seats. A few minutes later, the ship began to descend. Michael and Victor stood in front of the launch-bay doors, the deck rumbling under their boots.

"You remember this place well?" Michael asked.

"Yes, it was my home for many years," Victor said.

"Good."

Michael tapped the screen of his wrist computer to bring it online for a final systems check. All systems came back green.

"Pepper, upload the maps," he said.

"Stand by, sir."

The digital maps in the corners of their HUDs sizzled to life with the location of the light.

As the airship *Vanguard* lowered over the ocean, Michael watched out a porthole. He couldn't see anything on the horizon.

No glimmer of moonlight—nothing that would give them away. Still, Michael had ordered the airship to lower way out here, three miles away from the port of Arrecife. He wasn't taking any chances.

A green light brightened, and the launch-bay doors clicked unlocked. Victor and Michael climbed into the raft.

"Prepare for deployment," Timothy said.

The double doors opened, letting in a frigid gust of wind. The robotic crane arm swung out and began lowering them toward the ocean thirty feet below.

"Good luck," Timothy called down.

When they were floating on the water, Michael raised his hand and waved the ship off, and the beetle-like underbelly rose away, the AI's glow just visible behind the closing launch-bay doors.

Victor started the electric outboard motor and steered for shore. The raft thumped over the waves.

Lightning flashed as they picked up speed, but Michael still couldn't see land.

He turned to look up, but the airship was already gone, swallowed by the clouds. His heart fluttered with anxiety.

Don't worry, he repeated to himself, just as he had told Layla.

Victor pushed the throttle down as far as it would go, eating up the distance, and soon they got their first view of shore.

Just as Victor had described, a wall of dirt and rocks formed a barrier around the old seaport. Michael tried to imagine the force of the tsunamis that had ravaged this place centuries ago.

Victor eased off the throttle on approach. Michael scrambled forward and grabbed the bow rope from the bottom of the raft. The surf was breaking just ahead, waves slapping against the beach outside the wall that appeared to rise a hundred feet at its highest point.

With his night-vision optics, he scanned the beach for

anything moving. Nothing in either sweep. Infrared came back negative. The beach was clear.

Victor let a wave take them in to shore, pushing them all the way up onto the sand. Michael hopped out, and he and Victor pulled the raft up all the way to the base of the wall. Victor clove-hitched it to an exposed rebar.

Michael eased his pistol out while Victor unslung his laser rifle. He jerked the barrel to the right. They crouch-walked at double time along the base of the fortress surrounding the old boat city, passing collapsed structures and weaving around rubble and beach flotsam. Michael didn't see a way up, but Victor seemed to know of a secret passage.

Sure enough, he led them to some huge boulders at the base of the wall. He crouched in front of them, then got down on his stomach.

"Follow, please," he said.

He crawled inside, and Michael got down on his belly. The two men belly-crawled through a man-made tunnel under the rocks, to a space large enough to stand. A metal door was built into the rock wall. Victor opened it, then went into a vertical shaft with a ladder going up.

"Secret entry," he said.

They climbed the rungs all the way to the top, where they popped a dorsal hatch. Climbing out, they had a view of the boat city on the other side of the wall.

The first thing Michael checked for was the mysterious light among the ships and boats. He crouched and did a full search of the port. Most of it was enclosed by the berm of dirt and rubble that tsunamis had pushed up after the war and that was later fortified by the inhabitants. The eastern side was bordered by a concrete pier that had been a large slip for ships.

Three industrial cranes hung over the sides of that pier. It seemed the former occupants had once used them to construct this place. One of the cranes still had its cable claws gripping a container.

The steel cranes remained upright, but they had taken a beating over the years. There wasn't anything left of the buildings that Michael had seen on old pictures in the archives.

There were, however, what looked like three defensive emplacements built along the top of the concrete pier. Perhaps they were once used for cannons or machine guns. Two of them had been blown up and had debris scattered around them. The third was mostly intact, though the ceiling had collapsed. Razor-wire fences leaned at low angles among the destroyed structures.

He lowered the scope to the city and saw the scars from a massive battle years ago. Hundreds of rusted block-shaped containers littered the muddy terrain of detonation craters on the other side of the wall, across the bottom of what had once been a bay filled with water. Blasted chain-link fences and water-filled trenches formed a loose barrier around the boat city.

Beyond those, a graveyard of smaller boats lay across the ground. Most of the hulls had damage. Michael could almost picture the pirates advancing across the useless defenses toward the heart of the city.

That heart was once a sight to behold before the battle that destroyed this place. Boardwalks and platforms connected a container ship and a cruise ship positioned side by side. An entire colony of smaller boats was up on lifts around the massive vessels. They all displayed battle scars: bullet holes, busted frames, and burned hulls.

"There," Victor said. "I… born… there."

He pointed toward a weathered white ship between the two larger ships and the small colony of boats. A faded red cross marked the hull.

Michael checked his digital map. The coordinates for the light seemed to be on, or in, the container ship.

"Okay, let's go," he said.

Victor walked across the top of the dirt berm to where it connected with the concrete pier. The three cranes loomed overhead as they passed under. A skeletal body lay ahead. It was missing an arm and a foot.

The sight made Victor pause, but then he pushed onward. Michael kept his pistol at the ready. They approached one of the destroyed bunkers, and he glanced inside. The bent barrel of a machine gun lay buried in the rubble.

"Follow me," Victor said.

He went to the edge of the pier overlooking the boat city that was once a harbor, now a patchwork of muddy craters. There, a stairwell had collapsed down the other side. From his estimate, it had once been five or six stories from the bottom of the harbor to the top of the wall—all of it filled with water when this was once a port.

A single metal ladder provided a way down the concrete wall to what had been the bottom of the harbor. Michael figured the occupants had added the ladder after the water was gone, for access to the defenses above and the city below. Victor tested the top rung by jouncing a couple of times. It was a long drop down if it should snap free.

"Take it easy," Michael said. "We just want to test it—not demolish it."

Victor started down while Michael waited at the top, staring out at the container ship. There was still no light, no movement out here. Nothing on infrared either.

He looked down to see Victor moving quickly. Michael holstered his pistol and started down the ladder. The rungs were slick, and with only one arm he didn't feel confident. He took his time.

He was halfway down when Victor called up to him.

"Chief…"

He looked to see Victor pointing toward the ships. Glancing up quickly, Michael nearly lost his grip on the ladder. He held steady, then looked out to see a white light blink and then go off. For a few moments, he stood there unmoving, waiting for it to come again.

Seeing nothing, Michael continued all the way to the bottom, where he again unholstered his pistol. Victor led the way with his rifle up, moving around the craters from the battle with the pirates. He guided them around the collapsed razor-wire fence, then over the flooded trenches, leaping across at a run.

Something crunched under Michael's boot. Looking down, he found a crushed crab shell. When he got back up, he saw that the entire muddy field ahead was filled with the little crustaceans. Droves of crabs skittered away from the men as they entered the boneyard of boats.

A skeleton lay partially buried in the muck ahead. The crabs had picked it clean long ago.

Victor moved through the hull of a yacht snapped in two by monstrous forces an age ago. Crabs went skittering away with every step.

Finally, they made it to the heart of the city. Victor hunkered down behind planks from a destroyed boat that stuck out of the mud like rib bones.

"I go check out light," he said. "You stay here."

Michael didn't like splitting up and shook his head.

"I'll be okay, Chief," Victor said. "Please. It's better this way."

Finally, Michael nodded. He crouched down while Victor took off running. The man was fast, and he took an exterior ladder up to the mezzanines and platforms that formed bridges between the cruise ship and the container ship. A few minutes later, he had already made it onto the vessel.

Michael looked the way they had come, searching for motion

again. The only things moving were the crabs. There were enough of them to feed everyone indefinitely.

He turned back to the ship with his infrared. This time, he got a heat signature. It was Victor, standing on the top deck and waving.

"Chief, come in," he said over the comm.

"Copy," Michael said.

"I found light hooked up to a solar panel, like you thought. It's on timer. Goes off the same time every night."

"Weird. Okay, get back down here."

"On my way."

Michael didn't know what to make of it, but it was benign as far as he could tell. There wasn't anyone here. Soon, he would be back on the airship, and they could head back down to the cave and start rehabbing and retrofitting it.

He imagined the comfy home they could build here, falling asleep and waking up to the sound of waves. This place could be a real home for them—a safe and beautiful place to raise Bray.

But it hadn't been a safe haven for all. Crouching amid the devastation, he was reminded of the horrors that the pirates had visited on these people.

Michael got up and started toward the ship. Coming back here had to be hard for Victor. So many memories, so many losses…

He saw Victor now, already back on the ground and slogging his way back through the mud. Michael heard a squishing noise behind him.

He spun around—right into the muzzle of a sawed-off shotgun at chest level. The blade of a cutlass went to his wrist.

Michael dropped his pistol into the mud. The blade moved from his arm to his neck.

"Easy," he said.

The man wore a hood. A scarf covered his face, and a long black coat extended below his knees.

He motioned for Michael to turn around, the shotgun now at his back.

All sense of peace fled, replaced by dread and also self-judgment for letting his guard down.

The man behind him said nothing, and Michael waited for his heart to be blasted out of his chest.

"I mean you no harm," Michael said. "My wife and son..."

His words trailed when he saw Victor trot over and then stop suddenly.

"Whoa," he said.

"Relax," Michael said. "It's okay, no sudden movements."

Victor raised a hand and then lowered his rifle slowly to the ground.

The shotgun muzzle moved away from Michael's back to point over his shoulder at Victor. In that second, Michael considered trying to slip away, but he felt the sharp point of the cutlass at the back of his neck.

"Ground," said the captor in a muffled voice that sounded oddly female.

"Okay, okay," Victor said. He put his hands on his head. "Please, no hurt him. We come to look at light."

"Down!" yelled the captor.

A woman for certain.

Victor seemed to hesitate. "Gabi?"

The blade pulled back from Michael's neck. He seized on that and spun into his captor, using his helmet to smash her in the face and grab the arm with the sawed-off shotgun, shaking it loose.

They both went down in the mud. Michael landed on top and pushed himself up. The woman tried to raise her head, but he slammed her with his helmet again. The woman went back down, splashing in the mud.

Michael pried the blade from her hand. He turned the edge against her neck as she squirmed under him.

"Stop!" Victor yelled.

He rushed over, panting.

"Chief, *ies amiga!* Friend!"

Michael kept the blade against her neck as he looked down into a woman's frightened gaze.

It all came together. This was the fourth person from his group.

He pulled the blade back and stood over her as she gripped her bleeding nose.

Victor knelt down beside her, pushing up his visor to expose his eyes.

"*¡Gabi, Gabi! ¿Eres tú?*" He helped her sit up, and she pulled down her mask to reveal the face of a woman in her forties.

"Victor," she said. "*¡Qué milagro!*"

"Yes." He reached down and embraced her. Tears rushed down her bloody face as she looked over at Michael. Part of him felt bad for hurting her, but then, things could easily have ended up much worse.

You're lucky too, he thought.

Victor helped Gabi to her feet.

"Ask her if there is anyone else out there," Michael said.

Victor spoke again, and Gabi shook her head, then pointed to the horizon, speaking rapidly.

"What?" Michael asked.

Victor seemed to tense up. "She said not here, but there are out there."

She reached out for her cutlass, but Michael hesitated.

"You're sure we can trust her?" he asked.

"With our lives," Victor replied.

Michael handed the blade back to her, hoping he wouldn't regret it.

THIRTY-ONE

X woke up to a warm, wet kiss from Miles. It wasn't until he raised his head that he realized this wasn't the afterlife. Pain meant he was still alive. It took a few groggy moments to take in what he remembered last: up on the bluff, naked in the dirt, coughing his lungs up, seeing Magnolia in a dress, hearing barking, gunshots, then watching the mammoth Crixus fighting Jo-Jo.

What happened after that was murky, though he did recall picking up a shotgun and making the demented mutant shorter by about four inches.

"He's awake," someone called out.

X blinked, trying to place the voice.

A blue light produced a dim glow, spreading across a small room furnished with two chairs. Someone got up from one of those chairs. He squinted at the person, realizing that he wasn't on the *Sea Wolf*.

Approaching him was a face he hadn't expected. Corporal Valeria, in a black shirt tucked into cargo pants with medical pouches. She gave him a warm, kind grin.

"Rest," she said. "You're safe, King Xavier."

"Corporal," he rasped. "How did you…"

The hatch opened, and Magnolia looked inside.

"X," she said.

"Hey," he said quietly. His throat hurt, his chest too. And he was cold. He shivered in the wool sweater he was wearing.

"How are you feeling?" she asked.

"Fine," he lied.

"You're not fine. You were—"

"How's Jo-Jo?"

Magnolia looked to Valeria, who lowered her head.

"She's hurt bad," she said. "I'm not sure I can save her."

X got up, nearly stumbling as his feet hit the deck.

Magnolia reached out to help him. "Sit," she said.

"I want to see Jo-Jo. She saved us."

"You can see her later," Magnolia said. "Right now you need rest. You have a viral infection and you've been exposed to radiation. You might feel okay, but that's only the meds you're souped up on."

"All the more reason I should use this time to see Jo-Jo and start planning the next leg of our journey."

"Journey?"

"To find Michael and his family."

Magnolia stared at X with her jaw hanging open, perhaps thinking he was joking. X was not.

"Is it okay to move him?" she asked.

Valeria looked unsure.

"Fine," Magnolia said. "Let's go."

X patted his thigh, and Miles followed them out of the quarters into a small communal space with a stove. The boat was actually smaller than the *Sea Wolf* and appeared to be one of el Pulpo's former speedboats.

They climbed up into an enclosed cabin with a view of Rio

on one side and the bay on the other. The *Sea Wolf* was moored to a pier beside them, but there was another vessel in the water, this one many times the size of their boats. And it wasn't just any ship—this was a warship. Though only five hundred feet from stern to bow, the corvette had once been a potent weapon on the seas.

Two enclosed cannon turrets rose off the bow. Mounted machine guns provided the next line of defense. The ship had seen plenty of action over the years and had the scars to prove it, including entire sections of hull patched with steel plate, now rusted brick red.

"I take it that was Crixus's ride?" X muttered.

"Ours now," Magnolia said. "I wish it was me who got to blow off his dome, but hey, he's dead either way, and so are his followers. Only ones left are two guards who surrendered and seven slaves."

"What about his boy?"

X tried to remember what happened after he killed Crixus, but all he recalled was being carried down to the bluff. After that, it was pretty hazy.

"Lucca's on the ship," Magnolia explained. "He's locked up—tried to bite Valeria."

"He's going to be a problem, but he's just a boy."

"Yeah, and a baby Siren's just a cute li'l pet."

X took a long look at the ship.

"Any aircraft?"

"None," Magnolia said.

"Then I guess we'll continue the search for Tin on the sea."

Magnolia and Valeria exchanged a glance.

"What?" X asked.

They were keeping something from him, and it was starting to annoy him.

"We're preparing to set sail in the next hour for the Vanguard Islands," Magnolia said. "King Kade has requested that we return."

"Then tell him I'm not ready."

"Sir," Valeria said.

"They need us," Magnolia said. "Scouts in Panama detected two large ships coming up through the canal, bearing the trident emblem."

X remembered that symbol from the Sunshine Coast.

So the Forerunner had decided to go make the journey after all.

"We must put the search for the airship on hold," Magnolia said. "Our homeland needs us."

"How long do we have?"

"Not long enough."

X felt his blood pressure rising.

"I think we should take those speedboats back with Valeria while the rest of her crew brings back the warship and the *Sea Wolf*," Magnolia said. "Time is of the essence."

"*Sí, sí, muy rápido*," Valeria said. "We got to move fast."

She nodded at him respectfully. He suddenly realized he had yet to thank her. If it weren't for Valeria and the Cazador troopers who had come in search of them, he would be roasting over a low fire by now, along with Miles and Jo-Jo.

X reached out with his bandaged hand. "You have my gratitude, Corporal. Thank you. Thank you for making this trip and saving us."

"*De nada*. Anyway, King Kade send me to find you."

She shook his hand, then leaned in and gave him a kiss on his gray-stubbled cheek. Before he knew it, she was gone to check on something to do with Jo-Jo.

X stood there with Magnolia and Miles. The dog wagged his tail.

"Interesting," Magnolia said. "I figured King Kade had sent

her, but after that little kiss, I'm wondering if Valeria came to save your ass on her own."

X grumbled. "She came for the animals."

"'For the animals,' he says." Magnolia rolled her eyes.

X looked to the sky. Michael, Layla, Bray, Timothy, Steve, and Victor were out there somewhere, alive. He could feel it in his heart. But right now his duty was to the Vanguard Islands. They would need all the help they could get against this Forerunner and his knights.

"I need a suit and my helmet," he said.

"X," Magnolia said.

"Mags, just listen to me for once."

She stormed off, and returned a few minutes later. It gave X some time to calm down. When she opened up the hatch, he apologized.

"I'm sorry, Mags," he said. "I just want to see Jo-Jo, okay? Especially if she's going to be heading home with the other crew."

"I get it. It's just, you're in really bad shape."

He took a seat and gingerly put on his suit, wincing from shooting pains in his legs, back, and neck. It took a few minutes and some help from Magnolia, but he finally stood, fully dressed.

She led him outside, down the pier, to the gangplank that led up to the warship. A distant whining noise came from the deck above. Miles bolted ahead, tail down in his suit. X tried to move faster, then gripped his side and nearly bent double from a shooting pain.

"Let me help you," Magnolia said.

He put his arm around her, and she helped him the rest of the way to the top. A Cazador holding a sniper rifle stood there, dressed in light armor.

"This is Jonah," Magnolia said. "He's the sharpshooter who took out four of those bastards."

Jonah nodded.

"My deepest thanks," X said. "Stay sharp, because we may be needing your skills again soon."

X thought of the Forerunner. If he got the chance to put a bullet in the half man, half robot, he was going to take it.

Loud grunting came across the deck, where two camels were eating fodder from a trough. Both beasts looked up, chewing lazily. They weren't the source of the noise, but X had already figured that out. It was coming from a trailer on the deck. The truck that Crixus had used to pull it was also there—probably the same truck that had bashed X in the ribs.

He grimaced as he made his way over to the trailer. The back door was open, and Valeria was inside with Jo-Jo. The monkey lay on a stained mattress. She looked up as Miles came inside.

Valeria was bending down to check a wound. From what X could see, the hulking primate had several. The worst were burns on her arm and side from the flamethrower back in the city.

Patches of hair and skin had been scorched off. A clear coat of something shiny covered the wounds, but X could see they didn't have the proper equipment here.

Valeria glanced up, confirming what he could already see.

"She's dying," she whispered.

X bent down next to Jo-Jo, taking one of her paws in his hands. The heavy mitt covered his. He didn't squeeze hard, for fear of hurting her more.

Lying on her side, she fixed him with those big, gleaming black eyes.

"You're going to be okay," X said. "We're going to get you help."

He glanced down again, closer now, and noticed that several of her wounds already looked infected. Not just the burns—a few of the cuts she had gotten from the leviathan looked just as bad.

"She needs more and better meds," X said. "To fight the infection."

"*No hay mucha*," Valeria said. "We almost out."

X felt regret tugging at his heart. He should have let the monkey go, released her into the wild long ago.

But if he had, he would surely be dead right now.

"Load her onto the speedboat," X said. "We're taking her with us."

"X, wouldn't she be better off on the warship?" Magnolia asked.

"I'll personally look after her." X gripped her hand and stared into her eyes. "You're not dying yet, girl."

* * * * *

"Are you going to sit there in silence the entire flight?" Frank asked. "Should I speak in Spanish instead?"

"Tired," Gran Jefe said over the thump of the helicopter rotors. He sat in one of the ancient flight seats in the Jayhawk's cargo hold. The AI hologram known as Frank was in the cockpit, shining brightly in front of the colorful dashboard of controls.

They had left the *Angry 'Cuda* six hours ago after finally getting the helicopter airborne. It had taken a lot of patience on Gran Jefe's part as he scampered about following the AI's orders.

Slayer had remained on the ship, furious. Tia had never even come up from sickbay, where she tended Zuni. They both knew full well that the AI could lead them to their doom, and they both wanted the program destroyed permanently.

Unfortunately, Frank was also the only one who could help save them. Even King Kade saw that. If it meant that Gran Jefe had to make a deal with the devil, so be it. But that didn't mean he had to be the damned thing's *amigo*.

"I spent many years in solitude," Frank said. "It wasn't always that way. I was once friends—or comrades, you might say—with the people living in the mining installation you discovered. Long after my physical body died, I piloted this very Jayhawk with several of their leaders to look for survivors. That mission ended up bringing back a fungus. Eventually, it turned them all into the no-longer-human monsters you saw."

Gran Jefe found the story vaguely interesting, but he really just wanted to sleep. If this Forerunner was coming for the Vanguard Islands, Gran Jefe was going to need every bit of his strength to fight the knights.

He lowered his head and tried to rest his eyes. They still had another three hours to go before they got to the coordinates for Lucky's boat in the ocean.

"Do you have a family?" Frank asked. "A wife? A son or daughter?"

Gran Jefe glanced up, then wiped a strand of hair from his sweaty forehead.

"Son," he said.

"How old?" Frank asked.

"Toddler." Gran Jefe was ashamed to admit he didn't know Pablo's exact age.

"I had two sons, a daughter, and a wife," Frank said. "When the war started, it was chaos and I couldn't get to them. I was stuck on a ship during a mission to stop drug smugglers. By the time we found out what was happening, Houston was gone. My children, their mother, and their stepfather—gone in the blink of an eye."

He is a ghost, Gran Jefe thought. Just like Timothy Pepper.

"How? How you become *fantasma*?"

"Not by choice," Frank replied. "After the bombs started to fall, we rescued everyone we could, staging missions from the mining facility where you found me. We brought them back there."

He looked back at Gran Jefe.

"On one mission, I was deployed to extract an ITC scientist named Hesh and his team. I flew to a beach on Galveston, where they waited with equipment they claimed could help win the war."

"ITC?"

"Yes. Industrial Tech Corporation."

Gran Jefe nodded. It was the company that built the end-of-the-world bunkers that the Hell Divers and Cazadores often raided.

"For years, my comrades and I deployed to rescue people and bring them to our facility, which we continued to retrofit and modify under the direction of Hesh and his staff," Frank said. "One by one, my comrades were killed—by the machines, other survivors, radiation, et cetera."

He let out a grim sigh.

"Five years after the first bombs dropped, it was just me and a copilot that was sick with radiation poisoning," Frank explained. "When he died and I got sick, Hesh and his team decided for me that I couldn't afford to die. They hooked me up to a machine and turned me into what you see now."

Gran Jefe got the gist of what he said: Frank was never given the choice to live indefinitely. It was forced on him.

"I outlived all of them," he continued. "Eventually, raiders found us, killed our guards, broke inside, and murdered Hesh and his people. They took over, and they used me. Generations later, the descendants became infested when we brought the fungus back from a flight to California."

"Sorry," Gran Jefe said.

Frank nodded. "It's in my programming to protect myself. Otherwise, I'd have let your comrades destroy me."

Part of Gran Jefe wondered if this was all one big lie. If so, it was a hell of a good one.

"You still haven't told me your name," Frank said.

"Mata. Jorge Mata, or Gran Jefe."

"Gran Jefe. Okay, big boss man. You are going to tell me what we're doing out here, and tell me before we get to these coordinates, because we're almost there."

Gran Jefe had lost track of time talking with the AI. He unbuckled his harness and moved up to the cockpit. The chopper flew lower over the ocean, sweeping its searchlights over the endless whitecaps.

"We look for boat," he said. "I have to go down, find man, and bring back with us."

"Easy, just like old times." Frank jerked his chin. "Go grab a harness and secure it to a cable. I'll lower you down."

"Okay, okay."

Gran Jefe went into the cargo hold and climbed into a harness. By the time he had clipped in, the chopper was closing in on the coordinates.

"We're here," Frank said. "No boat, though."

Moving from viewport to viewport, Gran Jefe checked the surface below. Nothing broke the vast expanse of water.

"I'll do a few sweeps of the area," Frank said. "Stand by."

As he waited, Gran Jefe thought for the first time about what the king was asking him to do. His orders were to get the location of the Coral Castle from this knight, through whatever means necessary.

This wasn't the first time Gran Jefe had been tasked with beating information out of someone. And if it meant protecting his son, he would do whatever it took. It was Lucky's bad luck that Gran Jefe knew a lot of ways to inflict pain.

"Eyes on," Frank said. "Circling now."

Gran Jefe opened the sliding cargo door and spotted the boat bobbing in the rough water. The chopper's searchlight blazed against the hull.

"I don't see anyone down there," Frank announced.

"Lower me," Gran Jefe said.

"Copy that. Lowering in three, two, one…"

Gran Jefe waited until they were hovering over the boat, then stepped out into the air. The winch lowered him over the stern. He had his rifle trained on the cabin the whole way down.

His boots hit the deck, and he unbuckled from the harness. Then he went up the ladder to check the top cabin. He could see that it was empty before opening the hatch, but he looked in anyway.

A thermos sat in a cup holder, the top off and tea inside. He checked the controls—the knight had shut the boat off and removed the key.

Gran Jefe climbed back down and opened the hatch to the lower quarters. With his rifle barrel up and tac light on, he moved down the ladder.

The creak and groan of the boat was the only answer to his footfalls. He swept the light over the empty kitchen and a couch with a blanket. The bedroom was also empty.

No one was here. The knight had left.

Gran Jefe went back up to the deck, where he found a partially open aluminum box. He found blood inside, and human hair.

Bending down, he opened it and found a square plastic device covered in something sticky. Holding it up to the light between thumb and forefinger, he recognized it as a tracking device. Lucky must have discovered it somehow.

But where had the knight gone after leaving the boat, and whose blood and hair was this?

Gran Jefe went back up to the deck, thoroughly confused.

They were in the middle of the Caribbean Sea, fifty miles from the nearest land.

He looked up at the chopper, clipped back in to the harness, and motioned for Frank to pull him up. He had bad news for the cowboy king.

The knight was gone, and with him their chance of finding the Coral Castle.

THIRTY-TWO

At dawn, Imulah arrived with a note.

"Sorry to disturb you, sir, but this is from Pedro," he said.

Kade had fallen asleep at the council table turned war table, in the great chamber. His face was stuck to a map with a wet spot where he had drooled. He wiped his mouth, looking up groggily as the scribe handed him a folded piece of paper.

"What time is it?" Kade asked.

"Almost six, sir."

Kade lifted his head to see sunlight bleeding through the shuttered windows. He unfolded the paper and read the confidential message quickly. But it didn't make any sense. Gran Jefe had located the yacht, and it was empty.

"I don't understand." Kade racked his brain to come up with a theory of how Lucky could have gotten himself off that boat. There was no way the knight could have jumped overboard and swum to land. Perhaps a sea monster—no shortage of those—had snatched him out of the boat, or maybe Lucky had finally decided that life just wasn't worth it anymore.

But why?

No, not likely.

General Forge stepped back into the room, looking as though he too had been up all night.

"Sir," he said, "all of our vessels are moving into position, and we're prepared to start moving the children to the vault. The boat you requested is finished and has been relocated to the enclosed marina."

Kade nodded and then said, "Lucky's gone."

"Gone?"

Kade handed the note to the general. His eye squinted as he read.

"There's nothing we can do now but strengthen our defenses and prepare for these ships," Forge said. "Commander Slayer is on his way here with another helicopter, and Valeria is returning with X and Magnolia. The corvette they salvaged will be a few days behind them."

"Too late to help us," Kade said.

He felt despair getting the upper hand. Woody was dead, murdered by some freak AI that they were now counting on to fly their helicopters. If that was what it took to protect the Vanguard Islands, he would find a way to deal with it.

Kade grabbed his duty belt and slung it around his waist. General Forge was right—they had to proceed as planned.

Beau arrived just as Kade was about to leave the room. Dakota, still awake but looking somewhat the worse for wear, stood guard outside.

"Morning, sir," Beau said.

He still didn't know about Woody.

"Beau," Kade said.

"Yeah?"

"Wait for me outside," Kade said to Forge.

"Something bad happened, didn't it?" Beau asked.

"Yes, I'm afraid it did."

"Woody?"

Kade nodded. "Killed on the mission."

Beau glanced down at his boots. "Bloody hell, Kade." He looked back up. "I knew this was going to happen. He didn't stand a chance out there, even with those Barracudas or whatever the hell you call them."

"He didn't die for nothing. Both helicopters were extracted, and they will play a vital role in defending this place."

Beau reached up to scratch his forehead, then sighed.

"He's really gone?" he asked.

"Yes, I'm sorry. It hurts, I know. Trust me."

Beau sucked in a deep breath. "So who's going to fly the choppers, then?"

"For now, we have to rely on the AI they encountered. He'll have to teach the pilots." He left out the fact the AI was the reason Woody and Blackburn were dead. Only Forge knew the truth.

A knock came on the door, and it opened to admit Lieutenant Wynn.

"Sir, the chamber is ready," he said, saluting.

"Good work," Kade said. "Let's start moving the kids as soon as possible."

"Yes, sir. I'll get word out to each rig."

Kade left the chamber and took a stairwell to the rooftop. He wanted to check on the Hell Divers, but more than that, he needed some fresh air.

Beau and Dakota followed him up to the top hatch. Kade opened it and stepped out into morning sun. The first thing he saw was the rank of cannons positioned along the western platforms on the rooftop. Seeing the firepower reminded him that they were ready for the knights. If the two massive ships got past all the other defenses somehow, these cannons would punch their hulls below the waterline and sink them before they could get close.

He stepped out to a platform with an unmanned machine-gun nest. Boats chugged away from the marina, filled with civilians preparing to be soldiers. The *Frog* was already out there, patrolling to the south along with fishing trawlers and smaller, faster scout boats. Soon, the armada would deploy, ready for battle.

He turned to the east and raised a hand to the sky. The two hot-air balloons with the platform suspended beneath them were still up at five thousand feet. Two figures on the platform dived off, spearing down through the blue sky and arching back before assuming the stable falling position. The two parachutes deployed simultaneously, the black canopies blooming out and floating them down to the Sky Arena. The divers had trained through the night, jumping over and over in the darkness.

"Roman's getting good," Beau said. "He's landed ten dives without a hitch."

Kade nodded, though Roman had a lot to learn. This was basic-level training. Diving through electrical storms and landing in a radioactive hot zone was an entirely different level.

"Where to now, boss?" Beau asked.

It was time to check the last trick he had up his sleeve. They took the elevator cage down to the piers. A few boats were already motoring toward them in the distance, each loaded with kids being moved from the other rigs.

Wynn was waiting there with officers chosen for their gentle manner to help usher the children inside without scaring them.

Kade went to the side door of the enclosed marina. The clack and whir of machinery guided him down platforms of raised boats. At the very end was his secret weapon: a war boat that had been comprehensively transformed into an armor-plated yet very fast gunboat.

"Wow, looks like a tank on water," Beau said.

"That's the intention," Kade replied. "I want something strong for the Forerunner if he decides to attack."

They walked over a portable gangplank onto the deck, where the engineers had added a secret storage area on the bow. His first plan had been to install a bomb inside, but now he was going to arm the Jayhawk with the bombs. It was the one thing the Forerunner didn't have anymore: air superiority.

"Add this back to the fleet," Kade said. "I want it on the open water."

Wynn looked at the boat for a second but didn't question the orders.

By the time Kade got back to the marina, Cazador kids were already getting off the boats. Kids no older than Alton, clutching their belongings to their chests, hurried across the docks with their chaperones.

Kade stood by and watched, trying to extend reassuring nods to them. To his happy surprise, most of the girls and boys seemed unafraid. Some even smiled at him. One Cazador boy in particular gazed at Kade with a look of determination. He had never seen this child or the woman with him, who must be his mother.

They walked over in his direction, and the woman called out, "King Kade."

Dakota stepped forward to speak to the woman.

"She says you want to see her," he said.

"What's your name?" Kade asked.

"Jada," she said. "*Este muchacho es Pablo.*"

"Oh, I'm sorry, yes, I've been looking for you," Kade said. "Gran Jefe asked me to give you something from him."

Dakota translated for Kade.

Jada blanched visibly and stepped back. Speaking rapidly in Spanish, she glanced from the guard back to Kade.

"She wants to know if Jorge is dead," Dakota said.

She pulled Pablo close.

"Oh, no, no!" Kade said. "*Jorge está bien.* He's out on a very important mission."

Pablo glanced up with curious eyes as Dakota explained.

"A mission to keep us all safe," Kade said. He reached into his vest pocket and pulled out the ring. "He wanted me to give this to you if he doesn't come back. Truth is, I think I should give it to you now, in case something happens to *me.*"

After Dakota relayed the words, Jada looked at the ring with hesitation in her eyes.

"*Por favor,*" Kade said. He gently proffered it, and after a beat, she took it.

"*Gracias, Su Majestad.*" She nodded and then corralled Pablo back into the line with the other kids.

Kade took the stairs back up to the council chambers and throne room. He took his time walking down the hall of paintings and statues, stopping a few times to pay his respects. Seeing Captain Les "Giraffe" Mitchells's likeness gave him pause. He felt a wash of guilt for sharing a tender moment with Giraffe's widow, Katherine, the other night at the festivities on the trading post rig.

Dakota opened the large wooden door to the council chamber. Pedro was inside, setting up radio equipment with two scribes. Imulah was back at the war table, along with General Forge and several guards. Sofia had also arrived, on crutches until a guard quickly brought her a chair.

"We got word from Slayer," Forge announced. "They're about a day out, making good time. He should be here ahead of the enemy."

It was good news.

"Gran Jefe and the AI pilot will be back by midnight," Forge added. "Have you decided how to handle that murderous machine?"

Kade went over to the table with the maps. He knew how dangerous bringing an AI back here was, but he also knew that the only way to learn how to fly those helicopters was through this AI, this Frank.

"Why are we even discussing this?" Sofia asked. "After everything we went through with the defectors back at the camp?"

"I'll make my decision shortly," Kade said.

"Kade," Beau said, shaking his head. "You can't seriously be considering keeping the bloody thing around."

"Nothing's off the table right now."

Beau massaged his mustache—his nervous tic, his tell. "If you think I'm gonna allow Roman to get on one of those choppers with that thing..."

"The Hell Divers won't be going with me," Kade said.

Everyone around the table fell silent.

"I'm going alone," Kade said.

"I'm sending a team with you," Forge said.

"This isn't up for debate. I've made my decision. I'm going with the bomb, and I'm going to make peace. If peace isn't possible, then we get there another way."

He didn't need to spell it out for everyone here. They knew that it was likely a one-way trip.

"I'm going to go see the kids, then get cleaned up," Kade said. "I'll be back in a few hours to continue our planning."

Dakota followed Kade out of the chamber, with Beau hurrying after him. When they got to the hall, he stopped them. "King Kade," he said.

Kade looked at his old friend.

"I'm sorry," Beau said. "I've been a coward all this time, and after losing my son, and now Woody, I fear for Roman."

"I understand, Beau. Trust me, I understand."

Kade patted him on the back. Beau wasn't a weak man, but

he had never been a killer. It wasn't in his nature. And that was what Kade liked most about him.

"If you want me to go on the helicopter with you, I will," Beau said.

"I appreciate that, but this is something I've gotta do on my own," Kade replied.

He turned without another word and spent the next few minutes taking the stairs and corridors to the heart of the rig. There, el Pulpo once kept his treasures in a massive wheel-handled vault with the thickest walls anywhere on the islands. Two militia soldiers guarded it. Both had been personally assigned by Wynn, and approved by Forge after two days of vetting.

When he arrived, the door was open. Hundreds of bunks had been set up along the walls. Many were already occupied. Crates of food and barrels of water were set up in a storage room in back. Two mechanics were putting the finishing touches on an air-filtration system that would pump in fresh air and suck out any smoke in the event of a fire.

Kade walked inside to find a group of kids playing games at a low table.

"Cowboy King!" Alton yelled.

Phyl and Katherine made their way over as the other kids spoke in hushed voices. The other chaperones and teachers prepared games and lessons for the children.

"How long do we have to stay here?" Alton asked.

"Not very long—just until I can talk to the leader of the knights," Kade said.

Katherine eyed him.

"You're not a good liar, sir," Alton said. "I'm old enough to know the truth. Are we all going to die here?"

Kade squatted down in front of him so they were at eye level.

"No, we're not all going to die. You're going to be just fine," he said.

"How do you know?" Phyl asked.

Kade glanced over at the young girl. "I can't explain it. It's just something I know."

"Will you stay with us?" Alton asked.

"I'll come visit you after I finish some work later tonight," Kade said.

"I want to come with you, though."

Katherine put her arm around Alton. "The king's busy," she said softly. "He'll come back when he can."

Alton frowned. "Did X find Michael yet?"

The question took Kade off guard, and again Katherine came to his aid.

"Let's go play a game," she said. "Come on, now."

Kade nodded at her and smiled. He hoped the smile didn't look strained.

Exhausted, he left the vault and went back to his quarters, leaving Beau and Dakota to hold sentry outside his doors.

When he got into his room, he eyed his bed, longing to collapse on it and enter a vegetative state. Instead, he went to his desk and sat down. The window was open, letting in the ocean breeze. The sun was about to merge with the horizon, sending streaks of orange across the sky.

He pulled out a cracked leather journal and opened it. For years, he had considered what he would say to his family. An hour passed before he picked up the pen. By the time he put it to paper, it was dark outside.

Dear Mikah, Rich, Jack, and Sean,

He held the pen in a shaking hand. Just seeing their names brought back so many memories. Good ones, but all bittersweet.

I miss you so much. I miss your laughs. Your smiles. Lying on the floor with all three of you boys and wrestling while your mother told us to keep it down. I carry these moments in my heart. There, they will always live as long as I am here.

Here is a place I wish you could see. Then again, maybe you can.

Some of our people think this is heaven, but for me it can never be heaven without you. I hope that wherever you are, I'll be able to join you someday. Until then, I have a few things left to do.

A tear fell from his eye. Then another. The third exploded on the paper, smearing the ink.

Kade put the pen down and went to the sink, looked in the cracked mirror. He turned on the water and splashed it over his face. Then he gazed at his reflection. The lines cutting into his forehead and around his eyes seemed deeper, more sharply etched.

Grays were spreading along his temples and forelock. He swept back strands and looked away. Hearing something small hit the floor, he saw that his pen had fallen off the desk.

Kade wiped his face off with a towel and was reaching for his toothbrush when he noticed it rattling slightly in its glass on the sink.

"What in the bloody…"

He hurried over to the window just as a distant booming sounded. Pulling back the drapes, he stared out the window at the dark horizon. He saw nothing out there but the lights on the other rigs.

Heavy pounding on the door made him flinch.

Dakota swung it open.

"I'm coming," Kade said. He grabbed a bag and rushed after the guard and Beau. Neither of them knew what was going on as they ran back down to the council chambers, where Pedro was working the radios.

"Sitrep," Kade said.

"One of our ships went offline," Pedro said.

General Forge entered. "Which ship?" he demanded.

"The *Gannet*," Pedro said.

Kade and Forge went to the map. The *Gannet* was an old transport ship they had sent out to the front lines. It was slow, but it had armor, along with six Jet Skis aboard.

"Did they report anything?" Kade asked.

"They said there was something on the horizon," Pedro said. "Then nothing."

"Could it be those two enemy ships got here faster than we thought?" Kade asked.

"No, that's impossible," Forge said. "No ship moves that fast."

The radio crackled with a voice almost too faint to hear.

"We're under attack. Requesting reinforcements!"

The message was clear. The battle had started.

How didn't matter. They were out of time and had to respond.

Booming in the distance was loud enough to shake the interior of the rig.

Forge ran for the door. "I'm going to the rooftop!"

Kade ran after him, heart pounding.

Panicked voices filled the hallway as guards moved into a protective position outside the hall. Several joined the group with Kade, including Forge's two retainers. Six men marched up a stairwell to the rooftop.

Forge swung it open to a rumbling sound emanating from a fiery clump of clouds. The edges morphed and rolled outward like some sort of bulging, fiery apparition.

"What in the wastes is that?" Forge asked.

Kade picked up the scent of smoke.

This was no cloud. This was a disguise…

"It's an airship!" he shouted. "Aim the cannons! Shoot it down!"

By the time the crews rotated the barrels toward the fiery cloud formation, rockets shot out of the smoke screen, slamming into the cannons. Explosions rocked the rooftop.

A machine-gun nest opened fire, only to vanish in a cloud of black smoke. Shrapnel whined through the air as Kade hunched down.

Dakota brought up his shield in front of the king. Kade drew the Monster Hunter from its holster on his hip and raised it to the sky.

"Get back inside!" Forge yelled.

The men retreated into the stairwell, but Kade lingered outside, staring up as the clouds dissipated over the smooth hull of an enormous airship.

"My God," he murmured.

The Forerunner had arrived in his chariot. A gargantuan black vessel with two wings sporting turbofans, and a finned aft section. The cockpit was windowless and bare save for a single blinking light.

Rockets peeled away from hidden tubes on the underbelly while machine-gun turrets sent swarms of tracer bullets into the rooftop.

"Get back!" Dakota shouted.

He turned and pushed Kade with one hand while holding his shield in the other. Dirt sprayed up from the impacts of rounds, raining down on Kade and the Cazador soldiers as they raced to the stairwell.

A few steps down, Beau hunkered down, panicked. Kade grabbed his friend by the collar and gave him a good shake.

"Go tell Pedro to radio Gran Jefe. Tell him to link up with X. They might be our only hope. Get a second message to Slayer. Tell him to divert and meet up with the others. They can't return to the islands until they're ready to fight!"

Beau stared at Kade.

"Do you understand?"

"Yes."

"Go!" Kade released him.

Another fiery explosion billowed from the rooftop, and a machine-gun nest fell silent. The airship hovered directly over the plot of tropical forest on the capitol tower. A wide hatch like a mouth opened below the bow.

Kade waited for a bomb to drop to end it all, but instead, a ramp lowered.

In the shadowy interior, Kade spotted knights. A dozen warriors stood with submachine guns and assault rifles.

They weren't here to destroy the rig. They were here to *seize* it.

Forge shut the hatch and sealed it from the inside as Beau squeezed past the soldiers huddling in the stairwell with Kade. Frightened eyes watched the king, waiting for orders.

"What do we do?" one man asked.

"We have to surrender!" yelled a militia soldier. "They'll destroy us all!"

"No," Kade replied in a calm voice. He moved between the soldiers. "If they wanted to destroy us, they would have already. They want our food, our oil, and our home."

He drew his cutlass.

"Prepare to fight!" Kade yelled. "We can't let them inside. We must protect the children. We will defend these halls to the last drop of blood!"

THIRTY-THREE

"King Kade, do you copy?" Magnolia asked.

She held her hands over her headset, trying to block out the racket of the speedboat, but all she could hear was static.

"King Kade, do you copy?" she repeated.

She leaned forward in her seat in the cockpit, wearing her diving armor once again. And her twin curved blades were again sheathed on her back. She had recovered them from one of Crixus's mortally wounded goons, using one to put him out of his misery.

Behind the wheel was Jonah, the sharpshooter who, with Valeria, had saved their bacon at Rio.

"I'm going belowdecks," Magnolia said.

Jonah nodded his bald head. He didn't speak much, but he did wear the cross pendant of an ancient religion—the same religion that worshipped the statue overlooking Rio, Magnolia realized. He had held it in his hand with closed eyes before they sailed.

She slipped out of the hatch and made her way belowdecks. Just before she entered, her hand went to her stomach. All the thumping and rocking was making her feel queasy again.

She ducked down into the shallow belly of the speedboat. Miles trotted over, wagging his tail. Jo-Jo lay beneath a table on her side, covered with a blanket. Valeria poked her head out of the quarters where X was supposed to be resting.

Magnolia walked past the sleeping monkey and stood in the open hatch to the bedroom, where X sat up in his bunk. Valeria stepped back and let her inside.

"Well? Did you talk to King Kade?" X asked.

"I can't get through," Magnolia said. "It's like the signal just suddenly shut off."

"Probably the storms…"

She took a seat in a chair and put her head in her hands, sighing.

"It's gonna be okay," X said.

"Yeah, sorry, I just feel like shit," Magnolia said.

"You want medicine?" Valeria asked.

"No, save it for now," Magnolia said. She looked up and gave a weary smile. "Thanks, Corporal."

"De nada, comandante."

She walked away, leaving Magnolia and X alone.

"I don't think the islands can survive another war," she said.

X ran a hand through his greasy gray hair. "Maybe we can negotiate a peace. Give them a rig for their people like we did the sky people from—"

"And how'd that work out?"

X swung his legs over the bed. He looked a lot better than when Magnolia had seen him lying naked in the dirt, but he was a shell of his former self.

"Let me help you," she said.

X shook away her hand and, still bent over, walked out to the living quarters. Jo-Jo was awake, barely. She opened one eye. It went to Magnolia, then X.

"How you doing, girl?" X asked.

"She is strong but very sick," Valeria said. "I need *más medicina*. And *better* medicine."

X went over and sat next to the animal, reaching out to stroke the top of her head. She cooed peacefully.

Miles nudged in between X and Jo-Jo, not wanting to miss out on the affection.

"I love you too, boy," X said.

Valeria watched with a fond gaze, clearly taking a liking to the king. Magnolia approved. Xavier deserved a shot at love, if that was what he wanted.

Magnolia felt the nausea build toward the point of no return. A moment later, she rushed out of the cabin, swung open the hatch, and skidded on the wet deck outside.

She leaned over the gunwale of the thumping boat and heaved a torrent over the side. The acid made her throat burn, and she knelt down, wiping her mouth off.

She looked out over the dark water—whitecaps under the blue glow of storm clouds. This was going to be her view for the next four or five agonizing days. She just hoped she could kick this crud before they got back to the islands. She needed to be ready to fight.

"You okay?" X called out through the half-open hatch.

Magnolia raised a hand but didn't turn. "Yeah, yeah, fine."

After a pause, the hatch swung shut. Magnolia felt another surge of nausea. She pushed herself up to vomit over the gunwale again when she noticed something in the sky. A white light beamed down from the clouds to the water. It didn't blink off but remained strangely constant above them.

"What is…" Magnolia retched loudly again but quickly recovered to stare up at the sky. The light was gone now.

Maybe she imagined it.

Fairly confident that she was done throwing up, she wiped her mouth off and stood. For a few minutes, she lingered in case there was a third round. As she stepped away from the rail, a horn blared, making her flinch.

She looked up to the cabin. Jonah was waving frantically with one hand and steering with the other. She went over to the ladder, fearing he had spotted something monstrous.

A mutant shark or, worse, a leviathan.

As she grabbed the ladder, she noticed lights beaming through the storm clouds again. This time, she was certain they weren't in her mind.

She hurried up the ladder just as X burst through the lower hatch. He stood beneath her, draped in a blanket.

"What's going on?" he yelled.

Valeria came out of the cabin after X, holding a rifle.

"There!" She aimed at the sky.

As the boat slowed, Magnolia turned on the ladder to see a spear of light in the sky. She jumped down to the deck, staring at the white beam raking over the ocean.

"Airship!" Valeria yelled.

Magnolia stared up at what appeared to be some sort of aircraft.

"Where's my rifle!" X shouted.

Magnolia staggered over to a mounted speargun and angled it up at the light. Barking came from the open hatch as Miles poked his head out.

"Get back inside!" X shouted.

He closed the hatch and came back onto the deck with Valeria as the boat began to veer away from the approaching light.

"Get ready to open fire!" X yelled.

Valeria held her rifle as steady as she could, but her boots kept slipping on the shifting deck.

Magnolia aimed the spear at the belly of the ship. As she moved her finger to the trigger, she heard a beating sound—a faint but growing *wop, wop, wop* of a main rotor.

This was no airship. It was a helicopter.

Magnolia stared at a midsize chopper dipping over the water. Searchlights pierced the darkness and played over the surface, hitting the boat.

"Should I fire?" Magnolia yelled.

X staggered over, pulling himself along the rail. He turned to Valeria. "Tell Jonah to kill the engines!"

She climbed up and gave the order.

A moment later, the engines fell silent. The vessel bobbed in the waves. Magnolia kept the weapon trained on the chopper, leading it slightly as it circled.

Suddenly, it curved toward them and hovered directly overhead. The cargo hold's hatch slid open, revealing a hulking figure in the opening.

X gaped. "I'll be dipped in Siren shit."

"Gran fuckin' Jefe," Magnolia breathed.

The big Cazador cabled down to the deck and unclipped.

"King Xavier," he said, pounding his chest armor.

X turned to Valeria. "Keep Jo-Jo inside!"

Then he faced Gran Jefe.

"How'd you find us?" X asked.

"Tracker," Gran Jefe said.

Magnolia recalled Valeria telling her they had a tracker on the boat that Kade sent them out with, just in case they too went missing while trying to locate the *Sea Wolf.*

"The islands are under attack," Gran Jefe grunted. "Pedro say to come get you. We go meet Slayer and form offensive."

"Hold up a minute. What do you mean, the islands are under attack? I thought those ships were…"

"Not ships. Airship."

"An airship?" Magnolia asked. "The Forerunner has an *airship*?"

"*Sí.*"

X and Magnolia exchanged a glance. He had a look of shock in his eyes, and Magnolia knew she probably did too. They had to be thinking the same thing—that they had underestimated this Forerunner, and so had King Kade.

"We go now with Frank," Gran Jefe said, pounding his chest again. "We go save islands!"

*　　*　　*　　*　　*

Michael looked out from the cave's mouth. Rays of moonlight broke through the dense cloud cover in the distance.

The pirates who had raided the port of Arrecife were some-where out there where the sun was shining again. Three days had passed since they found Gabi—or, rather, since she found them—in the destroyed boat city. She was malnourished and had spent most of the time inside the airship keeping to herself, eating or sleeping. Building strength. When she was awake, she explained to Victor that the pirates had settlements along the Western Sahara and Morocco but rarely came this way.

After hearing that, Michael, Victor, and Layla had decided to continue their settlement plans in the ruins of Jameos del Agua. Layla was up on the airship resting with Bray while Michael and Victor put the finishing touches up on their new home in the caves.

The two men returned to the stack of building materials they had brought down from the airship. Waves bashed the shore, sending up sprays of ocean spume.

Michael planned on keeping safe down here by keeping Timo-thy as their aerial lookout. Always watching, always scanning for the pirates and other threats. With Pepper's help and Gabi's experience, they had a real shot at survival. Gabi had not only managed to escape when the pirates raided the caves at the former resort, but she had also managed to survive off the land. Seafood, plants, and fresh water had kept her alive. They really lucked out finding such a knowledgeable local.

But Michael couldn't fully trust her, not yet. A lot of time had passed since Victor last saw her. Years alone could change a person—especially years spent scavenging in the wastes. Michael thought of how it had changed X. He had come back to the airship half-crazed, half-dead, and barely able to speak.

Gabi seemed to be in better shape physically, perhaps mentally too, but not by much. Only time would tell whether she could fit in with their family.

"Will this work?" Victor asked, holding up a pipe fitting.

Michael looked at it and shook his head. "Too small."

He looked over the dwindling supply of construction materials: extra pipe, spools of conduit, hatches, leftover carpet, roofing felt. At this point, mostly scrap remained after they worked through the night to make the interior caves habitable.

They had added walls and ceilings to each room and installed a sink and a shit can. It was a work in progress.

Michael kicked aside a ragged scrap of sheet metal and found the pipe fitting he was looking for.

"Got it," he said.

Victor picked up a hatch salvaged from the airship. He grimaced from the arrow wound he had gotten weeks earlier, when they took the airship from Charmer's underlings.

"Let me help you," Michael said.

He stuffed the pipe fitting in his pack of tools, slung it over his arm, and grabbed the bottom of the metal door. They carried it down the passage and got it through the open gate in the fence they had strung back up. Soon, they would reinforce it with a better barrier, built of rock and perhaps spare parts from the airship.

Victor and Michael carried the hatch into the communal space. A table was already there with five chairs—one for each of them, including Bray. They leaned the hatch against a wall.

Michael got out a basin wrench from a bag of tools and went about installing the shit-can drain. It would incorporate an improvised P trap to keep the sewer smell out, and drain through the same hole in the floor as the sink.

Sweat dripped down Michael's face as he struggled with the tool. The construction process had been difficult without his prosthetic arm. But each time he found himself about to get angry, he reminded himself that they were alive and safe.

Victor worked on installing the hatch. An hour later, they both were finished. They stood back to look over their work.

"Good job, Chief," Victor said.

"You too," Michael said.

After a short look around to make sure everything was in place, Michael went to the radio. "Pepper, we're done," he said. "Do a scan, and then bring everyone down."

Static crackled from the receiver, followed by *"Copy, sir."*

Michael went into the bedroom he would share with Layla and Bray. They had already brought down a bed and a crib that Michael had put together. This space didn't look like much yet with walls and ceilings fashioned from airship panels, but they would make it their own with a little paint, some pictures, and some salvaged carpet.

The radio buzzed with a message from Timothy. "Scans are all clear," he said. "Proceeding with descent."

"On our way," Michael said.

He and Victor trekked through the dark passage and arrived

at the cave entrance, where the hum of the airship greeted them.

Michael looked out over the horizon, uneasy even after the all clear from Timothy. It was still possible that someone could be out there watching.

The airship lowered out of the clouds, hovering just above the rocky overlook beyond the cave's entrance. A hatch in the stern opened to the cargo hold, and the lightweight aluminum ramp with handrails extended downward.

Layla appeared in the cargo doorway above, with Bray in her arms. Gabi joined them, bathed in Timothy's blue glow.

Bray stuck his finger out to meet the holographic finger of the AI. They had really taken a liking to each other.

Gabi clipped in to the harness first, and Timothy lowered her to the rock outcropping in front of the cavern. She touched down, and Victor went out to help her out of the harness. He sent it back up to Layla and Bray.

"Welcome," Michael said to Gabi.

She looked up at him with anxious brown eyes. Michael understood her fear. As a Hell Diver, you had to be on your guard always. Even now he was watching the horizon and listening for anything that might be sneaking up on them.

Layla and Bray came down next, turning slowly in the air as they descended.

"Wheeee!" Bray yelled.

Michael and Victor smiled while Gabi remained stone faced.

"Gotcha," Michael said, grabbing the harness and pulling Layla and Bray over to him. Victor helped them unbuckle. Bray reached out to Michael. "Daddy," he said.

He took his son in his arm and kissed him on the cheek.

As soon as they were out of the way, Timothy began moving the final loads of supplies and materials with the cable pulley system.

A robotic arm swung outward, a crate suspended beneath it and lowering toward the cave. Each box was labeled: CLOTH- ING. BEDDING. TOWELS. Everything they would need to make this home comfortable.

While Michael took Bray, Layla, and Gabi into the dark, rocky corridor, Victor stayed outside to unhook the cable slings so Timothy could send the next load.

"You really finished with the bathroom?" Layla asked.

"Yup. I think we might actually have a working shit can," Michael said.

When they were all standing in the communal space, he handed Bray back to Layla.

"Shut off your lights," he said.

Layla did as instructed, but Gabi didn't seem to understand. Michael reached out to the switch he had installed on a conduit. A chain of light bulbs flickered to life, spreading over the room and the table.

"We have lights!" Layla proclaimed.

"Light, light!" Bray said, clapping his hands. Michael set him down, and the boy hurried across the room, twirling in circles and laughing.

"I rigged up some batteries and solar collectors," Michael said.

"I can't believe it, Tin," Layla said. She walked inside with Bray, who oohed and aahed, pointing at things.

Gabi, too, seemed surprised. She looked at Michael, and for the first time in the three days he had known her, she nodded.

Michael nodded back.

He beckoned to her and led her to the bedroom where she would stay. Then he went over to his room, where Layla stood with her arms over her chest.

Bray was already jumping on the bed and laughing.

"Come on, bud," Layla said. "Let's go get our stuff."

They left to help ferry in the crates and supplies. When they arrived at the cave's mouth, the airship and Timothy had already taken off.

Michael was going to miss being around the AI all the time, but it was best to have him up there, watching over them.

By suppertime, they had finished unpacking and making the beds. The scent of grilling meat and onions drew them out into the communal space. Even Gabi was there, peering curiously out of her room.

Victor stood behind the electric grill in the small kitchen, cooking something. The table, Michael saw, was already set with plates and utensils from the airship. A bowl of tomatoes from the airship's farm sat in the center of the table.

"Smells delicious," Layla said. "What is it?"

"Surprise," Victor said.

Bray walked over to investigate, but Layla scooped him up.

"Take a seat," Victor said, motioning with a spatula.

"Gabi, please join us," Layla said with a smile.

As they all sat down, Victor brought over a platter of grilled fish filets, and a big tureen of seaweed soup.

"I took out bones," he said.

Bray snatched up a ribbon of seaweed off his plate and stuffed it in his mouth. For a moment, his eyes seemed to widen as he decided whether he liked it.

Then he clapped his hands together and said, "More!"

Everyone laughed, and Gabi cracked the first hint of a smile Michael had ever seen from her. Bray reached out to her and waved.

She waved back—just once, but it was something.

Michael couldn't help feeling a wave of relief. He knew right then that she would be a good addition to the family.

Victor sat, and they all dug in. Gabi ate like a half-starved

Siren, practically inhaling the fish and the seaweed soup, using her fingers instead of a fork. Not that Michael was judging. He remembered one of his first meals at the Vanguard Islands after the war with el Pulpo. He had shoveled fruit and fish into his mouth, scarcely taking the time to chew.

"Timmatee," Bray said.

Michael leaned over. "Timothy isn't far, don't worry."

"He's making sure we're safe," Layla said.

Bray looked at them in turn, then popped another piece of fish in his mouth.

They spent a leisurely hour over dinner. Cleaning up was going to be trickier down here. Everything must be discarded away from the caves lest they attract people or monsters.

Soon, Bray was yawning.

"I'll go put him down," Layla said.

Michael kissed the boy good night. Bray took turns waving to Victor, then Gabi, saying, "Buh-bye."

Gabi went to her room, but Victor stayed with Michael. They picked up their rifles and took a stroll back out into the corridor, to the cave's mouth. Moonlight speared through a gap in the clouds on the horizon, lighting the rock bluff just outside the cavern.

Michael rested his rifle barrel against the wall, then took the radio from his belt.

"Pepper, you copy?" he asked.

"*Copy, sir. How are the new digs?*"

"Good! Bray misses you already. We all do."

"*I miss you all as well, but don't worry,*" Timothy said. "*I'll keep watch over your new home. You deserve this second chance.*"

Footsteps approached, Layla joining them in the shadows of the cave. "We're going to need a name for this place." She put an arm around Michael and Victor. "Got any ideas?"

"Not yet," Michael said.

"I have idea," Victor said.

They both turned from the view to hear his idea.

"How about Santuario?" he asked. "Means 'Sanctuary' in my language."

Layla seemed to like that, and Michael did too.

"Santuario," Michael said. "Let's hope that's what this place is for us."

THIRTY-FOUR
FOUR HOURS EARLIER . . .

Knights pounded on the hatch to the rooftop of the capitol tower. Soon they would break it down.

Kade felt each thumping impact in his chest. Part of him couldn't believe that the enemy had arrived. He wasn't ready—he wasn't prepared to fight them.

Snap out of it, Kade. Get your head on!

He stood in the uppermost level of the tower, right below the stairs to the rooftop hatch. Dakota stood in front of him, shield out in front. Behind them were six more soldiers. More were showing up by the second to defend this corridor. If they could hold the knights back here, they might have a chance of stopping them. But Kade had no idea how many knights there were. He had under-estimated the Forerunner. Not only did they have an airship, but they had far more forces than he had seen at the Coral Castle.

The pounding stopped.

"Here they come!" Kade shouted. "Give 'em hell!"

An explosion blew the hatch off its hinges and sent the blasted metal skidding down the steps to the landing. Kade raised the Monster Hunter as Dakota held up his shield to protect them.

"Sir, get back!" Forge shouted.

Kade felt hands on his shoulders pulling him backward.

For a moment, there was only the echo of the metal and the ringing from the blast.

Then came the deep, booming battle cry of the knights.

A Cazador soldier moved up to take Kade's place beside Dakota. The man raised an assault rifle and opened fire at the first sign of movement. In the tight space, the report was deafening. Then came the screams of agony. The first enemy blood was spilled.

Slumping over on the landing, the knight gave a long sigh and went still.

But there was no time to take in the scene. Return fire slammed into the shield Dakota held out. A Cazador in light armor peered around the side, and immediately his head flew apart from a well-placed burst of bullets.

Dakota fell as the man's dead weight toppled onto him. Another soldier with a shield took Dakota's place, allowing him to get back up. The two men stood together, holding the shields while militia and Cazador soldiers took turns firing through the gap between them.

Kade couldn't see what was going on in front of the shields, but he could hear the screams of pain in the respite of the gunfire.

Something rolled between Dakota's feet and the other shield carrier. There was only enough time for Dakota to shout, "Grenade!" and dive to the side. The other guard tried to run, but it exploded as he turned his back, sending him flying.

Blood flecked the walls as shrapnel hit other soldiers in the corridor. Something stung Kade in the chest. Looking down, he saw that it was a roofing nail.

The improvised grenade had been filled with them. Other soldiers lay around him, howling in anguish with hot metal jutting from their flesh.

Smoke churned down the hallway.

Kade scooped up an assault rifle and knelt, searching for a target. It came a second later—a knight with an armet covering his face. Kade sighted up and fired into the visor, killing the man instantly.

He tuned out the clanging metal, moans, and cries to give himself a moment of calm. He waited for the next target to loom out of the smoke screen.

They came, charging and firing at the same time. A round zipped past Kade's head. He heard a screech of pain to his left and felt warm blood on his face.

Two knights ran forward, one with a cutlass, the other firing a pistol. Kade slipped, falling onto his back. An axe slammed into the helmet of the knight with the handgun, knocking him backward.

Out of nowhere, a Cazador practically leaped over Kade, swinging a cutlass to check another in midswing toward Kade's neck. The sharp blades met, sparked.

Kade scooted away on his back as the Cazador swung sideways, hitting the knight in the hip with a sickening crunch. Blood spurted from the riven armor as the Cazador yanked the edge free of the bone. Then the Cazador wrested the hatchet from the armet of the knight with the handgun. He had gone down on his knees, head slumped against his chest.

As the Cazador rocked the bit free of the skull that held it, he turned to Kade. It was General Forge.

"Get the king to safety!" he shouted.

Forge ducked the next blade and brought his axe down diagonally against the knight's ankle, all but severing the foot. Rising up, he shoved his dagger through the soft flesh under the chin, through the palate, and into the brain.

Kade managed to get his rifle up, firing to give Forge time to back up with Dakota—the only other soldier still standing in the hallway. Three Cazadores and two militia soldiers were dead or dying on a deck slick with blood.

The knights had suffered too, Kade saw as the smoke cleared. Four armored bodies bearing the trident heraldry lay in their own pooling blood.

Forge, Dakota, and Kade retreated into the next corridor, where more reinforcements were arriving. Kade stopped to catch his breath. Gritting his teeth, he pulled the nail from his chest muscle.

Then he stood and checked his magazine—still half-full.

"Don't let them—" he began to shout.

The grenade exploded the same instant it rolled around the corner. Dakota stood in front of Kade, bearing the brunt of the blast. Kade hit the ground on his back, blinking with blurred vision. A smoldering hunk of armor lay by his side. Somewhere in his confused and concussed mind, Kade understood that this was what remained of Dakota, who had just given his life to save him. But the horror of the sight had not registered yet. It didn't seem real.

Kade felt motion and realized he was being dragged away.

When he regained consciousness, he was inside the council chamber. Imulah, Pedro, and General Forge were nearby. Six soldiers stood guard at the double doors. Kade couldn't make out what anyone was saying, including the crackly voice on the radio. He heard only a steady ringing tone.

He glanced over to a face that he recognized as Beau's. His lips were moving, but Kade couldn't hear him either.

Something crawled down Kade's cheek. He reached up to brush it away, and his fingers came away slick with blood.

"Oh God," Kade muttered. He tried to get up but stumbled.

Over the ringing in his ears, he heard Forge yell something about an airship. Adrenaline rushed through Kade as everything came crashing back to him. He pushed at the ground, and Beau helped him to his feet and over to the table.

Kade shook his head and put a hand on his left ear, where the ringing seemed to be worst. Squinting, he stared at Forge.

"How bad is it?" he asked.

"We're losing the fight," Forge said. "All our ships have been taken out by an EMP."

"What about the Jayhawk?" Kade asked.

"Right before they took out our signal boosters, we got an encrypted message out to Gran Jefe," Pedro said. "He's in the air with King Xavier and Magnolia, on their way. Still a few hours out. The others are still days away."

Kade shook his head. There was no time for any help to arrive.

An explosion rattled the rooftop. Dust rained from the ceiling as a guard ran through the doors guarded by two sentries.

"Lieutenant Wynn just reported knights two floors above the vault," Pedro said. "He says they can't hold them much longer!"

Kade understood in that moment that all his planning was in vain. He had underestimated the Forerunner and the knights. He had trusted Lucky, and Lucky betrayed him.

Not only that, but Kade had been the one to bring them here, sealing the fate of his people.

As their king, he had failed to safeguard them, just as he had failed to protect his family back at Kilimanjaro.

He thought of his sons and wife and missed them more than ever.

"Sir," Pedro said.

"King Kade," Forge said.

Kade snapped out of his bewilderment.

"I'm getting a message to you," Pedro said. "It's for you."

"Play it," he said.

Pedro turned up the volume on the speakers as Kade walked over.

"King Kade Long, we eliminated your air defenses, and your ships are dead in the water," said a voice. *"Lay down your weapons, surrender, and we will spare your civilians."*

Kade didn't believe that. Especially if the Forerunner thought his people were barbarians.

"We must fight," Forge said.

Chest heaving, Kade considered the kids in the vault. He would protect them whatever the cost.

"Get ready to send them a response," Kade said.

Pedro, Imulah, Forge, and the ten soldiers in the room looked at Kade.

"Tell them I will meet the Forerunner on the rooftop to negotiate," he said.

"They will kill you!" Forge shouted. "We must fight."

"I'm ready to die."

Forge stared at him. "No, King Kade—"

Another blast shook the chamber, followed by a new burst of gunfire. The enemy was getting closer to the children.

"Send the message, Pedro," Kade demanded.

Pedro obeyed, sitting back down with his headset on.

"Kade," Beau said. "You don't have to do this."

"Someone has to pay for Rolo's sins and for my mistake of bringing Lucky here," Kade said. He put a hand on his friend's shoulder. "For Roman, Tia, Alton, and everyone else—"

Pedro turned from the bank of radio equipment. "They are coming," he said.

"Coming where?" Imulah asked.

Gunfire answered him. The ten soldiers in the room took up position in front of the doors, aiming and waiting.

Screams rang out, closer now, silenced by more gunshots. Then came a low humming.

The hum grew to a roar, like a growing tsunami poised to slam onto the shore. Banging came from the doors.

"Hold fire until I give the order!" Forge shouted.

Not a week ago, Kade had said the same thing to Forge and the soldiers when they surrounded the last holdouts of Charmer supporters.

Now another enemy was about to break down their door.

The violence, it seemed, would never end.

The whirring rose into a raucous roar, as if a war boat were coming at full throttle, right outside the windows.

Kade turned as the shutters exploded inward, sending glass flying across the room.

This was no boat.

Five curved metal claws the length of a man crunched through the window frame and wall. A robotic limb pulled the claws back, taking part of the wall with it. The gaping hole exposed what the claws were attached to—the hull of the airship.

The armored behemoth lowered, and a hatch opened in the hull.

"Get back!" Kade shouted.

A ramp extended down, and knights charged down it, into the throne chamber as Kade brought up the Monster Hunter revolver.

He fell to the floor just as the double doors burst inward. An electrical current sizzled through the chamber, slamming into the soldiers and knocking everyone down.

Kade convulsed on the floor, his nerves on fire.

The knights poured in from both sides, weapons angled down at the disabled Cazador and militia soldiers.

Blinking, Kade tried to look through his dimmed vision. Four knights had him surrounded, and one was looming over him.

"Kade…"

The voice was familiar.

His eyes beheld a face that couldn't be real.

"Lucky," he whispered. "How…"

"*I* was the beacon, Kade," said the knight. "It's inside me, just like you put the tape inside him."

He tossed Charmer's head to the floor. It rolled a few feet, the baleful eye glazed over but still somehow staring up at Kade. The stench was awful, and Kade already felt nauseated by all the death. His stomach churned.

"Tell your people to surrender. There has already been enough bloodshed," Lucky said. "You can end this."

Kade slowly took in the room. Imulah and Pedro were both on the ground, blades to their throats. Beau had a spear to his chest. All the soldiers were pinned down by swords or rifle muzzles. Only one remained standing.

Somehow, General Forge had pushed himself up, brandishing a machete at three knights who had blades out.

"Put it down, General," Kade said. "It's over."

Forge moved his blade from knight to knight, falling into a defensive hunch, ready to strike.

"We must not—" he started to say.

Automatic gunfire cracked from the ramp of the airship. Bullets slammed into Forge, knocking him backward. All three knights closed in with their swords. Despite being severely injured, the general swiped with his cutlass, knocking away a sword and then stabbing that knight in the gut.

"Stop!" Kade shouted.

The other two enemy soldiers closed in, striking Forge in his side and arm. They pulled their blades back as the general hunched over, still on his feet. His helmet fell off, and he looked up at the soldier standing on the ramp with the machine gun.

Kade looked into the face of a man he had seen die back in Australia.

General Jack, leader of the knights.

He wore an armet with the visor flipped up, exposing his pale features. His emotionless face tightened.

Forge used his sword to push himself up. He staggered there, his armor dripping blood in several places.

"No!" Kade yelled.

Jack fired again, the bullets tearing into the great Cazador general. Forge looked at Kade one last time before toppling over. And yet, he still breathed. The three knights moved back in cautiously, like hunters around a wounded animal that could still bite.

Kade resisted the urge to close his eyes as the men thrust their swords into Forge. He watched each stroke until it was over and Forge lay still. Then his eyes flitted back to Jack as he announced, "All clear."

The zombie general strode down the ramp, leading a shadowy figure in an electric wheelchair. The Forerunner had arrived.

"The barbarian warrior is dead," he said. "Bring me the immortal king."

THIRTY-FIVE

Xavier Rodriguez watched the waves crash against the beach of Sint Eustatius. In his mind, he played the message Pedro had sent hours ago.

We have lost control of the capitol tower, General Forge is dead, and our fleet has been disabled. The Forerunner says he has an offer for peace but will speak only with the immortal king...

Offer, X thought. What kind of offer could it be?

He walked away from the surf, back to the Jayhawk. They had set down on Sint Eustatius, a training ground for new warriors that the Cazadores once called the Man Maker. The last time he was here, X had been strong, confident, and ready to expand the Vanguard Islands. Now he could move thanks only to the medicine Valeria had pumped into his system. It had reduced his fever and his cough, but he felt loopy, unsteady. Nowhere close to fighting condition.

X gazed out over the silos where Michael had moved the food supplies with Steve Schwarzer, Ton, and Victor. This was where they were betrayed by the Wave Runner's and Charmer's forces.

So much had happened since then.

Events flashed by in his mind. From the Panama mission to the Sunshine Coast in Australia. The trial of Michael back at the Vanguard Islands, where Charmer had framed him for murder.

In those months, X had been so focused on expansion, he had let his guard down, failing to see the threat from both Charmer and Rolo. They had betrayed him at home and on the seas back at the Sunshine Coast while he was busy fighting monsters—not realizing that human monsters were with him.

Now the devil had come for payback.

X had not yet decided what to do. Soon, Cazador troops would arrive. Slayer, Tia, Zuni, and a chopper flown by an AI that had killed Blackburn and Woody. The warship they had commandeered from Crixus and his cult would come a few days later.

It wouldn't be enough to fight the Forerunner, even if they could trust the AI to fly the Jayhawk into battle. But there was one wild card that Kade had sent them.

In the marina, not a thousand feet away, was an armored speedboat with a bomb big enough to sink an oil rig. A Cazador had piloted it here on King Kade's orders during the airship attack the night before. According to the warrior, Kade had planned on using it before he learned of the helicopters. The plan had changed to putting the bomb on a Jayhawk that he would ride out to meet the Forerunner. If negotiations went sour, then he would blow them all to hell. But Kade never got the chance.

X, however, had that option.

The boat pilot was here now, awaiting orders to remove the bomb from the vessel. Gran Jefe was on a pier in the marina, clearly anxious and wanting to return to the islands as quickly as possible. Valeria, Magnolia, and Jonah were huddled behind the tent they had pitched on the beach, where Jo-Jo and Miles rested.

For X, there would be no rest.

He looked at his comrades. Mags and Gran Jefe were indeed

renegades, but now all of them, X included, were something else—they were underdogs. Not by a little, but by a lot. They had almost zero chance of winning back the islands. Especially without taking massive casualties, including innocents like Alton, Phyl, and all the other children.

That was why Kade had surrendered, X realized. Too much blood had been spilled.

He walked over to Magnolia, his decision made.

"Gran Jefe, get over here!" X yelled.

The big lug came trotting across the sand. As soon as everyone had gathered around, X made his announcement.

"I'm going to meet the Forerunner," he said. "Alone."

"What!" Magnolia gasped. "If you do that, he'll *kill* you, X! You know this."

"Yeah, maybe."

"I fight with you, *Su Majestad*," Gran Jefe said. He pounded his chest and snorted.

Valeria nodded.

That was the Cazador way. To fight. To slay your enemy.

X had fought the warrior society, earning his place as their equal and then as their leader. Winning the respect and trust of many great warriors like General Rhino and General Forge. But the cowardly Captain Rolo had feared them and, out of cowardice, hit the Cazadores in the back.

The mere thought of the old bastard made X furious. Not good for his ailing health. He couldn't focus on the dead. He had to focus on keeping as many people alive as he could.

The question was, what did the cyborg have planned? Would he be like Rolo and annihilate them when they least expected it, or would he be like X and work to build trust?

One thing was certain: if X took the boat with the bomb, and the Forerunner somehow detected that bomb, then it destroyed any chance for peace—especially after Rolo poisoned the Coral Castle by nuking the supercarrier *Immortal*.

"Get the bomb off the boat," X said. "I'm taking it unarmed. If you don't hear from me in three days, then I failed and you must work with Slayer to come up with a different plan."

"X, you can't do this on your own," Magnolia said. "You need help. We're a team—"

"That's why I need you here, Mags. If I fail, we need a leader for this fight, and that leader has to be you. I need to know I can trust you."

She hesitated, her lip quivering. Finally, she nodded.

X nodded back and moved to Gran Jefe.

"If you die, I avenge you, King X," he said.

They interlocked arms in the traditional Cazador shake.

Finally, X turned to Valeria.

"Thank you for everything you've done for me," X said. "And for Miles and for Jo-Jo. Look after them both with Magnolia."

Valeria saluted but then reached out and embraced X. This time, he hung on to her and pulled her close. It had been a long time since he felt anything for a woman, but there was no denying that Valeria had started to mend his dark heart. Now wasn't the time for that, though. There might *never* be a time for that.

Gran Jefe whistled to the Cazador on the boat and relayed the instructions. X hoped this was the right move, because he could see no other choice. He walked to the tent where Jo-Jo was sleeping. Even at ten paces, he could hear her raspy breathing. She wasn't long for this world if they didn't get the infection under control.

He unzipped the tent and bent down.

"Hi, girl, how you doing?" X asked. He reached down and stroked a swatch of her hair that wasn't singed or otherwise abused. "I have to go away for a while, but Valeria, Mags, and Miles will be right here with you."

Jo-Jo glanced up, but only for a moment before laying her head back down. She was weak—too weak even to engage Gran Jefe, although X had made sure they were kept far apart just in case the animal did get a second wind.

X got up as Jo-Jo let out a low whimper. Watching her suffer made his heart hurt worse. He looked for another long moment, then zipped the tent up.

He grabbed his gear and slung it over his shoulder. Miles trotted over, tail wagging, ready to go. X bent down in front of him.

"You can't come with me this time, boy," he said quietly.

The dog whined as if he understood.

X leaned down and gave the dog a hug. This wouldn't be the last time, would it?

Miles whined more, and again X felt his heart breaking. His best friend knew he was going to be left behind, and as much as X wanted to bring him along, he couldn't. This time, X had to go on his own.

He glanced up at Magnolia, who nodded in understanding. She grabbed the dog by the collar on his suit and pulled him back.

"I love you, boy," X said. "And I love you, Mags."

"I love you too, X," she said.

Miles barked.

They embraced, and then X turned and didn't look back. Miles barked, his tone rising into a sad, desperate baying. X was glad when the boat's engines drowned out the plaintive howls.

He backed into the water, still looking away from his dog and his friends. Turning the wheel, he aimed the bow out to sea.

"Okay, X, time to meet this cyber motherfucker," he said.

The four big outboard motors purred like jungle cats. His

prosthetic hand pushed the throttle down, and those engines roared, launching the boat across the wave tops.

X held the wheel, looking out the reinforced viewport in the enclosed cockpit. The digital display put him 140 miles away from the capitol tower. At his top speed of sixty-five miles an hour, the fast-moving craft would get him there in just over two hours.

He pulled away from the island. It was all he could do not to look back, but he knew that if he did, he would break at the sight of Miles and Magnolia standing there. Along with Michael and his family, they were the two most important things in his world.

X looked to the sky. They were somewhere out there, drifting in the darkness, fighting for survival.

"If I survive this, I'll find you, Tin," X said. "Even if it takes me the rest of my life."

On the journey back to the islands, he lost himself in his thoughts. Almost two and a half hours later, the darkness began to pale.

Here we go, X thought.

He heaved a breath and eased off the throttle. Then he picked up the radio and transmitted on an open channel.

"This is Xavier Rodriguez," he said. For a moment, he held the mic, thinking about saying something snarky—maybe a play on *foreskin*. But he decided to keep it polite. "I'm here to see the Forerunner."

The outermost oil rigs came into view. But unlike on other homecomings, he saw no skiffs or fishing trawlers lazily motoring between the rigs.

In a few minutes, X could see the capitol tower. What he saw made him pause. It was the biggest damned airship he had ever seen—probably two thousand feet from bow to stern. Blocky structures protruded from the top, stern, and undercarriage, all of them sporting machine-gun turrets. An array of dishes and antennas rose off the bulbous cockpit, all of them protected by more machine guns.

This was no airborne lifeboat. This was a war machine.

And it was starting to fly toward him.

X picked up a pair of binoculars resting on the dashboard. All those missing boats and ships were now corralled around the bottom of the rig. He zoomed in on the docks, where knights held security.

Then he moved the binos over to the *Frog* and zoomed in on the deck. A flag with a trident had been raised on a mast.

The knights had control of everything, but from what X could see, there wasn't any damage to the boats or ships. Only the top of the capitol tower showed any sign of a battle. Tendrils of smoke rose away from destroyed machine-gun nests and cannons. It seemed the Forerunner had taken out the air defenses and disabled all the boats with an EMP.

X lowered the binos and grabbed the wheel.

The airship flew closer, its shadow passing over X and quickly enveloping his small boat. He pulled back the sliding hatch to gaze up right into the underbelly of the dark hull.

A hatch opened, and a dish with an antenna extended down. The light on the end flashed red, then turned green. It struck him that he was being scanned.

Had he brought the bomb, he would have been caught, no doubt.

X took off his helmet to stare at this monstrous machine. He counted ten machine-gun turrets on the ship's ventral surface alone, each with ample firepower to destroy his boat utterly.

The dish retracted back inside, the hatch closing.

Slowly the center of the ship crept until it hovered directly over his boat. A round hatch slid open, and a harness lowered on a cable.

When it came within reach, X slipped it under his arms, thinking, *I'm getting too old for this bullshit.*

As the cable drew him up toward the hovering fortress, he watched a score of dolphins looping through the waves.

X glanced up into the black interior of the chamber overhead. A few seconds later, he was inside. The hatch slid shut under his boots with a soft click.

In the utter darkness, a synthetic voice greeted him.

"So you are the Immortal..."

X looked about him for the source of the voice.

"My name is Xavier Rodriguez," he said. "I'm here to see the Forerunner."

Overhead lights clicked on one at a time, spreading a glow over a cargo hold. Not ten feet away, three men in body armor held crossbows pointed at X.

On his knees in front of him was Cowboy Kade.

Hearing movement behind him, X turned to face one of the knights—a big man with a shotgun.

"Back up," said the knight.

X moved over to Kade.

"You okay?" he whispered down.

Kade got to his feet. "Been better, mate."

"Silence!" shouted the synthesized voice.

Out of the darkness came a mechanical platform bearing a sickly-looking man in an electrical chair. A red tunic with a trident logo on the breast covered his frail body. Cords and tubes ran from a pair of complicated-looking machines flanking the chair, which seemed to be keeping him breathing.

X met the man's eyes—one natural, dark; the other a glowing blue prosthetic—set deep in sunken sockets. He felt as if he was being scanned, as the antenna had scanned his boat. The white mustache seemed to twitch.

Hydraulics clanked as robotic limbs lifted the chair off the platform and lowered the Forerunner to X. The wizened face and bald, liver-spotted scalp glistened in the bright light.

X stood firmly, despite his aching body.

"So you are the man your people call the Immortal?" asked the Forerunner.

"I'm just a Hell Diver," X said. "I'm here to make peace."

"Is that why you came for the Coral Castle?"

X held the ancient creature's gaze. "Yes—to expand and bring more people back here. We've brought hundreds from places around the world."

The blue eye flashed again, perhaps reading X for a lie.

"And yet your people dropped a nuclear warhead in our lands!" The synthetic voice resonated through the room, hurting X's ears.

"I'm sorry," X said after it echoed away. "The men responsible for that betrayal are dead, and we are prepared to make up for their sins."

"Their sins . . ." The Forerunner turned his chair slightly to look at Kade. "You are the one who killed this Rolo and Charmer."

Kade looked up and nodded.

"You sent this tape with Gaz." The blue eye flashed again.

A voice played from unseen speakers. X heard Charmer, admitting his crimes. Another track played, this one of Rolo, announcing he had dropped the bomb to destroy the Cazadores.

"You have removed these diseases from your ranks, and I have killed your barbarian general," said the Forerunner. "But why should I spare your people? I have two ships packed with followers of the Trident, heading here with a year of supplies."

"There's room for us all here," X said.

"That is up to you."

The Forerunner took a moment to take several breaths, as if he was struggling to fill his lungs.

"You have one chance to save your people and mine," he said, gasping. "Our home has been poisoned, and this place will never survive the storms over the long term. The last hurricane didn't destroy you, but what about the next one? The only way to survive is to activate the weather-modification units at the poles."

The robotic arms lowered the chair so close, X could smell his fetid breath.

"I sent a team there many years ago, but they never returned," he said. "I've seen these harsh places with my own eyes. It will take a hero to activate the technology—an immortal who has fought monsters, destroyed the killer machines, and survived in the wastes, as your people say of you."

The Forerunner looked from X to Kade.

"Two Hell Divers, two missions." The synthetic voice sounded almost fully human this time. "To me, this seems like fate."

X glanced over at Kade, who nodded back.

"All right," X said. "But if I do this, I bring my own team. And I need you to provide medicine for several who are currently sick. Then, if we're successful, I need something from you after the tech is activated."

The Forerunner let out a synthetic chuckle. "You're *negotiating* now?"

"You asked me to save the world," X replied. "The least you can do is hear me out."

"Speak."

"I've been away, looking for a friend and his family that the miscreant Charmer tried to kill," he said. "If I turn on the weather-mod units at the poles, I ask you to take me on this airship to find my friends."

The Forerunner stared at him for a long moment. Then he

raised his hands, the tunic falling back over an arm that was part flesh, part prosthesis.

"You have a deal, Xavier Rodriguez."

He reached out with a wrinkled hand. X took it and found the grip surprisingly strong. As he let go, the Forerunner looked to his knights.

"Prepare the medicine," he said. "Give them whatever gear they need."

Then the platform lifted him back into the shadows.

X stood there, unsure who, or what, he had just made a deal with. Time would tell, but right now they had work to do. He glanced over to Kade.

"Guess we got one last dive, Cowboy King," X said. "From renegades to heroes—it's time to save the world, mate."

HELL DIVERS XII

HEROES

The adventure comes to an end summer 2024
with *Hell Divers XII: Heroes*

ABOUT THE AUTHOR

Nicholas Sansbury Smith is the *New York Times* and *USA Today* bestselling author of the Hell Divers series, the Orbs series, the Trackers series, the Extinction Cycle series, the Sons of War series, and the new E-Day series. He worked for Iowa Homeland Security and Emergency Management in disaster mitigation before switching careers to focus on storytelling. When he isn't writing or daydreaming about the apocalypse, he enjoys running, biking, spending time with his family, and traveling the world. He is an Ironman triathlete and lives in Iowa with his wife, daughter, and their dogs.

Join Nicholas on social media:
Facebook: Nicholas Sansbury Smith
Twitter: @GreatWaveInk
Website: www.NicholasSansburySmith.com